THE SUMMER THEY NEVER FORGOT

BY
KANDY SHEPHERD

Kandy Shepherd swapped a fast-paced career as a magazine editor for a life writing romance. She lives on a small farm in the Blue Mountains near Sydney, Australia, with her husband, daughter and a menagerie of animal friends. Kandy believes in love at first sight and real-life romance—they worked for her!

Kandy loves to hear from her readers. Visit her website at: www.kandyshepherd.com.

CHAPTER ONE

ON SANDY ADAMS's thirtieth birthday—which was also the day the man she'd lived with for two years was getting married to another woman—she decided to run away.

No. Not run away. *Find a new perspective.*

Yes, that sounded good. Positive. Affirming. Challenging.

No way would she give even a second's thought to any more heartbreak.

She'd taken the first step by driving the heck out of Sydney and heading south—her ultimate destination: Melbourne, a thousand kilometres away. On a whim, she'd chosen to take the slower, scenic route to Melbourne on the old Princes Highway. There was time, and it went through areas she thought were among the most beautiful in the state of New South Wales.

Alone and loving it, she repeated to herself as she drove.

Say it enough times and she might even start to believe it.

Somewhere between the seaside town of Kiama and the quaint village of Berry, with home two hours behind her, she pulled her lime-green Beetle off onto a safe lay-by. But she only allowed herself a moment to stretch out her cramped muscles and admire the rolling green hills and breathtaking blue expanse of the Pacific Ocean before she got back in the car. The February heat made it too hot to stay outside for too long.

From her handbag she pulled out her new notebook, a birthday present from her five-year-old niece. There was a pink fairy on the cover and the glitter from its wings had already shed all through Sandy's bag. It came with a shocking-pink pen. She nibbled on the pen for a long moment.

Then, with a flourish, she headed up the page 'Thirtieth Birthday Resolutions' and started to scribble in pink ink.

1. Get as far away from Sydney as possible while remaining in realms of civilisation and within reach of a good latte.

2. Find new job where can be own boss.

She underscored the words 'own boss' three times, so hard she nearly tore the paper.

3. Find kind, interesting man with no hang-ups who loves me the way I am and who wants to get married and have lots of kids.

She crossed out 'lots of kids' and wrote instead '*three kids'*—then added, '*two girls and a boy'*. When it came to writing down goals there was no harm in being specific. So she also added, *'Man who in no way resembles That-Jerk-Jason'*.

She went over the word 'jerk' twice and finished with the date and an extravagant flourish. Done.

She liked making lists. She felt they gave her some degree of control over a life that had gone unexpectedly pear-shaped. But three goals were probably all she could cope with right now. The resolutions could be revisited once she'd got to her destination.

She put the notebook back into her bag and slid the car back onto the highway.

An hour or so later farmland had made way for bushland

and the sides of the road were lined with eucalypt forest. Her shoulders ached from driving and thoughts of a break for something to eat were at the front of her mind. When she saw the signpost to Dolphin Bay it took only a second for her to decide to throw the car into a left turn.

It was a purely reflex action. She'd planned to stop at one of the beachside towns along the way for lunch and a swim. But she hadn't given sleepy Dolphin Bay a thought for years. She'd adored the south coast when she was a kid—had spent two idyllic summer holidays at different resort towns with her family, revelling in the freedom of being let off the leash of the rigorous study schedule her father had set her during the school year. But one summer the family had stayed in Dolphin Bay for the first time and everything had changed.

At the age of eighteen, she'd fallen in love with Ben. Tall, blond, surfer dude Ben, with the lazy smile and the muscles to die for. He'd been exciting, forbidden and fun. At the same time he'd been a real friend: supportive, encouraging—all the things she'd never dreamed a boy could be.

Then there'd been the kisses. The passionate, exciting, first-love kisses that had surprised her for years afterwards by sneaking into her dreams.

Sandy took her foot off the accelerator pedal and prepared to brake and turn back. She'd closed the door on so many of the bittersweet memories of that summer. Was it wise to nudge it open again by even a fraction?

But how could it hurt to drop in to Dolphin Bay for lunch? It was her birthday, after all, and she couldn't remember the last proper meal she'd eaten. She might even book into Morgan's Guesthouse and stay the night.

She put her foot back to the accelerator, too excited at the thought of seeing Dolphin Bay again to delay any further.

As she cruised into the main street that ran between the rows of shops and the waterfront, excitement melted down in a cold rush of disappointment. She'd made a big mistake.

The classic mistake of expecting things to stay the same. She hadn't been to Dolphin Bay for twelve years. And now she scarcely recognised it.

Determined not to give in to any kind of let-down feelings, she parked not far from the wasn't-there-last-time information kiosk, got out, locked the car and walked around, trying to orientate herself.

The southern end of the bay was enclosed by old-fashioned rock sea walls to form a small, safe harbour. It seemed much the same, with a mix of pleasure boats and fishing vessels bobbing on the water. The typically Australian old pub, with its iron lace balconies was the same too.

But gone was the beaten-up old jetty. It had been replaced by a sleek new pier and a marina, a fishing charter business, and a whale-and dolphin-watching centre topped with a large fibreglass dolphin with an inane painted grin that, in spite of her shock, made her smile. Adjoining was a row of upmarket shops and galleries. The fish and chip shop, where she'd squabbled with her sister over the last chip eaten straight from the vinegar-soaked paper, had been pulled down to make way for a trendy café. The dusty general store was now a fashionable boutique.

And, even though it was February and the school holidays were over, there were people strolling, browsing, licking on ice cream cones—more people than she could remember ever seeing in Dolphin Bay.

For a moment disappointment almost won. But she laughed out loud when she noticed the rubbish bins that sat out on the footpath. Each was in the shape of a dolphin with its mouth wide open.

They were absolute kitsch, but she fell in love with them all over again. Surreptitiously, she patted one on its fibreglass snout. 'Delighted you're still here,' she whispered.

Then, when she looked more closely around her, she noticed that in spite of the new sophistication every business still sported a dolphin motif in some form or another, from a discreet sticker to a carved wooden awning.

And she'd bet Morgan's Guesthouse at the northern end of the bay wouldn't have changed. The rambling weatherboard building, dating from the 1920s, would certainly have some sort of a heritage preservation order on it. It was part of the history of the town.

In her mind's eye she could see the guesthouse the way it had been that magic summer. The shuttered windows, the banks of blue and purple hydrangeas her mother had loved, the old sand tennis court where she'd played hit-and-giggle games with Ben. She hoped it hadn't changed too much.

As she approached the tourist information kiosk to ask for directions on how to get there she hesitated. Why did she need the guesthouse to be the same?

Did it have something to do with those rapidly returning memories of Ben Morgan? Ben, nineteen to her eighteen, the surfer hunk all the girls had had wild crushes on.

Around from the bay, accessed via a boardwalk, was a magnificent surf beach. When Ben had ridden his board, harnessing the power of the waves like some suntanned young god, there had always been a giggling gaggle of admiring girls on the sand.

She'd never been one of them. No, she'd stood on the sidelines, never daring to dream he'd see her as anything but a guest staying for two weeks with her family at his parents' guesthouse.

But, to her amazement and joy, he'd chosen *her*. And then the sun had really started to shine that long-ago summer.

'Morgan's Guesthouse?' said the woman manning the information kiosk. 'Sorry, love, I've never heard of it.'

'The old wooden building at the northern end of the bay,' Sandy prompted.

'There's only the Hotel Harbourside there,' the woman said. 'It's a modern place—been there as long as I've been in town.'

Sandy thanked her and walked away, a little confused.

But she gasped when she saw the stark, modern structure of the luxury hotel that had replaced the charming old weatherboard guesthouse. Its roofline paid some kind of homage to the old-fashioned peaked roof that had stood there the last time she had visited Dolphin Bay, but the concrete and steel of its construction did not. The hotel took up the footprint of the original building and gardens, and rose several floors higher.

Hotel Harbourside? She'd call it Hotel Hideous.

She took a deep, calming breath. Then forced herself to think positive. The new hotel might lack the appeal of the old guesthouse but she'd bet it would be air conditioned and would almost certainly have a decent restaurant. Just the place for a solo thirtieth birthday lunch.

And as she stood on the steps that led from the beach to the hotel and closed her eyes, breathed in the salty air, felt the heat shimmering from the sand, listened to the sound of the water lapping at the edge of the breakwater, she could almost imagine everything was the same as it had been.

Almost.

The interior of the restaurant was all glass, steel and smart design. What a difference from the old guesthouse dining room, with its mismatched wooden chairs, well-worn old table and stacks of board games for ruthlessly played after-dinner tournaments. But the windows that looked out over the bay framed a view that was much the same as it had always been—although now a fleet of dolphin-watching boats plied its tourist trade across the horizon.

She found a table in the corner furthest from the bar and sat down. She took off her hat and squashed it in her bag but kept her sunglasses on. Behind them she felt safer. Protected. Less vulnerable, she had to admit to herself.

She refused to allow even a smidgeon of self-pity to intrude as she celebrated her thirtieth birthday all by herself whilst at the same time her ex Jason was preparing to walk down the aisle.

Casting her eye over the menu, Sandy was startled by a burst of masculine laughter over the chatter from the bar. As that sound soared back into her memory her heart gave an excited leap of recognition. No other man's laughter could sound like that.

Rich. Warm. Unforgettable.

Ben.

He hadn't been at the bar when she'd walked in. She'd swear to it. Unless he'd changed beyond all recognition.

She was afraid to look up. Afraid of being disappointed. Afraid of what she might say, do, to the first man to have broken her heart.

Would she go up and say hello? Or put her hat back on and try to slink out without him seeing her?

Despite her fears, she took off her sunglasses with fingers that weren't quite steady and slowly raised her head.

Her breath caught in her throat and she felt the blood drain from her face. He stood with his profile towards her, but it was definitely Ben Morgan: broad-shouldered, towering above the other men in the bar, talking animatedly with a group of people.

From what she could see from this distance he was as handsome as the day they'd said goodbye. His hair was shorter. He wore tailored shorts and a polo-style shirt instead of the Hawaiian print board shorts and singlet he'd favoured when he was nineteen. He was more muscular. Definitely more grown up.

But he was still Ben.

He said something to the guy standing near him, laughed again at his response. Now, as then, he held the attention of everyone around him.

Did he feel her gaze fixed on him?

Something must have made him turn. As their eyes connected, he froze mid-laugh. Nothing about his expression indicated that he recognised her.

For a long, long moment it seemed as if everyone and everything else in the room fell away. The sound of plates clattering, glasses clinking, and the hum of chatter seemed muted. She realised she was holding her breath.

Ben turned back to the man he'd been talking to, said something, then turned to face her again. This time he smiled, acknowledging her, and she let out her breath in a slow sigh.

He made his way to her table with assured, athletic strides. She watched, mesmerised, taking in the changes wrought by twelve years. The broad-shouldered, tightly muscled body, with not a trace of his teenage gangliness. The solid strength of him. The transformation from boy to man. Oh, yes, the teenage Ben was now very definitely a man.

And hotter than ever.

All her senses screamed that recognition.

He'd reached her before she had a chance to get up from her chair.

'Sandy?'

The voice she hadn't heard for so long was as deep and husky as she remembered. He'd had a man's voice even at nineteen. Though only a year older than her, he'd seemed light years ahead in maturity.

Words of greeting she knew she should utter were wedged in her throat. She coughed. Panicked that she couldn't even manage a hello.

His words filled the void. 'Or are you Alexandra these days?'

He remembered that. Her father had insisted she be called by her full name of Alexandra. But Alexandra was too much of a mouthful, Ben had decided. He'd called her by the name she preferred. From that summer on she'd been Sandy. Except, of course, to her father and mother.

'Who's Alexandra?' she said now, pretending to look around for someone else.

He laughed with what seemed like genuine pleasure to see her. Suddenly she felt her nervousness, her self-consciousness, drop down a notch or two.

She scrambled up from her chair. The small round table was a barrier between her and the man who'd been everything to her twelve years ago. The man she'd thought she'd never see again.

'It's good to see you, Ben,' she said, her voice still more choked than she would have liked it to be.

His face was the same—strong-jawed and handsome—and his eyes were still as blue as the summer sky at noon. Close-cropped dark blond hair replaced the sun-bleached surfer tangle that so long ago she'd thought was the ultimate in cool. There were creases around his eyes that hadn't been there when he was nineteen. And there was a tiny white crescent of a scar on his top lip she didn't remember. But she could still see the boy in the man.

'It's good to see you, too,' he said, in that so-deep-it-bordered-on-gruff voice. 'I recognised you straight away.'

'Me too. I mean, I recognised you too.'

What did he see as he looked at her? What outward signs had the last years of living life full steam ahead left on her?

'You've cut your hair,' he said.

'So have you,' she said, and he smiled.

Automatically her hand went up to touch her head. Of course he would notice. Her brown hair had swung below her waist when she'd last seen him, and she remembered how he'd made her swear never, *ever* to change it. Now it was cut in a chic, city-smart bob and tastefully highlighted.

'But otherwise you haven't changed,' he added in that husky voice. 'Just grown up.'

'It's kind of you to say that,' she said. But she knew how much she'd changed from that girl that summer.

'Mind if I join you?' he asked.

'Of course. Please. I was just having a drink…'

She sat back down and Ben sat in the chair opposite her. His strong, tanned legs were so close they nudged hers as he settled into place. She didn't draw her legs back. The slight pressure of his skin on her skin, although momentary, sent waves of awareness coursing through her. She swallowed hard.

She'd used to think Ben Morgan was the best-looking man she'd ever seen. The twelve intervening years had done nothing to change her opinion. No sophisticated city guy had ever matched up to him. Not even Jason.

She'd left the menu open on the table before her. 'I see you've decided on dessert before your main meal,' Ben said, with that lazy smile which hadn't changed at all.

'I was checking out the salads, actually,' she lied.

'Really?' he said, the smile still in his voice, and the one word said everything.

He'd caught her out. Was teasing her. Like he'd used to do. With no brothers, an all-girls school and zero dating experience, she hadn't been used to boys. Never hurtful or mean, his happy-go-lucky ways had helped get her over that oversensitivity. It was just one of the ways he'd helped her grow up.

'You're right,' she said, relaxing into a smile. 'Old habits die hard. The raspberry brownie with chocolate fudge sauce *does* appeal.' The birthday cake you had when you weren't having a birthday cake. But she wouldn't admit to that.

'That brownie is so good you'll want to order two servings,' he said.

Like you used to.

The unspoken words hung between them. Their eyes met for a moment too long to be comfortable. She was the first to look away.

Ben signalled the waiter. As he waved, Sandy had to suppress a gasp at the ugly raised scars that distorted the palms of his hands. What had happened? A fishing accident?

Quickly she averted her eyes so he wouldn't notice her shock. Or see the questions she didn't dare ask.

Not now. Not yet.

She rushed to fill the silence that had fallen over their table. 'It's been a—'

He finished the sentence for her. 'Long time?'

'Yes,' was all she was able to get out. 'I was only thinking about you a minute ago and wondering...'

She felt the colour rise up her throat to stain her cheeks. As she'd walked away from the information kiosk and towards the hotel hadn't she been remembering how Ben had kissed her all those years ago, as they'd lain entwined on the sand in the shadows at the back of the Morgan family's boat shed? Remembering the promises they'd made to each other between those breathless kisses? Promises she'd really, truly believed.

She felt again as gauche and awkward as she had the night she'd first danced with him, at a bushfire brigade fundraiser dance at the surf club a lifetime ago. Unable to believe that Ben Morgan had actually singled her out from the summer people who'd invaded the locals' dance.

After their second dance together he'd asked her if she had a boyfriend back home. When she'd shaken her head, he'd smiled.

'Good,' he'd said. 'Then I don't have to go up to Sydney and fight him for you.'

She'd been so thrilled she'd actually felt dizzy.

The waiter arrived at their table.

'Can I get you another drink?' Ben asked.

'Um, diet cola, please.'

What was wrong with her? Why was she so jittery and on edge?

As a teenager she'd always felt relaxed with Ben, able to be herself. She'd gone home to Sydney a different person from the one who had arrived for that two-week holiday in Dolphin Bay.

She had to stop being so uptight. This was the same Ben. Older, but still Ben. He seemed the same laid-back guy he'd been as her teenage heartthrob. Except—she suppressed a shudder—for the horrendous scarring on his hands.

'Would you believe this is the first time I've been back this way since that summer?' she said, looking straight into his eyes. She'd used to tell him that eyes so blue were wasted on a man and beg him to swap them for her ordinary hazel-brownish ones.

'It's certainly the first time I've seen you here,' he said easily.

Was he, too, remembering those laughing intimacies they'd once shared? Those long discussions of what they'd do with their lives, full of hopes and dreams and youthful optimism? Their resolve not to let the distance between Dolphin Bay and Sydney stop them from seeing each other again?

If he was, he certainly didn't show it. 'So what brings you back?' he asked.

It seemed a polite, uninterested question—the kind a long-ago acquaintance might ask a scarcely remembered stranger who'd blown unexpectedly into town.

'The sun, the surf and the dolphins?' she said, determined to match his tone.

He smiled. 'The surf's as good as it always was, and the dolphins are still here. But there must be something else to bring a city girl like you to this particular backwater.'

'B...backwater? I wouldn't call it that,' she stuttered. 'I'm sorry if you think I—' The gleam in his blue eyes told her he wasn't serious. She recovered herself. 'I'm on my way from Sydney through to Melbourne. I saw the turn to this wonderful non-backwater town and here I am. On impulse.'

'It's nice you decided to drop in.' His words were casual, just the right thing to say. Almost too casual. 'So, how do you find the place?'

She'd never had to lie with Ben. Still, she was in the habit of being tactful. And this *was* Ben's hometown.

'I can't tell you how overjoyed I was to see those dolphin rubbish bins still there.'

Ben laughed, his strong, even teeth very white against his tan.

That laugh. It still had the power to warm her. Her heart did a curious flipping over thing as she remembered all the laughter they'd shared that long-ago summer. No wonder she'd recognised it instantly.

'Those hellish things,' he said. 'There's always someone on the progress association who wants to rip them out, but they're always shouted down.'

'Thank heaven for that,' she said. 'It wouldn't be Dolphin Bay without them.'

'People have even started a rumour that if the dolphins are removed it will be the end of Dolphin Bay.'

She giggled. 'Seriously?'

'Seriously,' he said, straight-faced. 'The rubbish bins go and as punishment we'll be struck by a tsunami. Or some other calamity.'

He rolled his eyes. Just like he'd used to do. That hidden part of her heart marked 'first love' reacted with a painful lurch. She averted her gaze from his mouth and that intriguing, sexy little scar.

She remembered the hours of surfing with him, playing tennis on that old court out at the back of the guesthouse. The fun. The laughter. Those passionate, heartfelt kisses. Oh, those kisses—his mouth hard and warm and exciting on hers, his tongue exploring, teasing. Her body straining to his…

The memories gave her the courage to ask the question. It was now or never. 'Ben. It was a long time ago. But…but why didn't you write like you said you would?'

For a long moment he didn't answer and she tensed. Then

he shrugged. 'I never was much for letters. After you didn't answer the first two I didn't bother again.'

An edge to his voice hinted that his words weren't as carefree as they seemed. She shook her head in disbelief. 'You wrote me two letters?'

'The day after you went home. Then the week after that. Like I promised to.'

Her mouth went suddenly dry. 'I never got a letter. Never. Or a phone call. I always wondered why…'

No way would she admit how, day after day, she'd hung around the letterbox, hoping against hope that he'd write. Her strict upbringing had meant she was very short on dating experience and vulnerable to doubt.

'Don't chase after boys,' her mother had told her, over and over again. *'Men are hunters. If he's interested he'll come after you. If he doesn't you'll only make a fool of yourself by throwing yourself at him.'*

But in spite of her mother's advice she'd tried to phone Ben. Three times she'd braved a phone call to the guesthouse but had hung up without identifying herself when his father had answered. On the third time his father had told her not to ring again. Had he thought she was a nuisance caller? Or realised it was her and didn't want her bothering his son? Her eighteen-year-old self had assumed the latter.

It had been humiliating. Too humiliating to admit it even now to Ben.

'Your dad probably got to my letters before you could,' said Ben. 'He never approved of me.'

'That's not true,' Sandy stated half-heartedly, knowing she wouldn't put it past her controlling, righteous father to have intercepted any communication from Ben. In fact she and Ben had decided it was best he not phone her because of her father's disapproval of the relationship.

'He's just a small-town Lothario, Alexandra.' Her father's long-ago words echoed in her head. Hardly. Ben had treated

her with the utmost respect. Unlike the private school sons of his friends her father had tried to foist on her.

'Your dad wanted more for you than a small-town fisherman.' Ben's blue eyes were shrewd and piercing. 'And you probably came to agree with him.'

Sandy dropped her gaze and shifted uncomfortably in her seat. Over and over her father had told her to forget about Ben. He wasn't suitable. They came from different worlds. Where was the future for a girl who had academic talents like hers with a boy who'd finished high school but had no intention of going any further?

Underneath it all had been the unspoken message: *He's not good enough for you.*

She'd never believed that—not for a second. But she had come to believe there was no future for them.

Inconsolable after their summer together, she'd sobbed into her pillow at night when Ben hadn't written. Scribbled endless notes to him she'd never had the courage to send.

But he hadn't got in touch and she'd forced herself to forget him. To get over something that obviously hadn't meant anything to him.

'Men make promises they never intend to keep, Alexandra.' How many times had her mother told her that?

Then, once she'd started university in Sydney, Dolphin Bay and Ben Morgan had seemed far away and less and less important. Her father was right—a surfer boyfriend wouldn't have fitted in with her new crowd anyway, she'd told herself. Then there'd been other boys. Other kisses. And she'd been too grown up for family holidays at Dolphin Bay or anywhere else.

Still, there remained a place in her heart that had always stayed a little raw, that hurt if she pulled out her memories and prodded at them.

But Ben had written to her.

She swirled the ice cubes round and round in her glass, still unable to meet his eyes, not wanting him to guess how disconcerted she felt. How the knowledge he hadn't abandoned her teenage self took the sting from her memories.

'It was a long time ago…' she repeated, her voice tapering away. 'Things change.'

'Yep. Twelve years tends to do that.'

She wasn't sure if he was talking about her, him, or the town. She seized on the more neutral option.

'Yes.' She looked around her, waved a hand to encompass the stark fashionable furnishings. 'Like this hotel.'

'What about this hotel?'

'It's very smart, but not very sympathetic, is it?'

'I kinda like it myself,' he said, and took a drink from his beer.

'You're not upset at what the developers did on the site of your family's beautiful guesthouse?'

'Like you said. Things change. The guesthouse has… has gone forever.'

He paused and she got the impression he had to control his voice.

'But this hotel and all the new developments around it have brought jobs for a lot of people. Some say it's the best thing that's ever happened to the place.'

'Do you?'

Sandy willed him to say no, wanting Ben to be the same carefree boy who'd lived for the next good wave, the next catch from the fishing boats he'd shared with his father, but knew somehow from the expression on his face that he wouldn't.

But still his reply came as a surprise. 'I own this hotel, Sandy.'

'You…you do?'

'Yep. Unsympathetic design and all.'

She clapped her hand to her mouth but she couldn't take back the words. 'I'm…I'm so sorry I insulted it.'

'No offence taken on behalf of the award-winning architect.'

'Really? It's won awards?'

'A stack of 'em.'

She noted the convivial atmosphere at the bar, the rapidly filling tables. 'It's very smart, of course. And I'm sure it's very successful. It's just…the old place was so charming. Your mother was so proud of it.'

'My parents left the guesthouse long ago. Glad to say goodbye to the erratic plumbing and the creaking floorboards. They built themselves a comfortable new house up on the headland when I took over.'

Whoa. Surprise on surprise. She knew lots must have changed in twelve years, but this? 'You took over the running of the guesthouse?' Somehow, she couldn't see Ben in that role. She thought of him always as outdoors, an action man—not indoors, pandering to the whims of guests.

'My wife did.'

His wife.

The words stabbed into Sandy's heart.

His wife.

If she hadn't already been sitting down she would have had to. Stupidly, she hadn't considered—not for one minute—that Ben would be married.

She shot a quick glance at his left hand. He didn't wear a wedding ring, but then plenty of married men didn't. She'd learned that lesson since she'd been single again.

'Of course. Of course you would have married,' she babbled, forcing her mouth into the semblance of a smile.

She clutched her glass so tightly she feared it would shatter. Frantically she tried to mould her expression into something normal, show a polite interest in an old friend's new life.

'Did you…did you marry someone from around here?'

'Jodi Hart.'

Immediately Sandy remembered her. Jodi, with her quiet manner and gentle heart-shaped face. 'She was lovely,' she said, meaning every word while trying not to let an unwarranted jealousy flame into life.

'Yes,' Ben said, and a muscle pulled at the side of his mouth, giving it a weary twist.

His face seemed suddenly drawn under the bronze of his tan. She was aware of lines etched around his features. She hadn't noticed them in the first flush of surprise at their meeting. Maybe their marriage wasn't happy.

Ben drummed his fingers on the surface of the table. Again her eyes were drawn to the scars on his hands. Horrible, angry ridges that made her wince at the sight of them.

'What about you?' he asked. 'Did you marry?'

Sandy shook her head. 'Me? Marry? No. My partner… he…he didn't believe in marriage.'

Her voice sounded brittle to her own ears. How she'd always hated that ambiguous term *partner*.

'"Just a piece of paper," he used to say.' She forced a laugh and hoped it concealed any trace of heartbreak. 'Sure made it easy when we split up. No messy divorce or anything.'

No way would she admit how distraught she'd been. How angry and hurt and humiliated.

His jaw clenched. 'I'm sorry. Did—?'

She put her hand up to stop his words. 'Thank you. But there's no point in talking about it.' She made herself smile. 'Water under the bridge, you know.'

It was six months since she'd last seen Jason. And that had only been to pay him for his half of the sofa they'd bought together.

Ben looked at her as if he were searching her face for something. His gaze was so intense she began to feel uncomfortable. When—at last—he spoke, his words were slow and considered.

'Water under the bridge. You're right.'

'Yes,' she said, not sure what to say next.

After another long, awkward pause, he glanced at his

watch. 'It's been great to see you, Sandy. But I have a meeting to get to.' He pushed back his chair and got up.

'Of course.' She wanted to put out a hand to stop him. There was more she wanted to ask him. Memories she wanted to share. But there was no reason for him to stay. No reason for him to know it was her birthday and how much she would enjoy his company for lunch.

He was married.

Married men did not share intimate lunches alone with former girlfriends, even if their last kiss had been twelve years ago.

She got up, too, resisting the urge to sigh. 'It was wonderful to catch up after all these years. Please…please give my regards to Jodi.'

He nodded, not meeting her eyes. Then indicated the menu. 'Lunch is on the house. I'll tell the desk you're my guest.'

'You really don't have to, Ben.'

'Please. I insist. For…for old times' sake.'

She hesitated. Then smiled tentatively. 'Okay. Thank you. I'm being nostalgic but they were good old times, weren't they? I have only happy memories of Dolphin Bay.' *Of the time we spent together.*

She couldn't kiss him goodbye. Instead she offered her hand for him to shake.

He paused for a second, then took it in his warm grip, igniting memories of the feel of his hands on her body, the caresses that had never gone further than she'd wanted. But back then she hadn't felt the hard ridges of those awful scars. And now she had no right to recall such intimate memories.

Ben was married.

'I'm sorry I was rude about your hotel,' she said, very seriously. Then she injected a teasing tone into her voice. 'But I'll probably never stop wondering why you destroyed the guesthouse. And those magnificent gum trees—there's not one left. Remember the swing that—?'

Ben let go her hand. 'Sandy. It was just a building.'

Too late she realised it wasn't any of her business to go on about the guesthouse just because she was disappointed it had been demolished.

'Ben, I—'

He cut across her. 'It's fine. That was the past, and it's where it should be. But it really has been great seeing you again…enjoy your lunch. Goodbye, Sandy.'

'Good-goodbye, Ben,' she managed to stutter out, stunned by his abrupt farewell, by the feeling that he wasn't being completely honest with her.

Without another word he turned from her, strode to the exit, nodded towards the people at the bar, and closed the door behind him. She gripped the edge of the table, swept by a wave of disappointment so intense she felt she was drowning in it.

What had she said? Had she crossed a line without knowing it? And why did she feel emptier than when she'd first arrived back in Dolphin Bay? Because when she'd written her birthday resolutions hadn't she had Ben Morgan in mind? When she'd described a kind man, free of hang-ups and deadly ambition, hadn't she been remembering him? Remembering how his straightforward approach to life had helped her grow up that summer? Grow up enough to defy her father and set her own course.

She was forced to admit to herself it wasn't the pier or the guesthouse she'd wanted to be the same in Dolphin Bay. It was the man who represented the antithesis of the cruel, city-smart man who had hurt her so badly.

In her self-centred fantasy she hadn't given a thought to Ben being married—just to him always being here, stuck in a time warp.

A waitress appeared to clear her glass away, but then paused and looked at her. Sandy wished she'd put her sunglasses back on. Her hurt, her disappointment, her anger at herself, must be etched on her face.

The waitress was a woman of about her own age, with a pretty freckled face and curly auburn hair pulled back tightly. Her eyes narrowed. 'I know you,' she said suddenly. 'Sandy, right? Years ago you came down from Sydney to stay at Morgan's Guesthouse.'

'That's right,' Sandy said, taken aback at being recognised.

'I'm Kate Parker,' the woman said, 'but I don't suppose you remember me.'

Sandy dredged through her memories. 'Yes, I do.' She forced a smile. 'You were the best dancer I'd ever seen. My sister and I desperately tried to copy you, but we could never be as good.'

'Thanks,' Kate replied, looking pleased at the compliment. She looked towards the door Ben had exited through. 'You dated Ben, didn't you? Poor guy. He's had it tough.'

'Tough?'

'You don't know?' The other woman's voice was almost accusing.

How would she know what had gone on in Ben Morgan's life in the twelve years since she'd last seen him?

'Lost his wife and child when the old guesthouse burned down,' Kate continued. 'Jodi died trying to rescue their little boy. Ben was devastated. Went away for a long time—did very well for himself. When he came back he built this hotel as modern and as different from the old place as could be. Couldn't bear the memories…'

Kate Parker chattered on, but Sandy didn't wait to hear any more. She pushed her chair back so fast it fell over and clattered onto the ground. She didn't stop to pull it up.

She ran out of the bar, through the door and towards the steps to the shoreline, heart pumping, face flushed, praying frantically to the god of second chances.

Ben.

She just had to find Ben.

CHAPTER TWO

TAKING THE STEPS two at a time, nearly tripping over her feet in her haste, Sandy ran onto the whiter-than-white sand of Dolphin Bay.

Ben was way ahead of her. Tall and broad-shouldered, he strode along towards the rocks, defying the wind that had sprung up while she was in the hotel and was now whipping the water to a frosting of whitecaps.

She had to catch up with him. Explain. Apologise. Tell him how dreadfully sorry she was about Jodi and his son. Tell him… Oh, so much she wanted to tell him. Needed to tell him. But the deep, fine sand was heavy around her feet, slowing her so she felt she was making no progress at all.

'Ben!' she shouted, but the wind just snatched the words out of her mouth and he didn't turn around.

She fumbled with her sandals and yanked them off, the better to run after him.

'Ben!' she called again, her voice hoarse, the salt wind whipping her hair around her face and stinging her eyes.

At last he stopped. Slowly, warily, he turned to face her. It seemed an age until she'd struggled through the sand to reach him. He stood unmoving, his face rigid, his eyes guarded. How hadn't she seen it before?

'Ben,' she whispered, scarcely able to get the word out. 'I'm sorry… I can't tell you how sorry I am.'

His eyes searched her face. 'You know?'

She nodded. 'Kate told me. She thought I already knew. I don't know what to say.'

Ben looked down at Sandy's face, at her cheeks flushed pink, her brown hair all tangled and blown around her face. Her eyes were huge with distress, her mouth oddly stained bright pink in the centre. She didn't look much older than the girl he'd loved all those years ago.

The girl he'd recognised as soon as she'd come into the hotel restaurant. Recognised and—just for one wild, unguarded second before he pummelled the thought back down to the depths of his wounded heart—let himself exult that she had come back. His first love. The girl he had never forgotten. Had never expected to see again.

For just those few minutes when they'd chatted he'd donned the mask of the carefree boy he'd been when they'd last met.

'I'm so sorry,' she said again, her voice barely audible through the wind.

'You couldn't have known,' he said.

Silence fell between them for a long moment and he found he could not stop himself from searching her face. Looking for change. He wanted there to be no sign of the passing years on her, though he was aware of how much he had changed himself.

Then she spoke. 'When did…?'

'Five years ago,' he said gruffly.

He didn't want to talk to Sandy about what the locals called 'his tragedy'. He didn't want to talk about it anymore full-stop—but particularly not to Sandy, who'd once been so special to him.

Sandy Adams belonged in his past. Firmly in his past. *Water under the bridge*, as she'd so aptly said.

She bit down on her lower lip. 'I can't imagine how you must feel—'

'No, you can't,' he said, more abruptly than he'd intended, and was ashamed at the flash of hurt that tightened her face. 'No one could. But I've put it behind me...'

Her eyes—warm, compassionate—told him she knew he was lying. How could he ever put that terrible day of helpless rage and despair behind him? The empty, guilt-ridden days that had followed it? The years of punishing himself, of not allowing himself to feel again?

'Your hands,' she said softly. 'Is that how you hurt them?'

He nodded, finding words with difficulty. 'The metal door handles were burning hot when I tried to open them.'

Fearsome images came back—the heat, the smoke, the door that would not give despite his weight behind it, his voice raw from screaming Jodi's and Liam's names.

He couldn't stop the shudder that racked his frame. 'I don't talk about it.'

Mutely, she nodded, and her eyes dropped from his face. But not before he read the sorrow for him there.

Once again he felt ashamed of his harshness towards her. But that was him these days. Ben Morgan: thirty-one going on ninety.

His carefree self of that long-ago summer had been forged into someone tougher, harder, colder. Someone who would not allow emotion or softness in his life. Even the memories of a holiday romance. For with love came the agony of loss, and he could never risk that again.

She looked up at him. 'If...if there's anything I can do to help, you'll let me know, won't you?'

Again he nodded, but knew in his heart it was an empty gesture. Sandy was just passing through, and he was grateful. He didn't want to revisit times past.

He'd only loved two women—his wife, Jodi, and, before her, Sandy. It was too dangerous to have his first love around, reminding him of what he'd vowed never to feel again. He'd resigned himself to a life alone.

'You've booked in to the hotel?' he asked.

'Not yet, but I will.'

'For how long?'

Visibly, her face relaxed. She was obviously relieved at the change of subject. He remembered she'd never been very good at hiding her emotions.

'Just tonight,' she said. 'I'm on my way to Melbourne for an interview about a franchise opportunity.'

'Why Melbourne?' That was a hell of a long way from Dolphin Bay—as he knew from his years at university there.

'Why not?' she countered.

He turned and started walking towards the rocks again. Automatically she fell into step behind him. He waited.

Yes. He wasn't imagining it. It was happening.

After every three of his long strides she had to skip for a bit to keep up with him. Just like she had twelve years ago. And she didn't even seem to be aware that she was doing it.

'You're happy to leave Sydney?'

'There's nothing for me in Sydney now,' she replied.

Her voice was light, matter-of-fact, but he didn't miss the underlying note of bitterness.

He stopped. Went to halt her with a hand on her arm and thought better of it. No matter. She automatically stopped with him, in tune with the rhythm of his pace.

'Nothing?' he asked.

Not meeting his gaze, swinging her sandals by her side, she shrugged. 'Well, my sister Lizzie and my niece Amy. But…no one else.'

'Your parents?'

Her mouth twisted in spite of her effort to smile. 'They're not together any more. Turns out Dad had been cheating on my mother for years. The first Mum heard about it was when his mistress contacted her, soon after we got home from Dolphin Bay that summer. He and Mum patched it up that time. And the next. Finally he left her for his receptionist. She's two years older than I am.'

'I'm sorry to hear that.'

But he was not surprised. He'd never liked the self-righteous Dr Randall Adams. Had hated the way he'd tried to control every aspect of Sandy's life. He wasn't surprised the older man had intercepted his long-ago letters. He'd made it very clear he had considered a fisherman not good enough for a doctor's daughter.

'That must have been difficult for you,' he said.

Sandy pushed her windblown hair back from her face in a gesture he remembered. 'I'm okay about it. Now. And Mum's remarried to a very nice man and living in Queensland.'

During that summer he'd used to tease her about her optimism. 'You should be called Sunny, not Sandy,' he'd say as he kissed the tip of her sunburned nose. 'You never let anything get you down.'

It seemed she hadn't changed—in that regard anyway. But when he looked closely at her face he could see a tightness around her mouth, a wariness in her eyes he didn't recall.

Maybe things weren't always so sunny for her these days. Perhaps her cup-half-full mentality had been challenged by life's storm clouds in the twelve years since he'd last seen her.

Suddenly she glanced at her watch. She couldn't smother her gasp. The colour drained from her face.

'What's wrong?' he asked immediately.

'Nothing,' she said, tight lipped.

Nothing. Why did women always say that when something was clearly wrong?

'Then why did you stare at your watch like it was about to explode? Is it connected to a bomb somewhere?'

That brought a twitch to her lips. 'I wish.'

She lifted her eyes from the watch. Her gaze was steady. 'I don't know why I'm telling you this, but right at this very moment Jason—my…my former boyfriend, partner, live-in lover or whatever you like to call him—is getting married.'

Sandy with a live-in boyfriend? She'd said she'd had a partner but had it been that serious? The knowledge hit him in the gut. Painfully. Unexpectedly. Stupidly.

What he and Sandy had had together was a teen romance. Kid stuff. They'd both moved on. He'd married Jodi. Of course Sandy would have had another man in her life.

But he had to clear his throat to reply. 'And that's bad or good?'

She laughed. But the laugh didn't quite reach her eyes. 'Well, good for him. Good for her, I guess. I'm still not sure how I feel about coming home one day to find his possessions gone and a note telling me he'd moved in with her.'

'You're kidding me, right?' Ben growled. How could someone treat his Sandy like that. *His Sandy.* That was a slip. She hadn't been his for a long, long time.

'I'm afraid not. It was…humiliating to say the least.' Her tone sounded forced, light. 'But, hey, it makes for a great story.'

A great story? Yeah, right.

There went sunny Sandy again, laughing off something that must still cause her pain.

'Sounds to me like you're better off without him.'

'The further I get from him the more I can see that,' she said. But she didn't sound convinced.

'As far away as Melbourne?' he asked, finding the thought of her so far away unsettling.

'I'm not running away,' she said firmly. Too firmly. 'I need change. A new job, a new—'

'Your job? What is that?' he asked, realising how little he knew about her now. 'Did you study law like your father wanted?'

'No, I didn't. Don't look so surprised—it was because of you.'

'Me?' No wonder her father had hated him.

'You urged me to follow my dreams—like you were following yours. I thought about that a lot when I got back home. And my dream wasn't to be a solicitor.' She shuddered. 'I couldn't think of anything less me.'

He'd studied law as part of his degree and liked it. But he wasn't as creative as he remembered Sandy being. 'But you studied for years so you'd get a place in law.'

'Law at Sydney University.' She pronounced the words as though they were spelled in capital letters. 'That was my father's ambition for me. He'd given up his plans for me to be a doctor when I didn't cut it in chemistry.'

'You didn't get enough marks in the Higher School Certificate for law?'

'I got the marks, all right. Not long after we got back to Sydney the results came out. I was in the honour roll in the newspaper. You should have heard my father boasting to anyone who'd listen to him.'

'I'll bet he did.' Ben had no respect for the guy. He was a bully and a snob. But he had reason to be grateful to him. Not for ruining things with him and Sandy. But for putting the bomb under him he'd needed to get off his teenage butt and make himself worthy of a girl like Sandy.

'At the last minute I switched to a communications degree. At what my father considered a lesser university.'

'He must have hit the roof.'

Sandy's mouth tightened to a thin line. 'As he'd just been outed as an adulterer he didn't have a leg to stand on about doing the right thing for the family.'

Ben smiled. It sounded as if Sandy had got a whole lot feistier when it came to standing up to her father. 'So what career did you end up in?'

'I'm in advertising.' She quickly corrected herself. 'I *was* in advertising. An account executive.'

On occasion he dealt with an advertising agency to help promote his hotel. The account executives were slick, efficient, and tough as old boots. Not at all the way he thought of Sandy. 'Sounds impressive.'

'It was.'

'Was?'

'Long story,' she said, and started to walk towards the rocks again.

'I'm listening,' he said, falling into step beside her.

The wind had dropped and now the air around them seemed unnaturally still. Seagulls screeched raucously. He looked through narrowed eyes to the horizon, where grey clouds were banking up ominously.

Sandy followed his gaze. She wrinkled her cute up-tilted nose. 'Storm brewing,' she said. 'I wonder—'

'Don't change the subject by talking about the weather,' he said, stopping himself from adding, *I remember how you always did that.*

He shouldn't have let himself get reeled in to such a nostalgic conversation. There was no point in dredging up those old memories. Not when their lives were now set on such different paths. And his path was one he needed—wanted—to tread unencumbered. He could not survive more loss. And the best way to avoid loss was to avoid the kind of attachment that could tear a man apart.

He wanted to spend his life alone. Though the word 'alone' seemed today to have a desolate echo to it.

She shrugged. 'Okay. Back to my story. Jason and I were both working at the same agency when we met. The boss didn't think it was a good idea when we started dating…'

'So you had to go? Not him?'

She pulled a face. 'We…ell. I convinced myself I'd been there long enough.'

'So you went elsewhere? Another agency?'

She nodded. 'And then the economy hit a blip, advertising revenues suffered, and last one in was first one out.'

'That must have been tough.'

'Yeah. It was. But, hey, one door closes and another one opens, right? I got freelance work at different agencies and learned a whole lot of stuff I might never have known otherwise.'

Yep, that was the old Sandy all right—never one to allow adversity to cloud her spirit.

She took a deep breath. He noticed how her breasts rose under her tight-fitting top. She'd filled out—womanly curves softened the angles of her teenage body. Her face was subtly different too, her cheekbones more defined, her mouth fuller.

He wouldn't have thought it possible but she was even more beautiful than she'd been when she was eighteen.

He wrenched his gaze away, cleared his throat. 'So you're looking at a franchise?'

Her eyes sparkled and her voice rose with excitement. 'My chance to be my own boss, run my own show. It's this awesome candle store. A former client of mine started it.'

'You were in advertising and now you want to sell candles? Aren't there enough candle stores in this world?'

'These aren't ordinary candles, Ben. The store is a raging success in Sydney. Now they're looking to open up in other towns. They're interviewing for a Melbourne franchise and I put my hand up.'

She paused.

'I want to do something different. Something of my own. Something challenging.'

She looked so earnest, so determined, that he couldn't help a teasing note from entering his voice. 'So it's candles? I don't see the challenge there.'

'Don't you?' she asked. 'There's a scented candle for every mood, you know—to relax, to stimulate, to seduce—'

She stopped on the last word, and the colour deepened in her cheeks, flushed the creamy skin of her neck. Her eyelashes fluttered nervously and she couldn't meet his gaze.

'Well, you get the story. I wrote the copy for the client. There's not much I don't know about the merits of those candles.' She was almost gabbling now to cover her embarrassment.

To seduce.

When he'd been nineteen, seducing Sandy had been all he'd thought about. Until he'd fallen in love with her. Then respecting her innocence had become more important than his own desires. The number of cold showers he'd been forced to take…

Thunder rumbled ominously over the water. 'C'mon,' he said gruffly, 'we'd better turn back.'

'Yes,' she said. 'Though I suppose it's too late now for my birthday lunch…' She hesitated. 'Please—forget I just said that, will you?'

'It's your birthday today?'

She shrugged dismissively. 'Yes. It's nothing special.'

He thought back. 'It's your *thirtieth* birthday.'

And she was celebrating alone?

'Eek,' she said in an exaggerated tone. 'Please don't remind me of my advancing years.'

'February—of course. How could I forget?' he said slowly.

'You remember my birthday?'

'I'd be lying if I said I recalled the exact date. But I remember it was in February because you were always pointing out how compatible our star signs were. Remember you used to check our horoscopes in your father's newspaper every day and—?'

He checked himself. Mentally he slammed his hand against his forehead. He'd been so determined not to indulge in reminiscence about that summer and now he'd gone and started it himself.

She didn't seem to notice his sudden reticence. 'Yes, I remember. You're Leo and I'm Pisces,' she chattered on. 'And you always gave me a hard time about it. Said astrology was complete hokum and the people at the newspaper just made the horoscopes up.'

'I still think that and—' He stopped as a loud clap of thunder drowned out his voice. Big, cold drops of water started pelting his head.

Sandy laughed. 'The heavens are angry at you for mocking them.'

'Sure,' he said, but found himself unable to resist a smile at her whimsy. 'And if you don't want to get drenched we've got to make a run for it.'

'Race you!' she challenged, still laughing, and took off, her slim, tanned legs flashing ahead of him.

He caught up with her in just a few strides.

'Not fair,' she said, panting a little. 'Your legs are longer than mine.'

He slowed his pace just enough so she wouldn't think he was purposely letting her win.

She glanced up at him as they ran side by side, her eyes lively with laughter, fat drops of water dampening her hair and rolling down her flushed cheeks. The sight of her vivacity ignited something deep inside him—something long dormant, like a piece of machinery, seized and unwanted, suddenly grinding slowly to life.

'I gave you a head start,' he managed to choke out in reply to her complaint.

But he didn't get a chance to say anything else for, waiting at the top of the stairs to the hotel, wringing her hands anxiously together, stood Kate Parker.

'Oh, Ben, thank heaven. I didn't know where you were. Your aunt Ida has had a fall and hurt her pelvis, but she won't let the ambulance take her to hospital until she's spoken to you.'

CHAPTER THREE

SANDY WAS HALFWAY up the stairs, determined to beat Ben to the top. Slightly out of breath, she couldn't help smiling to herself over the fact that Ben had remembered her birthday. Hmm… Should she be reading something into that?

And then Kate was there, with her worried expression and urgent words, and the smile froze on Sandy's face.

She immediately looked to Ben. Her heart seemed to miss a beat as his face went rigid, every trace of laughter extinguished.

'What happened?' he demanded of the red-haired waitress.

'She fell—'

'Tap-dancing? Or playing tennis?'

Kate's face was pale under her freckles. 'Neither. Ida fell moving a pile of books. You know what she's like. Pretends she's thirty-five, not seventy-five—'

Ida? A seventy-five-year-old tap-dancing aunt? Sandy vaguely remembered Ben all those years ago talking about an aunt—a great-aunt?—he'd adored.

'Where is she?' Ben growled, oblivious to the rain falling down on him in slow, heavy drops, slicking his hair, dampening his shirt so it clung to his back and shoulders, defining his powerful muscles.

'In the ambulance in front of her bookshop,' said

Kate. 'Better hurry. I'll tell the staff where you are, then join you—'

Before Kate had finished speaking, Ben had turned on his heel and headed around to the side of the hotel with the long, athletic strides Sandy had always had trouble keeping up with.

'Ben!' Sandy called after him, then forced herself to stop. Wasn't this her cue to cut out? As in, *Goodbye, Ben, it was cool to catch up with you. Best of luck with everything. See ya.*

That would be the sensible option. And Sandy, the practical list-maker, might be advised to take it. Sandy, who was on her way to Melbourne and a new career. A new life.

But this was about Ben.

Ben, with his scarred hands and scarred heart.

Ben, who might need some support.

Whether he wanted it or not.

'I'm coming with you,' she called after him, all thoughts of her thirtieth birthday lunch put on hold.

Quickly she fastened the buckles on her sandals. Wished for a moment that she had an umbrella. But she didn't really care about getting wet. She just wanted to be with Ben.

She'd never met a more masculine man, but the tragedy he had suffered gave him a vulnerability she could not ignore. Was he in danger of losing someone else he loved? It was an unbearable thought.

'Ben! Wait for me!' she called.

He turned and glanced back at her, but made no comment as she caught up with him. Good, so he didn't mind her tagging along.

His hand brushed hers as they strode along together. She longed to take it and squeeze it reassuringly but didn't dare. Touching wasn't on the agenda. Not any more.

Within minutes they'd reached the row of new shops that ran down from the side of the hotel.

There was an ambulance parked on the footpath out of

the rain, under the awning in front of a shop named Bay Books. When she'd driven past she'd admired it because of its charming doorframe, carved with frolicking dolphins. Who'd have thought she'd next be looking at it under circumstances like this?

A slight, elderly lady with cropped silver hair lay propped up on a gurney in front of the open ambulance doors.

This was Great-Aunt Ida?

Sandy scoured her memories. Twelve years ago she'd been so in love with Ben she'd lapped up any detail about his family, anything that concerned him. Wasn't there a story connected to Ida? Something the family had had to live down?

Ben was instantly by his aunt's side. 'Idy, what have you done to yourself this time?' he scolded, in a stern but loving voice.

He gripped Ida's fragile gnarled hand with his much bigger, scarred one. Sandy caught her breath at the look of exasperated tenderness on his face. Remembered how caring he'd been to the people he loved. How protective he'd been of *her* when she was eighteen.

Back then she'd been so scared of the big waves. Every day Ben had coaxed her a little further from the shore, building her confidence with his reassuring presence. On the day she'd finally caught a wave and ridden her bodyboard all the way in to shore, squealing and laughing at the exhilaration of it, she'd looked back to see he had arranged an escort of his brother and his best mates—all riding the same break. What kind of guy would do that? She'd never met one since, that was for sure.

'Cracked my darn pelvis, they think. I tripped, that's all.' Ida's face was contorted with annoyance as much as with pain.

Ben whipped around to face the ambulance officer standing by his aunt. 'Then why isn't she in the hospital?'

'Point-blank refused to let me take her. Insisted on seeing you first,' the paramedic said with raised eyebrows and admirable restraint, considering the way Ben was glaring at him. 'Tried to get her to call you from hospital but she wasn't budging.'

'That's right,' said Ben's aunt in a surprisingly strong voice. 'I'm not going anywhere until my favourite great-nephew promises to look after my shop.'

'Absolutely,' said Ben, without a second's hesitation. 'I'll lock it up safely. Now, c'mon, let's get you in the ambulance and—'

His aunt Ida tried to rise from the gurney. 'That's not what I meant. That's not good enough—' she said, before her words were cut short by a little whimper of pain.

Sandy shifted from sodden sandal to sodden sandal. Looked away to the intricately carved awning. She felt like an interloper, an uninvited witness to Ben's intimate family drama. Why hadn't she stayed at the beach?

'Don't worry about the shop,' said Ben, his voice burred with worry. 'I'll sort something out for you. Let's just get you to the hospital.'

'It's not life or death,' said the paramedic, 'but, yes, she should be on her way.'

Ida closed her eyes briefly and Sandy's heart lurched at the weariness that crossed her face. *Please let her be all right—for Ben's sake.*

But then the older lady's eyes snapped into life again. They were the same blue as Ben's and remarkably unfaded. 'I can't leave my shop closed for all that time.'

The paramedic interrupted. 'She might have to lie still in bed for weeks.'

'That's not acceptable,' continued the formidable Ida. 'You'll have to find me a manager. Keep my business going.'

'Just get to the ER and I'll do something about that later,' said Ben.

'Not later. *Now*,' said Aunt Ida, sounding nothing like a

little old lady lying seriously injured on a gurney. Maybe she was pumped full of painkillers.

Sandy struggled to suppress a grin. For all his tough, grown-up ways she could still see the nineteen-year-old Ben. He was obviously aching to bundle his feisty aunt into the ambulance but was too respectful to try it.

Aunt Ida's eyes sought out Kate, who was now standing next to Sandy. 'Kate? Can you—?'

Kate shook her head regretfully. 'No can do, I'm afraid.'

'She's needed at the hotel. We're short-staffed,' said Ben, with an edge of impatience to his voice.

Ida's piercing blue gaze turned to Sandy. 'What about you?'

'Me?' Was the old lady serious? Or delirious?

Before Sandy could stutter out anything more, Kate had turned to face her.

Her eyes narrowed. 'Yes. What about you, Sandy? Are you on holiday? Could you help out?'

'What? No. Sorry. I'm on my way to Melbourne.' She was so aghast she was gabbling. 'I'm afraid I won't be able to—'

'Friend of Kate's, are you?' persisted the old lady, in a voice that in spite of her obvious efforts was beginning to tire.

Compelled by good manners, Sandy took a step forward. 'No. Yes. Kind of… I—'

She looked imploringly at Ben, uncertain of what to say, not wanting to make an already difficult situation worse.

'Sandy's an…an old friend of mine,' he said, stumbling on the word friend. 'Just passing through.'

'Oh,' said the older lady, 'so she can't help out. And I can't afford to lose even a day's business.'

Her face seemed to collapse and she looked every minute of her seventy-five years.

Suddenly she reminded Sandy of her grandmother—

her mother's mother. How would she feel if Grandma were stuck in a situation like this?

'I'm sorry,' she said reluctantly.

'Pity.' Ida sighed. 'You look nice. Intelligent. The kind of person I could trust with my shop.' Wearily she closed her eyes again. 'Find me someone like her, Ben.'

Her voice was beginning to waver. Sandy could barely hear it over the sound of the rain drumming on the awning overhead.

Ben looked from Sandy to his aunt and then back to Sandy again, his eyes unreadable. 'Maybe…maybe Sandy can be convinced to stay for a few days,' he said.

Huh? Sandy stared at him. 'But, Ben, I—'

Ben held her with his glance, his blue eyes intense. He leaned closer to her. 'Just play along with me and say yes so I can get her to go to the hospital,' he muttered from the side of his mouth.

'Oh.' She paused. Thought for a moment. Thought again. 'Okay. I'll look after the shop. Just for a few days. Until you get someone else.'

'You promise?' asked Ida.

Promise? Like a cross-your-heart-and-hope-to-die-type promise? The kind of promise she never went back on?

Disconcerted, Sandy nodded. 'I promise.'

What crazy impulse had made her come out with that? Wanting to please Ben?

Or maybe it was the thought of what she would have liked to happen if it was her grandmother, injured, in pain, and having to beg a stranger to help her.

Ida's eyes connected with hers. 'Thank you. Come and see me in the hospital,' she said, before relaxing with a sigh back onto the gurney.

'Right. That's settled.' Ben slapped the side of the ambulance, turned to the ambulance officer. 'I'll ride in the back with my aunt.'

A frail but imperious hand rose. 'You show your friend around Bay Books. Settle her in.'

Sandy had to fight a smile as she watched Ben do battle with his great-aunt to let him accompany her to the hospital.

Minutes later she stood by Ben's side, watching the tail-lights of the ambulance disappear into the rain. Kate was in the back with Ida.

'Your aunt Ida is quite a lady,' Sandy said, biting her lip to suppress her grin.

'You bet,' said Ben, with a wry smile of his own.

'Isn't she the aunt who…?' She held up her hand. 'Wait. Let me remember. I know!' she said triumphantly. 'The aunt who ran off with an around-the-world sailor?'

Ben's eyes widened. 'You remember that? From all that time ago?'

I remember because you—and the family I fantasised about marrying into—were so important to me. The words were on the tip of her tongue, but she didn't—couldn't—put her voice to them. 'Of course,' she said instead. 'Juicy scandals tend to stick in my mind.'

'It *was* a scandal. For these parts anyway. She was the town spinster, thirty-five and unmarried.'

'Spinster? Ouch! What an awful word.' She giggled. 'Hey, I'm thirty and unmarried. Does that make me—' she made quotation marks in the air with her fingers '—a spinster?'

'As if,' Ben said with a grin. 'Try *career woman about town*—isn't that more up to date?'

'Sounds better. But the message is the same.' She pulled a mock glum face.

Ben stilled, and suddenly he wasn't joking. He looked into her face for a long, intense minute. An emotion she didn't recognise flashed through his eyes and then was gone.

'That boyfriend of yours was an idiot,' he said gruffly.

He lifted a hand as if he was about to touch her, maybe run his finger down her cheek to her mouth like he'd used to.

She tensed, waiting, not sure if she wanted him to or not. Awareness hung between them like the shimmer off the sea on a thirty-eight-degree day.

He moved a step closer. So close she could clearly see that sexy scar on his mouth. She wondered how it would feel if he kissed her…if he took her in his arms…

Her heart began to hammer in her chest so violently surely he must hear it. Her mouth went suddenly dry.

But then, abruptly, he dropped his hand back by his side, stepped away. 'He didn't deserve you,' he said, in a huskier-than-ever voice.

She breathed out, not realising she had been holding her breath. Not knowing whether to feel disappointed or relieved that there was now a safe, non-kissing zone between her and the man she'd once loved.

She cleared her throat, disconcerted by the certain knowledge that if Ben had kissed her she wouldn't have pushed him away. No. She would have swayed closer and…

She took a steadying breath. 'Yeah. Well… I…I'm better off without him. And soon I'll be living so far away it won't matter one little bit that he chose his mega-wealthy boss's daughter over me.'

She wouldn't take cheating Jason back in a million years. But sometimes it was difficult to keep up the bravado, mask the pain of the way he'd treated her. It was a particular kind of heartbreak to be presented with a *fait accompli* and no opportunity to make things right. It made it very difficult for her to risk her heart again.

'Still hurts, huh?' Ben said, obviously not fooled by her words.

She remembered how he'd used to tease her about her feelings always showing on her face.

She shook her head. After a lacklustre love life she'd thought she'd got things right with Jason. But she wasn't going to admit to Ben that Jason had proved to be another disappointment.

'You talk the talk, Sandy,' Jason had said. *'But you always held back, were never really there for me.'*

She couldn't see the truth in that—would never have committed to living with Jason if she hadn't believed she loved him. If she hadn't believed he would change his mind about marriage.

'Only my pride was hurt,' she said now to Ben. 'Things between us weren't right for a long time. I wasn't happy, and he obviously wasn't either. It had to end somehow….' She took a deep breath. 'And here I am, making a fresh start.' She nodded decisively. 'Now, that's enough about me. Tell me more about your aunt Ida.'

'Sure,' he said, glad for the change in subject. 'Ida got married to her wayfaring sailor on some exotic island somewhere and sailed around the world with him on his yacht until he died. Then she came back here and started the bookshop—first at the other end of town and now in the row of new shops I built.'

'So you're her landlord?'

'The other guy was ripping her off on her rent.'

And Ben always looked after his own.

Sandy remembered how fiercely protective he'd been of his family. How stubbornly loyal. He would have been just as protective of his wife and son.

No wonder he had gone away when he'd lost them. What had brought him back to Dolphin Bay, with its tragic memories?

He turned to face her, his face composed, no hint from his expression that he might have been about to kiss her just minutes ago.

'It was good of you to play along with me to make her happy. I just had to get her into that ambulance and on her way. Thank you.'

She shrugged. 'No problem. I'd like someone to do the same for my grandmother.'

He glanced down at his watch. 'Now you'd better go have your lunch before they close down the kitchen. Sorry I can't join you, but—'

'But what?' Sandy tilted her head to one side. She put up her hand in a halt sign. 'Am I missing something here? Aren't you meant to be showing me the bookshop?'

Ben swivelled back to face her. He frowned. 'Why would you want to see the bookshop?'

'Because I've volunteered to look after it for your aunt until you find someone else. I promised. Remember? Crossed my heart and—'

He cut across her words. 'But that wasn't serious. That was just you playing along with me so she'd go to the hospital. Just a tactic…'

Vehemently, she shook her head. 'A tactic? No it wasn't. I meant it, Ben. I said I'd help out for a few days and I keep my word.'

'But don't you have an interview in Melbourne?'

'Not until next Friday, and today's only Saturday. I was planning on meandering slowly down the coast…'

She thought regretfully of the health spa she'd hoped to check in to for a few days of much needed pampering. Then she thought of the concern in Ida's eyes.

'But it's okay. I'm happy to play bookshop for a while. Really.'

'There's no need to stay, Sandy. It won't be a problem to close the shop for a few days until I find a temporary manager.'

'That's not what your aunt thinks,' she said. 'Besides, it might be useful for my interview to say I've been managing a shop.' She did the quote thing again with her fingers. '"Recent retail experience"—yes, that would look good on my résumé.' An update on her university holiday jobs working in department stores.

Ben was so tight-lipped he was bordering on grim. 'Sandy, it's nice of you, but forget it. I'll find someone. There are agencies for emergency staff.'

Why was he so reluctant to accept such an easy solution to his aunt's dilemma? Especially when he'd been the one to suggest it?

It wasn't fair to blame her for not being aware of his 'tactic'. And she wasn't—repeat *wasn't*—going to let his lack of enthusiasm at the prospect of her working in the bookshop daunt her.

Slowly, she shook her head from side to side. 'Ben, I gave my word to your great-aunt and I intend to keep it.'

She looked to the doorway of Bay Books. Forced her voice to sound steady. 'C'mon, show me around. I'm dying to see inside.'

Ben hesitated. He took a step forward and then stopped. His face reminded her of those storm clouds that had banked up on the horizon.

Sandy sighed out loud. She made her voice mock scolding. 'Ben, I wouldn't like to be in your shoes if you have to tell your aunt I skipped out on her.'

His jaw clenched. He looked at her without speaking for a long second. 'Is that blackmail, Sandy?'

She couldn't help a smile. 'Not really. But, like I said, if I make a promise I keep it.'

'Do you?' he asked hoarsely.

The smile froze on her face.

Ben stood, his hands clenched by his sides. Was he remembering those passionately sworn promises to keep their love alive even though she was going back to Sydney at the end of her holiday?

Promises she hadn't kept because she'd never heard from him? And she'd been too young, too scared, to take the initiative herself.

She'd been wrong not to persist in trying to keep in touch

with him. Wrong not to have trusted him. Now she could see that. Twelve years too late she could see that.

'Yes,' she said abruptly and—unable to face him—turned on her heel. 'C'mon, I need to check out the displays and you need to show me how to work the register and what to do about special orders and all that kind of stuff.'

She knew she was chattering too quickly, but she had to cover the sudden awkwardness between them.

She braced herself and looked back over her shoulder. Was he just going to stay standing on the footpath, looking so forbidding?

No. With an exhaled sigh that she hoped was more exasperated than angry, he followed her through the door of Bay Books.

As Ben walked behind Sandy—forcing himself not to be distracted by the sway of her shapely behind—he cursed himself for being such an idiot. His impulsive ploy to placate Idy with a white lie about Sandy staying to help out had backfired badly.

How could he have forgotten just what a thoughtful, generous person Sandy could be? In that way she hadn't changed since she was eighteen, insisting on helping his mother wash the dishes at the guesthouse even though she'd been a paying guest.

Of course Sandy wouldn't lie to his great-aunt. He should have realised that. And now here she was, insisting on honouring her 'promise'.

The trouble was, the last thing he wanted was his old girlfriend in town, reminding him of what he'd once felt for her. What he didn't want to feel again. Not for her. Not for anyone.

Point-blank, he did *not* want Sandy helping out at Bay Books. Did not want to be faced by her positive get-up-and-go-for-it attitude, her infectious laugh and—he couldn't deny it—her lovely face and sexier-than-ever body.

He gritted his teeth and determined not to fall victim to her charm.

But as she moved through the store he couldn't help but be moved by her unfeigned delight in what some people called his great-aunt's latest folly.

He saw the familiar surrounds afresh through her eyes—the wooden bookcases with their frolicking dolphin borders, the magnificent carved wooden counter, the round tables covered in heavy fringed cloths and stacked with books both bestsellers and more off-beat choices, the lamps thoughtfully positioned, the exotic carpets, the promotional posters artfully displayed, the popular children's corner.

'I love it—I just love it,' she breathed. 'This is how a bookshop should be. Small. Intimate. Connected to its customers.'

Reverently, she stroked the smooth wooden surface of the countertop, caressed with slender pink-tipped fingers the intricate carved dolphins that supported each corner.

'I've never seen anything like it.'

'It's different, all right. On her travels Aunt Ida became good friends with a family of Balinese woodcarvers. She commissioned them to fit out the shop. Had all this shipped over.'

Sandy looked around her, her eyes huge with wonder. 'It's unique. Awesome. No wonder your aunt wants it in safe hands.'

Some people might find the shop too quaint. Old-fashioned in a world of minimalist steel and glass. Redundant at a time of electronic everything. But obviously not Sandy. He might have expected she'd appreciate Aunt Ida's eccentric creation. Just as she'd loved his family's old guesthouse.

She twirled around in the space between the counter and a crammed display of travel paperbacks.

'It even smells wonderful in here. The wood, of course. And that special smell of books. I don't know what it is—the paper, the binding.' She closed her eyes and inhaled with a look of ecstasy. 'I could just breathe it in all day.'

No.

His fists clenched tight by his sides. That was not what he wanted to hear. He didn't want Sandy to fit back in here to Dolphin Bay as if she'd never left.

He wanted her gone, back on that highway and heading south. Not connecting so intuitively with the magic his great-aunt had tried to create here. Not being part of his life just by her very presence.

How could he bear to have her practically next door? Every day she'd be calling on him to ask advice on how to run the shop. Seeking his help. Needing him.

And he wouldn't be able to resist helping her. Might even find himself looking in on the off chance that she needed some assistance with Aunt Ida's oddball accounting methods. Maybe bringing her a coffee from the hotel café. Suggesting they chat about the business over lunch.

That couldn't happen. He wouldn't let it happen. He needed his life to stay just the way it was. He didn't want to invite love into his life again. And with Sandy there would be no second measures.

Sandy threw herself down on the low, overstuffed sofa his aunt provided for customers to sit on and browse through the books, then jumped up again almost straight away. She clasped her hands together, her eyes shining with enthusiasm. 'It's perfect. I am *so* going to enjoy myself here.'

'It's only for a few days,' he warned. 'I'll talk to the agency straight away.' Again his voice was harsher than he'd intended, edged with fear.

She frowned and he winced at the quick flash of hurt in her eyes. She paused. Her voice was several degrees cooler when she replied.

'I know that, Ben. I'm just helping out until you get a manager. And I'm glad I can, now that I see how much of her heart your aunt has put into her shop.'

Avoiding his eyes, she stepped behind the counter, placed her hands on the countertop and looked around her. Despite his lack of encouragement, there was an eagerness, an excitement about her that he found disconcerting. And way too appealing.

She pressed her lips firmly together. 'I'll try not to bother you too much,' she said. 'But I'll need your help with operating the register. Oh, and the computer, too. Is all her inventory in special files?'

He knew he should show some gratitude for her helping out. After all, he'd been the one to make the ill-conceived suggestion that she should stay. But he was finding it difficult when he knew how dangerous it might be to have Sandy around. Until now he'd been keeping everything together in his under-control life. Or so he'd thought.

'I can show you the register,' he said grudgingly. 'The computer—that's a mystery. But you won't be needing to operate that. And, besides, it's only temporary, right?'

'Yeah. *Very* temporary—as you keep reminding me.'

This time she met his gaze head-on.

'But what makes you think I won't want to do as good a job as I can for your aunt Ida while I'm here? You heard what she said about needing every day of business.'

'I would look after her if she got into trouble.'

The truth was he didn't need the rent his great-aunt insisted on paying him. Could easily settle her overheads.

'Maybe she doesn't want to be looked after? Maybe she wants to be totally independent. I hope I'll be the same when I'm her age.'

Sandy at seventy-five years old? A quick image came to him of her with white hair, all skewered up in a bun on top of her head, and every bit as feisty as his great-aunt.

'I'm sure you will be,' he said, and he forced himself

not to smile at the oddly endearing thought. Or, by way of comparison, look too appreciatively at the beautiful woman who was Sandy now, on her thirtieth birthday.

'What about paying the bills?' she asked.

'I'll take care of that.'

'In other words,' she said with a wry twist to her mouth, 'don't forget that I'm just a temporary caretaker?'

'Something like that,' he agreed, determined not to make it easy for her. Though somewhere, hidden deep behind the armour he wore around his feelings, he wished he didn't have to act so tough. But if he didn't protect himself he might fall apart—and he couldn't risk that.

She looked up at him, her expression both teasing and serious at the same time. But her voice wasn't as confident as it had been. There was a slight betraying quiver that wrenched at him.

'You know something, Ben? I'm beginning to think you don't want me in Dolphin Bay,' she said, her eyes huge, her luscious mouth trembling. She took a deep breath. 'Am I right?'

He stared at her, totally unable to say anything.

Images flashed through his mind like frames from a flickering cinema screen.

Sandy at that long-ago surf club dance, her long hair flying around her, laughing as she and her sister tried to mimic Kate's outrageously sexy dancing, smiling shyly when she noticed him watching her.

Sandy breathless and trembling in his arms as he kissed her for the first time.

Sandy in the tiniest of bikinis, overcoming her fear to bravely paddle out on her body-board to meet him where the big waves were breaking.

Sandy, her eyes red and her face blotchy and tear-stained, running to him again and again to hurl herself in his arms for just one more farewell kiss as her father impatiently honked the horn on the family car taking her back to Sydney.

Then nothing. *Nothing.*

Until now.

He fisted his hands so tightly it hurt the harsh edges of the scars. Scars that were constant reminders of the agony of his loss.

How in hell could he answer her question?

CHAPTER FOUR

HE SAID *SHE* showed her emotions on her face? She didn't need a PhD in psychology to read his, either. It was only too apparent he was just buying time before spilling the words he knew she wouldn't want to hear.

For an interminable moment he said nothing. Shifted his weight from foot to foot. Then he uttered just one drawn-out word. 'Well…'

He didn't need to say anything else.

Sandy swallowed hard against the sudden, unexpected shaft of hurt. Forced her voice to sound casual, light-hearted. 'Hey, I was joking, but…but you're serious. You really *don't* want me around, do you?'

She pushed the rain-damp hair away from her face with fingers that weren't quite steady. Gripped the edge of the countertop hard, willing the trembling to stop.

When he finally spoke his face was impassive, his voice schooled, his eyes shuttered. 'You're right. I don't think it's a great idea.'

She couldn't have felt worse if he'd slapped her. She fought the flush of humiliation that burned her cheeks. Forced herself to meet his gaze without flinching. 'Why? Because we dated when we were kids?'

'As soon as people make the connection that you're my old girlfriend there'll be gossip, speculation. I don't want that.'

She swallowed hard against a suddenly dry throat, forced the words out. 'Because of your…because of Jodi?'

'That too.'

The counter was a barrier between them but he was close. Touching distance close. So close she could smell the salty, clean scent of him—suddenly heart-achingly familiar. After their youthful making out sessions all those years ago she had relished the smell of him on her, his skin on her skin, his mouth on her mouth. Hadn't wanted ever to shower it away.

'But…mainly because of me.'

His words were so quiet she had to strain to hear them over the noise of the rain on the metal roof above.

Bewildered, she shook her head. 'Because of you? I don't get it.'

'Because things are different, Sandy. It isn't only the town that's changed.'

His voice was even. Too even. She sensed it was a struggle for him to keep it under control.

He turned his broad shoulders so he looked past her and through the shop window, into the distance towards the bay as he spoke. 'Did Kate tell you everything about the fire that killed Jodi and my son, Liam?'

'No.' Sandy shook her head, suddenly dreading what she might hear. Not sure she could cope with it. Her knees felt suddenly shaky, and she leaned against the countertop for support.

Ben turned back to her and she gasped at the anguish he made no effort to mask.

'He was only a baby, Sandy, not even a year old. I couldn't save them. I was in the volunteer fire service and I was off fighting a blaze somewhere else. Everything was tinder-dry from years of drought. We thought Dolphin Bay was safe, but the wind turned. Those big gum trees near the guesthouse caught alight. And then the building. The guests got out. But…but not…' His head dropped as his words faltered.

He'd said before that he didn't want to talk about his tragedy—now it was obvious he couldn't find any more words. With a sudden aching realisation she knew it would never get easier for him.

'Don't,' she murmured, feeling beyond terrible that she'd forced him to relive those unbearable moments. She put her hand up to halt him, maybe to touch him, then let it drop again. 'You don't have to tell me any more.'

Big raindrops sat on his eyelashes like tears. She ached to wipe them away. To do something, anything, to comfort him.

But he'd just said he didn't want her here in town.

He raised his head to face her again. 'I lost everything that day,' he said, his eyes bleak. 'I have nothing to give you.'

She swallowed hard, glanced again at the scars on his hands, imagined him desperately trying to reach his wife and child in the burning guesthouse before it was too late. She realised there were scars where she couldn't see them. Worse scars than the visible ones.

'I'm not asking anything of you, Ben. Just maybe to be… to be friends.'

She couldn't stop her voice from breaking—was glad the rain meant they had the bookshop all to themselves. That no one could overhear their conversation.

He turned his tortured gaze full on to her and she flinched before it.

The words were torn from him. 'Friends? Can you really be "just friends" with someone you once loved?'

She picked up a shiny hardback from the pile to the left of her on the counter, put it back without registering the title. Then she turned back to face him. Took a deep breath. 'Was it really love? We were just kids.'

'It was for me,' he said, his voice gruff and very serious, his hands clenched tightly by his sides. 'It hurt that you never answered my letters, never got in touch.'

'It hurt me that you never wrote like you said you would,' she breathed, remembering as if it were yesterday the anguish of his rejection. Oh, yes, it had been love for her too.

But a small voice deep inside whispered that perhaps she had got over him faster than he had got over her. She'd never forgotten him but she'd moved on, and the memories of her first serious crush had become fainter and fainter. Sometimes it had seemed as though Ben and the times she'd had with him at Dolphin Bay had been a kind of dream.

She hadn't fully appreciated then what was apparent now—Ben wasn't a player, like Jason or her father. When he loved, he loved for keeps. In the intervening years she'd been attracted to men who reminded her of him and been bitterly disappointed when they fell short. She could see now there was only one man like Ben.

They both spoke at the same time.

'Why—?'

'Why—?'

Then answered at the same time.

'My father—'

'Your father—'

Sandy gave a short nervous laugh. 'And my mother, too,' she added, turning away from him, looking down at a display of mini-books of inspirational thoughts, shuffling them backwards and forwards. 'She told me not to chase after you when you were so obviously not interested. Even my sister, Lizzie, got fed up with me crying over you and told me to get over it and move on.'

'My dad said the same thing about you. That you had your own life in the city. That you wouldn't give me a thought when you were back in the bright lights. That we were too young, anyway.' He snorted. '*Too young.* He and my mother got married when they were only a year older than I was then.'

She looked up to face him. 'I phoned the guesthouse, you know, but your father answered. I was too chicken to speak to him, though I suspect he knew it was me. He told me not to call again.'

'He never said.'

Sandy could hear the beating of her own heart over the sound of the rain on the roof. 'We were young. Maybe too young to doubt them—or defy them.'

An awkward silence—a silence choked by the echoes of words unspoken, of kisses unfulfilled—fell between them until finally she knew she had to be the one to break it.

'I wonder what would have happened if we had—'

'Don't go there, Sandy,' he said.

She took a step back from his sudden vehemence, banging her hip on the wooden fin of a carved dolphin. But she scarcely felt the pain.

'Never torture yourself with *what if?* and *if only*,' he continued. 'Remember what you said? Water under the bridge.'

'It…it was a long time ago.'

She didn't know what else she could say. Couldn't face thinking of the 'what ifs?' Ben must have struggled with after the fire.

While he was recalling anguish and irredeemable loss, she was desperately fighting off the memories of how much fun they'd had together all those years ago.

She'd been so serious, so strait-laced, so under her father's thumb. For heaven's sake, she'd been old enough to vote but had never stayed out after midnight. Ben had helped her lighten up, take risks—be reckless, even. All the time knowing he'd be there for her if she stumbled.

He hadn't been a bad boy by any means, but he'd been an exciting boy—an irreverent boy who'd thumbed his nose at her father's old-fashioned edicts and made her question the ways she'd taken for granted. So many times she'd snuck out to meet him after dark, her heart thundering with both fear of what would happen if she were caught and anticipation of being alone with him.

How good it had felt when he'd kissed her—kissed her

at any opportunity when they could be by themselves. How his kisses, his caresses, had stirred her body, awakening yearnings she hadn't known she was capable of.

Yearnings she'd never felt as strongly since. Not even for Jason.

Saying no to going all the way with Ben that summer was one of the real regrets of her life. Losing her virginity to him would have been an unforgettable experience. How could it not have been when their passion had been so strong?

She couldn't help remembering their last kiss—with her father about to drag her into the car—fired by unfulfilled passion and made more poignant in retrospect because she'd had no idea that it would be her last kiss from Ben.

Did he remember it too?

She searched his face, but he seemed immersed in his own dark thoughts.

Wearily, she wiped her hand over her forehead as if she could conjure up answers. Why had those kisses been printed so indelibly on her memory? Unleashed passion? Hormones? Pheromones? Was it the magic of first love? Or was it a unique power that came only from Ben?

Ben who had grown into this intense, unreadable, tormented man whom she could not even pretend to know any more.

The rain continued to fall. It muffled the sound of the cars swishing by outside the bookshop, made it seem as if they were in their own world, cocooned by their memories from the reality of everyday life in Dolphin Bay. From all that had happened in the twelve years since they'd last met.

Ben cleared his throat, leaned a little closer to her over the barrier of the counter.

'I'm glad you told me you never got my letters, that you tried to phone,' he said, his voice gruff. 'I never understood how you could just walk away from what we had.'

'Me too. I never understood how you didn't want to see me again, I mean.'

She thought of the tears she'd wept into her pillow all those years ago. How abandoned she'd felt. How achingly lonely. Even the agony of Jason's betrayal hadn't come near it.

Then she forced her thoughts to return to today. To Ben's insistence that he didn't want her hanging around Dolphin Bay, even to help his injured aunt at a time of real need for the old lady.

It was beyond hurtful.

Consciously, she straightened her shoulders. She forced a brave, unconcerned edge to her voice. 'But now we know the wrong my father did maybe we can forget old hurts and… and feel some kind of closure.'

'Closure?' Ben stared at her. 'What kind of psychobabble is *that*?'

Psychobabble? She felt rebuffed by his response. She'd actually thought 'closure' was a very well-chosen word. Under the circumstances.

'What I mean is…maybe we can try to be friends? Forgive the past. Forget there was anything else between us?'

She was lying. *Oh, how she was lying.*

While her mind dictated emotion-free words like 'closure' and 'friends' her body was shouting out that she found him every bit as desirable as she had twelve years ago. More so.

Just months ago—when she'd still had a job—she'd worked on a campaign for a hot teen surf clothing label. Ben at nineteen would have been perfectly cast in the lead male role, surrounded by adoring bikini-clad girls.

Now, Ben at thirty-one could star as a hunky action man in any number of very grown-up commercials. His face was only improved by his cropped hair, the deep tan, the slight crinkles around his eyes and that intriguing scar on his mouth. His damp shirt moulded to a muscled chest and powerful shoulders and arms.

Now they were both adults. Experienced adults. She'd

been the world's most inexperienced eighteen-year-old. What would she feel if she kissed him now? A shudder ran deep inside her. There would be no stopping at kisses, that was for sure.

'You may be able to forget we were more than friends but I can't,' he said hoarsely. 'I still find you very attractive.'

So he felt it too.

Something so powerful that twelve years had done nothing to erode it.

Her heart did that flippy thing again, over and over, stealing her breath, her composure. Before she could stutter out something in response he continued.

'That's why I don't want you in Dolphin Bay.'

She gasped at his bluntness.

'I don't mean to sound rude,' he said. 'I…I just can't deal with having you around.'

What could she say in response? For all her skill as an award-winning copywriter, she couldn't find the right words in the face of such raw anguish. All she could do was nod.

That vein throbbed at his temple. 'I don't want to be reminded of what it was like to…to have feelings for someone when I can't…don't want to ever feel like that again.'

The pain behind his confession made her catch her breath in another gasp. It overwhelmed the brief flash of pleasure she'd felt that he still found her attractive. And it hurt that he was so pointedly rejecting her.

'Right,' she said.

Such an inadequate word. Woefully inadequate.

'Right,' she repeated. She cleared her throat. Looked anywhere but at him. 'I hear what you're saying. Loud and clear.'

'I'm sorry, I—'

She put up her hand in a halt sign. 'Don't be. I…I appreciate your honesty.'

Her heart went out to him. Not in pity but in empathy. She had known pain. Not the kind of agony he'd endured, but pain just the same. Her parents' divorce. Jason's callous dumping. Betrayal by the friends who'd chosen to be on Jason's side in the break-up and had accepted invitations to today's wedding of the year at St Mark's, Darling Point, the Sydney church famed for society weddings.

But the philosophy she'd evolved in those years when she'd been fighting her father's blockade on letting her lead a normal teenage life had been to refuse to let hurt and disappointment hold her back for long. She now firmly believed that good things were always around the corner. That light always followed darkness. But you had to take steps to invite that light into your life. As she had in planning to leave all the reminders of her life with Jason behind her.

Ben had suffered a tragedy she could not even begin to imagine. Would he ever be able to move out of the shadows?

'Honesty is best all round,' he said, the jagged edge to his voice giving a terrible sincerity to the cliché.

She gritted her teeth against the thought of all Ben had endured since they'd last met, the damage it had done to him. And yet…

From what she remembered of sweet-faced Jodi Hart, she couldn't imagine she would want to see the husband she'd loved wrapping himself in a shroud of grief and self-blame, not allowing himself ever again to feel happiness or love.

But it was not for her to make that judgement. She, too, belonged to Ben's yesterday, and that was where he seemed determined to keep her. He did not want to be part of her tomorrow in any way.

If only she could stop wondering if the magic would still be there for them…if they could both overcome past hurts enough to try.

She had to force herself not to sigh out loud. The attraction she felt for him was still there, would never go away. It was a longing so powerful it hurt.

'Now I know where I stand,' she said, summoning the strength to make her voice sound normal.

He was right. It was best to get it up-front. Ben was not for her. Not any more. The barriers he had up against her were so entrenched they were almost visible.

But in spite of it all she refused to regret her impulsive decision to return to Dolphin Bay. It was healing to meet up with Ben and discover that he hadn't, after all, heartlessly ditched her all those years ago. Coming after the Jason fiasco, that revelation was a great boost to her self-esteem.

She forced a smile. 'That's sorted, then. Let's get back on track. Tell me more about Bay Books. I'm going to be the best darn temporary manager you'll ever see.'

'So long as you know it's just that. Temporary.'

She nodded. She could do this. After all, she loved reading and she loved books—e-books, audiobooks, but especially the real thing. Added to that, the experience of looking after the bookshop might help her snag the candle store franchise. Maybe her reckless promise to Ida might turn out to benefit herself as much as Ben's great-aunt.

Yes, making that swift exit off the highway this morning had definitely been a good idea. But in five days she would get back into her green Beetle and put Dolphin Bay and Ben Morgan behind her again.

Five days of wanting Ben but knowing it could never be.

Five days to eradicate the yearning, once and for all.

But the cup-half-full part of her bobbed irrepressibly to the surface. There was one other way to look at it: five days to convince him they should be friends again. And after that who knew?

CHAPTER FIVE

BEN WATCHED THE emotions as they played across Sandy's face. Finally her expression settled at something between optimistic and cheerful.

He might have been fooled if he hadn't noticed the tight grip of her hands on the edge of the countertop. Even after all these years and a high-powered job in advertising she hadn't learned to mask her feelings.

He had hurt her. Hurt her with his blunt statements. Hurt her with his rejection of her friendship, his harsh determination to protect himself from her and the feelings she evoked.

He hated to cause her pain. He would fight with his fists anyone who dared to injure her in any way. But he had to be up-front. She had to know the score. The fire had changed him, snatched his life from him, forged a different person from the one Sandy remembered. *He had nothing left to give her.*

Her eyes were guarded, the shadows beneath them more deeply etched. She tilted her head to one side. A wispy lock of rain-damp hair fell across her face. He had to force himself not to reach out and tenderly push it aside, as he would have done twelve years ago.

She took a deep breath and again he couldn't help but appreciate the enticing swell of her breasts. She'd been sizzling at eighteen. As a woman of thirty she was sexual dynamite. Ignite it and he was done for.

Finally she spoke. 'Okay, so maybe promising to help your aunt wasn't such a great idea. But I crossed my heart. I'm here in Dolphin Bay. Whether you like it or not.'

Her lovely pink-stained mouth trembled and she bit down firmly on her lower lip. She blinked rapidly, as if fighting back tears, sending a wrenching shaft of pain straight to his heart.

She choked out her words. 'Don't be angry at me for insisting on staying. I couldn't bear that.'

'Like I'd do *that*, Sandy. Surely you know me better?'

She shook her head slowly from side to side. Her voice broke like static. 'Ben, I don't know you at all any more.'

A bruised silence fell between them. He was powerless to do anything to end it. Each breath felt like an effort.

Sandy's shoulders were hunched somewhere around her ears. He watched her make an effort to pull them down.

'If you don't want to be friends, where does that put us?'

'Seems to me we're old friends who've moved on but who have been thrown together by circumstance. Can't we leave it at that?'

Before she had a chance to mask it, disappointment clouded her eyes. She looked away. It was a long moment before she nodded and looked back up at him. Her voice was resolute, as if she were closing on a business deal, with only the slightest tremor to betray her. 'You're right. Of course you're right. We'll be grown-up about this. Passing polite for the next five days. Is that the deal?'

She offered him her hand to shake.

He looked at it for a long moment, at her narrow wrist and slender fingers. Touching Sandy wasn't a good idea. Not after all these years. Not when he remembered too well how good she'd felt in his arms. How much he wanted her—had always wanted her.

He hesitated a moment too long and she dropped her hand back by her side.

He'd hurt her again. He gritted his teeth. What kind of a man was he that he couldn't shake her hand?

'That's settled, then,' she said, her voice brisk and businesslike, her eyes not meeting his. 'By the way, I'll need somewhere to sleep. Any suggestions?'

Wham! What kind of sucker punch was that? His reaction was instant—raw, physical hunger for her. Hunger so powerful it knocked him for six.

He knew what he ached to say. *You can sleep in my bed. With me. Naked, with your legs twined around mine. On top of me. Beneath me. With your face flushed with desire and your heart racing with passion. Sleep with me so we can finish what we started so long ago.*

Instead he clenched his fists by his sides, looked somewhere over her head so he wouldn't have to see her face. He couldn't let her guess the thoughts that were taking over his mind and body.

'You'll be my guest at the hotel. I'll organise a room for you as soon as I get back.'

She put up her hand. 'But that won't be necessary. I—'

He cut short her protest. 'No buts. You're helping my family. You don't pay for accommodation. You'll go in a penthouse suite.'

She shook her head. 'I'm happy to pay, but if you insist—'

'I insist.' He realised, with some relief, that the rain had stopped pelting on the roof. 'The weather has let up. We'll get you checked in now.'

The twist to her mouth conceded defeat, although he suspected the argument was far from over. Like Idy, she was fiercely independent. Back then she'd always insisted on paying her way on their dates. Even if she only matched him ice cream for ice cream or soft drink for soft drink.

'Okay. Thanks. I'll just grab my handbag and—' She felt around on the counter, looked around her in panic. 'My bag!'

'It's at Reception. Kate picked it up.'

Kate, her eyes wide with interest and speculation, had whispered to him as they were helping Ida into the ambulance. She said Sandy had been in such a hurry to follow him out of the restaurant and onto the sand she'd left her bag behind.

Kate obviously saw that as significant. He wondered how many people now knew his old girlfriend was back in town.

The phone calls would start soon. His mother first up. She'd liked Sandy. She'd never pried into his and his brother Jesse's teenage love lives. But she'd be itching to know why Sandy was back in town.

And he'd wager that Sandy would have a stream of customers visiting Bay Books. Customers whose interest was anything but literary.

Sandy went to move from behind the counter.

'Sandy, before you go, there's something I've been meaning to tell you.'

She frowned. 'Yes?'

He'd been unforgivably ill-mannered not to shake her hand just to avoid physical contact. So what inexplicable force made him now lean towards her and lightly brush his thumb over her mouth where it was stained that impossibly bright pink? He could easily tell her what he had to without touching her.

His pulse accelerated a gear at the soft, yielding feel of her lips, the warm female scent of her. She quivered in awareness of his touch, then stood very still, her cheeks flushed and her eyes wide.

He didn't want her around. Didn't want her warmth, her laughter, falling on his heart like drops of water on a spiky-leaved plant so parched it was in danger of dying. A plant that needed the sun, the life-giving rain, but felt safe and comfortable existing in the shadows, living a half-life that until now had seemed enough.

'Sandy….' There was so much more he wanted to say. But couldn't.

She looked mutely back at him.

He drew a deep, ragged breath. Cleared his throat. Forced his voice into its usual tone, aware that it came out gruffer but unable to do anything about it.

'I don't know if this is the latest city girl look, but your mouth…it's kinda pink in the middle. You might want to fix it.'

She froze, then her hand shot to her mouth. 'What do you mean? I don't use pink lipstick.'

Without saying a word he walked around to her side of the counter and pulled out a drawer. He handed her the mirror his aunt always kept there.

Sandy looked at her image. She stared. She shrieked. 'That's the ink from my niece Amy's feather pen!'

It was difficult not to grin at her reaction.

Then she glared at him, her eyes sparking, though she looked about as ferocious as one of the stray puppies his mother fostered. '*You!* You let me go around all this time looking like this? Why didn't you tell me?'

He shrugged, finding it hard not show his amusement at her outraged expression. 'How was I to know it wasn't some fashion thing? I've seen girls wearing black nail polish that looks like bruises.'

'But this…' She wiped her hand ineffectively across her mouth. 'This! I look like a circus clown.'

He shrugged. 'I think it's kinda cute. In a…circusy kind of way.'

'You!' She scrutinised her image and scrubbed hard at her mouth.

Now her lips looked all pouty and swollen, like they'd used to after their marathon teen making out sessions. He had to look away. To force himself not to remember.

She glared again. 'Don't you ever, *ever* let me go out in public again looking weird, okay?'

'I said cute, not weird. But okay.' He couldn't help his mouth from lifting into a grin.

Her eyes narrowed into accusing slits. 'Are you laughing at me, Ben Morgan?'

'Never,' he said, totally negating his words by laughing.

She tried, but she couldn't sustain the glare. Her mouth quirked into a grin that spilled into laughter chiming alongside his.

After all the angst of the morning it felt good to laugh. Again he felt something shifting and stirring deep inside the seized and rusted engine of his emotions. He didn't want it to fire into life again. That way led to pain and anguish. But already Sandy's laughter, her scent, her unexpected presence again in his life, was like the slow drip-drip-drip of some powerful repair oil.

'C'mon,' he said. 'While the rain's stopped let's get you checked into the hotel. Then I have to get back to work.'

As he pulled the door of Bay Books closed behind him he found himself pursing his mouth to whistle. A few broken bars of sound escaped before he clamped down on them. He glanced to see if Sandy had noticed, but her eyes were focused on the street ahead.

He hadn't whistled for years.

CHAPTER SIX

SANDY SAT IN her guest room at Hotel Hideous, planning a new list. She shivered and hugged her arms to herself. The room was air conditioned to the hilt. There was no stinting on luxury in the modern, tasteful furnishings. She loved the dolphin motif that was woven into the bedcover and decorative pillows, and repeated discreetly on the borders of the curtains. And the view across the old harbour and the bay was beyond magnificent.

But it wasn't a patch on the charm of the old guesthouse. Who could have believed the lovely building would come to such a tragic end? She shuddered at the thought of what Ben had endured. Was she foolish to imagine that he could ever get over his terrible losses? Ever be able to let himself love again?

She forced herself to concentrate as she turned a new page of her fairy notebook. The pretty pink pen had been relegated to the depths of her handbag. She didn't have the heart to throw Amy's gift in the bin, even though she could never use it again.

She still burned at the thought of not just Ben but Kate, Ida and who-knew-who-else seeing her with the hot pink stain on her mouth. It was hardly the sophisticated image she'd thought she was putting across. Thankfully, several minutes of scrubbing with a toothbrush had eliminated the stain.

But maybe the ink stain had, in a roundabout way, served a purpose. Thoughtfully, she stroked her lip with her finger, where Ben's thumb had been. After all, hadn't the stain induced Ben to break out of his self-imposed cage and actually touch her?

She took a pen stamped with the Hotel Harbourside logo—which, of course, incorporated a dolphin—from the desk in front of her and started to write—this time in regulation blue ink.

1. *Reschedule birthday celebrations.*

No.

Postpone indefinitely.

Was turning thirty, with her life such a mess, actually cause for celebration anyway? Maybe it was best left unmarked. She could hope for better next year.

2. *Congratulate self for not thinking once about The Wedding.*

She scored through the T and the W to make them lower case. It was her friends who had dramatised the occasion with capital letters. Her so-called friends who'd gone over to the dark side and accepted their invitations.

She could thank Ben's aunt Ida for pushing all thoughts of That-Jerk-Jason and his lucrative trip down the aisle out of her mind.

Or—and she must be honest—was it really Ida who'd distracted her?

She realised she was gnawing the top of the pen.

3. *Quit chewing on pens for once and for all. Especially pens that belong to first love.*

First love now determined not even to be friends.
Which brought her to the real issue.

4. *Forget Ben Morgan.*

She stabbed it into the paper.

Forget the shivery delight that had coursed through her when his finger had traced the outline of her mouth. Forget how he'd looked when he had laughed—laughed at her crazy pink ink stain—forget the light in his eyes, the warmth of his smile. Forget the stupid, illogical hope that sprang into her heart when they joked together like in old times.

She slammed the notebook shut, sending glitter shimmering over the desk. Opened it again. She underscored the last words.

Then got on to the next item.

5. *Visit Ida and get info on running bookshop.*

She had to open Bay Books tomorrow and she didn't have a clue what she should be doing. This was scary stuff.

She leaned back in her chair to think about the questions she should ask the older lady when the buzzer to her room sounded.

'Who is it?' she called out, slamming her notebook shut again in a flurry of glitter.

'Ben.'

In spite of her resolutions her heart leaped at the sound of his voice. 'Just give me a second,' she called.

Her hands flew to her face, then smoothed her still-damp-from-the-shower hair. She tightened the belt on the white towelling hotel bathrobe. She ran her tongue around suddenly dry lips before she fumbled with the latch and opened the door.

Ben filled the doorway with his broad shoulders and impressive height. Her heart tripped into double time at the sight of him. He had changed into jeans and a blue striped shirt that brought out the colour of his eyes. Could any man be more handsome?

She stuttered out a greeting, noticed he held a large brown paper grocery bag in one hand.

He thrust the bag at her. 'For you. I'm not good at gift wrapping.'

She looked from the bag up to him. 'Gift wrapping?'

'I feel bad your birthday turned out like this.'

'This is a birthday gift?'

He shrugged. 'A token.'

She flushed, pleased beyond measure at his thoughtfulness. 'I like surprises. Thank you.'

Not sure what to expect, she delved into the bag. It was jam-packed with Snickers bars. 'Ohmigod!' she exclaimed in delighted disbelief.

He shifted from foot to foot. 'You used to like them.'

She smiled at him. 'I still do. They're my favourite.'

She didn't have the heart to add that when she was eighteen she'd been able to devour the chocolate bars by the dozen without gaining weight, but that at thirty they were an occasional indulgence.

'Thank you,' she said. 'You couldn't have given me anything I'd like more.'

She wasn't lying.

Ben's thoughtfully chosen gift in a brown paper bag was way more valuable than any of the impersonal 'must-have' trinkets Jason had used to choose and have gift wrapped by the shop. Her last present from him had been an accessory for her electronic tablet that he had used more than she ever had.

Her heart swelled with affection for Ben. For wounded, difficult, vulnerable Ben.

She looked up at him, aching to throw her arms around him and kiss him. Kiss him for remembering her sweet tooth. Kiss him for the simple honesty of his brown-bagged gift. Kiss him for showing her that, deep down somewhere beneath his scars and defences, her Sir Galahad on a surfboard was still there.

But she felt too wary to do so. She wasn't sure she could handle any more rejection in one day. His words echoed in her head and in her heart: *'I don't want you in Dolphin Bay.'*

'Thank you,' she said again, feeling the words were totally inadequate to express her pleasure at his gesture.

He looked pleased with himself in a very male, tell-me-again-how-clever-I-was way she found endearing.

'I bought all the shop had—which just happened to be thirty.'

She smiled up at him. 'The shopkeeper must have thought you were a greedy pig with a desperate addiction to chocolate.'

'Nah. They know chilli corn chips are more to my taste.'

She hugged the bag of chocolate bars to her chest. 'So I won't have to share? Because you might have to fight me for them.'

'That makes *you* the greedy pig,' he said. 'They're all yours.' He stood still, looking deep into her eyes. 'Happy birthday, Sandy.'

She saw warmth mixed with wariness—which might well be a reflection of what showed in her own eyes.

Silence fell between them. She was aware of her own quickened breathing over the faint hum of the air-conditioning. Felt intoxicated by the salty, so familiar scent of him.

Now.

Surely now was the moment to kiss him? Suddenly she desperately wanted to feel his mouth—that sexy, sexy mouth—on hers. To taste again the memory that had lingered through twelve years away from him.

She felt herself start to sway towards him, her lips parting, her gaze focusing on the blue eyes that seemed to go a deeper shade of blue as he returned her gaze. Her heart was thudding so loudly surely he could hear it.

But as she moved he tensed and took an abrupt step backwards.

She froze. *Rejection again.* When would she learn?

She stepped back too, so hastily she was in danger of tripping backwards into the room. She wrapped her robe tighter around her, focused on the list of hotel safety instructions posted by the door rather than on him. A flush rose up her neck to sting her cheeks.

She couldn't think of a word to say.

After an excruciatingly uncomfortable moment Ben cleared his throat. 'I've been sent on a mission from Aunt Ida to find and retrieve you and take you to the hospital to meet with her.'

Sandy swallowed hard, struggled to make her voice sound light-hearted. 'Sounds serious stuff. Presumably an urgent briefing on the Bay Books project?'

He snapped his fingers. 'Right first guess.'

She smiled, knowing it probably looked forced but determined to appear natural—not as if just seconds ago she'd been longing for his kiss.

'Let me guess again. She's getting anxious about filling me in on how it all works?'

'Correct again,' he said. 'I promised to return with you ASAP to complete the mission.'

'Funnily enough I have no other pressing social engagements in Dolphin Bay.' She turned and started to walk back into the room, then stopped and looked back over her shoulder at him. 'Do you want to come in while I get dressed?'

His glance went briefly to her open neckline. He cleared his throat. 'Not a good idea.'

She blushed even redder and clutched the robe tighter. 'I mean… I didn't mean…' she stuttered.

'How about I come back to get you in half an hour?'

Her voice came out an octave higher. 'Twenty minutes max will be fine. Where will you be if I'm ready earlier?'

'Downstairs in my office.'

'Pick me up in twenty, then.'

He turned to go.

She swallowed against the sudden tension in her throat. 'Ben?' she said.

He swung back to face her, a question on his face.

'Thank you for the Snickers. I won't say I'll treasure them for ever, because they'll be devoured in double quick time. But…thank you.'

'You're welcome,' he said. 'It was—'

Afterwards she wondered at the impulse that had made her forget all caution, all fear of rejection. Before she could think about whether it was a good thing or not to do, propelled by pure instinct, she leaned up on her bare toes and kissed him lightly on his cheek.

Then she staggered at the impact of his closeness, at the memories that came rushing back in a flood of heat and hormones. The feel of his beard-roughened cheek beneath her lips, the strength of his tightly muscled body, the out-and-out maleness of him. She clung to him, overwhelmed by nostalgia for the past, for when she'd had the right to hold him close. *How could she ever have let go of that right?*

His hands grasped her shoulders to steady her. She could feel their warmth on her skin through the thick cloth of her robe. Swiftly, he released her. He muttered something inarticulate.

Reeling, she lifted her head in response, saw the shutters come down over his eyes—but not before she'd glimpsed something she couldn't read. It could have been passion but was more likely panic.

Bad, bad idea, Sandy, she berated herself. *Even a chaste peck is too much for him to handle.*

Too much for you *to handle.*

But no way was she was going to let herself feel ashamed

of a friendly thank-you kiss. She was used to spontaneous expressions of affection between friends.

She forced her breath to steady, tilted her chin upwards. 'See you in twenty,' she said, praying he didn't notice the tremor in her voice.

Ben stood back and watched as Sandy talked with his great-aunt in her room at the brand new Dolphin Bay Memorial Hospital. He might have known they would hit it off.

On doctor's orders, Ida was lying flat on her back in her hospital bed. She'd been told she had to hold that position for six weeks to heal her cracked pelvis.

Sandy had pulled up a chair beside her and was chatting away as if she and Ida were old friends.

Why, although they were talking about authors and titles of favourite books, did he sense this instant alliance could mean trouble for him? Trouble not of the business kind—hell, there was nothing he couldn't handle *there*—but a feminine kind of trouble he was not as well equipped to deal with.

Sandy was laughing and gesticulating with her hands as she spoke. His aunt was laughing too. It pleased him to see a warm flush vanquishing the grey tinge of pain from her face.

'What do you think, Ben?' Sandy asked.

'Me?'

'Yes. Who is the primary customer for Bay Books?'

He shrugged. 'People off the boats looking for something to read? Retirees?'

His aunt nodded. 'They're important, yes. But I sell more books to the telecommuters than to anyone else. They're crazy for book clubs. A book club gives them human contact as an antidote to the hours they spend working away on their computers, reporting to an office somewhere miles and miles away.'

Ben rubbed his hands together in simulated glee. 'All

those people fleeing the cities, making a sea-change to live on the coast—the lifeblood of commerce in Dolphin Bay. They're buying land, building houses, and spending their socks off.'

Sandy wrinkled up her nose in the way he remembered so well. It was just as cute on her at thirty as it had been at eighteen.

'That seems very calculating,' she said.

'What do you expect from the President of the Dolphin Bay Chamber of Commerce?' said Aunt Ida, her voice dripping with the pride all his family felt at his achievement. 'The town has really come on under his leadership.'

Sandy's eyes widened. 'You're full of surprises, Ben.'

On that so expressive face of hers he could see her wondering how he'd come from fisherman's son to successful businessman. Her father had judged him not good enough, not wealthy enough. He'd had no idea of how much land Ben's family owned. And Sandy didn't know how spurred on to succeed Ben had been by the snobby older man's low opinion of him.

'We have a lot to catch up on,' she said.

No.

More than ever he did *not* want to spend more time than was necessary with Sandy, reviving old feelings that were best left buried.

She was modestly dressed now, in a neat-fitting T-shirt and a skirt of some floaty material that covered her knees. But she'd answered the door to him at the hotel wrapped in nothing more than a Hotel Harbourside bathrobe.

As she'd spoken to him the robe had slid open to reveal the tantalising shadow between her breasts. Her face had been flushed and her hair damp. It was obvious she'd just stepped out of the shower and the thought of her naked had been almost more than his libido could take.

Naked in one of his hotel bathrooms. Naked under one of his hotel's bathrobes. It hadn't taken much to take the thought a step further to her naked on one of his hotel's beds. With the hotel's owner taking passionate possession.

He'd had to grit his teeth and force his gaze to somewhere above her head.

When she'd kissed him it had taken every ounce of his iron-clad self-control not to take her in his arms and kiss her properly. Not on the cheek but claiming her mouth, tasting her with his tongue, exploring her sexy body with hungry hands. Backing her into the room and onto the bed.

No.

There'd be no catching up on old times. Or letting his libido lead him where he had vowed not to go.

He cleared his throat. 'Isn't this conversation irrelevant to you running the bookstore for Aunt Ida?'

Sandy met his gaze in a way that let him know she knew only too well he was steering the conversation away from anything personal.

'Of course. You're absolutely right.'

She turned to face the hospital bed.

'Ida, tell me about any special orders.' Then she looked back at him, her head at a provocative angle. Her eyes gleamed with challenge. 'Is that better, Mr President?'

He looked to Ida for support, but her eyes narrowed as she looked from him to Sandy and back again.

It was starting. The speculation about him and Sandy. The gossip. And it looked as if he couldn't count on his aunt for support in his battle to protect his heart.

In fact she looked mighty pleased at the prospect of uncovering something personal between him and her temporary manager.

'You can tell me more about your past friendship with Sandy some other time, nephew of mine,' she said.

Sandy looked as uncomfortable as he felt, and had trouble meeting his gaze. 'Can we get back to talking about Bay Books, Ida?' she asked.

His aunt laughed. 'Back to the not nearly so interesting

topic of the bookshop? Okay, my dear, have you got something you can take some notes in? The special orders can get complicated.'

Looking relieved, Sandy dived into her handbag. She pulled out a luminous pink notebook and with it came a flurry of glitter that sparkled in the shafts of late-afternoon sun falling on his aunt's hospital bed.

'Sorry about the mess,' she said, biting down on her bottom lip as the particles settled across the bedcovers.

Ida seemed mesmerised by the glitter. 'It's not mess, it's fairy dust!' she exclaimed, clapping her hands with delight. Her still youthful blue eyes gleamed. 'Oh, this is wonderful, isn't it, Ben? Sandy will bring magic to Dolphin Bay. I just know it!'

Ben watched the tiny metallic particles as they glistened on the white hospital sheets. Saw the pleasure in his aunt's shrewd gaze, the gleam of reluctant laughter in Sandy's eyes.

'Magic? Well, it *did* come from my fairy notebook,' she said.

Something called him to join in their complicity, to believe in their fantasy.

Hope he'd thought long extinguished struggled to revive itself. Magic? *Was* it magic that Sandy had brought with her? Magic from the past? Magic for the future? He desperately wanted to believe that.

But there was no such thing as magic. He'd learnt that on a violently blazing day five years ago, when he had been powerless to save the lives of his family.

He would need a hell of a lot more than some so-called fairy dust to change his mind.

CHAPTER SEVEN

THE FIRST THING Sandy noticed on the beach early the next morning was the dog. A big, shaggy golden retriever, it lay near a towel on the sand near the edge of the water with its head resting on its paws. Its gaze was directed out to the surf of Big Ray Beach, the beach she'd reached via the boardwalk from the bay.

Twelve years ago she'd thought 'Big Ray' must refer to a person. No. Ben had informed her the beach had another name on the maps. But the locals had named it after the two enormous manta rays that lived on the northern end of the beach and every so often undulated their way to the other end. He had laughed at her squeals and hugged her close, telling her they were harmless and that he would keep her safe from anything that dared hurt her.

This morning there were only a few people in the water; she guessed one of them must be the dog's owner. At six-thirty, with strips of cloud still tinged pink from sunrise, it was already warm, the weather gearing up for sultry heat after the previous day's storm. Cicadas were already tuning up their chorus for the day.

Sandy smiled at the picture of doggy devotion. *Get dog of own once settled in Melbourne,* she added in a mental memo for her 'to do' list. That-Jerk-Jason had allergies and wouldn't tolerate a dog in the house. How had she been so in love with him when they'd had so little in common apart from their jobs?

She walked up to the dog and dropped to her knees in the sand. She offered it her hand to sniff, then ruffled the fur behind its neck. 'Aren't you a handsome boy?' she murmured.

The dog looked up momentarily, with friendly, intelligent eyes, thumped his plumed tail on the sand, then resumed his vigil.

She followed the animal's gaze, curious to see the object of such devotion. The dog's eyes were fixed on a man who was body-surfing. His broad, powerful shoulders and athletic physique were in perfect sync with the wave, harnessing its energy as it curled behind him and he shot towards shore.

The man was Ben.

She knew that even before he lifted his head from the water, a look of intense exhilaration on his face as he powered down the face of the wave. He was as at home on a wave as he had been when he was nineteen, and for a moment it was as if she were thrown back into the past. So much of her time with him that summer had been spent on this beach.

She was transported back to a morning like this when she'd run from the guesthouse to the sand and found him riding a wave, accompanied by a pod of dolphins, their grey shapes distinct on the underside of the wave. Joy and wonder had shone from his face. She'd splashed in to meet him and shared a moment of pure magic before the pod took off. Afterwards they'd lain on their backs on the beach, holding hands, marvelling over the experience. Did he remember?

Now he had seen her watching, and he lifted off the wave as it carried him into shore. She wanted to call out to him not to break off his ride on her account, but knew he wouldn't hear her over the sound of the surf.

He waved a greeting and swam, then strode towards her through the small breaking waves that foamed around his legs. Her breath caught in her throat at his near-naked magnificence. He was so tall and powerfully built that he seemed to dominate the vastness of the ocean and the horizon behind him.

His hair was dark and plastered to his head. The water was streaming off his broad shoulders and honed muscles. Sunlight glistened off the drops of water on his body so he seemed for one fanciful moment like some kind of mythical hero, emerging from the sea.

Desire, sudden and overwhelming, surged through her. Her nipples tensed and she seemed to melt inside. She wanted him. Longed for him. How could she ever have left him? She should have defied her parents and got back to Dolphin Bay. Somehow. Anyhow. Just to be with him.

That was back then. Now they were very different people who just happened to have found themselves on the same beach. But the attraction was as compelling as ever, undiluted by the years that had passed.

Why couldn't she forget that special time they had shared? What kept alive that fraction of hope that they could share it again? It wasn't just that she found him good-looking. This irrational compulsion was more than that. Something so powerful it overrode his rejection of her overtures. He didn't want her here. He had made that clear from the word go. She should just return his acquaintance-type wave and walk on.

But she ran in to the knee-deep waves to meet him. The dog splashed alongside her, giving a few joyous barks of welcome. She squealed at the sudden chill of the water as it sprayed her.

Remember, just friends, she reminded herself as she and Ben neared each other. Give him even a hint of the desire that had her so shaky and confused and he might turn back to that ocean and swim all the way to New Zealand.

'Good morning, Mr President,' she said. Ben as leader of the business community? It took some getting used to.

And yet the air of authority was there when he dealt with his staff at the hotel—and they certainly gave him the deference due to a well-respected boss.

'Just Ben will do,' he said as he walked beside her onto the dry sand. As always, she had trouble keeping up with his stride.

She was finding it almost impossible not to look at his body, impressive in red board shorts. Kept casting sideways glances at him.

'So you've met Hobo,' he said, with an affectionate glance at the dog.

'No formal introductions were made, but we said hello,' she said, still breathless at her physical reaction to him. 'Is he yours?'

She felt self-conscious at Ben's nearness, aware that she was wearing only a bikini covered by the skimpiest of tank tops.

'My mother helps out at a dog shelter. Sometimes she brings dogs home to foster until they find permanent homes. This one clapped eyes on me, followed me to my house and has been with me ever since.' He leaned down to pat the dog vigorously. 'Can't get rid of you, can I, mate?' He spoke with ill-concealed affection.

So he had something to love.

She was glad.

'He's adorable. And he guarded your towel like a well-trained soldier.'

Ben picked up the towel from the sand and flung it around his neck. *How many times had she seen him do that in just the same way? How many times had he tucked his towel solicitously around her if her own towel was damp?*

'What brings you to the beach so early?' he asked.

She pulled a face. 'Had to walk those Snickers bars off.'

'How many gone?'

'Only two.'

'One for dinner and one for breakfast?'

'Chocolate for breakfast? I've got a sweet tooth, but I'm not a total sugar freak.' She scuffed her foot in the sand. 'I couldn't sleep. Kept thinking of all I don't know about managing a bookstore.' *Kept thinking about you.*

He picked up a piece of driftwood and threw it for Hobo. The dog bounded into the water to retrieve it.

'You took a lot of notes from Aunt Ida yesterday.'

'It's just nerves. Bay Books is so important for Ida and I want to get it right.'

'You'll be fine. It's only for a few days.'

No doubt he meant to sound reassuring. But it seemed as if he was reminding her yet again that he wanted her out of Dolphin Bay.

'Yes. Just a few days,' she echoed. 'I guess I won't bankrupt the place in that time.'

Hobo splashed out of the shallows with the driftwood in his mouth, grinning a doggy grin and looking very pleased with himself. He dropped it between their feet.

Sandy reached down to pick it up at the same time as Ben did. She collided with his warm, solid shoulders, felt her head connect with his. 'Ouch!' She rubbed the side of her temple.

'Are you okay?' Ben pulled her to her feet and turned her to face him.

They stood very close, her hands on his shoulders where she'd braced herself for balance. He was damp and salty and smelled as fresh and clean as the morning. It would be so easy to slide her hands down, to tangle her fingers in his chest hair, test the strength of his muscles. Every cell in her body seemed to tingle with awareness where his bare skin touched hers.

She nodded, scarcely able to speak. 'That's one tough skull you've got there. But I'm fine. Really.'

He gently probed her head, his fingers sending currents of sensation coursing through her. 'There's no bump.'

'I think I'll live,' she managed to choke out, desperately attempting to sound flippant.

His big scarred hands moved from her scalp to cradle her face. He tilted her head so she was forced to look up into his eyes. For a long moment he searched her face.

'I don't want to hurt you, Sandy,' he said, his voice hoarse.

She knew he wasn't talking about the collision. 'I realise that, Ben,' she whispered.

Then, with her eyes drowning in his, he kissed her.

She was so surprised she stood stock-still for a moment. Then she relaxed into the sensation of Ben's mouth on hers. It felt like coming home.

When Ben had lifted his head from the wave and had seen Sandy standing on the beach, it had been as if the past and the present had coalesced into one shining moment. A joy so unexpected it was painful had flooded his heart.

And here he was, against all resolutions, kissing her.

Her lips were warm and pliant beneath his. Her breasts were pressed to his chest. Her eyes, startled at first, were filled with an expression of bliss.

He shouldn't be kissing her. Starting things he could not finish. Risking pain for both of them. But those thoughts were lost in the wonder of having her close to him again.

It was as if the twelve years between kisses had never happened.

He twined his hands in her shiny vanilla-scented hair, tilted her head back as he deepened the kiss, pushed against her lips with his tongue. Her mouth parted to welcome him, to meet the tip of his tongue with hers.

She made a small murmur of appreciation and wound her arms around his neck. His arms slid to her waist, to the smooth, warm skin where her top stopped, drawing her close. He could feel her heart thudding against his chest.

He wanted her. She could surely feel his arousal. But

this wasn't just about sex. It had always been so much more than that with Sandy.

The world shrank to just him and her, and the surf was a muted pounding that echoed the pulsing of their hearts, the blood running hot through his veins.

He could feel her nipples hard against him. Sensed the shiver of pleasure that vibrated through her. He pulled her tighter, wanting her as close to him as she could be.

But then something landed near his foot, accompanied by a piteous whining. Hobo. The driftwood. *Damn!*

He ignored it. Sand was dug in a flurry around them, stinging his legs. The whining turned to sharp, demanding barks.

Inwardly he cursed. Willed Hobo to go away. But the dog just kept on digging and barking. Ben broke away from the first time he'd kissed Sandy in twelve years for long enough to mutter, 'Get lost, boy.'

But when he quickly reclaimed Sandy's lips she was trembling. Not with passion but repressed laughter. 'He's not going to go away, you know,' she murmured against his mouth.

Ben groaned. He swore. He leaned down, grabbed the driftwood and threw it as far away as he could—so hard he nearly wrenched his shoulder.

Now Sandy was bent over with laughter. 'He wasn't going to let up, was he?'

Ben cursed his dog again.

'I know you don't really mean that,' she said, with a mischievous tilt to her mouth. 'Poor Hobo.'

'Back to the shelter for him,' Ben growled.

'As if,' said Sandy.

She looked up to him, her eyes still dancing with laughter. She looked as though she'd been thoroughly kissed. He didn't shave until after his morning surf and her chin was all pink from his beard. He felt a surge of possessiveness so fierce it was primal.

'That…that was nice, Ben.'

Nice? He struggled for a word to sum up what it had meant to him. When he didn't reply straight away, the soft, satisfied light of a woman who knew she was desired seemed to dim in her eyes.

'More than nice,' he said, and her eyes lit up again.

He reached out to smooth that wayward lock of hair from her eyes. She caught his hand with hers and dropped a quick kiss on it before she let it go.

'Why did you kiss me, Ben, when with every second breath you're telling me go away?'

Did he know the answer himself? 'Because I—'

He couldn't find the words to say, *Because you're Sandy, and you're beautiful, and I still can't believe you've come back to me, but I'm afraid to let you in because I don't want to love you and then lose you again.*

Her eyes were huge in her flushed face. She'd got damp from hugging him while he was still wet from the surf. Her tank top clung to her curves, her nipples standing erect through the layers of fabric.

She ran the edge of her pink pointy tongue along her lips to moisten her mouth. He watched, fascinated, aching to kiss her again.

A tremor edged her voice. 'It's still there, isn't it, Ben? That attraction. That feeling there isn't anyone else in this world at this moment but you and me. It was like that from the start and it hasn't changed.' She took a deep gulp of air. 'If only…'

He clenched his fists so hard his scars ached. 'I told you—no if-onlys. That—the kiss—it shouldn't have happened.'

'Why not?' Her eyes were still huge. 'We're both free. Grown-up now and able to choose what we want from our lives, choose who we want to be with.'

Choose to leave when we want to.

Even after that one brief kiss he could feel what it would

be like, having found her, to lose her again. He'd managed fine these past years on his own. He couldn't endure the pain of loss again.

She looked very serious, her brow creased. 'That time we had together all those years ago was so special. I don't know about you, but I was too young to appreciate just how special. I never again felt that certainty, that rightness. Maybe this unexpected time together is a gift. For us to get to know each other again. Or…or…maybe we have to try it again so that we can let it go. Have you thought of that?'

He shook his head. 'It's not that easy, Sandy.'

'Of course it isn't easy. It isn't easy for me either. I'm not in a rush to get my heart broken again.'

He noticed again the shadows under her eyes. Remembered her ex had got married yesterday. Typically, she wasn't letting on about her pain. But it was there.

'I can see that,' he said.

He was glad the beach was practically deserted, with just a few people walking along the hard, damp sand at the edge of the waves, others still in the surf. Hobo romped with another dog in the shallows.

Her voice was low and intense. 'Maybe if we gave it a go we'd…we'd burn it out.'

'You think so?' He couldn't keep the cynicism from his voice.

She threw up her hands. 'Who knows? After all this time we don't really know what the other is like now. Grown-up Sandy. Grown-up Ben. We might hate each other.'

'I can't see that happening.' Hate Sandy? No way. Never.

She scuffed the sand with her bare toes, not meeting his eyes. 'How do you know? I like to put a positive spin on things when I can. But, fact is, I haven't had a lot of luck with men. When I started dating—after I gave up on us seeing each other again—it seemed to me there were two types of men: nice ones, like you, who would ultimately betray me—'

He growled his protest.

She looked back up at him. 'I know now it was a misunderstanding between us, but I didn't know that then. If anyone betrayed me it was my father. By lying to me about you. By cheating on our family.'

He didn't disagree. 'And the second type of man?'

'Forceful, controlling guys—'

'Like your father?'

She nodded. 'They'd convince me they knew what was best for me. I'd be in too deep before I realised they had anything but my interests at heart. But obviously I must have been at fault, too, when things went wrong.'

'You're too hard on yourself.' He hated to see the tight expression on her face.

Her mouth twisted into an excuse of a smile. 'Am I? Even little things about a person can get annoying. Jason used to hate that I never replaced the empty toilet roll. It was only because the fancy holder he installed ruined my nails when I tried, but—'

Ben couldn't believe what he was hearing. 'What kind of a loser *was* this guy?'

'He wasn't a loser. He was smart. Clever. It seemed I could be myself with him. I thought at last I'd found Mr Perfect. But that was one of the reasons he gave for falling out of love with me.' She bit down hard on her lower lip. 'And he said I was noisy and a show-off.'

Ben was so astounded he couldn't find an appropriate response.

Her eyes flickered to his face and then away. 'When I first knew him he said I lit up a room just by coming into it. *Effervescent* was the word he used. By the end he said I embarrassed him with my loud behaviour.'

Her voice was forcedly cheerful but there was a catch to it that tore at Ben.

'But you don't want to hear about that.'

Anger against this unknown man who had hurt Sandy

fuelled him. 'You're damn right I don't. It's crap. That jerk was just saying that to make himself feel better about betraying you.'

She pulled a self-deprecating face. 'I tell myself that too. It made me self-conscious around people for a while—you know…the noisy show-off thing. I couldn't help wondering if people were willing me to shut up but were too polite to say so. But…but I've put it behind me.'

With his index finger he tilted her face upwards. 'Sandy. Look at me. I would never, ever think you were an embarrassing show-off. I never have and I never will. Okay? You're friendly and warm and you put people at ease. That's a gift.'

'Nice of you to say so. Kind words are always welcome.' Her voice made light of what she said.

'And I would never give a damn about a toilet roll.'

Her mouth twitched. 'It sounds so dumb when you say it out loud. A toilet roll.' The twitch led to a smile and then to full-blown giggles. 'What a stupid thing for a relationship to founder over.'

'And what a moron he was to let it.'

Ben found himself laughing with her. It felt good. Again, like oil on those rusty, seized emotions he had thought would never be kick-started into life again.

'I was just using the toilet roll as an example of how little things about a person can get annoying to someone else,' she said. Her laughter died away. 'After a few days of my company you might be glad to see the end of me.'

'And vice-versa?' The way he'd cut himself off from relationships, she was more likely to get the worst end of the bargain. He was out of the habit of being a boyfriend.

She nodded. 'Then we could both move on, free of… free of this thing that won't let go of us. With…with the past washed clean.'

'Maybe,' he conceded.

She wanted to rekindle old embers to see if they burned

again or fizzled away into lifeless ash. But what if they raged away like a bush fire out of control and he was the one left scorched and lifeless? *Again.*

She took hold of his arm. Her voice was underscored with urgency. 'Ben, we should grab this second chance. Otherwise we might regret it for the rest of our lives. Like I regret that I didn't trust in what we had. I should have come back to you to Dolphin Bay. I was eighteen years old, for heaven's sake, not eight. What could my parents have done about it?'

'I came looking for you in Sydney.' He hadn't meant to let that out. Had never intended to tell her.

Her brows rose. 'When?'

'A few months after you left.'

'I didn't know.'

'You wouldn't. My mates were playing football at Chatswood, on the north shore. I had my dad's car to drive down with them.' He'd been up from university for the Easter break. 'After the game I found your place.'

'The house in Killara?'

He nodded. It had been a big house in a posh northern suburb, designed to show off her father's social status. 'I parked outside, hoping I'd see you. Not sure what I'd do if I did.'

'Why didn't you come in?'

'I was nineteen. You hadn't written. Or phoned. For all I knew you'd forgotten all about me. And I knew your father wouldn't welcome me.'

'Was I there? I can't believe while you were outside I might have been in my room. Probably sobbing into my diary about how much I was missing you.'

'Your hat was hanging on the veranda. I could see it from outside. That funny, stripy bucket hat you used to wear.'

She screwed up her face. 'I remember… I lost that hat.'

'No, you didn't. I took it. I jumped over the fence and snatched it.'

Her eyes widened. 'You're kidding me? My old hat? Do… do you still have it?'

'Once I was back in the car my mates grabbed it from me. When we crossed the Sydney Harbour Bridge they threw it out of the window.'

'Hey! That hat cost a whole lot of hard-earned babysitting money.'

She pretended outrage, but he could tell she was shaken by his story.

'I didn't steal it to see it squashed by a truck. I wanted to punch my mates out. But they told me to stop bothering with a girl who didn't want me when there were plenty who did.'

Sandy didn't say anything for a moment. Then she sighed. 'Oh, Ben, if only…' She shook her head. 'I won't say it. You're right. No point.'

'That's when I gave up on you.'

He'd said enough. He could never admit that for years afterwards when he'd driven over that spot on the bridge he'd looked out for her hat.

'And there *were* other girls?' She put her hand up in her halt sign. 'No. Don't tell me about them. I couldn't bear it.' Her eyes narrowed. 'I used to imagine all those blonde surfer chicks. Glad the city interloper was gone. Able to have their surf god all to themselves again.'

He stared at her incredulously. 'Did you just call me a surf god?'

Colour stained her cheeks. 'Hey, I'm in advertising. I get creative with copy.' But when she looked up at him her eyes were huge and sincere. 'I adored you, Ben. You must know that.' Her voice caught in her throat.

Ben shifted from foot to foot in the sand. 'I… Uh… Same here.' *He'd planned his life around her.*

'Let's spend these four days together,' she urged. 'Forget all that's happened to us since we last saw each other. Just go back to how we were. Sandy and Ben. Teenagers again. Carefree. Enjoying each other's company. Recapturing what we had.'

'You mean a fling?'

'A four-day fling? No strings? Why not? I'm prepared to risk it if you are.'

Risk. Was he ready to risk the safe life he'd so carefully constructed around himself in Dolphin Bay? He'd done so well in business by taking risks. But taking this risk—even for four days—could have far greater complications than monetary loss.

'Sandy. I hear what you're saying. But I need time.'

'Ben, we don't have time. We—'

Hobo skidded at their feet, the driftwood in his mouth, wet and eager and demanding attention.

Sandy glared at the animal. 'You have a great sense of timing, dog.'

'Yeah, he's known for it.' Ben reached down for the driftwood and tossed it just a short distance away. 'I've got to get him back. Dogs are only allowed unleashed on the beach before seven a.m.'

'And you can't be seen to be breaking the rules, can you?'

Was she taunting him?

No. The expression in her eyes was wistful, and he realised how she'd put herself on the line for him. For them. Or the possibility of them.

He turned to her. 'I'll consider what you said, Sandy.'

Her tone was again forcedly cheerful. 'Okay, Mr President.'

He grinned. 'I prefer surf god.'

'I'm going to regret telling you I called you that, aren't I? Okay, surf god. But don't take too long. These four days will be gone before we know it and then I'm out of here. Let's not waste them.' She turned to face the water. 'Are the mantas still in residence?'

'Yes. More likely their descendants, still scaring the hell out of tourists.'

He remembered how she'd started off being terrified of the big black rays. But by the end of that summer she'd been snorkelling around them. She had overcome her fears. Could he be as brave?

She reached up and hugged him. Briefly, he held her bare warmth to him before she pushed him away.

'Go,' she said, her voice not quite steady. 'Me? I'm having my first swim at Big Ray Beach for twelve years. I can't wait to get into the surf.'

With unconscious grace she pulled off her skimpy tank top, giving him the full impact of her body in a brief yellow bikini. *Her breasts were definitely bigger than they'd been when she was eighteen.*

Was he insane not to pull her back into his arms? To kiss her again? To laugh with her again? To have her as part of his life again?

For four days.

She headed for the water, treating him to a tantalising view of her sexy, shapely bottom. 'Come see me when you've done your thinking,' she called over her shoulder, before running into the surf.

She squealed as the cold hit her. Water sprayed up over her slim brown legs and the early sunlight shattered into a million glistening crystals. *More fairy dust.*

He looked at the tracks her feet had made in the sand. After the fire he had felt as if he'd been broken down to nothing—like rock into sand. Slowly, painfully, he had put himself back together. But there were cracks, places deep inside him, that still crumbled at the slightest touch.

If he let it, could Sandy's magic help give him the strength to become not the man he had been but someone better, finer, forged by the tragedy he had endured? Or would she break him right back down to nothing?

CHAPTER EIGHT

EVERY TIME THE old-fashioned bell on the top of the entrance door to Bay Books jangled Sandy looked up, heart racing, body tensed in anticipation. And every time it wasn't Ben she felt so let down she had to force herself to smile and cheerfully greet the customers, hoping they wouldn't detect the false note to her voice.

When would he come? Surely he wanted to be with her as much as she ached to be with him?

Or was he staying away because she had driven him away, by coming on too strong before he was ready? His reaction had both surprised and hurt her. Why had he been so uncertain about taking this second, unexpected chance with her? It was only for four days. Surely they could handle that?

She knew she should stop reliving every moment on the beach this morning over and over again, as if she were still eighteen. But she couldn't stop thinking about the kiss. That wonderful, wonderful kiss. After all those years it could have been a let-down. But kissing Ben again had been everything she had ever fantasised about. In his arms, his mouth claiming hers, she'd still felt the same heady mix of comfort, pleasure and bone-melting desire. It was as if their twelve-year separation had never happened.

Although there was a difference. Now she wanted him with an adult's hunger—an adult's sensual knowledge of the pleasures that could follow a kiss.

She remembered how on fire with first-time desire she'd felt all that time ago, when they'd been making out behind the boat shed. Or in the back seat of his father's car, parked on the bluff overlooking the ocean. They hadn't even noticed the view. Not that they could have seen it through the fogged-up windows.

And yet she hadn't let him go all the way. Hadn't felt ready for that final step. Even though she had been head-over-heels in love with him.

Her virginal young self hadn't appreciated the effort it must have taken for Ben to hold back. 'When you're ready,' he'd always said. Not like her experiences with boys in Sydney—'suitable' sons of her fathers' friends—all grabby hands and then sulks when she'd slapped them away. No. Ben truly had been her Sir Galahad on a surfboard.

Would a four-day fling include making love with Ben? That might be more than she—or Ben—could handle. They should keep it to kissing. And talking. And lots of laughing. Like it had been back then. Carefree. Uncomplicated.

She refused to listen to that nagging internal voice. *Could anything be uncomplicated with the grown-up Ben?*

She forced her thoughts back to the present and got on with her work. She had to finish the job Ida had been in the middle of when she'd fallen—unpacking a delivery and slotting the books artfully onto the 'new releases' table.

Just minutes later, with a sigh of satisfaction, she stepped back to survey her work. She loved working in the bookshop. Even after just a few hours she felt right at home. The individuality and quirkiness of Ida's set-up connected with her, though she could immediately see things she'd like to change to bring the business model of this bricks-and-mortar bookstore more in step to compete with the e-bookstores. That said, if she could inject just a fraction of Bay Books' charm into her candle shop she'd be very happy. She must write in her fairy notebook: *Ask Ida about Balinese woodcarvers.*

But it wasn't just about the wooden dolphins with their enchanting carved smiles. The idyllic setting was a vital part of Bay Books. Not, she suspected, to be matched by the high-volume-retail-traffic Melbourne mall the candle people would insist on for their shop. It might be hard to get as excited about that.

Here, she only had to walk over to the window to view the quaint harbour, with the old-fashioned stone walls that sheltered it from the turquoise-blue waters of the open sea—only had to push the door open to hear the squawk of seagulls, breathe in the salt-tangy air.

This morning, in her hotel room, she had been awoken by a chorus of kookaburras. When she'd opened the sliding doors to her balcony it had been to find a row of lorikeets, the small, multi-coloured parrots like living gems adorning the balcony railing. On her way to the beach she'd surprised two small kangaroos, feeding in the grass in the bushland between the boardwalk and the sand dunes of Big Ray. It was good for the soul.

What a difference from fashionable, revitalised inner-city Surry Hills, where she lived in Sydney. It had more restaurants, bars and boutiques than she would ever have time to try. But it was densely populated and in summer could be stiflingly hot and humid. Driving round and round the narrow streets, trying to find somewhere to park her car, she'd sometimes dreamed of living in a place closer to nature.

And here she was back in Dolphin Bay, working in a stranger's bookshop, reconnecting with her first love.

It seemed surreal.

She paused, a paperback thriller in her hand. Remembered her pink-inked resolution. *Get as far away from Sydney as possible.*

That didn't necessarily have to mean moving to Melbourne.

But she had only ever been a city girl. Could she settle for small-town life and the restrictions that entailed?

The bell sounded again. She looked up, heart thudding, mouth suddenly dry. But again it wasn't Ben. It was red-haired Kate, the waitress from the hotel.

'Hey, nice to see you, Kate,' she said, masking her disappointment that the woman wasn't her tall blond surf god.

'You too,' said Kate. 'We all love this shop and the personal service Ida gives us. It's great you're able to help her out.'

'Isn't it? I'm getting the hang of things. Can I help you with a book?' she asked.

Kate smiled and Sandy wondered if she could tell how inexperienced a shopkeeper she was.

'Ida ordered some titles for me, but in all the drama yesterday I didn't get a chance to see if they were in.'

'Sure,' said Sandy, heading behind the counter to access Ida's computer. She had the special orders file open when Kate leaned towards her over the carved wooden counter.

'So, I heard you and Ben were kissing on the beach this morning.'

Sandy was so flabbergasted she choked. She coughed and spluttered, unable to utter a word in response.

Kate rushed around the counter and patted Sandy's back until her breath came more easily.

'Thanks,' Sandy finally managed to choke out.

'Don't be so surprised. News travels fast in Dolphin Bay.'

Sandy took another ragged breath. 'I'm beginning to see that.'

Kate's green eyes gleamed. 'So you *were* kissing Ben?'

Again Sandy was too aghast to reply. 'Well, I…' she started.

'She who hesitates is thinking of how to tell me to mind my own business,' said Kate with a grin.

Sandy laughed at her audacity. 'Well, now that you mention it…'

'Feel free to tell me to keep my big mouth shut, but… well, I love Ben to pieces and I don't want—'

Ben and Kate?

Sandy felt dizzy—not from lack of air but from the feeling that her heart had plummeted to the level of her ballet flats. 'I'm sorry, Kate, I didn't know… He didn't say…'

Kate's auburn eyebrows rose. 'I don't mean *that* kind of love. My mum and Ben's mum are friends. I grew up with Ben. It's his brother, Jesse, I have a thing for. Unrequited, unfortunately.'

'Oh,' said Sandy, beyond relieved that Kate hadn't marched into the bookshop to stake a claim on Ben.

Kate leaned closer. 'You *do* realise that for Ben to be kissing a woman in public is a big, big deal?'

Sandy took a step back. 'It was six-thirty in the morning on a practically deserted beach.'

'That might be private in Sydney, but not in a place like Dolphin Bay. Here, it takes one person to see for everyone to know.'

'I had no idea.' Sandy felt suddenly dry in the mouth. What kind of pressure did this put on Ben? On her?

'You and Ben together is big news.'

'Then next time—if there is a next time—I'll make sure we're completely alone.'

She spoke with such vehemence that Kate frowned and took a step back from her. 'I'm sorry, Sandy. But this is a small town. We all look out for each other. If you're not serious about Ben don't start something you're not prepared to see through.'

Sandy gripped the edge of the counter. She knew Ben had been to hell and wasn't yet all the way back. She didn't need anyone to tell her.

Pointedly, she scrolled through the special orders file on Ida's computer, looked up again at Kate. 'I don't see your order here, but your contact number is. How about I call you when it comes in?'

Kate shifted from foot to foot. 'You must think I'm the nosiest busybody you've ever met.'

Sandy didn't disagree.

'But I've only got Ben's interests at heart,' Kate continued, sounding hurt.

Sandy gentled her tone of voice. 'I appreciate that.'

She was gratified at Kate's smile as she said goodbye. Despite the redhead's total lack of tact, she thought she could get to like her.

But Kate's visit, with her revelation about the undercurrents of small-town life, had left her reeling. She'd had no idea that any reunion would be conducted under such watchful eyes. What had seemed so simple on the beach at dawn suddenly seemed very complicated.

It made her self-conscious when dealing with the customers who came in dribs and drabs through the doors. Were they genuinely interested in browsing through the books—or in perusing her? Her doubts were realised when two older ladies, hidden from full view behind a display of travel books, spoke in too-loud whispers they obviously thought she couldn't hear.

'She seems nice, and Ida likes her,' said the first one. 'That's a point in her favour.'

Sandy held her breath when she realised they were talking about her.

'It might be a good thing. Ben's been in mourning for too long. His mother's worried about him,' said the other.

'I wonder what Jodi's parents will think.' The first lady sighed. 'Such a sweet girl. What a loss. No wonder Ben's stayed on his own all this time.'

Sandy slammed her hand over her mouth so the ladies wouldn't hear her gasp. *Jodi.* Ben's late wife. The gentle woman Ben had loved enough to marry and have a child with.

She stared ahead without seeing. Noticed a poster promoting a bestselling new celebrity biography had come adrift at one corner. But she felt too shaken to do anything about it. Would there always be the memory of another woman coming between her and Ben? *Could she cope with coming second? With being just a disposable fling while his wife always held first place in his heart?*

She couldn't meet the ladies' eyes when they scurried out through the door without buying a book.

An old familiar panic had started to overwhelm her—the same panic she'd used to feel when she'd been faced with those big waves rearing up so aggressively as she'd stood dry-mouthed with terror on the beach. Ben had helped her conquer that fear and discover the joy of riding the waves—and she'd used the memory to help her deal with any number of challenges she'd faced in her career. But now what she'd thought would be smooth water ahead might be filled with swirling undercurrents. Did she have the strength to battle through the rough water?

Was it worth it for a four-day fling?

The bell on the top of the door jangled again. She jumped. More ladies to check her out and assess her suitability?

Ben shouldered his way through the door, carrying two large take-away coffee containers. The smile he gave her made her heart do the flippy thing—backwards, forwards and tumbling over itself. Her breath seemed to accelerate, making her feel light-headed, giddy.

Her surf god. In the flesh and hotter than ever.

He was back in shorts, and a blue polo shirt that hugged the breadth of his shoulders and brought out the blue of his eyes. She preferred the semi-naked beach look, but in true surf god manner he looked wonderful in anything he wore.

She smiled back in her joy at seeing him again. It was four hours and thirty-five minutes since she'd said goodbye to him on the beach.

She prayed no customers would intrude. More than ever she needed to be alone with Ben. To be reassured that the thing between them was worth taking the risks of which she'd been so blithely ignorant.

Kate's words had hit home. Made her all too aware of

the power she had to wound Ben. After all, she was the one who had left him all those years ago. Then he'd been young and untroubled, and still she had hurt him. Now he was anything but untroubled.

Could he deal with a walk-away-from-it fling?

Could *she*?

The expectations of her were frightening. But what if the reality of Ben didn't match up to her memories? What if they didn't have a thing in common and she wanted to run after the first twenty-four hours? What if he wanted her to stay and she hurt him all over again? Or if she fell hard for him again but couldn't match up to his wife? Then it would be her with her heart broken again.

She caught her breath in what felt dangerously like a sob.

Could she do this?

'You okay?'

His marvellous blue eyes were warm with concern for her. That sexy, sexy mouth was set in a serious line that just made her want to kiss it into a smile. Wordlessly, she nodded.

Could she not do it?

'Apparently we were seen on the beach this morning,' she said.

'Seen and duly noted. Makes you wonder what else people have to do with their time.'

'You're big news in Dolphin Bay.'

He put the coffee down on the counter. 'You're bigger news.'

'Tell me about it. The predatory city slicker hunting down the town's favourite son.'

She'd meant that to sound like a joke. But as soon as it came out she knew it was anything but funny.

Ben frowned. 'Did someone say that?'

'Yes. Well, not in so many words. Kate dropped in.' She couldn't help the wobble in her voice.

Why had Kate and those women come in and ruined

everything? Made her feel suddenly so self-conscious with Ben?

She just wanted to fall back into his arms and continue where they'd left off this morning. But the exchange she'd overheard had unsettled her.

She bit down on her lower lip and looked up at Ben, not certain what to do next. How could she tell him she was having cold feet because she was so terrified of hurting him? Could she find the courage to ask him about Jodi?

CHAPTER NINE

To Ben, Sandy looked as if she'd always stood behind the counter of Bay Books. The short hair he was still getting used to was tucked behind her ears. Just below her left shoulder she had pinned a round metal badge that urged people to get involved with a local literacy campaign. She looked smart, efficient—every inch the professional salesperson. Yet her yellow dress seemed to bring the sunlight right into the corners of the dark wooden carvings so favoured by Aunt Ida, and her vanilla scent brought a sweet new warmth.

She fitted right in.

Ida would be delighted.

But Sandy looked anything but happy—she was wary, guarded, with a shadow behind her eyes. She was chewing her lip so hard she was in danger of drawing blood.

Fear gripped him deep in his gut. What gave here?

'Hey,' he said, and went around the counter to pull her into his arms, expecting her warm curves to relax against him. Instead she stiffened and resisted his embrace.

Why the sudden cold change? Hell, he'd worked damn hard to pull down a chink in those barriers he'd built up. Had she now decided to put up a few of her own?

It didn't figure.

'What's going on?' he asked.

Sandy took a step back, her struggle to decide what to tell

him etched on her face. She picked up a waxed paper coffee cup, took a sip. Her hand wasn't quite steady and the froth on the top wobbled dangerously. She put it down and the foam slid over the lid of the cup and dribbled down its side.

'Leave it,' he said as she reached for a cloth to wipe it up.

'No. It might damage the wood,' she said.

She cleaned the spill too thoroughly. A delaying tactic if ever he'd seen one.

She put the cloth away, started to speak way too rapidly. 'Why don't we take our coffee over to the round table?' She was gabbling, her eyes blinking rapidly as she looked everywhere but at him. 'It's a cosier place to have coffee. Y'know, I'm thinking it would be great for Ida to have a café here. Maybe knock through to the vacant shop next door so that customers—'

She went to pick up the coffee cup again, but he closed his hand around her wrist to stop her. He wouldn't give her an excuse to evade him. Her hand stilled under his. 'Tell me. Now.'

Her eyes flickered up to meet his and then back down. When she spoke, her words came out in a rush. 'Kate told me the whole town is watching to see if I hurt you.'

In his relief, he cursed. 'Is that all?' He let go her wrist.

'What do you mean, *is that all*?' Hands on hips, she glared at him with the ferocity of a fluffed-up kitten. 'Don't you patronise me, Ben Morgan. Kate really freaked me out.'

He used both hands to push down in a gesture of calm. 'Kate exaggerates. Kate and the old-school people who were here before Dolphin Bay became a hotspot for escapees from the city. They all mind each other's business.'

Sandy's chin tilted upwards. 'And your business in particular, if Kate's to be believed.'

He shook his head. 'It's no big deal.'

'Are you telling me that's part and parcel of living in a small town?'

He picked up his coffee. Drank a few mouthfuls to give

him time to think. It was just as he had predicted. *Ben's old girlfriend is back.* He could practically hear the hot news humming through cyberspace. 'Yeah. Better get used to it.'

'I don't know if I can.' Her voice rose to a higher pitch. 'I'm used to the don't-give-a-damn attitude of the city.'

Ben thought back to how the town had pulled together for him after the fire. How it had become so stifling he'd had to get away. He'd thrown himself into high-risk money-making ventures because he'd had nothing to lose when he'd already lost everything. They'd paid off in spades. And he'd come back. Dolphin Bay would always be home. No matter that sad memories haunted him at every turn.

But why should that hothouse concern for him bother Sandy?

Her arms were crossed defensively against her chest. Was she using her fear of the townfolk's gossip to mask some deeper reluctance? Some concern she had about him?

He chose his words carefully. 'I can see that. But you're only here for four more days. We're not thinking beyond that, right? Why worry about what they think?'

'I just do,' she said, in a very small voice.

He put down his coffee, put his finger under her chin and tilted it upwards so she was forced to meet his gaze. 'What else did Kate say?'

'It wasn't Kate. There were some other women. Customers. They...they were talking about...about Jodi.'

Pain knifed through him at the sound of Jodi's name. People tended to avoid saying it in front of him.

His feelings must have shown on his face, because Sandy looked stricken.

'Ben, I'm so sorry...'

She went to twist away from him, but he stopped her.

'I should tell you about Jodi.'

The words would be wrenched from him, but he had to tell Sandy about his wife. There should be no secrets between them. Not if they were to enjoy the four days they had together.

'Ben. No. You don't have to—'

He gently put his hand over her mouth to silence her and she nodded.

He dropped his hand. 'I loved Jodi. Don't ever think otherwise. She was a good wife and a wonderful mother.'

'Of course.' Sandy's eyes were warm with compassion—and a touch of wariness.

'I'd known her all my life. But I didn't date her until I'd finished university and was working in Melbourne.'

Sandy's brows rose. 'University? You said—'

'You wouldn't catch me in a classroom again?'

'That's right. You said it more than once. I remember because I was looking forward to going to uni.'

'You can thank your father for my business degree.'

She frowned. 'My father? I—'

'He used to look at me as if I were something scraped off the bottom of his shoe. Left me in no doubt that I wasn't worthy of his daughter.' Ben would have liked to apply some apt swear words to his memories of Dr Randall Adams, but Sandy might not appreciate that.

Sandy protested. 'Surely he didn't say that to you? I can't believe he—'

'He didn't have to say it. I saw his sneer.'

Her mouth twisted. 'No wonder I never got your letters.'

Teen testosterone had made him want to flatten the guy. 'But he had a point. To be worthy of his daughter I needed to get off my surfboard and make something of myself. I had deferred places at universities in both Sydney and Melbourne to choose from.'

'You never said...'

'At the time I had no intention of taking either. I just wanted to surf every good break at Big Ray Beach and work for my dad when I needed money to travel to other surf beaches. That summer... I guess it made me grow up.'

He'd been determined to prove Dr Adams wrong. And broadening his horizons had been the right choice, even if made for the wrong reasons. And now fate had brought Sandy back to him. Now they met as equals in every way.

'You could have been studying at the same uni as me,' Sandy said slowly. She pulled a face that looked sad rather than funny. 'I won't say *if only* again.'

They both fell silent. But Ben refused to give in to musing about what might have been. He had tortured himself enough.

Sandy cleared her throat. 'What happened after you finished uni?'

'I was offered a job in a big stockbroking firm in Melbourne. Got an apartment and stayed down there.'

'But you came home for holidays? And…and met up with Jodi again?'

He could tell Sandy was finding the conversation awkward. She twisted the fabric of her skirt between the fingers of her right hand without seeming to be aware she was doing it.

'I had an accident in the surf. Got hit in the face with the fin of my board.' His hand went to the scar on his lip. 'Jodi was the nurse who looked after me at the hospital.'

And it had started from there. A relaxed, no-strings relationship with a sweet, kind-hearted girl that had resulted in an unplanned pregnancy.

He'd said there were to be no secrets from Sandy, but Liam's unexpected conception was something he didn't want to share with her. Not yet. Maybe never.

'Jodi moved down to Melbourne with me after we got married.'

'What…what brought you both back to Dolphin Bay?'

'I'm not a city guy. I'd had it with Melbourne. The insane work hours, the crowds, the traffic. Mum and Dad were tired of running the guesthouse. Jodi wanted to be with family when she had the baby.'

He gritted his teeth, trying not to let himself be overwhelmed by emotion when he thought of his baby son. The son he'd loved so fiercely from the moment he'd been placed in his arms as a newborn and yet hadn't been able to protect.

'I could trade shares from here. Start business projects here.'

There was another pause. Sandy twisted the edge of her skirt even tighter. 'Those ladies… They…they said Jodi's parents wouldn't be happy with me coming onto the scene.'

Ben clenched his hands into fists. Who *were* these busybody troublemakers? If he found out he'd tell them to damn well butt out of his business.

He shook his head. 'Not true. Jodi's mum and dad are good people. They want me to…to have someone in my life again.'

Sandy's eyes widened. 'You know that for sure?'

'Yes. They've told me not to let the…the tragedy ruin my life. That…that it's not what Jodi would have wanted.'

'And you believe that? About Jodi?'

He nodded. His words were constricted in his throat. 'The night Liam was born she told me that if anything happened to her—she was a nurse and knew there could be complications in childbirth—she didn't want me to be on my own. She…she made me promise I would find someone else…'

'Oh, Ben.'

Sandy laid her hand on his arm. He realised she was close to tears. When she spoke again her voice was so choked he had to strain to hear her.

'How can I live up to such a wonderful woman?'

In a few shaky steps she made her way around the counter and stood with her back to him. She picked up a book from the display and put it back in exactly the same place.

'Sandy, it isn't a competition.'

Her voice was scarcely a murmur. 'There would always

be a third person in our relationship. I don't know that I could deal with that…'

'Sandy, didn't you hear what I said? Jodi would *want* me to take this chance to spend time with you.'

She turned to face him, the counter now a barrier between them. Her eyes, shadowed again, searched his face. 'Jodi sounds like…like an angel.'

Ben forced himself to smile through the pain. 'She'd laugh to hear you say that. Jodi *was* special, and I loved her. But she was just a human being, like the rest of us, with her own strengths and weaknesses.'

'Ben, I'm no angel either. Don't expect me to be. I'm quick to make judgements, grumpy when I'm hungry or tired—and don't dare to cross me at my time of the month. Oh, and there's the toilet roll thing.'

Despite the angst of talking about Jodi, Sandy made him smile. Just as she'd done when she was eighteen. 'You can let me deal with that.'

She pushed the hair away from her forehead in a gesture of weariness. 'I…I don't know that I've thought this through very well.'

'What do you mean?' he asked.

Fear knifed him again.

He'd had five major turning points in his life. One when he'd decided to go to university. The second when he'd married Jodi. The third when Liam was born. Fourth, the fire. And the fifth when he'd looked up from that wave this morning and seen Sandy standing on the shore next to his dog, as if she were waiting for him to come home to her.

Since he'd kissed her he'd thought of nothing but Sandy. Of the impact she'd made in less than twenty-four hours on his safe, guarded, ultimately sterile life.

He hadn't wanted her here. But her arrival in town had forced him to take stock. And what he saw was a bleak, lonely future—a half-life—if he continued to walk the solitary path he had mapped for himself. He had grieved. A part of him would always grieve. But grief that didn't heal could twist and turn and fester into something near madness—if he let it.

He would *not* allow Sandy to back away from him now. She'd offered four days and he was going to take them.

She took a deep breath. 'The you-and-me thing. What if it doesn't work out and I…and I hurt you again? You've endured so much. I couldn't bear it if I caused you more pain.'

'Leave that to me. It's a gamble I'll take.'

Sandy was his best bet for change. The ongoing power of his attraction to her improved the odds. Her warmth, her vivacity, made him feel as though the seized-up machinery that was his heart was slowly grinding back to life.

She gave him hope.

Maybe that was her real magic—a magic that had nothing to do with shop-bought fairy glitter.

There were four more days until she had to leave for Melbourne. He didn't know what he brought to the table for *her* in terms of a relationship. But he'd be a fool not to grab the second chance she'd offered him. No matter the cost if he lost her again.

'Are you still worried about the townsfolk? They're nothing to be scared of.'

She set her shoulders, tossed back her head. 'Scared? Who said I'm scared?' Her mouth quirked into the beginnings of a smile. 'Maybe…maybe I *am* a little scared.'

Scared of him? Was that the real problem? Was she frightened he would rush her into something before she was ready?

He ached to make love to Sandy. Four days might not be enough to get to that stage. But he could wait if that was what she needed. Even though the want, the sheer physical ache to possess her, was killing him.

'No need to be. I'm here to fight battles for you. Never forget that.'

At last her smile reached her eyes. 'You're sure about that?'

She looked so cute he wanted to kiss the tip of her nose.

He stepped around the counter towards her at the same time she moved towards him. He took both her hands in his and pulled her to him. This time she didn't resist. Her face was very close. That warm vanilla scent of hers was already so familiar.

'As sure as I am about taking that second chance we've been offered. Let's give it everything we've got in the next four days. Turn back the clock.'

She stared at him. He couldn't blame her for being surprised at his turnaround. The shadow behind her eyes was not completely gone. Had she told him everything that was worrying her?

'Are you serious?' she choked out.

'Very.'

She reached up her hand to stroke the side of his cheek. As if checking he was real. When it came, her smile was tender and her eyes were warm. 'I'm so happy to hear you say that. It's just that…' She paused

'What?' he asked.

'All these expectations on us. It…it's daunting. And what will we tell people?'

'Nothing. Let them figure it out for themselves.' He gripped her hands. 'This is just about you and me. It's always just been you and me.'

'And we—'

'Enough with the talking,' he growled, and he silenced her with a kiss.

A kiss to seal their bargain. A kiss to tell her what words could not.

But the kiss rapidly escalated to something hot and hungry and urgent. She matched his urgency with lips, teeth, tongue. He let go her hands so he could pull her tight. Her curves shaped to him as though they were made to fit and she wound her arms around his neck to pull him closer. The strap of her yellow dress slid off her shoulder. He wanted to slide the dress right off her.

He broke away from the kiss, his breath hard and ragged. 'We're out of here. To get some privacy.'

'Wh…what about the shop?' Her own ragged breathing made her barely coherent.

'How many books have you sold today?'

'Just…just a few.'

'Yeah. Not many customers. Too many gossips.' He stroked the bare warm skin on her shoulder, exalted in her shiver of response.

'They did seem to spend more time lurking around corners and looking at me than browsing,' she admitted.

Her hands slid through his hair with an unconscious sensuality that made him shudder with want.

'You shut down the computer. I'll set the alarm.'

'But Ida…'

'Don't worry about Ida.' He could easily make up to his aunt for any drop in sales figures.

Sandy started to say something. He silenced her with another kiss. She moaned a throaty little sound that made him all the more determined to get her out of here and to somewhere private, where he could kiss her without an audience.

The old-fashioned doorbell on the top of the shop door jangled loudly.

Sandy froze in his arms. Then she pulled away from him, cheeks flushed, eyes unfocused. Her quiet groan of frustration echoed his. She pressed a quick, hard kiss on his mouth and looked up wordlessly at him.

To anyone coming into the store they would look as guilty as the pair of teenagers they'd once been. He rolled his eyes. Sandy started to shake with repressed giggles.

He kept his arm firmly around her as they turned to face the two middle-aged women who had entered the shop. Both friends of his mother.

Two sets of eyebrows had risen practically to their hairlines.

News of kiss number two for the day would be rapidly telegraphed through the town.

And he didn't give a damn.

'Sorry, ladies,' he said, in a voice that put paid to any argument. 'This shop is closed.'

CHAPTER TEN

DESTINATION? SOMEWHERE THEY could have privacy. Purpose? To talk more freely about what had happened to each other in the twelve years since she'd left Dolphin Bay. And Sandy didn't give a flying fig that the two bemused ladies Ben had ousted from Bay Books stood hands on hips and watched as she and Ben hastened away from the shop.

Even just metres down the street she fell out of step with Ben and had to skip to catch up. He turned to wait for her, suppressed laughter still dancing around his mouth, and extended his hand for her to take.

Sandy hesitated for only a second before she slid her fingers through his. Linked hands would make quite a statement to the good folk of Dolphin Bay. Anticipation and excitement throbbed through her as he tightened his warm, strong grip and pulled her closer. She smiled up at him, her breath catching in her throat at his answering smile.

When she'd very first held hands with Ben the simple act had been a big deal for her. Most of her schoolfriends had already had sex with their boyfriends by the age of eighteen. Not her. She'd never met a boy she'd wanted to do more with than kiss. When she'd met Ben she'd still been debating the significance of hands held with just palms locked or, way sexier, with fingers entwined.

And Ben?

Back then he'd had no scars.

'Where are we going?' she asked, surprised when her voice came out edged with nervousness.

'My place,' he said. His voice didn't sound nervous in the slightest.

Did he live at the hotel? That would make sense. Maybe in an apartment as luxurious as the room where she was staying.

'Do you remember my family's old boathouse?' he asked as he led her down the steps in front of the hotel.

'Of course I do,' she said, and she felt herself colour. Thirty years old and blushing at the memory of that ramshackle old boathouse. Dear heaven, she hoped he didn't notice.

On the sand outside the boathouse, in the shelter of Ben's father's beached dinghies, she and Ben had progressed from first base to not-ready-to-progress-further-than-third.

She glanced quickly up at Ben. Oh, yes, he remembered too. The expression in those deep blue eyes made that loud and clear.

She blushed a shade pinker and shivered at the memory of all that thwarted teen sexuality—and at the thought of how it might feel to finally do something about it if she and Ben got to that stage this time around.

'I live in the boathouse,' he said.

'You *live* there?' She didn't know what else to say that would not come out sounding ill-mannered.

Instead, she followed Ben across the sand in silence, wondering why a successful businessman would choose to live in something that was no more than a shack.

But the structure that sat a short distance to the right of the hotel bore little resemblance to the down-at-heel structure of her memory. Like so much of Dolphin Bay, it had changed beyond recognition.

'Wow! I'm impressed,' she said.

Ben's remodelled boathouse home looked like something that could star on a postcard. Supported by piers on the edge of the bay, its dock led out into the water. Timber-panelled walls were weathered to a silvery grey in perfect harmony with the corrugated iron of the peaked roof. Window trim and carriage lamps had been picked out in a deep dusky blue. Big tubs of purple hydrangeas in glazed blue pots sat either side of the door.

Ben leaned down to pluck a dead leaf from one of the plants without even seeming to realise he did it. She wouldn't have taken him for a gardener—but then she knew so very little of what interests he might have developed in the years since they'd last been together at this rich-in-memories part of the beach.

'The boathouse was the only part of the guesthouse to survive the fire,' Ben said. He pushed open the glossy blue door. 'Jesse lived here before he went away. I had it remodelled as guest accommodation, but liked it so much I kept it for myself.'

'I can see why,' she said. 'I envy you.'

A large ceramic dog bowl filled with water, hand-painted with the words 'Hobo Drinks Here', sat just outside the door. She remembered the look of devotion in the dog's big eyes and Ben's obvious love for him.

'Where's your adorable dog?' she asked, stepping through the door he held open for her, fully expecting the retriever to give Ben a boisterous greeting.

'Mum dog-sits him the days I can't take him to work with me,' he said. 'Seems she always has a houseful of strays. He fits right in.'

Sandy was about to say something about his mother, but the words were stopped by her second, 'Wow!' as Ben stepped aside and she got her first glimpse of the interior of the boathouse.

She only had a moment to take in a large open-plan space, bleached timber and shades of white, floor-to-ceiling windows facing the water at the living room end and a vast wooden bed at the other.

The thought that it would be a fabulous location for an advertising shoot barely had time to register in her mind, because the door slammed shut behind them and she was in Ben's arms.

Ben didn't want to give a tour of the boathouse. He didn't want to talk about the architectural work Jesse had done on the old building. He just wanted, at last, to have Sandy to himself.

For a long, still moment he held her close, his arms wrapped tightly around her. He closed his eyes, breathed in the vanilla scent of her hair, scarcely able to believe it was real and she was here with him. He could feel the warm sigh of her breath on his neck, hear the thud-thud-thud of her heartbeat. Then he kissed her. He kissed the curve of her throat. He kissed the delicate hollow beneath her ear. He pressed small, hungry kisses along the line of her jaw. Then he kissed her on the mouth.

Without hesitation Sandy kissed him right back. She tasted of coffee and chocolate and her own familiar sweetness. As she wound her arms around his neck, met his tongue with hers, she made that sexy little murmur deep in her throat that he remembered from a long time ago. It drove him nearly crazy with want.

Secure in the privacy of the boathouse, he kissed her long enough for them to catch right up on the way they'd explored kissing each other all those years ago. Until kissing no longer seemed enough.

The straps of her yellow dress gave little resistance as he slid them down her smooth shoulders. She shrugged to make it easier for him. Without the support of the straps, the top of her dress fell open. He could see the edge of her bra, the swell of her breasts, the tightness of her nipples. He kissed down her neck and across the roundness of her breasts, until she gasped and her hands curled tightly into his shoulders.

He couldn't get enough of her.

But with an intense effort he forced himself to pull back. 'Do you want me to stop?'

'No,' she said immediately. 'Not yet. I couldn't bear it if you stopped.'

In reply, he scooped her up into his arms. Her eyes widened with surprise and excitement. Her arms tightened around his neck and she snuggled her cheek against his shoulder.

She laughed as he marched her towards the bedroom end of the boathouse. 'Even more muscles than when you were nineteen,' she murmured in exaggerated admiration, her voice husky with desire.

She was still laughing as he laid her on the bed—his big, lonely bed. Her dress was rucked up around her slender tanned thighs, giving him a tantalising glimpse of red panties. She kicked off her shoes into the air, laughed again as they fell to the wooden floor with two soft thuds. Then she held out her arms to urge him to join her. Warm, vibrant Sandy, just as he remembered her. Only more womanly, more confident, more seductive.

He kicked off his own shoes and lay down next to her. He leaned over her as she lay back against the pillows, her face flushed, her eyes wide.

'I never thought I'd see you back here.' His voice was hoarse with need for her.

She kissed him. 'Do you remember the sand outside this place? How scratchy it was?' she asked. 'How we'd sneak off there whenever we could get away from everyone.'

'How could I forget?' he replied. Ever since she'd walked into the hotel and back into his life he'd thought of little else.

'This is so much more comfortable,' she said, with on-purpose seduction in her smile. She pulled him down to her to kiss him again. 'And private,' she murmured against his mouth.

Her kiss was urgent, hungry, and he responded in kind.

Outside on that sand as teenagers they'd fooled around as though they had all the time in the world. Now they had a clock ticking on their reunion. And they were playing grown-up games.

Within minutes he'd rid her of her dress and her bra. He explored the lush new fullness of her breasts. Kissed and teased her nipples.

He lifted his head and she made a murmur of protest. His voice was ragged. 'You sure you're ready for this?'

Sandy's eyes were huge. 'I should say no. I should say we need to spend more time together first, that we can't rush into anything we might regret.' Her voice broke. 'But I can't say no. I want you too much. Have always wanted you… Don't stop, Ben. Please don't stop.'

What she'd said about not rushing made sense. This was going faster than he could have anticipated. He should be the sensible one. Should stop it. But he was beyond thinking sensibly when it came to Sandy. *He only had four days with her.*

She kissed him. He kissed her back and was done for. The last restraints gone. He stroked down the curve of her belly, felt her tremble at his touch. Then her panties were gone and he explored there too.

'Not fair. I want to get you naked as well,' she murmured as she started to divest him of his clothes.

She kissed a hot trail across his chest as she slid off his shirt, stroked right down his arms. Her fingers weren't quite steady as she fumbled with the zipper on his shorts. It made the act of pulling them over his hips a series of tantalising caresses along his butt and thighs that made his body harden so much it ached.

Then they were naked together.

Sandy's heart was doing the flipping over thing so rapidly she felt dizzy. Or maybe the dizziness was from the desire that throbbed through her, that made her press her body close to Ben. Close. Closer. *Not close enough.*

Did that urgent whimper come from her as Ben teased her taut nipples with his tongue? As he stroked her belly and below until she bucked against his hand with need? She gasped for breath as ripples of pleasure pulsed everywhere he touched. Revelled in the intensity of the intimacy they were sharing.

This was further than they'd gone the last time they'd been on this beach together. Now she wanted more. Much more. He was as ready for her as she was for him. She shifted her hips to accommodate him, to welcome him—at last.

Then she stilled at the same time as he did. Spoke at the same time as he did.

'Protection.'

'Birth control.'

He groaned, pressed a hard, urgent kiss against her mouth, then swung himself off the bed.

Sandy felt bereft of his warmth and presence. The bed seemed very big and empty without him. *Hurry, hurry, hurry back!* She wriggled on the quilt in an ecstasy of anticipation, pressed her thighs together hard. Twelve years she'd waited, and she didn't want to wait a second longer.

But she contained her impatience enough to watch in sensual appreciation as Ben, buck naked, strode without a trace of self-consciousness towards the tall dresser at the other side of the bed. He was magnificent, her surf god, in just his skin. Broad shoulders tapering to the tight defined muscles of his back; firm, strong buttocks, pale against the tan of the rest of him; long, muscular legs. A wave of pure longing for him swept through her and she gripped her hands tight by her sides.

He reached the dresser, pulled out the top drawer.

Yes! Get the protection and get back here. Pronto!

But he hesitated—that taut, magnificent body was suddenly very still. Then he reached for a small framed photo that stood on the top of the dresser. It was too far away for Sandy to make out the details, just that there was a woman. Ben picked it up and slid it into the drawer, face downwards.

Sandy caught her breath.

Jodi. The photo must be of Jodi.

Ben didn't want her to see it. Didn't want Jodi seeing her naked on his bed.

And that was okay. Of course it was.

She had absolutely no reason to be upset by his action. He'd told her his late wife had loved him so unselfishly that she didn't want him to be alone. Sandy couldn't allow herself even a twinge of jealousy that Jodi had been the perfect wife.

But the desire that had been simmering though her suddenly went right off the boil. Despite the warmth of the day, she shivered. She pulled herself up on her elbows, looked around for something to cover her nakedness. She found his shirt, clutched it against her. It was still warm from his body heat.

Ben's gaze caught hers in a long, silent connection. Sandy's throat tightened. He knew she'd seen. But he didn't say anything. She knew he wouldn't. Knew she couldn't ask—in spite of his earlier frankness.

She realised with a painful stab of recognition that Ben had gone so far away, in such a different direction from the youth they'd shared, that she didn't know him at all any more. For all they'd shared over the last twenty-four hours, today's Ben had been forged by loss and grief beyond her comprehension.

She'd loved Ben back then, with the fierce intensity of first love. But now? How could she love him when she didn't know him any more? Wasn't this just physical attraction she was feeling? She had never had sex without love. The fact was, though, she was the one who had encouraged this encounter. How could she back down now?

And yet his look of excited yet respectful anticipation made her swell with emotion. Did she love him again already? Was that what the heart-flipping thing was all about? Had her heart just taken up where it had left off twelve years ago? What if these four days were all she would ever have of him?

Desire warmed her again. She wanted him. She would take the chance.

She smiled as Ben impatiently pulled open the drawer. But the smile froze as he continued to dig through the contents. He swore. Slammed the door shut. Looked through another drawer. Then another. He threw out his hands in a gesture to indicate emptiness.

'None. No protection. You got any?' His voice was a burr of frustration and anger and something that could have been despair.

'No. I…uh…don't carry it with me.'

She'd had no use for protection for a long time. Seemed as if Ben was in the same boat.

He strode back and sat on the bed next to her. He smoothed back a lock of hair that had drifted across her cheek in a caress that was both gentle and sensual.

'I want you so much. But I won't risk getting you pregnant.'

An unplanned pregnancy wasn't on her agenda either. No way would she suggest taking that risk, much as she yearned for him. 'I'm not on the pill. S…sorry.'

'Why should you apologise?' He groaned. 'I should have—'

'Could we…could we go buy some?' As soon as the words were out of her mouth she knew that was a ridiculous idea. Ben acknowledged it with a grim smile. No doubt some busybody citizen of Dolphin Bay would be behind the counter at the pharmacy and only too eager to broadcast the news that Ben and his old girlfriend were in need of contraceptives.

'Okay…bad idea.' She didn't know what else she could say.

Ben's handsome face was contorted with frustration, his voice underscored with anguish. 'Sandy. You have to know I won't be a father again. Won't have another child. Not after what happened to my little boy. Can't risk that loss…that pain.'

Oh, Ben. Her heart felt as if it was tearing in sorrow for him, for the losses she couldn't even begin to imagine.

'I…I understand,' she stuttered. But did she? Could she ever comprehend the agony he felt at losing his child? 'D… do you want to talk about it?'

He shifted his body further from her. But more than a physical distance loomed between them. He took a deep, shuddering breath.

'You have a right to know why I feel this way.'

'Of course,' she murmured.

'When my mother knew Liam was on the way she told me that I wouldn't know what love was until I held my first child in my arms. I scoffed at her. I thought I knew what it was to love.'

'Lizzie said something similar after Amy was born.'

Ben swallowed hard. It must be agony for him to relive his memories.

'A father's love—it was so unexpected. So overwhelming. My mother was right. I would have done anything for my son.'

'Of course you would have,' she murmured, feeling helpless. She didn't know what to say—a thirty-year-old single whose only experience of loving a child was her niece.

'Changing nappies. Getting up at all hours of the night the minute I heard a whimper. Rocking him in my arms for hours to soothe him when he was teething. I did all that. But…but I couldn't save his life.'

Survivor's guilt. Post-traumatic stress. Labels she thought might apply—but what did she know about how to help him?

'Ben, you're carrying a big burden. Did you have counselling to help you come to terms with your loss?'

As soon as the question left her mouth she knew it was a mistake. Ben so obviously *hadn't* come to terms with it.

His eyes were as bleak as a storm-tossed sea. 'I had counselling. But nothing can change the fact I couldn't save my baby son. End of story. On the day I buried him I vowed I would never have another child.'

'Because…because you think you don't deserve another child?'

'That too. But I couldn't bear the agony of loss again.'

She knew it wasn't the time to say that new life could bring new hope. That there was the possibility of loss any time you put your heart on the line. But how could she possibly understand what he'd gone through? Could she blame him for never wanting to risk finding himself in that unimaginably dark place again?

'Ben, I'm so sad for you.' She took his scarred, damaged hand in hers and squeezed it, wanting him to know how much she felt for him but was unable to express. He put his arms around her and pulled her tight. She nestled her face just below his shoulder, against the warm, solid muscle of his chest.

But she was sad for herself, too.

She thought back to her birthday goals. *Get married and have lots of kids. Three kids—two girls and a boy.*

It was as if Ben had read her mind. 'Remember how we used to talk about having kids? When were barely more than kids ourselves?'

'Yes,' she said. She swallowed hard against the lump of disappointment that threatened to choke her. She'd always seen being a mother in her future. Had never contemplated any other option.

He pulled back from her and she was forced to meet his gaze.

'So me not wanting kids could be a deal-breaker?'

She had to clear her throat before she answered, trying not to let him guess how shaken she was. 'Perhaps. For something long-term. But we're only talking four days, aren't we? It doesn't matter for…for a fling.'

'I guess not. But I wanted to make sure you knew where I stood.'

At the age of thirty she couldn't afford to waste time on any relationship—no matter how brief—that didn't have the possibility of children. Knowing that parenthood wasn't an option for Ben should make her pack up and leave Dolphin Bay right now. But she didn't have to think further than four days—and nothing could stop her from having this time with Ben. Come what may.

'I'm sorry, Sandy,' said Ben. 'This wasn't the way I thought things would pan out today.'

'It doesn't matter. I…I've lost the mood,' she confessed.

Suddenly she felt self-conscious being naked. With a murmur about being cold she disengaged herself from his arms. Fumbled around on the bed and found her dress. Pulled it over her head without bothering about wasting minutes with her bra. Wiggled into her panties. Found his clothes and handed them to him.

She felt very alone when he turned his back to her and dressed in awkward silence.

She sat on the edge of the bed and wondered how everything could have gone so wrong. 'Sunny Sandy', Ben had used to call her. But it was hard to see the glass-half-full side of finding out that he didn't ever want to have another child. And then there was that photo. How ready was he *really* to move on to another woman?

Ben wanted to pound the wall with his fists to vent his frustration and anger. He wanted to swear and curse. To fight his way through raging surf might help, too.

But he could do none of that. Sandy looked so woebegone sitting there, biting on her lip, her arms crossed defensively across her beautiful breasts. He had to control himself. Do anything in his power to reignite her smile.

His revelation that he didn't want more children had knocked the sunshine out of her. He appreciated how kind she'd been, how understanding, but dismay had shown on her face. But he'd had to put his cards on the table about a future with no children. He couldn't mislead her on such an important issue. Not that they were talking beyond these four days.

He reached out, took both her hands and pulled her to her feet.

'Sandy, I'm sorry—' he started.

'Don't say it again,' she said with a tremulous smile, and put her finger to his mouth. 'I'm sure we'll laugh about it one day.'

He snorted his disbelief. He would never see the humour in what had happened. Or had not happened.

'So what now?' she asked. 'Do I go back to the bookshop?'

He tightened his grip on her hands. 'No way. It's shut for the day. You're staying with me. We'll have lunch, then tonight I want to take you to a dinner dance.'

Her eyebrows rose. 'A dinner dance? In Dolphin Bay?'

She was such a city girl. She had no idea of how much the town had grown. How big his role as a business leader had become.

'The Chamber of Commerce annual awards night is being held at the hotel. As president, I'm presenting the awards. I'd like you to come.'

'As…as your date?'

'As my date.'

Her smile lit the golden sparks in her eyes in the way he remembered. 'I'd like that. This could be fun.'

'The speeches? Not so much. But there'll be a band and dancing afterwards.'

'Do you remember—?' she started.

'The dance?'

'I couldn't believe it when you asked me to dance with you.'

'I wasn't sure you'd say yes. You were the most beautiful girl there.'

She leaned up and kissed him on the mouth. 'Thank you for saying that.'

'You'll be the most beautiful girl there tonight.'

That earned him another kiss.

'Will I know anyone?'

'My parents. My brother, Jesse—he's back home for a couple days. Kate…'

Sandy's face tightened at the sound of Kate's name.

'Kate has a big mouth, but she also has a big heart,' he said.

'She can be confrontational.'

'Don't judge her too harshly. She means well.' He didn't want Sandy to feel alienated during her time in Dolphin Bay. That was one of the reasons he'd asked her to be his date for tonight, to go public with him. Encouraging a friendship with Kate was another.

'I'm sure she does. It's just that…'

'Yes?'

'Nothing,' she said, with an impish twist to her mouth.

He wasn't in the mood to argue with a female 'nothing'. 'C'mon. I'll make us some lunch.'

He kept her hand in his as he led her towards the kitchen.

'I didn't know you could cook,' she said.

She didn't know a lot about him. Some things she might never know. But his cooking prowess—or lack of it—was no secret.

'Basic guy-type stuff. Mostly I eat at the hotel. We could order room service if you want.'

'No. I like the idea of you cooking for me.'

She started to say something else but stopped herself.

He wondered if her ex had ever cooked for her. He sounded like a selfish creep, so that was probably a no.

'What's on the menu, chef?' she asked.

'Take your pick. Toasted cheese sandwich or…' he paused for dramatic emphasis '…toasted cheese sandwich.'

'With ketchup? And Snickers for dessert? I have some in my handbag.'

'Done,' he said as he headed towards the fridge.

Without realising it, he started to whistle. He stopped himself. Why would he want to whistle when he was furious at himself for the disaster in the bedroom and fresh with the memories of his loss?

'That's a sound I haven't heard for a long time,' Sandy said as she settled herself on one of the bar stools that lined the kitchen counter.

'It's rusty from disuse,' he said.

'No, it isn't. I like it. Don't stop. Please.'

Her eyes were warm with concern and understanding. Her yellow dress flashed bright in the cool, neutral tones of the kitchen. Her brown hair glinted golden in the sunshine that filtered through the porthole windows. Sandy. Here in his home. The only woman he had brought here apart from his mother and the maids from the hotel who kept it clean.

He picked up the tune from where he had left off and started to whistle again.

CHAPTER ELEVEN

SANDY WAS ONLY too aware that every detail of her appearance would be scrutinised by the other guests at the Chamber of Commerce dinner dance. Every nuance of her interaction with Ben would be fuel for the gossipmongers of Dolphin Bay.

In one way it amused her. In another it scared her witless.

In spite of Ben's reassurances Kate's warning still disconcerted her. All the people who would be there tonight knew Ben. Had known Jodi. Had even—and her heart twisted painfully at the thought—known his baby son. She wouldn't be human if that didn't worry her.

She wished she and Ben could spend the entire time they had together alone in his boathouse home. Just him and her, and no one else to poke their noses into the one step forward and two steps back of their reunion. But it seemed it would be played out on the open stage of Ben's tight-knit community.

Thank heaven she'd packed a take-her-anywhere outfit for Melbourne. She checked her image in the mirror of her hotel room with a mega-critical eye. Dress? Red, strapless, short but not too short. Jewellery? A simple yet striking gold pendant and a blatantly fake ruby-studded gold cuff from one of her fashion accessory clients. Shoes? Red, sparkling, towering heels. She thought she would pass muster.

The look in Ben's eyes when he came to her room to pick her up told her she'd got it right.

For a moment he stood speechless—a fact that pleased her inordinately. He cleared his throat. 'You look amazing,' he said.

Amazing was too inadequate a word to describe how Ben looked in a tuxedo. The immaculately tailored black suit emphasised his height and the breadth of his shoulders, and set off the brilliant blue of his eyes. There was little trace of the teen surfer in the urbane adult who stood before her in the doorway to her room, but she didn't mourn that. The crinkles around his eyes when he smiled, the cropped darker hair, only added to his appeal. It struck her that if she met the grown-up Ben now, for the first time, as a total stranger, she'd be wildly attracted to him.

For a moment she was tempted to wind her arms around his neck and lure him into her room with whispered words of seduction. She thought of the birth control she had discovered tucked into a corner of her suitcase, accompanied by a saucy note from her sister, Lizzie: *In case you get lucky in Melbourne.*

But Ben had official duties to perform. She couldn't make him late.

'You look amazing yourself,' she said. She narrowed her eyes in a mock-appraising way. 'Kinda like a surf god crossed with a tycoon god.'

He rolled his eyes at her words but smiled. 'If you say so.'

Her stratospheric heels brought her to kissing distance from his face. She kissed him lightly on the cheek, but he moved his face so her lips connected with his mouth. She nearly swooned at the rush of desire that hit her. As she felt his tongue slip familiarly into her mouth she calculated how much time they had before they were due at the dinner dance. Ten minutes. Not enough time for what she needed from Ben if things were going to get physical again.

Besides, she wasn't so sure that was the way to go when

their time together was so short. She didn't want to leave Dolphin Bay with a pulverised heart.

With a deep sigh of regret, she pulled away.

'C'mon, haven't you got awards to present?' she said.

She slipped her arm through his and they headed towards the elevator.

The first person Sandy saw when she walked with Ben into the hotel conference room where the dinner dance was being held was his mother. She clutched Ben's arm, shocked at the feeling of being cast back in time.

Maura Morgan had been wearing jeans and a T-shirt the last time she'd seen her; now she was wearing an elegant brocade dress. She was handsome, rather than beautiful, and she'd hardly changed in the intervening years. Her hair held a few more strands of grey, her figure was a tad more generous, but her smile was the same warm, welcoming smile that had made Sandy's stay at the guesthouse all those years ago so happy. And her voice still held that hint of a lyrical Irish accent that was a legacy of her girlhood in Dublin.

'Eh, Sandy, it's grand to see you. Who would have thought we'd see you here after all these years?' The older woman swept her into a warm hug.

'It's wonderful to see you again.' It was all Sandy could think of to say. But she meant every word. That summer, so long ago, there had been a wire of tension between her parents that at times had come close to snapping. Maura had been kind to her, and covered for her with her father when she'd snuck out to meet Ben.

Maura stepped back, with her hands still on Sandy's shoulders. 'Look at you, all grown up and even lovelier than when you were a girl—and friends with Ben again.' Her face stilled. 'Fate works in amazing ways.'

'It sure does,' Sandy agreed, reluctant to talk more deeply with Ben's mother. Not wanting to bring up the tragedies that had occurred since her last visit. She didn't know what

Ben had told Maura about her reasons for staying in Dolphin Bay. The reignited feelings between her and Ben were so fragile—still just little sparks—she wanted to hug them close.

Maura released her. 'Your mum and dad…?'

Sandy shrugged. 'Divorced.'

Maura shook her head slowly. 'Why does that not surprise me? And your sister?'

'Lizzie's still my best friend. She has a little girl, Amy, who's five years old and a real cutie.'

As soon as she mentioned Amy, Sandy wished she hadn't. Ben's son Liam had been Maura's only grandchild. But Maura's smile didn't dim. 'It's lovely to hear that,' she said. 'And do you—?'

Ben interrupted. 'Mum, I've sat you and Dad at my table so you'll get a chance to talk to Sandy during the evening.

Maura laughed. 'So quit the interrogation? I hadn't yet asked Sandy if she has room in her heart for a homeless puppy.'

Ben groaned, but Sandy could hear the smile in his protest.

'A puppy? I'd love one,' she said without hesitation. 'That is if…' Her voice trailed away. *Get dog of own once settled in Melbourne.* Could she really commit to a dog when her future had become so uncertain? Until she knew exactly how she felt about Ben at the end of the four days?

Maura patted her hand. 'I won't hold you to the puppy until we've talked some more.'

The genuine warmth in her voice did a lot to reassure Sandy that Maura did not appear to have any objection to her reunion with Ben.

She felt she could face the rest of the evening with a degree less dread.

Sandy outshone any other woman in the room, Ben thought as he watched her charm the bank manager and his wife.

It wasn't just the red dress, or the way the light caught her glittery shoes just like that darn fairy dust. It had more to do with the vivacity of her smile, the way her eyes gleamed with genuine interest at the details of the couple's daughter's high school results. He knew she was nervous, but no one would guess it.

It was a big, public step to bring her tonight—and he was glad he'd made it. It felt good to have her by his side. Instead of ill-disguised sorrow or embarrassed pity, he saw approval in the eyes of his family and friends. It was a big step forward.

But for the first time since he'd been elected president of the chamber Ben resented his duties. He didn't want to make polite chit-chat with the guests. He didn't want to get up there on stage and make a speech about the business community's achievements. Or announce the awards. He wanted to spend every second of the time he had left with Sandy—alone with her. They had less than four days—three days now—of catching up to do. If that included being behind closed doors, slowly divesting Sandy of that red dress and making love to her all night long, that was good too.

'We must catch up for coffee some time,' the banker's wife gushed in farewell to Sandy as Ben took Sandy's elbow to steer her away towards his table. He wanted her seated and introduced to everyone else at the table before he had to take his place on stage for the awards presentation.

'I'd like that,' Sandy called over her shoulder to the banker's wife as Ben led her away.

'Would you?' he asked in an undertone.

'Of course. She seems like a nice lady. But not any time soon.' She edged closer so she could murmur into his ear. 'We've only got a few days together. I want to spend every second of my spare time with you.'

'I'll hold you to that,' he said.

It felt unexpectedly good, being part of a couple again—even if only temporarily. He'd been on his own for so long.

Maybe too long. But his guilt and regret still gnawed at him, punishing him, stopping him from getting close to anyone.

And now Sandy was back with him in Dolphin Bay.

The president's table was at the front of the room. His parents were already seated around it, along with Kate, his brother, Jesse, and two of the awards finalists—both women.

If his father remembered how disparaging he had been all those years ago about the sincerity of a city girl's feelings towards his son, he didn't show it. In his gruff way he made Sandy welcome.

Jesse couldn't hide the admiration in his eyes as he rose from his seat to greet Sandy. 'I would have recognised you straight away,' his brother said as he kissed her on the cheek.

Ben introduced Sandy to the awards finalists, then settled her into the seat between him and Kate. 'I have to finalise the order of proceedings. I'll be back in five minutes—in time for the appetiser,' he said.

He wanted to kiss Sandy. Claim her as more than a friend in front of all eyes. But it wasn't the right time. Instead, he brushed his hand over her bare shoulder in parting before he headed backstage. Only Kate's big grin made him realise the simple gesture was more a sign of possession than a friendly kiss on Sandy's cheek would ever have been.

Sandy heaved a quiet sigh of relief as she sank into her chair. The worst of the ordeal was behind her. From the moment she'd entered the room she'd been aware of the undercurrent of interest in her presence beside Ben. Her mouth ached from smiling. From formulating answers in reply to questions about how long she intended to be in town. Even though Ben had smoothed the way, she felt she was being judged on every word she spoke. She reached gratefully for her glass of white wine.

Ben's empty seat was to her left, between her and Kate. Tall, dark-haired Jesse—every bit as handsome as in her memories of him—sat on the other side of her, engaged in conversation with his mother.

Kate sidled close enough to whisper to Sandy. 'Note that Ben didn't sit me next to Jesse. Probably worried I'd fling myself on his brother, wrestle him to the ground and have my way with him under the table.'

Sandy nearly choked on her drink. 'Really?'

'Nah. Just kidding. I actually asked him not to put me near Jesse.' Kate's green eyes clouded. 'It's hard to make small-talk with the guy I've wanted all my life when he sees me as more sister than woman.'

'Can't he see how gorgeous you are?' Sandy asked. In an emerald silk dress that clung to her curves and flattered the auburn of her hair, Kate looked anything but the girl next door.

Kate pulled a self-deprecating face. 'Thanks. But it doesn't matter what I wear. To Jesse I'll always just be good old Kate, his childhood pal.'

'You never dated him?'

'We kissed when I was thirteen and he was fourteen. I never stopped wanting him after that.'

'And Jesse?'

Kate shrugged. 'He was a shy kid, and I guess I was a convenient experiment. It never happened again. Though I must have relived it a million times.'

'He certainly doesn't look shy now.'

Jesse's full attention was beamed on the attractive blonde award finalist.

'Yep. He's quite the man of the world these days, and quite the flirt.' Kate kept her gaze on Jesse for a moment too long before returning it to Sandy.

Sandy's heart went out to Kate. 'That must be so tough for you. Ben told me Jesse's only visiting for a few days.'

'Yes. Jesse leads a construction team that builds low-cost housing in areas that have been destroyed by natural disasters. Think India, Africa, New Orleans. He only ever comes here between assignments.'

Sandy glanced again at Jesse. 'Good looks *and* a kind heart. No wonder you're hooked on him.'

'Kind hearts run in the Morgan family—as I think you well know.'

Was Kate about to give her another lecture about Ben? If so, she wasn't in the mood to hear it. 'Kate, I—'

Kate laughed and threw her hands up in a gesture of self-defence. 'I'm staying right out of the you-and-Ben thing. I've been warned.'

'Warned? By Ben?'

'Of course by Ben. You're important to him. Ben protects the people he cares about.'

Sandy loved the feeling Kate's words gave her. But, again, she sensed she might be getting out of her depth. Three more days in Dolphin Bay. That was all she was talking about after this evening. Deep in her heart, though, she knew there was a chance it could end up as so much more than that. She didn't know whether to be excited or terrified at the prospect.

After the starter course Ben took his place on stage. To Sandy, he looked imposing and every inch the powerful executive as he took the microphone to give a brief review of the year's past business activities. From the applause and occasional catcall from the audience it was apparent Ben was still very much the town's favourite son.

As he made a particularly pertinent point about the growth in revenue tourism had brought to Dolphin Bay Sandy thought she would burst with pride at his achievements, and at the way he had overcome such tragedy to get to this place. She wanted to get up from her seat and cheer. She caught his mother Maura's eye and saw the same pride and joy reflected in her face.

Maura acknowledged the thread of emotion that united

them with a smile and a brief nod, before turning back to face the stage and applaud the end of Ben's speech.

Sandy smiled back—a wobbly, not very successful smile. *Maura knew.* She bit her lip and shredded the edge of her dolphin-printed serviette without really realising she was doing so.

Could she kid herself any further that all she wanted from Ben was a fling? Could she deny that if she didn't protect her heart she might fall right back in love? And then where would she be, if Ben decided four days of her was enough?

CHAPTER TWELVE

BUT SANDY'S HEART was singing as she danced with Ben. He danced as he'd danced with her that first time twelve years ago, and it seemed as if the years in between had never happened. Although they kept a respectable distance apart their bodies were in tune, hips swaying in unison with each other, feet moving to the same beat.

Most of the people in the room had also got up to dance once the formalities of the evening were done, but Sandy was scarcely aware of them. She couldn't keep her eyes off Ben or stop herself from 'accidentally' touching him at any opportunity—shoulders brushing, hips bumping, her hand skimming his as they moved their bodies in time to the music of a surprisingly good local band. And, in spite of the other guests' ill-concealed interest in the fact they were dancing together, Ben did nothing to move away.

She longed to be alone with him. He had rhythm, he had energy, he had power in that big, well-built body—and she ached to have it all directed to *her*. Upstairs in her bedroom.

When the band changed to slow dancing music, she was done for. As Ben pulled her into his arms and fitted his body close to her she wound her arms around her neck and sighed. 'How much longer do we have to endure this torture? If I have to explain to one more person than I'm just here for a few more days, I'll scream.'

'Same. The strain of all this focus on us is too much.'

'How much longer do we have to stay?'

He nuzzled into her neck, murmured low and husky. 'See those doors that open up to the balcony?'

She looked across the room. 'Yes.'

'We're going to dance our way over there and out on to the balcony, as if we're going for some fresh air—'

'Won't everyone think we've gone to make out?'

'Who cares?' He pulled her tighter. 'That way we don't have to announce our escape by exiting through the main doors.'

'What about your duties?'

'I'm done with duty.'

'So now you're all mine for the rest of the evening?' she murmured, with a provocative tilt of her head.

His eyes darkened to a deeper shade of blue and his grip tightened on her back. 'From the balcony we'll take the door to the empty conference room next door and then to the foyer.'

'And then?' Her voice caught in her throat.

'That's up to you.'

Her heart started doing the flippy thing so fast she felt dizzy. She pulled his head even closer to hers, brushed her lips across his cheek. 'Let's go,' she murmured.

He steered her through the crowd, exchanging quick greetings with the people they brushed past, but not halting for a moment longer than necessary. Sandy nodded, smiled, made polite responses, held on to his hand and followed his lead.

They sidled along the balcony, then burst into the empty conference room next door, laughing like truant schoolkids. Ben shut the door behind him and braced it in mock defence with an exultant whoop of triumph.

Sandy felt high on the same exhilaration she'd felt as a teenager, when Ben and she had successfully snuck away from their parents. She opened her mouth to share that thought with him, but before she could form the words to congratulate him on their clever escape he kissed her.

His kiss was hard and hungry, free of doubt or second thoughts. She kissed him back, matching his ardour. Then broke the kiss.

She took a few deep breaths to steady her thoughts. 'Ben, I'm concerned we're moving too fast. What do you think?'

Ben glanced at his watch. 'This day is nearly over. That leaves us three days. I want you, Sandy. I've always wanted you.'

'But what if we regret it? What if you—?' She was so aware of how big a deal it was for him to be with her. And the heartbreak she risked by falling for him again. She feared once she made love with him she would never want to leave him.

'I'll regret it more if we don't take this chance to be together. On our terms. No one else's.'

'Me too,' she said. No matter what happened after these three remaining days, she never wanted to feel again the regret that had haunted her all those years ago.

Please, let this be our time at last.

'My room or yours?' she said, putting up her face to be kissed again.

Ben couldn't bear to let go of Sandy even for a second. Still kissing her, he walked her through the door, out of the conference room and into the corridor. Still kissing her, he punched the elevator's 'up' button.

As soon as the doors closed behind them he nudged her up against the wall and captured her wrists above her head with one of his so much bigger hands. The walls were mirrored and everywhere he looked he saw Sandy in that sexy red dress, her hair tousled, her face flushed, her lips swollen from his kisses. Beautiful Sandy, who had brought hope back into his life.

The raising of her arms brought her breasts high out

of her strapless dress to tease him. In the confines of the elevator the warm vanilla female scent of her acted like a mainline hit of aphrodisiac. He could make love to her there and then.

But, as it always had been with Sandy, this was about so much more than sex. This step they were about to take was as much about intimacy and trust and a possible move towards a future beyond the next three days. The responsibility was awesome.

It was up to him to make it memorable. He'd waited so long for her and he wanted their first time to be slow and thorough, not a heated rush that might leave her behind.

He trailed kisses down her throat to the swell of her breasts. She gasped and he tightened his grip on her hands. She started to say something but he kissed her silent. Then the elevator reached her floor.

Still kissing her, he guided Sandy out of the elevator and towards her room. He fished his master keycard out of his pocket, used it, then shouldered the door open. They stumbled into the room and he kicked the door shut behind them.

Sandy had imagined a sensual, take-their-time progression through the bases for her first-time lovemaking with Ben. But she couldn't wait for all that. It felt as if the entire day had been one long foreplay session. Every sense was clamouring for Ben. *Now.* Her legs were so shaky she could hardly stand.

She pulled away from the kiss, reached up and cradled his chin in her hands, thrilled at the passion and want in his eyes that echoed hers. Her breathing was so hard she had to gulp in air so her voice would make sense.

'Ben. Stop.'

Immediately, gentleman that he was, he made to pull away from her. Urgently she stilled him.

'Not stop. I mean go. Heck, that's not what I mean. I mean stop delaying. I swear, Ben, I can't wait any longer.'

She whimpered. Yes, she whimpered—something she'd never thought she'd do for a man. 'Please.'

His eyes gleamed at the green light she'd given him. 'If you knew how difficult it's been to hold back…' he groaned.

'Oh, I have a good idea what it's been like,' she said, her heart pounding, her spirit exulting. 'I feel like I've been waiting for this—for you—all my life.'

She kicked off her shiny shoes, not caring where they landed. Ben yanked down the zipper of her dress. She tugged at his tuxedo jacket and fumbled with the buttons on his shirt. Before she knew it she stood in just the scantiest red lace thong and Ben was in nothing at all—his body strong and powerful and aroused, his eyes ablaze with need for her.

Beautiful wasn't a word she'd usually use to describe a man. But all her copywriting skills deserted her as she sought to find another word.

He was her once-in-a-lifetime love and she knew, no matter what happened tomorrow or the day after or the day after that, that tonight she would be irrevocably changed. As she took a step towards him she froze, overwhelmed—even a little frightened—of what this night might unleash. Then desire for this man took over again. Desire first ignited twelve long years ago. Desire thwarted. Desire reignited. Desire aching to be fulfilled.

Ben swept her into his arms and walked her towards the bed. Soon she could think of nothing but him and the urgent rhythm of the intimate dance they shared.

Ben didn't know what time it was when he woke up. There was just enough moonlight filtering through the gaps in the curtains for him to watch Sandy as she slept. He leaned on his elbow and took in her beauty.

She lay sprawled on her back, her right arm crooked above her head, the sheet tucked around her waist. Her hair was all mussed on the pillow. He was getting used to seeing it short, though he wished it was still long. In repose, her face had lost the tension that haunted her eyes. A smile danced at the corners of her mouth. She didn't look much older than the girl he'd thought he'd never see again.

It didn't seem real that she was here beside him. Magic? Coincidence? Fate? Whatever—being with Sandy made him realise he had been living a stunted half-life that might ultimately have destroyed him.

How could he let her go in three days' time?

But if he asked Sandy to stay he had to be sure it would be to stay for ever.

With just one finger he traced the line of her cheekbones, her nose, her mouth.

She stirred, as he'd hoped she would. Her eyelids fluttered open and her gaze focused on him. His heart leapt as recognition dawned in her eyes. She smiled the slow, contented smile of a satisfied woman and stretched languorously.

'Fancy waking up to you in my bed,' she murmured. She took his hand and kissed first each finger in turn and then his palm with featherlight touches over the scars he hated so much. She placed his hand on her breast and covered it with her own.

'You were *so* worth waiting twelve years for,' she whispered.

'Yes.' He couldn't find any more words. Just kissed her on her forehead, on her nose, finally on her mouth.

Want for her stirred again. He circled her nipple with his thumb and felt it harden. She moaned that sweet moan of pleasure. She returned his kiss. Softly. Tenderly. Then she turned her body to his.

Afterwards she lay snuggled into him, her head nestled on his chest, their legs entwined. The sweet vanilla scent of her filled his senses. He held her to him as tightly as he could without hurting her. He didn't want to let her go.

Did she feel the same way about what had just happened—a connection that had been so much more than physical?

Did she know she had ripped down a huge part of the barricade that had protected him against feeling anything for anyone?

Hoarsely, he whispered her name.

The tenor of her breathing changed and he realised she was falling back to sleep. Had she heard him?

'Ben…' she murmured as her voice trailed away.

As Sandy drifted back into sleep, satiated not just with sexual satisfaction but with joy, she realised a profound truth: she'd never got it right with anyone but Ben. Not just the physical—which had been indescribably wonderful—but the whole deal.

Right back when she was eighteen she'd thought she'd found the man for her—but those close to her, those who had thought they knew what was best for her, had dissuaded her.

She tightened her grip on his hand and smiled.

Her heart had got it right the first time.

CHAPTER THIRTEEN

'SO, IS THE sex with my nephew good?'

Sandy nearly fell off the chair near Aunt Ida's hospital bed, too flummoxed even to think about a reply.

Ida laughed. 'Not a question you expect a little old lady to ask?'

'Uh…not really,' Sandy managed to splutter as hot colour flooded her cheeks. She'd come to talk about the Bay Books business, not her private life with Ben.

Ida shifted her shoulders and resettled herself on the pillows, a flash of pain tightening her face. Sandy ached to help her, but Ben's great-aunt was fiercely independent.

'You don't actually have to answer me,' said Ida. 'But great sex is so important to a healthy relationship. If you don't have those fireworks now, forget having a happy future together.'

Sandy realised she had blushed more times since she'd been back in Dolphin Bay than she had in her entire life.

'I… Uh… We…' How the heck did Ida know what had happened with Ben last night? How did she know there'd been fireworks aplenty?

Ida chuckled. 'I'll take that as a yes, then. Any fool can see the chemistry between you two. Good. No matter what the world dishes up to you, you'll always have that wonderful intimacy to keep your love strong. It was like that for me and Mike.'

'Oh?' Sandy literally did not know where to look. To talk about sex with someone of her grandmother's age was a new and unnerving experience.

'I suppose you know about my scandalous past?'

'I heard that you—'

'But I guess you don't want to hear about that.'

The expression in Ida's eyes made it clear that Ida wanted very much to tell her story. And Sandy was curious to hear it. There hadn't been much talking about relationships in her family's strait-laced household. No wonder she'd been so naïve at the age of eighteen, when she'd met Ben.

Sandy settled herself back in her chair. 'Did you really run away with a sailor, like Ben says?'

'Indeed I did. Mike was sailing up the coast. We clicked instantly. I went back to his boat with him and—'

Sandy found herself gripping the fabric of her skirt where it bunched over her knees. She wanted to hear the story but she didn't—she *really* didn't—want to hear the intimate details.

'I never left. I quit my job. Threw my hat in with Mike. We got married on an island in Fiji.'

One part of Sandy thought it romantic, another thought it foolhardy.

'Even though you hardly knew him?' *But how well did she actually know Ben? Enough to risk her heart the way she'd done last night?*

'I knew enough that I wanted to spend every waking and sleeping moment with him. I was thirty-five; he was five years older. We didn't have time to waste.'

Was that message aimed at her and Ben? The way she felt right now Sandy hated being parted from him even for a minute. But there were issues still unresolved.

'What about…what about children? Did you regret not having kids?'

'Not for a moment. We couldn't have had the life we had with kids. Mike was enough for me.'

Could Ben be enough for her? Right now her heart sang with the message that he was all she wanted. But what about in years to come? If things worked out with Ben, could she give up her dreams of a family?

Ida continued. 'And I don't have time to waste now. Once I'm over this injury I want to go back to the places I visited with Mike. It might be my last chance.'

Sandy put up a hand in protest. 'Surely not. You—'

'Still have years ahead of me? Who knows? But what I *do* know is I need to sell Bay Books—and I want you to buy it from me.'

Again, Sandy was too flabbergasted to reply to the old lady. Just made an incoherent gasp.

'You told me you want to run your own business,' said Ida. 'And I'm talking a good price for stock, fittings and goodwill.'

'Yes… But…'

But why not?

Candles came a poor second to books. And she already had so many ideas for improving Bay Books. Hadn't she thought, in the back of her mind, that if there were a chance she might stay in Dolphin Bay she would need to earn her living?

'Why the "but"?' Ida asked.

'The "but" is Ben,' said Sandy. 'We're not looking beyond these next few days right now. I have to take it slowly with him. I'm interested in your proposition. But I can't commit to anything until I know if there might be anything more with Ben.'

Ida's eyes were warm with understanding. 'I know what Ben's been through. I also know he needs to look to the future. I'm hoping it's with you.'

'Thank you,' said Sandy, touched by the older lady's faith in her.

'I'll keep my offer on the table. But I'll be selling—if not to you, to someone else.'

'Can we keep this between us?' Sandy asked. 'I'd rather not mention it to Ben just yet. I don't want him to think I'm putting any pressure on him.'

'Of course,' said Ida.

Sandy felt guilty, putting a 'Back in One Hour' sign on the door of Bay Books—but meeting Ben for lunch was more important.

Ida's words echoed through her head. *She didn't have time to waste.*

She made her way to the boathouse to find the door open and Ben unpacking gourmet sandwiches from the hotel café and loading cold drinks into the refrigerator.

Again, he was whistling, and she smiled at the carefree sound. He hadn't realised she was there and she was struck by the domesticity of the moment. Did she want this with Ben? Everyday routine as well as heart-stopping passion? Much, much more than a few days together?

The answer was in his eyes when he looked up and saw she was there. *Yes. Yes. Yes.*

Yes to sharing everything.

Everything but the rearing of kids.

He put down the bottle he was holding, she dropped her handbag, and they met in the middle of the room. Ben held her close. She stood in his arms, exulting in the warm strength of him, the thudding of his heart, the way he smelled of the sea.

'I'm glad you're here,' he said.

'Me too,' was the only reply she could manage.

Her heart started a series of pirouettes—demanding its message be heard.

She loved him.

Emotion, overwhelming and powerful, surged through her. So did gratitude for whatever power had steered her back to him.

But could wounded, wary Ben love her back in the way she needed?

He kissed her—a brief, tender kiss of welcome—then pulled away.

'How did it go with Ida at the hospital?'

When she told him about Ida's questioning about their love-life he laughed, loud and uproariously.

'The old girl is outrageous,' he said, with more than a hint of pride. 'So what did you say to her?'

'I was so embarrassed I didn't know where to look.'

He pulled her close again. His voice was deep and husky and suggestive. 'What *would* you have told her?'

She twined her arms around his neck. 'I think you know last night was the most amazing experience of my life.' She had trouble keeping her voice steady. 'Why didn't I say yes all those years ago? Why, why, *why* didn't I fight harder for you?'

'Water under the bridge, remember?'

'Yes, but—'

'It mightn't have been such an amazing experience when I was nineteen.'

'Not true. You were the best kisser. Still are.'

'Always happy to oblige,' he said.

She smiled. 'Last night…the dinner dance…it was fun, wasn't it?'

'You were a big hit.'

'Was I? I'm still not quite sure how to handle the townfolk. In particular the way they compare me to Jodi.' *And I'm not sure how, if we have a future, I'll handle being second in your life.*

'You're still worrying about that?' He took her hand and led her to the bedroom. 'There's something I want to show you.'

'And I'm quite happy to see it,' she quipped. 'We can eat lunch afterwards.'

He laughed. 'That's not what I meant. But we can do that too.'

He went to the dresser. He opened the top drawer and pulled out the framed photo he had put there yesterday—the yesterday that seemed a hundred years ago. She braced herself, not at all sure she could cope with seeing Jodi and Ben together in happy times. She prayed the baby wouldn't be in the photo. One day she would have to go there. But not now. Not when this was all too raw and new.

Ben held the photo so she couldn't see what it was. 'It concerned me when you said you were worried about coming second with me. About being in the shadow of the memory of another woman. It's ironic that Jodi felt the same way about you.'

Sandy frowned. 'What do you mean?'

He handed her the photo. Astounded, she looked from it to him and back again. 'But it's of me. Of you. Of *us*.'

The simple wooden frame held a faded snap of her very young self and Ben with their arms around each other. She—super-slim—was wearing a tiny pink floral-patterned bikini; her hair was wet and tangled with salt and fell almost to her waist. She was looking straight at the camera with a confident, happy smile. Ben's surfer hair was long and sun-streaked and he was wearing blue Hawaiian print board shorts. He wasn't looking at the camera but rather down at her, with an expression of pride and possession heartrendingly poignant on a teenager.

She had to clear her throat before she spoke. 'Where did you get this from?'

'From you. Don't you remember?'

Slowly the memory returned to her. 'Lizzie took this photo. We had to get the film developed at the chemist in those days. I bought the frame from the old general store. And I gave it to you to…to remember me by.' She'd had a copy, too. Had shoved it in the back of an old photo album that was heaven knew where now.

'Jodi found it at the bottom of a drawer in my room just before we got married. She brought it to me and said we needed to talk.'

'I…I thought you would have thrown it out.'

'She thought so too. She asked me was I still carrying a torch for you.'

'Wh…what did you say?'

'I said I'd cared for you once but was now totally committed to her.'

Sandy swallowed hard against a kick of that unwarranted jealousy. 'You…you were getting married. Wouldn't she *know* that?'

'We were getting married because she was pregnant with Liam.'

Sandy let out a gasp of surprise. 'I…I didn't know that.'

'Of course you didn't. But she was sensitive about it. Wanted me to reassure her that I wasn't marrying her just because I "had to".'

'Poor Jodi.' Her heart went out to the lovely girl who had cared so much for Ben, and she wished she had more than vague memories of her.

'So, you see, as far as Jodi was concerned you were the "third person", as you put it, in our marriage.'

'I…I don't really know what to say. If…if you were married I wouldn't come anywhere near you.'

'I know that. You know that. And I'm sure Jodi knew that. But no matter how much I reassured her that we would have got married anyway, just maybe not so soon, she had that little nagging doubt that she was my second choice.'

'And yet you…you didn't throw out the photo.' She was still holding the frame in her hands, her fingers tightly curled around the edge.

'No. I went to put it in the bin, to prove my point, but Jodi stopped me. Said it was unrealistic to expect we wouldn't each come into the marriage with a past. She just wanted to make sure you stayed in the past.'

'And here I am…in…in the future.'

'I hadn't thought about this photo in years. Then, after that morning on the beach with you and Hobo, I dug it out from a box in the storeroom at the hotel.'

'And put it on display?'

Ben took the photo frame from her hands and placed it back on top of the dresser. 'Where it will stay,' he said.

'So…so why did you hide it from me yesterday?'

'I thought you'd think it was strange that I'd kept it. It was too soon.'

'But it's not too soon now?'

'We've come a long way since yesterday.'

'Yes,' she said. She made a self-conscious effort to laugh. But it came out as something more strangled. 'Who knows where we'll get to in the next three days?'

It was a rhetorical question she wished she hadn't uttered as soon as she'd said it. But Ben just nodded.

He picked up the photo frame and then put it back down again. 'If you're okay with it, I'll keep it here.'

'Of course,' she said, speaking through a lump of emotion in her throat. 'And I don't expect you to keep photos of Jodi buried in a drawer while I'm around.'

But, please, no photos of Liam on display. No way could she deal with that while she was dealing with the thought that if it worked out with Ben she would see the demise of her dream of having her own kids.

'She was a big part of my life. I'm glad you don't want to deny that.'

'Of course I recognise that. Like…like she did about me.'

She looked again at the long-ago photo and wondered how Jodi had felt when she'd seen it. How sensible Jodi had been not to deny Ben his past. She had to do the same. But there was still that nagging doubt.

'I still can't help but wonder if I can compete with the memory of someone so important to you.'

He cupped her chin with his big scarred hands. 'As I said

Dolphin Bay was four hours away from Sydney, and Ben's hotel café did excellent coffee. But her stay depended on a rekindled relationship of uncertain duration.

2. Find new job where can be own boss.

Tick.

The possibility of owning Bay Books exceeded the 'new job' expectations. She scribbled, *Add gift section to bookshop—enquire if can be sub-franchisee for candles.*

But, again, the possible job depended entirely on her relationship with Ben. She wouldn't hang around in Dolphin Bay if they kissed goodbye for good on Wednesday.

She hesitated when she came to resolution number three. As opposed to the flippy thing, her heart gave a painful lurch.

3. Find kind, interesting man with no hang-ups who loves me the way I am and who wants to get married and have three kids, two girls and a boy.

She'd found the guy—though he came with hang-ups aplenty—and maybe he was the guy on whom she'd subconsciously modelled the brief. But as for the rest of it....

Could she be happy with just two out of three resolutions fulfilled? How big a compromise was she prepared to make?

Now her heart actually ached, and she had to swallow down hard on a sigh. Children had always been on the agenda for her—in fact she'd never imagined a life that didn't include having babies. Then her mother's oft-repeated words came to mind: '*You can't have everything you want in life, Alexandra.*'

She put down her pen, then picked it up again. Channelled 'Sunny Sandy'. Two out of three was definitely a cup more than half full. Slowly, with a wavering line of ink, she scored through the words relating to kids, then wrote: *If stay in DB, ask Maura about puppy.* She crossed out the word 'puppy' and wrote *puppies.*

Unable to bear any further thoughts about shelving her dreams of children, she slammed the fairy notebook shut.

As she did so the doorbell jangled. She looked up to see a very small person manfully pushing the door open.

'Amy! *Sweetpea!*'

Sandy flew around the counter and rushed to meet her niece, then looked up to see her sister, Lizzie, behind her. 'And Lizzie! I can't believe it.'

Sandy greeted Lizzie with a kiss, then swept Amy up into her arms and hugged her tight. Eyes closed at the bliss of having her precious niece so close, she inhaled her sweet little-girl scent of strawberry shampoo and fresh apple.

'I miss you, bub,' she said, kissing Amy's smooth, perfect cheek.

'Miss you too, Auntie Ex.'

Her niece was the only person who called her that—when she was tiny Amy hadn't been able to manage 'Alexandra' and it had morphed into 'Ex', a nickname that had stayed.

'But you're squashing me.'

'Oh, sorry—of course I am.' Sandy carefully put her niece down and smoothed the fabric of Amy's dress.

Amy looked around her with wide eyes. 'Where are the books for children?' she asked.

'They're right over here, sweetpea. Are your hands clean?'

Amy displayed a pair of perfectly clean little hands. 'Yes.'

'Then you can take books and look at them. There's a comfy purple beanbag in the corner.'

Amy settled herself with a picture book about a crocodile. Sandy had trouble keeping her eyes off her little niece. Had she grown in just the few days since they'd said goodbye in Sydney? Amy had been a special part of her life since she'd been born and she loved being an aunt. She'd looked forward to having a little girl just like her one day.

Her breath caught in her throat. *If she stayed with Ben no one would ever call her Mummy.*

'Nice place,' said Lizzie, looking around her. 'But what the heck are you doing here? You're meant to be on your way to Melbourne.'

'I could ask the same about you. Though it's such a nice surprise to see you.'

'Amy had a pupil-free day at school. I decided to shoot down here and see what my big sis was up to!'

'I texted you.'

'Just a few words to say you were spending some time in Dolphin Bay. Dolphin Bay! Why *this* end-of-nowhere dump? Though I have to say the place has smartened itself up. And Amy loves the dolphin rubbish bins.'

'I took the scenic route down the coast. It was lunchtime when I saw the turn-off, and—'

Lizzie put up her hand to halt her. 'I suspected it, but now I get it. This is about Ben Morgan, isn't it? What else would the attraction be here? And don't even *think* about lying, because you're blushing.'

'I have caught up with Ben. Yes.'

Lizzie took a step closer. 'You've done a lot more than "caught up" with Ben, haven't you?'

Sandy rolled her eyes skyward and laughed. Then she filled her sister in on what had happened since she'd driven her Beetle down the main street of Dolphin Bay. Including Ida's offer to sell her Bay Books, but excluding Ben's decision not to have any more children.

'So, are you going to stay here with Ben?' Lizzie asked.

Sandy shrugged. 'We're testing the waters of what it might be like. But I feel the same way about him as I did back then.'

Lizzie stayed silent for a long moment before she spoke

again. 'You're not just getting all sentimental about the past because of what happened with Jason?'

Sandy shook her head. 'Absolutely not. It's nothing to do with that. Just about me and Ben.'

Just mentioning their names together made her heart flip.

'I remember what it was like between you. Man, you were crazy about each other.'

Sandy clutched her sister's arm. Lizzie had to believe that what she'd rediscovered with Ben was the real deal. 'It's still there, Lizzie, that feeling between us. We took up where we left off. I'm so happy to have found him again. Even if these few days are all we have. And I don't give a toss about Jason.'

'I'm thrilled for you—truly I am. I always liked Ben. And I love this shop. It would be cool to own it. Way better than candles.' Lizzie shifted from foot to foot. 'But now I've brought up the J word I have to tell you something. You're going to hear it sooner or later, and I'd rather you heard it from me.'

Sandy frowned. 'Is it about the wedding?' She hadn't given it another thought.

'More about the bump under What's-Her-Name's wedding gown.'

Sandy had to hold on to the edge of the closest bookshelf. 'You mean—?'

'They're not admitting to it. But the wedding guests are betting there'll be a J-Junior coming along in about five months' time.'

Sandy felt the blood drain from her face. Not that she gave a flying fig for That-Jerk-Jason. But envy of his new bride shook her. Not envy of her having Jason's baby. The thought of anyone other than Ben touching her repulsed her. But envy because *she* would never be the one with a proudly displayed bump, would never bear Ben's child.

'Are you okay, Sandy?'

Sandy took a deep breath, felt the colour rush back into her face. 'Of course I'm okay. It's a bit of a shock, that's all.'

Lizzie hugged her. 'Maybe you'll be next, if you end up with Ben. You're thirty now—you won't want to leave it too long.'

'Of course not,' said Sandy, her voice trailing away.

Lizzie was just the first to say it. If, in some hypothetical future, she and Ben decided to stay together it would start. First it would be, *So when are you two tying the knot?* followed by, *Are you putting on weight or have you got something to tell us?*

Would she would be able to endure her friends' pregnancy excitement, birth stories, christenings, first-day-at-school sob-stories? All the while knowing she could never share them?

She understood Ben's stance against having another child. Was aware of the terrible place it came from. But she couldn't help but wonder if to start a relationship with Ben predicated on it being a relationship without children would mean a doomed relationship. It might be okay to start with, but as the years went by might she come to blame him? To resent him?

'You sure you're okay?' asked Lizzie. 'You look flushed.'

'Really, I'm fine.' Sandy fanned her face with both hands. 'It's hot. I suspect this rattly old air-conditioner is on its last legs.'

'You could put in a new one if you bought the business.'

'I guess…' she said, filled with sudden new doubt.

Holding Amy in her arms, hearing about Jason's bride's bump, had shaken her confidence in a long-term relationship with Ben that didn't include starting a family.

She changed the subject. 'What are you guys planning on doing? Can you stay tonight?'

'That depends on you. I promised Amy I'd take her to see the white lions at Mogo Zoo. Then we could come back here, have dinner with you and Ben, stay the night and go home tomorrow.'

'That would be amazing. Let's book you into Ben's gorgeous hotel.'

When had her thoughts changed from Hotel Hideous to 'Ben's gorgeous hotel'?

She didn't feel guilty about putting the 'Back in Ten Minutes' sign up on the bookshop door—Ida had quite a collection of signs, covering all contingencies. It was hot and stuffy inside Bay Books and she was beginning to feel claustrophobic.

And she wanted to see Ben again, to be reassured that loving him would be enough.

Ben was stunned to see Sandy coming towards Reception with a little girl. The child was clutching one of Bay Books' brown paper bags with one hand and holding on tight to Sandy's hand with the other. All the while she kept up a steady stream of childish chatter and Sandy looked down to reply, her face tender and her eyes warm with love.

That newly tuned engine of his heart spluttered and stalled at the sight. It looked natural and right to see Sandy hand in hand with a child. The little girl might be her daughter.

Anguish tore through him. Liam would have been around the same age if he'd lived. *He could not go there.* Getting past what would have been Liam's first birthday had seen him alone in his room with a bottle of bourbon. The other anniversaries had been only marginally better.

Sandy caught sight of him and greeted him with a big smile. Was he imagining that it didn't reach her eyes? He forced himself to smile back, to act as though the sight of her with a child had not affected him.

He pulled her into a big hug. His need to keep their relationship private from the gossiping eyes of Dolphin Bay was in the past. He'd been warmed and gratified by the good wishes he'd been given since the night of the Chamber of Commerce dance. He hadn't realised just how concerned his family and friends had been about him.

'This is my niece, Amy,' Sandy said. 'Amy, this is my friend Ben.'

Ben hunkered down to Amy's height. 'Hi, Amy. Welcome to Dolphin Bay.'

'I like dolphins,' Amy said. 'They smile. I like crocodiles too. I've got a new crocodile book.' She thrust the brown paper bag towards him.

'That's good,' Ben said awkwardly. He was out of practice with children. Hadn't been able to deal with them since he'd lost Liam.

Sandy rescued him from further stilted conversation. 'Do you remember my sister, Lizzie?' she asked, indicating the tall blonde woman who had joined them.

'Of course I remember you, Lizzie,' he said as he shook hands. Though, truth be told, back then he'd been so caught up with Sandy he'd scarcely noticed Lizzie, attractive though she was.

'Who would have thought I'd see you two together again after all these years?' said Lizzie.

'Yes,' he said.

He looked down at Sandy and she smiled up at him.

'Can we book Lizzie and Amy into a room with a water view?' she asked.

We. She'd said 'we'. And he wasn't freaked out by it as much as he'd thought he would be. In fact he kind of liked it.

He put his arm around her and held her close. She clutched onto him with a ferocity that both pleased and worried him. There was that shadow again around her eyes. *What gave?*

He booked Lizzie and Amy into the room adjoining Sandy's, talking over their protests when he told them that the room was on the house.

'Dinner tonight at the hotel?' he asked, including Lizzie and Amy in the invitation.

Sandy nodded. 'Yes, please—for all of us. Though it will have to be early because of Amy's bedtime.'

'I'm good with that.'

The sooner Lizzie and Amy were settled in their room, the sooner he could be alone with Sandy. Their time together was ticking down.

Lizzie glanced at her watch. 'We have to get to the zoo.' She took Amy's book and packed it in her bag. 'C'mon, Amy, quick-sticks.'

Amy indicated for Sandy to pick her up and Sandy obliged. She embraced Sandy in a fierce hug.

'I'll bring you a white lion, Auntie Ex,' she said.

Auntie Ex? Ben was about to ask for an explanation of the name when Amy leaned over from her position in Sandy's arms and put her arms up to be hugged by him.

'Bye-bye, Ben,' she said. 'Do you want a white lion, too?'

Ben froze. He hadn't held a child since he'd last held Liam. But Amy's little hands were resting on his shoulders, her face close to his. For a moment it was the three of them. A man. A woman. A child.

He panicked. Had to force himself not to shake. He looked to Sandy over the little girl's blonde head. Connected with her eyes, both sad and compassionate.

He cleared his throat and managed to pat the little girl gently on the back. 'A white lion would be great—thanks, Amy.'

'A girl one or a boy one?' Amy asked.

Ben choked out the words. 'A…a boy one, please.'

'Okay,' she said, and wiggled for Sandy to put her down.

Amy ran over to her mother.

'How are you going to get the white lions back here, Amy?' asked Sandy.

'In the back of the car, of course, silly,' Amy replied.

The adults laughed, which broke the tension. But Ben was still shaken by the emotion that had overtaken him when he'd stood, frozen, in that group hug with Sandy and Amy. And he couldn't help but notice how Sandy's eyes never left her delightful little niece. There was more than being a doting aunt in her gaze.

'Okay, guys, I have to get back to the bookshop,' Sandy said. She hugged Amy and Lizzie. Then turned to him and hugged him. 'I'm going to stay back for a little while after I shut up shop and flick through Ida's files. I'll see you for dinner.'

He tightened his arms around her. Something was bothering her—and that bothered him. 'Don't be too long,' he said, wanting to urge her to stay.

Lizzie and Amy headed for their car. Ben watched Sandy as she walked through the door. Her steps were too slow, her head bowed. She seemed suddenly alone, her orange dress a flash of colour in the monochrome decor of the reception area.

Was she thinking about how much she'd miss Lizzie and Amy if she settled in Dolphin Bay?

He suspected it was more than that.

Sandy had accepted his reasons for not wanting to risk having another child. But he'd seen raw longing in her eyes when she'd been with Amy.

When she was eighteen she'd chattered on that she wanted three kids. He'd thought two was enough—but he hadn't argued about wanting to be a parent. Fatherhood had been on his future agenda, too.

The ever-present pain knifed deeper. Being father to Liam had been everything he'd wanted and more. He'd loved every minute of his son's babyhood.

He took in a deep, shuddering breath. By denying Sandy her chance to be a mother he could lose her. If not now, then later.

It might make her wave goodbye and leave for Melbourne

on Wednesday, never to return to Dolphin Bay. Or, if she decided to stay with him, she might come to resent him. Blame him for the ache in her heart that only a baby could soothe.

Could he let that happen?

CHAPTER FIFTEEN

THE NEXT AFTERNOON Sandy trudged towards the hospital entrance. Fed up with the muggy atmosphere in Bay Books, and the rattling, useless air-conditioner, she'd shut up shop on the dot of five o'clock. To heck with going through more of Ida's files. She'd talk to Ida in person.

Whether or not she'd be able to have a sensible business conversation was debatable. She was too churned up with anxiety about the reality that a long-term relationship with Ben meant giving up her dream of having children. She tried summoning the techniques Ben had taught her to overcome her fear of monster waves but without any luck.

Her anxiety was like a dark shadow, diminishing the brilliance of her rediscovered love for Ben. Even memories of their heavenly lovemaking the night before, the joy of waking again in his arms, was not enough.

It felt like that long-ago summer day when she had been snorkelling with Ben at Big Ray Beach, out in the calm waters of the headland. It had been a perfect day, the sun shimmering through the water to the white sand beneath them, illuminating shoals of brightly coloured little fish darting in and out of the rocks. She and Ben had dived to follow some particularly cute orange and white clown fish.

Then suddenly everything had gone dark. Terrified, she'd gripped Ben's arm. He'd pointed upwards and she'd seen one of the big black manta rays that had given its name to the beach swim directly above them. She'd panicked, thinking she didn't have enough air to swim around it and up to the surface. But the ray had cruised along surprisingly quickly and she and Ben had been in sunshine again. They'd burst through to the top, spluttering and laughing and hugging each other.

Right now she felt the way she had when the light had been suddenly cut off.

She couldn't ignore Ben's stricken reaction when Amy had reached out to him yesterday. Her niece was discerning when it came to the adults she liked. She'd obviously picked Ben as a good guy and homed in like a heat-seeking missile. But all it had done was bring back painful memories for Ben.

If Sandy had held on to any remnant of hope that Ben might change his mind about having a child she'd lost it when she'd seen the fear and panic in his eyes.

And it hadn't got any better during dinner. She'd seen what an enormous effort it had been for Ben to take part in Amy's childish conversation. Amy, bless her, hadn't noticed. Her little niece had been too pleased she'd managed to get a toy girl white lion for her Auntie Ex and a boy one for Ben.

It must be so painful for Ben to endure—every child he encountered a reminder to him of what he had lost.

But it was painful for her, too, to know that Amy would be the only child she would ever have to love if she and Ben became a long-term couple.

Could she really do this? Put all her hopes of a family aside?

Would she be doomed to spend the next ten years or so hoping Ben might change his mind? Counting down the fertile years she had left? Becoming embittered and resentful?

She loved Ben; she didn't want to grow to hate him.

If she had any thought that her relationship with Ben might founder over the children issue should she think seriously of breaking it off now, to save them both future pain?

Her heart shrivelled to a hard, painful knot at the thought of leaving him.

She couldn't mention her fears to Lizzie—now back home in Sydney. Lizzie would tell her to run, not walk, away from Dolphin Bay. Her sister had often said giving birth to Amy was the best thing that had ever happened to her. She wouldn't want Sandy to miss out on motherhood.

Ben's decision not to have more children really could be a deal-breaker. Tomorrow was Wednesday and their future beyond tonight had become the elephant in the room. No. Not just an elephant but a giant-sized woolly mammoth.

As she neared the big glass doors of the hospital entrance she knew she had to tell Ida to take her out of the Bay Books equation. She couldn't consider her offer while she had any doubt at all about staying in Dolphin Bay.

But almost as soon as she was inside the hospital doors she was waylaid by the bank manager's wife, a hospital administrator, who wanted to chat.

By the time she got to Ida's bedside it was to find Ben's aunt in a highly agitated state.

'Why haven't you answered your mobile? There's smoke pouring out of Bay Books. Ben's there, investigating.'

It was nothing Ben could put his finger on, but he could swear Sandy had distanced herself from him last night. Especially through that awkward dinner. At any time he'd expected outspoken Lizzie to demand to know what his intentions were towards Sandy. And Sandy's obvious deep love for Amy had made him question again the fairness of depriving her of her own children.

But tomorrow was Wednesday. He *had* to talk with Sandy about her expectations—and his—if they were to go beyond these four awesome days.

She wasn't picking up her mobile. Seeing her would be better. He headed to Bay Books.

Ben smelled the smoke before he saw it—pungent, acrid,

burning the back of his throat. Sweat broke out on his forehead, dampened his shirt to his back. His legs felt like lead weights. Terror seized his gut.

Sandy. Was she in there?

He was plunged back into the nightmare of the guest-house fire. The flames. The doorknob searing the flesh of his hands. His voice raw from screaming Jodi's name.

His heart thudded so hard it made him breathless. He forced his paralysed legs to run down the laneway at the side of the shop, around to the back entrance. Dark grey smoke billowed out through a broken pane in the back window.

The wooden carvings. The books. So much fuel for the fire. A potential inferno.

Sandy could be sprawled on the floor. Injured. Asphyxiated. He had to go in. Find her.

Save her.

He shrugged off his jacket, used it to cover his face, leaving only a slit for his eyes. He pushed in his key to the back door and shoved. The door gave. He plunged into the smoke.

'Sandy!' he screamed until his voice was hoarse.

No response.

Straight away he saw the source of the smoke. The old air-conditioning unit on the wall that Ida had refused to let him replace. Smouldering, distorted by heat, but as yet with no visible flames.

The smoke appeared to be contained in the small back area.

But no Sandy.

Heart in his mouth, he shouldered open the door that led through into the shop. No smoke or flames.

No Sandy there either.

All the old pain he'd thought he'd got under control gripped him so hard he doubled over. What if it had been a different story and Sandy had died? By opening up to Sandy he'd exposed himself again to the agony of loss.

He fought against the thought that made him wish Sandy had never driven so blithely back into Dolphin Bay. Making him question the safe half-life that had protected him for so long.

Like prison gates clanging shut, the old barriers against pain and loss and anguish slammed back into place. He felt numb, drained.

How could he have thought he could deal with loving another woman?

A high-pitched pop song ringtone rang out, startling him. It was so out of place in this place of near disaster. He grabbed Sandy's mobile phone from next to the register and shoved it in his pocket without answering it. Why the *hell* didn't she have it with her?

He headed back to the smouldering air-conditioning unit, grabbed the fire extinguisher canister from the nearby wall bracket and sprayed fire retardant all over it.

Then he staggered out into the car park behind the shop.

He coughed and spluttered and gulped in huge breaths of fresh air.

And then Sandy was there, her face anguished and wet with tears.

'Ben. Thank heaven. *Ben.*'

Sandy never wanted to experience again the torment of the last ten minutes. All sorts of hideous scenarios had played over and over in her head.

She scarcely remembered how she'd got from the hospital to Bay Books, her heart pounding with terror, to find horrible black smoke and Ben inside the shop.

But Ben was safe.

His face was drawn and stark and smeared with soot. His clothes were filthy and he stank of acrid smoke. But she didn't care. She flung herself into his arms. Pressed herself to his big, solid, blessedly alive body. Rejoiced in the pounding of his heart, the reassuring rise and fall of his chest as he gulped in clean air.

'You're okay…' That was all she could choke out.

He held her so tightly she thought he would bruise her ribs.

'It wasn't as bad as it looked. There's just smoke damage out the back. It didn't reach the books.'

He coughed. Dear heaven, had the smoke burned his throat?

Relief that he was alive morphed into anger that he'd put himself in such danger. She pulled back and pounded on his chest with her fists. 'Why did you go in there? Why take the risk? Ida must have insurance. All that wood, all that paper… If it had ignited you could have been killed.' Her voice hiccupped and she dissolved into tears again.

He caught her wrists with his damaged hands. 'Because I thought you were in there.'

She stilled. 'Me?'

'You weren't answering your phone. I was worried.'

The implication of his words slammed into her like the kind of fast, hard wave that knocked you down, leaving you to tumble over and over in the surf. His wife and son had been trapped inside a fire-ravaged building. What cruel fate had forced him to face such a scenario again? Suffer the fear that someone he cared for was inside?

She sniffed back her tears so she was able to speak. 'I'd gone to visit Ida. To talk…to talk business with her.' *And to mull over what a future without kids might mean.* 'I'm so sorry. It was my fault you—'

'It was my choice to go in there. I had to.'

His grip on her hands was so tight it hurt.

'All I could think about was how it would be if I lost you.'

He let go her hands and stepped back.

Something was wrong with this scenario. His eyes, bluer than ever in the dark, smoke-dirtied frame of his face, were tense and unreadable. He fisted his hands by his sides.

She felt her stomach sink low with trepidation. 'But you didn't lose me, Ben. I'm here. I'm fine.'

'But what if you hadn't been? What if—?'

She fought to control the tremor in her voice. 'I thought we'd decided not to play the "what-if?" game.'

Beads of sweat stood out on his forehead. 'It was a shock.'

She heard the distant wail of a fire engine and was aware of people gathering at a distance from the shop.

Ben waved and called over to them. 'Nothing to worry about. Just smoke—no fire.'

He wiped his hand over his face in a gesture of weariness and resignation that tore at her. A dark smear of soot swept right across his cheek.

'Sandy, I need to let the fire department know they're not needed. Then go get cleaned up.'

'I'll come with you,' she said immediately.

This could be their last evening together.

He hesitated for just a second too long. 'Why don't you go back to the hotel and I'll meet you there?' he said.

One step forward and two steps back? Try ten steps forward and a hundred steps back.

'Sure,' she said, forcing the fear out of her voice.

He went to drop a kiss on her cheek but she averted it so the kiss landed on her mouth. She wound her arms around his neck, clung to him, willing him with her kiss to know how much she cared for him. How much she wanted it to work out.

'Woo-hoo! Why don't you guys get a room?'

The call—friendly, well-meant—came from one of the onlookers. She laughed, but Ben glared. She dropped her arms; he turned away.

So she *wasn't* imagining the change in him.

She forced her voice to sound Sunny-Sandy-positive. 'Okay. So I'll see you back at the hotel.'

She headed back towards Hotel Harbourside, disorientated by a haunting sense of dread.

Ben hated the confusion and hurt on Sandy's face. Hated that he was the cause of it. But he felt paralysed by the fear of losing her. He needed time to think without her distracting presence.

Thanks to this special woman he'd come a long way in the last few days. But what came next? Sandy deserved commitment. Certainty. But there were big issues to consider. Most of all the make-or-break question of children. He'd been used to managing only his own life. Now Sandy was here. And she'd want answers.

Answers he wasn't sure he could give right now.

CHAPTER SIXTEEN

SANDY WAS JUST about to turn in to the hotel entrance when she stopped. It wasn't exactly anger towards Ben that made her pause. More annoyance that she was letting herself tip-toe around vital issues she and Ben needed to sort out if they were to have any hope of a future together.

Ben needed to be treated with care and consideration for what he'd been through. But she had to consider her own needs, too. Decision time was looming. If she was to go to Melbourne and interview for the candle shop franchise she had to leave here by the latest tomorrow morning.

She turned right back around and headed down the steps to the beach.

The heat was still oppressive, the sand still warm. At this time of year it wouldn't get dark until nearly nine.

Before the sun set she needed answers.

She found Ben sitting on the wooden dock that led out from the boathouse into the waters of the bay. His broad shoulders were hunched as he looked out towards the breakwater.

Without a word she sat down beside him. Took his hand in hers. In response, he squeezed it tight. They sat in silence. Her. Ben. And that darn woolly mammoth neither of them seemed capable of addressing.

Beyond the breakwater a large cargo ship traversed the horizon. Inside the harbour walls people were rowing dinghies to shore from where their boats were anchored. A large seagull landed on the end pier and water slapped against the supporting posts of the dock.

She took a deep breath. 'Ida wants to sell me Bay Books.'

'Is that what you want?' His gaze was intent, the set of his mouth serious.

She met his gaze with equal intensity. 'I want to run my own business. I think I could make the bookshop work even better than it already does. But you're the only reason for me to stay in Dolphin Bay.'

'An important decision like that should be made on its own merits.'

'The bookshop proposition's main merit is that it allows me to stay here with you.' *Time to vanquish that mammoth.* 'We have to talk about where we go from here.'

His voice matched the bleakness of his face. 'I don't know that I can give you what you want.'

'I want you, Ben. Surely you know that.'

'I want you too. More than you can imagine. If it wasn't for…for other considerations I'd ask you to stay. Tell you to phone that candle guy and cancel your interview in Melbourne. But…but it's not that straightforward.'

'What other considerations?' she asked, though she was pretty sure she knew the answer.

He cleared his throat. 'I saw how you were with Amy.'

'You mean how I dote on her?'

He nodded. 'You were meant to be a mother, Sandy. Even when you were eighteen you wanted to have kids.'

'Two girls and a boy,' she whispered, the phrase now a desolate echo.

'I can't endure loss like that again. Today brought it all back.'

She wanted to shake him. Ben was smart, educated, an astute businessman. Why did he continue to run away from life? From love.

'I appreciate your loss. The pain you've gone through. But haven't you punished yourself enough for what happened?'

He made an inarticulate response and she knew she had hurt him. But this had been bottled up for too long.'

'Can't you see that any pleasure involves possible pain? Any gain possible risk. Are you *never* going to risk having your heart broken again?'

His face was ashen under his tan. 'It's too soon.'

'Do you think you'll ever change your mind about children?'

She held her breath in anticipation of his answer.

'Since you've been back I've thought about it. But four days isn't long enough for me to backtrack on something so important.'

Deep down she knew he was only giving voice to what she already knew. She wanted Ben. She wanted children. But she couldn't have both.

Slowly she exhaled her breath in a huge sigh. 'I can take that as a no then. But, Ben, you're only thirty-one. Too young to be shutting down your life.'

His jaw set in a stubborn line. 'It wouldn't be fair for me to promise something I can't deliver.'

'I...I understand.' But she didn't. Not really.

She shifted. The hard boards of the dock were getting uncomfortable.

'And I appreciate your honesty.'

His gaze was shrewd. 'But it's not good enough for you?'

She shook her head. 'No. It's not.'

Now she felt the floodgates were open. 'It was compromise all the way with Jason. I wanted marriage and kids. He said he had to get used to the idea. I moved in with him when I didn't want to live together without being married. Fine for other people. Too insecure for me. But I went along with him, put my own needs on hold.' Her attempt at laughter came out sharp-edged and brittle. 'Now I hear he's not only married, but his wife is pregnant.'

'That…that must have been a shock.'

'I can't go there again, Ben. Can't stay here waiting for heaven knows how long for you to get the courage to put the past behind you and commit to a future with me.'

Ben looked down at where the water slapped against the posts. She followed his gaze to see a translucent jellyfish floating by to disappear under the dock, its ethereal form as insubstantial as her dreams of a life with Ben.

'I'm sorry,' he said.

She didn't know whether he was apologising for Jason or because he couldn't give her the reassurances she wanted.

'I…I won't make all the compromises again, Ben,' she said brokenly. 'No matter how much I love you.'

She slapped her hand to her mouth.

The 'L' word.

She hadn't meant to say it. It had just slipped out.

Say it, Ben. Tell me you love me. Let me at least take that away with me.

But he didn't.

Maybe he couldn't.

And that told her everything.

'I'm sorry,' he said again, his voice as husky as she'd ever heard it. 'I can't be what you want me to be.'

If he told her she could do better than him she'd scream so loud they'd hear it all the way to New Zealand.

Instead he pulled her to him, held her tight against his powerful chest. It was the place she most wanted to be in the world. But she'd learned that compromise which was all one way wouldn't make either of them happy.

'I'm sorry too,' she murmured, fighting tears. 'But I'm not sorry I took that turn-off to Dolphin Bay. Not sorry we had our four-day fling.'

He pulled her to her feet. 'It's not over. We still have this evening. Tonight.'

She shook her head. 'It's perfect the way it is. I don't want to ruin the memories. I…I couldn't deal with counting down the hours to the last time we'll see each other.'

With fingers that trembled she traced down his cheek to the line of his jaw, trying to memorise every detail of his face. She realised she didn't have any photos to remember him by. Recalled there'd been a photographer at the dinner dance. She would check the website and download one. But not until she could look at his image and smile rather than weep.

'Sandy—' he started.

But she silenced him with a kiss—short, sweet, final.

'If you say you're sorry one more time I'll burst into tears and make a spectacle of myself. I'm going back to my room now. I've got phone calls to make. E-mails to send. Packing to do.'

A nerve flickered near the corner of his mouth. 'I'll call by later to…to say goodbye.'

'Sure,' she said, fighting to keep her voice under control. 'But I'm saying my goodbye now. No regrets. No what-ifs. Just gratitude for what we had together.'

She kissed him again. And wondered why he didn't hear the sound of her heart breaking.

Ben couldn't bear to watch Sandy walk away. He turned and made his way to the boathouse. Every step was an effort, as if he were fighting his way through a rip.

His house seemed empty and desolate—the home of a solitary widower. There was a glass next to the sink with Sandy's lipstick on the rim, but no other trace of her. He stripped off his smoke-stained clothes, pulled on his board shorts and headed for Big Ray Beach.

He battled the surf as if it were a foe, not the friend it had always been to him. He let the waves pound him, pummel him, punish him for not being able to break away from his self-imposed exile. The waves reared up over him, as if harnessing his anger at the cruel twist of fate that had brought Sandy back into his life but hadn't given him the strength to take the second chance she had offered him.

Finally, exhausted, he made his way back to the boathouse.

For one wild moment he let himself imagine what it would be like to come back to the house to find Sandy there. Her bright smile, her welcoming arms, her loving presence.

But the house was bare and sterile, his footsteps loud and lonely on the floorboards. That empty glass on the draining board seemed to mock him. He picked up the photo of him and Sandy on the beach that long-ago summer. All their dreams and hopes had stretched out ahead of them—untainted by betrayal and pain and loss.

He put down the photo with its faded image of first love. He'd lost her then. And he'd been so damned frightened of losing her at some undefined time in the future he'd lost her now.

He slammed his fist down so hard on the dresser that the framed photo flew off the top. He rescued it from shattering on the floor only just in time.

What a damn fool he was.

He'd allowed the fears of the past to choke all hope for the future.

Sandy had offered him a second chance. And he'd blown it.

Sandy. Warm, vibrant, generous Sandy. With her don't-let-anything-get-you-down attitude.

That special magic she'd brought into his life had nothing to do with the glitter she trailed around with her. Sandy's magic was hope, it was joy, but most of all it was love.

Love he'd thought he didn't deserve. With bitterness and self-loathing he'd punished himself too harshly. And by not forgiving himself he'd punished Sandy, too.

The final rusted-over part of him shifted like the seismic movement of tectonic plates deep below the floor of the ocean. It hurt. But not as much as it would hurt to lose Sandy for good.

He had to claim that love—tell her how much she meant to him. Show her he'd found the courage and the purpose to move forward instead of tripping himself up by looking back.

He showered and changed and headed for the hotel.

Practising in his head what he'd say to her, he rode the elevator to Sandy's room. Knocked on the door. Once. Twice. But no reply.

'Sandy?' he called.

He fished out the master key from his wallet and opened the door.

She was gone.

The suitcase with all her stuff spilling out of it was missing. Her bedlinen had been pulled down to the end of the bed. There was just a trace of her vanilla scent lingering in the air. And on the desk a trail of that darn glitter, glinting in the coppery light of the setting sun.

In the midst of the glitter was a page torn out from the fairy notebook she always carried in her bag. It was folded in two and had his name scrawled on the outside.

His gut tightened to an agonising knot. With unsteady hands he unfolded the note.

Ben—thank you for the best four days of my life. I'm so glad I took a chance with you. No regrets. No 'what ifs'. Sandy xx.'

He fumbled for his mobile. To beg her to come back. But her number went straight to voicemail. Of course it did. She wouldn't want to talk to him.

He stood rooted to the ground as the implications of it all hit him.

He'd lost her.

Then he gave himself a mental shaking.

He could find her again.

It would take at least ten hours for her to drive to Melbourne. More if she took the coastal road. It wasn't worth pursuing her by car.

In the morning he'd drive to Sydney, then catch a plane to Melbourne.

He'd seek her out.

And hope like hell that she'd listen to what he had to say.

Sandy had abandoned her plan to mosey down the coastal road to Melbourne. Instead she cut across the Clyde Mountain and drove to Canberra, where she could connect to the more straightforward route of the Hume Highway.

She didn't trust herself to drive safely in the dark after the emotional ups and downs of the day. A motel stop in Canberra, then a full day's driving on Thursday would get her to Melbourne in time to check in to her favourite hotel and be ready to wow the candle people on Friday morning.

She would need to seriously psyche herself up to sound enthusiastic about a retail mall candle shop when she'd fallen in love with a quaint bookshop on a beautiful harbour.

Her hands gripped tight on the steering wheel.

Who was she kidding?

It was her misery at leaving Ben that she'd have to overcome if she was going to impress the franchise owners.

She'd cried all the way from Dolphin Bay. Likely she'd cry all the way from Canberra to Melbourne. Surely she would have run out of tears by the time she faced the interview panel?

She pulled into the motel.

Ben would have read her note by now. Maybe it had been cowardly to leave it. But she could not have endured facing him again, knowing she couldn't have him.

No regrets. No regrets. No regrets.

Ben was her once-in-a-lifetime love. But love couldn't thrive in a state of inertia.

She'd got over Ben before. She'd get over him again.

Soon her sojourn in Dolphin Bay would fade into the realm of happy memories. She had to keep on telling herself that.

And pray she'd begin to believe it.

CHAPTER SEVENTEEN

BEN REMEMBERED SANDY telling him about her favourite hotel in the inner-city Southbank district of Melbourne—all marble, chandeliers and antiques. He'd teased her that it sounded too girly for words. She'd countered that she liked it so much better than his preferred stark shades of grey.

He'd taken a punt that that was where she would be staying. A call to Reception had confirmed it. He walked from his ultra-contemporary hotel at the other end of the promenade that ran along the banks of the Yarra River. He'd wait all day at her hotel to see her if he had to.

It was a grey, rainy morning in Melbourne, mitigated by the brilliant colours of a myriad umbrellas. Ben watched a hapless duck struggling to swim across the wide, fast-flowing brown waters of the Yarra.

Was his mission doomed to such a struggle?

He found the hotel and settled in one of the comfortable velvet chairs in the reception area. He didn't have to wait for long. He sensed Sandy was there before he glanced up.

He was shocked at how different she looked. She wore a sleek black suit with a tight skirt that finished above her knees and high-heeled black shoes. A laptop in a designer bag was slung across her shoulder. Her hair was sleek, her mouth glossy with red lipstick.

She looked sexy as hell and every inch the successful businesswoman.

Sandy the city girl.

It jolted him to realise how much he'd be asking her to give up. Now she was back in her own world would she want to settle for running a small-town bookshop in Dolphin Bay?

She must have felt his gaze on her, and stopped mid-stride as he rose from the chair. He was gratified that her first reaction was a joyous smile. But then she schooled her face into something more neutral.

For a moment that seemed to stretch out for ever they stood facing each other in the elegant surrounds of the hotel. He had to get it right this time. There wouldn't be another chance.

Sandy's breath caught.

Ben.

Unbelievably handsome and boldly confident in a superbly cut charcoal-grey suit. Her surf god in the city. She had trouble finding her voice.

'What are you doing here?' she finally managed to choke out.

He stepped closer. 'I've come to tell you how much I love you. How I always loved the memory of you.'

Ben. This troubled, scarred man she adored. He had come all the way to Melbourne to tell her he loved her, smack in the middle of a hotel lobby.

She kept her voice low. 'I love you too. But it doesn't change the reasons why I left Dolphin Bay.'

'You gave me the kick in the butt I needed. I'm done with living with past scars. I want a future. With you.'

He looked around. Became aware they were attracting discreet interest.

'Can we talk?'

'My room,' she said.

They had the elevator to themselves and she ached to kiss him, to hold him. That would only complicate things, but for the first time she allowed herself a glimmer of hope for a future with Ben.

Ben was grateful for the privacy of Sandy's hotel room. He took both her hands in his. Pulled her close. Looked deep into her eyes. 'More than anything I want a life with you.'

'Me too, Ben.'

'That life would be empty without a child. *Our* child.'

He watched her face as the emotions flashed over it. She looked more troubled than triumphant.

'Oh, Ben, you don't have to say that. I don't want you to force yourself to do something so important as having children because you think it's what *I* want. That…that won't work.'

The fear he'd been living with for five years had been conquered by her brave action in walking away from him.

'It's for your sake, yes. But it's also for my own.' He took a deep breath. 'I want to be a dad again some day.'

The loss of Liam had been tragic. All potential for that little life gone in a terrible, pointless fire. But no matter how much he blamed himself, he knew deep in his gut he had not been responsible for those out-of-control flames. No one could have predicted how the wind had changed. No one could have saved Jodi and his son.

'I know you were a brilliant father in the little time you were granted with Liam. Everyone told me that.'

'I did my best.'

The four words echoed with sudden truth.

He deserved a second chance. Another son. A daughter. A baby who would grow into a child, like Amy, and then a teenager like he and Sandy had been when they met. It would not diminish the love he'd felt for Jodi and Liam.

'I want a family again, Sandy, and I want it with you. We'll be good parents.'

Exulting, he kissed her—a long, deep kiss. But there was more he needed to talk about before he could take her back home with him. He broke the kiss, but couldn't bear to release her hands from his.

'How did your interview go?' he asked.

'The Melbourne store is mine if I want it.' She was notably lacking in enthusiasm.

'*Do* you want it? Because if your answer is yes I'll move to Melbourne.'

Her eyes widened. 'You'd do that?'

'If it's what it takes to keep you,' he said.

She shook her head. 'Of course I don't want it. I want to buy Bay Books from Ida and knock through into the space next door to make a bookshop/café. I want to have author talks. Cooking demonstrations. A children's storyteller.'

The words bubbled out of her—and they were everything he wanted to hear.

'I want to ask Ida to order matching carvings for the café from her Balinese woodcarver.'

'That can be arranged. I own the café. The lease is yours.' He ran his finger down her cheek to the corner of her mouth. 'Will you come back to Dolphin Bay with me?'

Sandy was reeling from Ben's revelations. But he hadn't mentioned marriage—and she wanted to be married before she had children.

She'd feared he was too damaged to love again—and look what had happened. What was to stop her proposing?

'Yes,' she said. 'I want to come back to Dolphin Bay. Be with you. But I—'

He silenced her with a finger over her mouth. 'One more thing.'

'Yes?' she said.

'Life is short. There's no time to waste. We could date some more. Live together. But I'd rather we made it permanent. Marry me?'

In spite of all his pain and angst and loss he'd come through it strong enough to love again. To commit.

But she didn't kid herself that Ben's demons were completely vanquished. He'd still need a whole lot of love, support and understanding. As his wife, she could give it to him by the bucketload. Ben still had scars—and she'd help him to heal.

'Yes, I'll marry you. Yes, yes and *yes*.'

He picked her up and whirled her around until she was dizzy.

They were laughing and trying to talk at the same time, interspersing words with quick, urgent kisses.

'I don't want a big white wedding,' she said.

'I thought on the beach?'

'Oh, yes! In bare feet. With Amy as a flower girl. And Hobo with a big bow around his neck.'

Her fairy notebook would be filling up rapidly with lists.

'We can live in the boathouse.'

'I'd love that.'

'Build a big, new house for when we have kids.'

Maybe it was because her emotions had been pulled every which way, but tears welled in her eyes again. Ben had come so far. And they had so far to go together.

She blinked them away, but her voice was wobbly when she got the words out. 'That sounds like everything I've ever dreamed of…'

She thought back to her goals, written in pink.

Tick. Tick. Tick.

* * * * *

THE SURGEON'S FAMILY MIRACLE

BY

MARION LENNOX

Marion Lennox was born on an Australian dairy farm. She moved on—mostly because the cows weren't interested in her stories! Marion writes Medical Romance as well as Cherish novels. Initially she used different names, so if you're looking for past books, search also for author Trisha David. In her non-writing life Marion cares (haphazardly) for her husband, kids, dogs, cats, chickens and anyone else who lines up at her dinner table. She fights her rampant garden (she's losing) and her house dust (she's lost!). She also travels, which she finds seriously addictive. As a teenager Marion was told she'd never get anywhere reading romance. Now romance is the basis of her stories, her stories allow her to travel, and if ever there was one advertisement for following your dream, she'd be it! You can contact Marion at www.marionlennox.com.

PROLOGUE

LILY stared at the thin blue line in consternation. Her plane ticket was right beside her on the bed. In three hours she'd be flying back to Kapua, her Pacific island home, and from now on she and Ben would be nothing but friends.

She was pregnant.

She gazed at herself in the mirror, horror building. They'd been so careful for the past four years, but last week she'd had a tummy bug, and this week, knowing she might never see him again… Well, the only sure contraceptive was abstinence and how could she bear to be apart if this final week was all she had?

She was having Ben's baby.

She needed to tell him.

The thought made her blench. He'd hate it. She knew how much he'd hate it. Ben who held himself aloof, who backed away at the first sign of need—how could he be a father? Maybe the biggest reason he'd let himself be drawn into their relationship had been that at the end of four years he'd known she had to go home.

She loved him with all her heart.

She closed her eyes, overwhelmed with panic. How could she leave him, knowing she was carrying his child? How could she leave him at all?

He wouldn't let her leave if he knew she was pregnant. She knew that about him. He might hold himself apart; he might admit he needed no one; but her lovely Ben was an honourable man. He'd suffered a desperately lonely childhood himself, and to have a child grow up without a father… He wouldn't do it.

But neither could he love a child, she thought bleakly. He didn't know what loving was. They'd been together now for almost all their medical training, and for all that time her loving had been a one-way deal.

Oh, she couldn't complain. Ben had been honest with her from the start. 'Lily, I love you as much as I'll ever love a woman, but I don't want a permanent relationship.' He'd spelt it out repeatedly, making sure she'd understood. 'This time together is great, but as soon as we finish medical school I need to go and see the world.'

But now…

Ben would feel the same about abortion as she did, she thought, but anything else… She'd seen the flare of panic whenever she'd come close to admitting she needed him, and a child would make no difference. Or maybe it would make him decide to marry her, she thought bleakly, and that would be worse than loneliness. He'd be trapped by his own sense of decency.

The clock ticked on. She should be packing.

Ben didn't need her, she told herself. He didn't need anyone. And back home in Kapua, her fellow islanders truly did. She continued staring into the mirror, thinking of the girl she'd been ten minutes ago and the woman she'd suddenly become.

She was a woman with obligations.

Kapua, her island home since she was eight years old, had never had a doctor. Islanders were dying because of it. But Lily had excelled at school, and she'd been desperate to study medicine. Somehow the islanders had supported that wish. Kapua's economy was subsistence level, which meant the islanders' decision to fund her medical training had been huge. Her family and neighbours had gone without basic necessities to give her—and themselves—this chance.

The further her training had progressed, the more the islanders' anticipation had built. Their telephone calls over the last few months had been jubilant. They'd built a hospital because they knew she was coming. She was qualified. The island would have its first doctor.

She was carrying Ben's child.

Appalled, she let the test strip fall and her hand dropped to her waistline. She was feeling for a pregnancy that was hardly there. This was so new. So tiny. A fragment of human life.

Pregnancy didn't always end in a live birth, she thought, trying not to cry. To tell Ben now…

Impossible. He was off at the end of this week on his first mission with the armed forces. He'd react with forcefulness, she thought. He'd decide on marriage. He'd organise a date for a wedding during his first leave.

But if she left—as she had to leave—he wouldn't follow, she thought bleakly. She'd tried so hard to persuade him to visit her island but he'd reacted with incomprehension. The islanders were her family? How could that be? He didn't know what a family was.

Family…. Yes, the islanders were her family. They'd love this child to bits, she thought.

Ben would see a child as nothing more than chains.

She was rocking back and forth now, distressed beyond measure. How could she tell him? If she told him then he'd insist on marriage, and how could she refuse him? But how could she not go home?

'So tell him and go anyway,' she told her reflection.

'I'm not brave enough.'

There were footsteps on the outside stairs. The door was

flung open, and Ben was there. Her lovely Ben. Big and strong and tanned, and laughing for the sheer joy of living.

The father of her child.

'Lily, they've accepted me into SAS training,' he said before she could say a word, and he was across the room, lifting her, swinging her round and round in his excitement. 'It's the crack army assault team—the best in the world. You'll be off saving your little island but I'll be seeing the world.' He spun her round and round until she felt dizzy, and when he finally set her on her feet she had no choice but to lean against him, to feel the strength of him one last time.

'Sweetheart, we've each achieved our dream,' he said, and she could tell that his thoughts were already off in the exciting future where she played no part. 'I'll miss you like hell, my love.'

'I'll miss you,' she managed, but only just.

'Will you?' He cupped her chin, forcing her to look at him, but his eyes were alive with excitement, and he didn't see the change in hers.

'I can't understand how you can want to go back to such a place as Kapua,' he said. 'When the whole world is yours.'

'The island is my world.'

He nodded. 'I guess,' he said, hugging her against him. 'I guess we're both driven, but in different directions. But I wish we could share.'

'No, you don't,' she whispered, but so softly he didn't hear. She whispered it from her heart to his. 'You don't wish we could share, my love. You're my darling Ben Blayden—who walks alone.'

CHAPTER ONE

'ISN'T Kapua where Lily Cyprano lives?'

Ben was running to a tight schedule, and he sighed as Sam Hopper joined him. Sam was a skilled surgeon but he talked too much. The first Chinook was leaving in an hour. Normally the adrenalin was kicking in by now, making him move with lightning speed, but lately… Hell, what did it mean when preparation for disaster seemed routine?

'What?' he asked without looking up, and Sam poured himself coffee and hiked his frame onto the bench where Ben was sorting drugs.

'Lily,' he repeated patiently. 'Cute as a button. Half islander, half French. We all thought she looked like Audrey Hepburn, only curvier. Sexiest thing on two legs. She went through med school, then went home to work on the little island where she'd been raised. Wasn't that Kapua?' He paused, sorting old memories. 'Hey, weren't you two an item? I was a couple of years above you but I seem to remember… I'm right, aren't I?'

Ben's hands stilled. For a moment—just for a moment—a surge of remembered pain washed through him. Lily.

Then he regrouped. 'We're talking about seven years ago,' he snapped. 'The trivia you keep in that tiny mind of yours…'

'But Kapua is Lily's island?'

'Yeah,' Ben said, remembering. He'd been so caught up in the urgency of the job that until now he hadn't thought of the link between Kapua and Lily. But, yes, Kapua was definitely the place Lily called home.

'Is she still there?'

'How would I know? I haven't heard from her for years.'

'It'd be a joke if she was among the insurgents.'

'A great joke,' he said dryly, starting to pack again.

They were moving fast. News had hit that morning of an insurgent attack in Kapua. The islanders needed help, desperately.

Kapua was the biggest of a small group of Pacific islands. Its population was an interracial mix of the original Polynesians and the Spaniards who'd decided to colonise the place centuries ago. There was little sign of that colonisation now. The Spaniards had obviously decided the Polynesian lifestyle suited them much better than their own, and the island's laid-back lifestyle continued to this day.

But things were changing. Ignored by the rest of the world for centuries, the island had recently been made more interesting to other countries by the discovery of oil. The island's rulers had shown minimal interest in selling it. To sell the oil could change their lifestyle, but it would leave their descendants without resources when it was finished. The islanders had therefore decided to make the oil last maybe a hundred years or more, and so far they'd sold nothing.

That decision seemed to suit most islanders, but greed did dreadful things. It took few brains to guess that the insurgents who'd stormed the capital would be interested in only one thing—oil money.

'It's just as well the island has big friends,' Sam said, moving on, and Ben nodded. The call for help had been frantic. The insurgents had blasted their way into Kapua's council compound, and there were reports of deaths and chaos across the island. This wasn't a political take-over where oil wealth would be shared among the whole population. The opinion of those who knew was that this would be a group with outside backing—backing that could potentially cause instability in the entire Pacific region.

With such destruction—with human loss and chaos—there was little choice for Kapua's political allies. Troops were therefore flying in immediately. Among them would be Lieutenant Ben Blayden, M.D.

She's probably forgotten me, he thought grimly. What's the bet she'll be a fat island mama by now, with six or seven kids?

That thought made him smile. Domesticity would have made Lily happy. All through her medical training she'd ached to be home.

'My island's family to me,' she'd told him. 'Come and see what it's like.'

Not him. He was in too much of a hurry to get where he wanted, and he wanted action. The thought of settling on a remote island and raising children made him shudder.

But Lily…

'Lily was great,' he told Sam. 'She was a good-looking lady.'

'Look her up when you get there.'

'Pop in and make a social call during the gunfire?'

'Maybe it's not as serious as reported,' Sam said optimistically. 'Maybe you can persuade the nasty men to put away their guns, pour marguerítas for everyone and go lie on the beach.'

'As if.'

'You never know,' Sam said, yawning. 'But at least it'll be action. See if you can find a few bodies that need sewing up. Nice interesting cases. I'll be there in a flash.'

'You want to take my place?'

'After you persuade the boys to put their guns away,' Sam said, grinning. 'You're the front-line doctor. Not me.'

* * *

'I can't find Benjy.'

Lily was making her way through the crowded hospital, terror making her numb. All around her were people who needed her. The criminals who'd taken over the compound had shot indiscriminately, seeming to relish the destruction they were creating. The death count at the moment stood at twenty but there were scores of injured, scores of people Lily should be caring for right now.

But Benjy…

At first sign of trouble, when Kapua's finance councillor had stumbled through Lily's front door that morning, clutching her bloodied arm, Lily had told Benjy to run to Kira's house.

Kira was Lily's great-aunt, a loving, gentle lady who was like a grandmother to Benjy. She lived well away from the town centre, in an island-style bure by the beach. Benjy would be safe there, Lily had thought as she'd worked her way through the chaos of that morning.

Then, at midday, an elderly man had stumbled into the hospital, weeping. Kira's neighbour.

'Kira,' the man had wept. 'Kira.'

Somehow Lily had finished treating an islander she'd been working on. A bullet had penetrated the man's thigh, causing massive tissue damage. He'd need further surgery but for the moment the bleeding had been controlled. As soon as she'd been able to step away from the table she'd run, to find that Kira's hut had been burned, to find Kira dead and to find no sign of her son.

She'd stood on the beach and looked at the carnage and felt sick to the stomach. Dear God…

Where was her little boy? Nowhere. By the time she returned to the hospital she was shaking so badly that her chief nurse took control, holding her arms in his broad hands and giving her a gentle shake.

'What do you mean, you can't find Benjy? Isn't he with Kira?'

'Kira's dead. Shot in the back, Pieter. That kind, loving old lady. And Benjy's gone. There's no one on the beach at all.' Her breath caught on a sob of terror. 'Where would he have gone? Why isn't he here?' She was close to collapse, and the big islander pushed her into a chair, knelt before her and took both her hands in his.

'Maybe he's with Jacques.'

'I don't know where Jacques is either. Oh, God, if he's…' She buried her face in her hands.

But Pieter was hauling her hands down, meeting her gaze head on. He was the island's most senior nurse, sixty or so, big and gentle and as patient as any man she'd met. The look of fear in his eyes now made her more terrified than she'd been in her life. If Pieter was scared…

But he had himself more together than she did. 'So Benjy's probably with Jacques,' he told her. 'Or he'll be hiding. It's a good sign, Lily. Benjy's the most sensible six-year-old I know. If we look for him or for Jacques, it'll only jeopardise us all. You were crazy to have left the hospital yourself.'

He hesitated then, but they had to face facts. 'I'm sorry, but you need to block Benjy out, Lily. You're our only doctor and we need you. Trust Jacques to take care of him. For now Benjy's on his own and so are we.'

It was dusk as the Chinook carrying Ben hovered over the northern beach, its searchlights illuminating the sweep of sand while they assessed whether it was safe to land.

'We have the north beach secured,' they'd been told on a shaky radio connection by a deputy head of council who'd seemed to be having trouble speaking. 'They don't seem to be near. And the hospital's ours. That's all.'

A problem with an idyllic island existence, thought Ben grimly, was that it left everyone exposed to the nasties of this world. Life in paradise is all very well if everyone feels that way. The majority of islanders hadn't owned guns. They'd never dreamed of needing them and it had left the way for the few to run riot.

A burst of gunfire came from their left and the pilot swung the Chinook round so the floodlights pierced the forest.

'That's M16s,' the sergeant sitting beside Ben told them. 'I recognise the firing pattern. They sound too far away to be accurate. Reports are that most of these guys were already on the ground. We're therefore acting on the assumption that they won't have high-calibre weapons. They'll give us trouble on the ground but if that's all they have… I say land.'

'OK, we're going in,' the pilot said. 'You know your job, guys. Let's go.'

Pieter had personally brought another two units of plasma into the operating theatre. He was needed outside, Lily knew, but she also knew he was treating her as a patient—a patient who he needed to stay on her feet. The woman under her hands was the island's housing councillor. The wound to her chest was deep and ugly. It was a miracle the shot had missed her heart. All Lily's attention had to be on her, but Pieter knew that she needed at least some hope.

He was giving it to her now.

'Friendly troops are landing on Fringe Beach,' he said. 'A couple of new patients have come in from the rainforest and they saw them land. We've radioed for help and it's come.'

Lily was hardly listening. 'Benjy,' she was whispering over and over again. 'Benjy…'

'How many?' one of the theatre nurses asked, and Lily focused enough to hear terror in her voice that matched her own. Any minute now the few armed men they had could be subdued. The insurgents could take this place over.

And outside… Somewhere in this island was her six-year-old son.

'Three helicopters so far.'

Lily could feel a tiny lessening of terror in the theatre staff at the news. Outside help?

'These men are cowards,' Pieter said into the stillness. 'They've left this place alone because they know we have guns here. They'll shoot us but they won't risk being shot themselves. They won't have counted on outside help so soon. I'm guessing they hoped to bring more military supplies—maybe more men—onto the island before that.'

'If they're not already here…'

'If they had full military capability, they'd have shot down the helicopters,' Pieter said soundly and Lily thought, Benjy, Benjy, Benjy.

'Many of the islanders are hiding,' Pieter added, glancing at her. 'Long may they stay hidden.'

Benjy.

'Is there any news from the council compound?' a nurse asked, and Lily clamped off a blood vessel and waited for the site to be swabbed. She felt sick.

'We don't know what's happened there,' Pieter said. 'All we know is that those who ran from the building were shot.'

'Were those inside shot, too?'

'Who would know?' Pieter said heavily. 'There's no access. Anyone who goes near the place is met with gunfire.' He handed over the plasma, glanced at Lily to see if she was OK—was anyone OK just now?—and turned away.

'There are three more urgent cases,' he told Lily dully. 'Hand over here as soon as you can.'

She worked all that night and into the next morning, blocking out everything but medical imperatives. Or she almost blocked out everything. There was so much need. They needed a dozen doctors and there was only her. She worked like an automaton, her silent plea a background throbbing that could never stop.

Benjy, Benjy, Benjy.

'You need to sleep,' Pieter told her at four in the morning, and she shook her head.

'How can I sleep?'

'I feel the same. But we're no good to anyone if we collapse.'

'We're good until we collapse,' Lily said bleakly, turning to the next stretcher. A burst of gunfire in the distance made her wince. 'That's the way it's going to be.'

It was almost dawn. There were two platoons with full military and medical gear on the ground now, brought in under cover of darkness. Crack SAS troops, with more on the way.

'How can they hope to have had a successful coup?' Ben demanded. He was treating a corporal who'd been hit in the face. A bullet aimed at him had hit a tree and sheared off what had essentially been an arrow. The man's face was grazed, and once the splinter was out he'd be fine. If this was the extent of their casualties, they'd be lucky.

'The guess is that they'd never expect us to act this quickly,' the corporal told him. 'First rule of warfare—never mess with a country who shares our passion for cricket.'

The man left and Ben rechecked his gear. As soon as the island was secured they could search for wounded, but for now, when the road into the township was still under insurgent hands, there was time to think.

About Lily?

Ever since Sam's comment yesterday she'd been drifting in and out of his mind. At such a time, with her medical training, she had to be at the hospital. When could they reach the hospital?

He worked on, sorting gear so that when they moved into the township the urgent stuff could be moved first and he wouldn't be left without imperative supplies. His job was partly about good medicine, but it was also a lot about good organisation.

'Hey, Doc, we've got the road clear,' a voice called, and he turned to see a corporal emerge from the shadows. Graham was a sometime paramedic, depending on need. 'I've just been talking to the big boys,' he said. 'We're heading for the hospital now. It seems to have become a refuge. The locals we've found are saying there's been a recent drug problem on the island, so the hospital orderlies have been trained to be security guards. The first insurgents got a reception of gunfire and they've left the place alone. That's where our initial radio report came from and we're in contact with the radio operator now. He's telling us it's safe to come in.'

Lily, Ben thought.

She wasn't necessarily at the hospital, he told himself. She could be anywhere. He glanced across at the few canvas-shrouded figures on the beach. She could even be…

Don't go there.

Dawn. She was still operating, but without much hope. They were out of plasma, low on everything, and the child under her hands had lost so much blood that she almost hadn't started operating. But therein lay defeat and somewhere in the back of her exhausted mind lay a cold fury that had grown so great that if any of the insurgents had been close to her scalpel right this minute, they would have feared for their lives.

The boy she was operating on—Henri—was a friend of Benjy's. Three nights ago she'd made pizza for the pair of them and they'd watched a silly movie, she in the middle of the settee, with a little boy at either side.

Henri had been with his father on the beach where Kira had been killed. Henri's father had fled with the wounded boy into the rainforest and had waited far too long before he dared bring the boy for treatment.

Benjy and Henri…

'I'm sorry. I didn't see what happened to Benjy,' Henri's father had told her, but all his attention had been on his son, and Lily's must, be too.

The wound on Henri's thigh was massive, tissue torn clear and jagged fragments of bone embedded in what remained. It was well beyond Lily's area of expertise. She was sweating as she worked, and as she looked at the heart monitor and saw that she was failing, she knew tears were mixing with the sweat.

Damn them. Damn them, damn them, damn them.

Then the door slammed open. The theatre staff jerked to attention. In truth they'd spent the last twenty four hours expecting gunmen to burst in, and these were gunmen—but they were dressed in khaki uniforms she recognised. Friends.

'Keep still, everyone,' drawled a voice as armed men, pointed machine-guns and the officer in command assessed what was before him. Checking that the place wasn't an insurgent stronghold. But here was no disguising that a very real operation was taking place. There was also no disguising that they were operating on a child. The officer in charge made a lightning assessment and obviously decided this was no place for warfare. 'Who's in charge?' he said, and Lily checked the monitor, winced again and managed to reply.

'I'm operating. This child is critical. We have to continue.'

'What do you need, Doctor?' he asked, and her heart, which had almost stopped beating, started to thump again.

'Plasma,' she said, and she made no attempt to disguise the desperation in her voice. 'Now. And help. If you have anyone with medical training…'

'Right.' This was a man of few words and plenty of action and Lily blessed him for it. 'Everyone out except theatre staff. Let's keep this place as aseptic as possible. Someone find the medical supplies now, and get Ben in here, pronto.'

The machine-guns disappeared. Lily turned her attention to the wound again as the door slammed open once more.

'Plasma's on its way,' a voice said. 'I'm a doctor. Do you want me to scrub?'

She didn't look up. She couldn't. 'Yes, please,' she managed, and the man hauled off his outer uniform, let it fall to the floor and crossed to the sinks.

'Lily's exhausted,' Pieter told him. 'She's been operating for almost twenty-four hours and her hands are shaking.'

'That's what I'm here for,' the voice said. 'More medics are on their way but I'm the forerunner. I'm a Lieutenant in the SAS, and I have surgical training. What do you want me to do?'

'Ben,' Lily whispered, and she lifted her hands clear. Her fingers were trembling so much she couldn't go on.

'Doctor,' Pieter said urgently, and magically Ben was there, lifting the clamps from Lily's fingers and checking the monitor.

'Get that plasma here now,' he roared in a voice that could be heard in the middle of next week. He glanced at Pieter, who was acting as anaesthetist. 'Are you a doctor?'

'I'm a nurse with the basic training Lily's taught me. I'm Pieter.'

'Then, Lily, you take over the anaesthetic,' Ben snapped. 'Pieter, no offence but…'

'Of course there's no offence,' Pieter said, motioning to Lily to take over. 'If you knew how pleased I am to leave this to you guys…'

'I can imagine,' Ben said, and fixed his gaze on Lily, forcing her to steady. 'You can do this,' he said.

She took a deep breath. 'I can.'

'Right,' he snapped. 'Don't you dare collapse. There's no time. Let's get this kid out of danger and worry about everything else later.'

Ben was there.

She was so exhausted she could hardly think, but the knowledge settled in her heart and stayed. It made her feel…not better but somehow less hopeless.

Which was crazy. It was ridiculous to think that Ben Blayden could make all right with her world. Though he'd thought so from the start. He was loud and bossy and sure that his way was right.

'There are no easy answers,' she'd told him at the end of med school. They'd been discussing their future, but they'd already accepted their future didn't involve each other.

'Of course there are easy answers. You follow your vocation and you don't get distracted,' he'd said, and she'd wanted to agree with him but she hadn't been able to. She had already been distracted.

And now here he was again, just as distracting. She could hardly see him under his mask and theatre cap, but she'd glimpsed enough to see that he'd hardly changed. Still with that mass of jet-black curls that always looked unruly, that always looked supremely sexy. Still with those deep brown eyes, creased at the edges from constant laughter. Still with that body that said he worked hard and he played hard, strongly physical.

Ben was just who they needed right now.

He'd always been just who she needed.

'Blood pressure,' he snapped, and she responded fast, the medical side of her working once more on automatic.

'Seventy on forty-five.'

'We're clamping this and waiting,' he snapped. 'There's muck further down but to clear it involves further blood loss. We have to get that pressure up first.'

Muck further down…

She'd never intended to clear it. The bullet that had smashed into Henri had obviously blasted though wood first, as there were shards of splintered timber in the wound. She'd decided her only option was to get the bleeding vessels clamped and the wound closed, then hope like hell they could get him off the island to a competent surgeon before the wound festered.

Now here was Ben, saying let's take our time, let's use the plasma, get his blood pressure up and get this wound properly cleaned.

The tiny frisson of hope built, both for Henri and for them all.

He wouldn't operate this way unless he knew that things weren't hopeless outside, she thought. He wasn't closing fast and moving on to the next disaster.

Right. She firmed and made her tired mind find its third or fourth or maybe its twentieth wind. She could do this.

'Thank you, Ben,' she whispered, and he flashed her a look of concern.

She looked away. She didn't need sympathy now. If he said just one word… Her world could collapse, she thought.

Dear God, where was Benjy?

Now that Henri's blood pressure was rising Ben worked swiftly, knowing the anaesthetic itself was a strain on this desperately injured child. But now they had plasma he thought he'd make it. The child was strong and otherwise healthy, and Lily had done the hard part.

Lily.

This was no contented mama with six or seven babies. He glanced along the table to where she stood at Henri's head. All he could see of her was her eyes. They were the same eyes he'd fallen hard for more than ten years before, when they had still been kids at university. But they'd changed. She seemed haunted. She looked exhausted beyond all limits, exhausted by something that went beyond this present drama.

If he'd had another doctor he'd have ordered her away from the table. Even if she wanted to work, having such an exhausted colleague had its own risks. But the rest of the medical team wasn't flying in until they were sure it was safe to do so. Ben was the forerunner, sent to deal with frontline casualties, and there'd be no more medics here for the next few hours.

So he worked on, and Lily watched Henri's obs like a hawk, and monitored the anaesthetic as if she'd been trained to the job.

She'd been practising here for seven years, Ben thought. She'd been a lone doctor here for seven years. She'd need so many skills…

She'd fall over if he didn't hurry.

'I'm closing now,' he said at last, and saw Lily's shoulders sag under her theatre gown. Was it just exhaustion?

'Before I came here I did a rough check of the wards,' he told her, trying to alleviate a terror he only sensed. 'Unless more have come in, there's nothing else urgent. The rest of my medical team will probably be here in the next few hours. Why don't I take over and you guys get some sleep?'

'We won't sleep,' Pieter said gruffly, speaking for them all. 'We don't know what's gone on outside. Until we know what's happened to the rest of the islanders, there'll be no sleep for anyone.'

Lily was reversing the anaesthetic. Henri coughed and gagged his way into consciousness and as soon as he did so she stepped away from the table.

'I need to go.'

'Stay,' Ben said urgently. 'I need to talk to you.'

'There's no outstanding surgery?'

'Not as far as I know, but—'

'I'm sorry Ben,' she faltered, looking down at Henri. Maybe

she was thinking she should stay. But her gaze moved to Ben and her shoulders straightened. 'I have to go. Now. Please, look after him. Pieter, will you talk to his father?'

'Of course we will,' Pieter said, and he put his hands on Lily's shoulders and propelled her out of the room. 'You go,' he said. 'And find him safe.'

Who was she worried about?

He couldn't follow. It was a complex wound and dressing it took time. Then he worked out antibiotic doses and started them running through the drip. Then the moment he walked out the door he was clutched by a man who turned out to be Henri's father.

'Is he…?'

'He'll be fine,' Ben said gently. 'As I'm sure Lily told you. You can see him in a minute. Just take that shirt off first, will you?' He grimaced at the gore over the man's clothes. He'd carried his desperately injured son to the hospital and it showed. 'You'll scare Henri into a relapse if he sees you like that.' Then, as the man's terror didn't fade, he took him by the arm and led him into the theatre. Henri was still coming round. There were tubes going everywhere, but his breathing was strong and steady and colour was seeping back into his face.

'He's not quite awake,' Ben said. 'Change your shirt and you can sit with him while he wakes.'

'His mother,' the man muttered.

Ben thought, Uh-oh, and braced himself for another tragedy. But it seemed none was coming.

'His mother's in Sydney,' he whispered. 'My daughter's won a scholarship to boarding school there. Our daughter's very clever, you know. She's fourteen and she's…' He broke off and buried his face in his hands.

'Let me give you something to help the trembling,' Ben said, even though all he wanted to do right now was find Lily.

'I want…'

'We all want, mate,' Ben said softly. 'Let's just do what comes next.'

What came next—treating him for shock and dressing a jagged cut across his elbow that the man hadn't noticed until Ben helped him off with his shirt—took time. Then, just as he'd settled Henri's dad into a chair by Henri's bedside and wondered who'd sleep the deepest, a private came to find him.

'One of our men's got a flash burn to the arm,' he told him. 'They're chucking out Molotov cocktails and he got hit.'

'From where?'

'From that place they call the council compound.' He shrugged. 'We're mopping up now—there doesn't seem to be any aggressive fire from anywhere else on the island except from there. Paul was just real unlucky to be hit.'

'So what's happening?' Ben asked. 'Did our guys storm the place?'

'Dunno about that,' the private told him, leading the way back to his friend with the burns. 'They're saying there are hostages. The sergeant reckons when they saw how many of us had arrived they took fright, grabbed as many people as they could and barricaded themselves in. The powers that be have had us fall back out of range. My mate here's the last one injured. We sit and wait, Sarge reckons.'

They'd reached his mate now, a lanky corporal with an arm that was blistered and raw. 'Ouch,' Ben said. 'You've been playing with matches?'

The corporal gave him a sickly grin and Ben looked round to find Pieter, anyone, to prepare him a syringe of morphine.

Pieter appeared as if he'd known he was being looked for. His face, though, was more grim than the last time Ben had seen it.

'What's up?' he asked.

'I hope not much,' Pieter said. 'My wife and daughters are

OK. Word is that order's being restored, except at the council compound.'

'Do we know how many people are in there?'

'I have no idea,' Pieter said brusquely. 'Lily's gone to find out.'

'Lily…' Ben frowned. 'She might be needed here. If she's anywhere else, she ought to be asleep.'

'You can't expect that of her,' Pieter said. 'Her son's missing and her fiancé. They've been missing for twenty-four hours now and Lily's going out of her mind.'

CHAPTER TWO

HE WAS caught for the next few hours. At mid morning the roads were declared open. A no go area was declared around the complex of buildings called the Council Compound—a series of bungalows surrounding a palm filled conclave used for island gatherings. Here the insurgents had holed up. There was no clear idea how many were there, or who was insurgent and who was hostage, but a cursory sweep had now been made of the entire island. The insurgents were either laying down their arms and declaring this had been a mistake, or they were with their comrades in the compound.

It had surely been a mistake, Ben thought grimly as more injured made their way to the hospital.

Where was Lily? He couldn't leave the hospital.

At midday a plane landed on the island's small airstrip, bringing Ben's colleagues—people like Sam, who relished trauma surgery. Ben's role was hands on if necessary but it was mostly organisational, getting on the ground first, assessing what was needed, doing hands-on treatment in the first few hours but then handing over to those more qualified in various specialties. These guys were good and their arrival meant he could often stand aside.

Not today. There was too much to be done. There was a

sports oval beside the island's hospital. The hospital was tiny, totally inadequate to cope with the influx of wounded. Four hours after the arrival of his team and equipment Ben had a massive field hospital erected as an annexe. Operating theatres, a triage centre, ward beds… They'd erected this hospital before and his team knew their stuff.

As well as the hospital itself there was the need to organise supplies. Was there enough plasma? Were there enough body bags?

Would he ever get used to this? Ben wondered, as he worked on into the afternoon.

These were Lily's people.

Where was she? Every time anyone approached he looked up, hoping it was her.

She'd be aware that she was no longer desperately needed. She'd be searching for her son and for her fiancé.

Her son and her fiancé.

Well, he'd expected her to be married with babies. Why did those two words have the capacity to make him feel as if he'd been kicked?

It was only because he didn't know where she was, he told himself as the day progressed. It was only because he couldn't help her.

He was helping her now, doing her work for her.

He wanted, quite desperately, to find her.

Finally, as dusk was falling, the bulk of the organisational work had been done and the urgent cases had been treated. It was time to hand over. Sam was available to take charge.

'I'm taking some sleep,' he told Sam, and Sam looked down to where Ben was changing his theatre slippers for military boots.

'Sleeping quarters for med staff are right through the canvas,' Sam said cautiously. 'You're expecting to die with your boots on?'

'There's no threat.'

'So you're putting your boots on, why?'

'I'm taking a walk.'

'To take in the sights,' Sam said, smiling. They'd worked together for a long time now, and Sam knew him well. 'You've been on your feet since last night. You're dropping where you stand. But you're going for a walk.'

'No one knows where Lily is.'

Sam's smile faded. 'Our Lily?'

'She was here when I first arrived,' Ben said. 'She was close to collapse when I arrived but her kid's missing.'

'Her kid.' Sam's brow creased. 'What sort of kid?'

'How the hell would I know? A kid kid. Pieter—the head nurse—told me she's got a kid she can't find but Pieter's gone home and won't be back on duty till tomorrow. I can't find anyone who knows where she is so I'm taking a look.'

'Grab some men,' Sam told him. 'There's lurgies out in that dark forest.'

He wasn't kidding. There was rainforest everywhere. Who knew what rebels were still out there, wanting to…?

Kill Lily?

It was a dumb thought, brought about by exhaustion, but even so the thought wouldn't go away. He felt sick.

'I'll be careful,' he told Sam.

'You want me to come with you and hold your hand?'

'You're afraid of the dark.'

'There is that,' Sam said peaceably, with just the faintest rueful grin to show Ben wasn't far off the mark. 'But for the gorgeous Lily…I'll risk it.'

'Look, she's an old friend and she's in trouble,' Ben said, exasperated. 'Unless you have any more dumb comments, you're holding me back.'

'Off you go, then,' Sam said, standing aside. He'd almost

been laughing but as Ben rose from lacing his boots Sam put a hand on his shoulder. There was a long line of grim reminders out the back of the hospital, reminding them both just how serious this situation was.

'Find her,' he said.

Dusk had given way to darkness when Ben made it to the road leading to the compound. He'd been hailed three times on the way.

'Ben, this lady's got a kid who got badly mosquito bitten while they were hiding.'

'Ben, I reckon I'm allergic to the water. You got something to settle my stomach?'

And finally the worst, which was: 'Ben, we've found another body. You want to come and take a look before we shift it to the morgue?'

It didn't make sense, Ben thought. The insurgents had appeared at dawn and had stormed toward the compound, shooting everything in their path. If they'd hoped to achieve pandemonium and terror then they'd succeeded, but in doing so they'd created a situation where the islander's allies had been forced to act immediately. This reeked of fools' work, Ben thought grimly, and a hostage situation, negotiating with fools was a nightmare.

Where the hell was Lily?

The question became a mantra, running through his head over and over. He asked everywhere. The islanders all knew her, but everywhere he asked he received headshakes.

'Her boy is missing and also her man. We saw her earlier but she's no longer here.'

He rounded the last corner to the roadblock before the compound. Here were the men and women he worked with, stopping anyone fool enough to risk their lives by trying to get nearer. There was someone in their midst, a woman, her voice raised.

'I know some were hurt. Let me ask. I'm a doctor. They'll let me in. Please, please, I beg you…'

Lily.

And he knew his colleagues' answer before he heard it. First rule of hostage situations—damage limitation. However many were in there, don't make it worse by sending more.

He saw Lily's shoulders slump. There was little light out here—all lights had been ordered off—and she was just a dark shadow in the moonlight. But he knew it was Lily.

She was still in theatre garb.

She looked like Lily.

'Lily,' he said, and she looked up and saw who it was. He saw the flash of recognition, but he also saw the defeat, despair and exhaustion.

'Lily,' he said again, and reached her and held her, and it was just as well.

'Ben,' she whispered, and crumpled where she stood.

He carried her back to the hospital. She'd gone past protesting; she'd gone past anything but lying limply in his arms.

What had happened to his vision of Lily as a fat mama with a brood of happy children? he asked himself. She was thinner even than he remembered. She was only five feet four, a woman of half French parentage, and that parentage showed. She'd stood out from every other medical student in their course, looking elegant and somehow right whatever she wore.

He gazed down at her now as they approached the hospital. Here, well out of range of the hostage-takers, lights were permitted on the roads and he could clearly see her features.

Her jet-black curls were still cut into that elfin style he'd loved, tendrils clinging to her face, making her Audrey Hepburn type features seem even lovelier than he remembered. But this was a new Lily, a battered Lily. There was nothing elegant about the bloodstained jeans and T-shirt and theatre over-gown she was wearing. Dark smudges marred her lovely eyes. There was a scratch across her cheek and she'd bled a little. She looked like…like…

Lily.

Why had he let her go?

That was a dumb question. There had never been any thought of staying together, he remembered. They each had their own path in life and they hadn't coincided.

'Ben,' she managed, rousing a little as he reached the entrance to the field hospital. He kicked aside a canvas barrier and found a stretcher-bed. He set her down and her eyes widened as if she'd suddenly remembered she had to do something. 'I can't,' she whispered.

'You can,' he said. 'You have to rest. It's OK.'

'It's not OK.' She tried to sit up, and as he gently guided her back on the pillows she shoved her hands against his chest and pushed. 'I need to—'

'You need to sleep, Lily,' he said firmly. 'You've worked for thirty-six hours or more without a rest. You're exhausted past the point of collapse.'

'I must.'

'You can't.'

'Then will you do it for me?' she said wildly. 'Please… Find…Ben.'

He'd thought she'd been talking about her son. What was she talking about now? 'I'm here,' he said, but she was staring straight through him.

'Please.'

'I'll look for your son,' he told her, figuring she was verging on the delirious. 'I'll have the men start a search. Tell me about him. How old is he?'

She was focusing on the point where the canvas had been

pulled aside to form a door, as if she was expecting any minute that someone would appear.

'He'll be with Jacques. He must be.'

'Jacques?'

'Benjy,' she whispered, and the effort she'd made was too much and it was too much effort to hold her eyes open a moment longer. 'My Ben. He's six years old,' she said, defeated. 'He's six years old and he looks like you. His name's Benjy. I called him after his father.'

She slept. Just like that she faded, sinking into a sleep that was almost unconsciousness. Ben stared down at her, incredulous, questions crowding his mind.

The silence stretched out. He stared at Lily as if staring could elicit information, but of course it couldn't, and the longer he stared the more questions formed.

A six-year-old boy called Benjy…

Could it be?

No. They'd always been careful. They had been medical students, not a pair of uninformed teenagers.

She hadn't meant it. He said that to himself, thinking there were more Bens than him in the world. She could have been referring to anyone.

He thought suddenly of the last time he'd seen Lily, seven years back. He'd been excited about the life ahead of him, and he'd thought she'd been just as excited about returning here. But at the last moment she'd clung and wept and then closed her eyes and pushed him away. There'd been half an hour until her flight. But…

'Go now,' she'd whispered. 'Go.'

'Lily—'

'I can't bear it. If you stay I'll break. Please. Go.'

And suddenly, finally, he knew in his heart that what he was thinking was right. Somewhere in the chaos outside, in the dark and frightening rainforest or worse, in the midst of the hostage situation, was a little boy who was his son.

I called him after his father.

He felt…ill.

There was nothing more for him to do here. Dazed, he made his way back through the triage station to the entrance to the island's permanent hospital. Sam was sitting out on the steps, smoking.

'That'll kill you,' Ben said, but he said it almost automatically, with no passion behind it, and Sam took a couple of drags on his cigarette and ground it out under his heel.

'Don't I know it. But seeing I only smoke when I lose a patient, I'm not likely to die any time soon. Damn, the kid had been left too long.'

'Another kid?' Ben said, and his heart missed a beat. 'Who…?' It was suddenly hard to ask the question but it had to be asked. 'Not a six-year-old boy called Benjy?'

When Sam shook his head his heart started again but only just.

'A ten-year-old girl called Sophia,' Sam said. 'Head injury. She was hit with shrapnel. We drilled a burrhole to try and alleviate pressure but she died under our hands.' He shifted his foot and stared at his stubbed-out cigarette as if he regretted extinguishing it. 'What were these bastards thinking?' he exploded. 'This isn't like any sort of military coup I've ever seen. They shot anything that moved. Kids, women… I've even seen a couple of shot dogs.'

'They're mad,' Ben agreed.

'I don't like our chances of negotiating,' Sam said morosely. 'God help the hostages.'

'No.' Ben hesitated and then sat down on the step beside Sam. Sam cast him a look that was suddenly concerned and moved aside to give him room.

'Do we know how many are being held hostage?' Sam

asked, and Ben shook his head. He was trying to think straight and it wasn't working.

I called him after his father.

'I need to get a search party together,' he said and rose.

Sam rose with him. 'There are search parties from one end of the island to the other,' Sam reminded him. 'Looking for injured islanders and rounding up anyone remotely connected to a gun. Why do you need another? Are you still looking for Lily?'

'I found her,' he said. 'Her son's missing. She's just passed out on me—she's been operating for thirty-six hours straight and she's closer to being unconscious than asleep. I promised I'd look for the kid.'

'A littlie?' Sam asked, concerned, and Ben took a deep breath, knowing it had to be said. Knowing it had to be acknowledged.

'A six-year-old boy,' he managed, and took a deep breath to give him strength to say the next few words. 'A six-year-old boy called Benjy. Lily named him after his father.'

The next few hours passed in a blur. At headquarters the officers listened to Ben's story—the local doctor's son was missing, as was her fiancé—a man called Jacques—and they consulted lists.

'We're searching for them already,' the captain told him. 'Others have reported them missing. Jacques is the island's financial administrator. His bungalow's in the compound and he hasn't been seen since the uprising. He's either a hostage or dead. And Dr Lily told us about the little boy. He was sent to the beach at the first sign of trouble but he would have found his great-aunt dead and everyone gone. Maybe he was forcibly taken to the compound. Or more likely…' He didn't need to complete the sentence. 'I've pulled the searchers back now. We'll search again in the morning.'

'Why not now?'

'You know why,' the captain said patiently. 'There might still be armed men in hiding, and I'll not risk our team being picked off. If I knew for sure the kid was there and alive then I'd risk it, but I know no such thing and neither do you.' His voice softened. 'Hell, Ben, you know the rules. Is this doctor putting pressure on you?'

'She's an old friend,' Ben said heavily. 'And she's been a hero here. In the last two days she's performed medicine that'd put us to shame.'

'We'll comb the forest again at first light,' the captain promised. 'I'll double the contingent to that area. I can't promise more than that.'

'And the hostage situation?'

'There's no communication,' the captain said grimly. 'So we sit and wait for them to make the first move. The last thing we need is another bloodbath.'

'There's nothing anyone can do?'

'For the moment I'm guessing the best thing for you to do is get some sleep,' the captain said, studying his friend's face and seeing a strain there he'd never seen before. 'Hell, Ben, it's not like you to get personally involved.'

'It's not, is it?' Ben said.

'Go to bed,' the captain said, roughly concerned. 'If there's any news, I'll let you know.'

'Thanks.'

'And, Ben?'

'Yeah?'

'This lady doctor…'

'Mmm?'

'How well did you know her?' And there was suddenly a hint of an understanding smile behind the captain's bland enquiry.

But Ben didn't feel like smiling. 'I knew her well enough. But I'm going to bed,' he muttered. 'Just keep the lid on the hostage situation. That's all I ask.'

CHAPTER THREE

BEN woke at dawn, and five minutes later he was striding into the original hospital, looking for Lily.

For she was gone. The first thing he'd done had been to check her stretcher-bed and the sight of its neatly folded blanket had made him feel ill.

Hell, he'd slept six hours and he'd needed that sleep. She'd had little more than that and she'd had a lot more to catch up on.

'Where's Dr Lily?' he snapped at the first person he saw. It was Pieter. The big nurse assessed Ben's face and nodded, as if he now understood something that had been worrying him.

'You'll be Dr Ben Blayden?'

'Yes.'

'I should have realised yesterday,' the nurse told him. 'I'm afraid I wasn't thinking.'

'You should have realised what?'

'That you're our Lily's Ben. That you're our Benjy's father.'

It took the wind out of Ben's lungs, so much so that he felt as if he'd been punched. After seven years…

'Where is she?' he managed, and Pieter shook his head, troubled.

'She came in here about four a.m. I wasn't here. One of your men said she should go back to sleep but I doubt she followed instructions. Her son is missing.' Pieter's voice softened. 'If I'm not mistaken, your son is missing.'

Ben flinched. He stood, stunned, letting the words sink in.

Last night there'd been room for doubt. Lily's words had been almost incoherent, the desperate words of a woman who'd gone past the point of sense. But now… 'She's told you about me?'

'She told me that Benjy was the son of a man she met at medical school. That you'd elected to be an emergency doctor with the SAS. That she'd chosen to come home, to raise your son alone because your worlds could never meet. And then yesterday…while Lily was scouring the island she went to my wife. She sobbed to her that you were here and how could she tell you about a son when she didn't know if he was alive?'

'She never told me,' Ben whispered, trying to rid himself of this sense of unreality, not sure whether he was angry or confused or just…bereft. He should be angry, he thought. The appropriate emotion should definitely be anger, but bereft was winning.

He had a son.

Where the hell was he?

'She'd only just learned she was pregnant when she came home,' Pieter was saying, watching his face. 'This island is a very easy place to raise a child without a father. In a sense we're a huge family where parenting is done by all. She wouldn't have seen the need…'

He had it now. Anger in spades, sweeping through him with a ferocity he found breathtaking.

'She wouldn't have seen the need to tell me? She didn't think I had the right to know?'

'She said you feared relationships,' Pieter said, 'But she also said you were a moral man who'd want to do the right thing by your son. She said her decision was not to load you with that responsibility.'

'But even you know…'

'Lily and I have worked side by side for almost seven years,' Pieter said, reassuringly, as if Ben was a little unhinged and he had to settle him. Which maybe wasn't far from the truth. 'I'm the cousin of her mother. There's little about Lily I don't know.'

'So she told you and she didn't tell me.'

'I believe she thought you wouldn't want to know.' Pieter looked grave. 'This is a conversation you should be having with Lily, but this is maybe not the time for considering feelings. Lily's in desperate trouble. She needs all the help she can get.'

'Where is she now?'

The big man's face clouded. 'I don't know. Maybe that's why I'm telling you this. I should be out looking for her. She should be here helping with our wounded. As I need to be. There are shoulds everywhere.'

'There's been no word about the hostages?'

'No.'

'And this Jacques?'

'He will be fine, that one,' Pieter said, and his expression grew even more grim. 'He must be a hostage but if he is…maybe he'll be the first one to talk his way out. He is not an islander, you understand. Jacques came here when the oil was found. He helps us with our administration.'

'You don't like him?'

'He's not one of us.'

And there it was, Ben thought grimly. The reason Lily had said she could never leave the island. The islanders were family.

But even though Jacques was an outsider, Lily had agreed to marry him. He must have something.

If I'd come to her island maybe she would have married me, he thought suddenly, but it was a dumb thought. He'd never have wanted to come here, and he had a lot more to think about right now than a seven-year-old romance that had gone astray

'Ben,' a voice called from the end of the corridor, and it was Sam, wearing theatre gear again.

'Yes?'

'They've released three of the hostages,' he said. 'Or at least they opened the front doors and shoved them out. Each of them has gunshot wounds. We need all hands in Theatre and that means you.'

Which meant another six hours operating. Six hours where they somehow managed to stabilise the injured islanders.

'But things have settled,' Ben was told by the sergeant in charge when, with surgery completed, he'd made his way to temporary headquarters. 'We've done a comprehensive sweep of the island. There are no more injured.'

'Have you seen the island doctor?'

'Lily,' the sergeant said. 'Yes. She's working in the original hospital. She knows you guys are thorough, but most of the families want to talk to her.' He hesitated. 'They've had a succession of English teachers on the island and English is spoken by everyone. But maybe if my kin had been shot I'd want my family doctor to talk me through it.'

Damn. Ben had just come from the field hospital which was next door to the original building. He turned to leave but then he remembered. It wasn't just Lily he was concerned about.

'The hostage situation?'

'We're negotiating,' the sergeant told him. 'They want transport out of here.'

'Do we know who's in there?'

'Ten islanders. The most badly injured they've tossed out. Ten fits with the number of islanders who remain missing. We don't know how many rebels.'

'Is Lily's son there?'

'Yes,' the sergeant said, and Ben felt suddenly light-headed.

'We know he's alive?' he demanded.

'One of the injured men saw him. Yes.'

'And you've told Lily?'

'She was here when we heard. She'd been everywhere on the island, checking with each search team as they came in, checking herself. We were almost as glad as she was when we heard the kid was alive.'

'And…Jacques someone?' he ventured, and there was a nod.

'We assume so. He wasn't seen by the guy we talked to but he said he heard him talking.'

'So they're both safe. And you'll negotiate transport in exchange for the hostages?'

'We don't know yet,' the sergeant said. 'These guys are dangerous. We need to get permission from higher up the line. Our politicians are talking to the only people here who are fit to speak. That's the deputy head of council and the finance councillor, and they're both still in a state of shock. But the decision to negotiate isn't up to us.'

'It has to be.'

'You want to storm the place?'

'No, but…'

'Then…' The sergeant was watching him curiously, sensing his tension. This was the team sent in as a front line at every crisis, and he knew Ben well. Ben usually worked efficiently, with little emotion. He was emotional now.

He couldn't stop being emotional.

'I need to talk to Lily.'

'We need your written assessment by dusk,' the sergeant said mildly.

'You'll have it. But the priority is Lily.'

He found her sitting outside the hospital, under a group of palms in the hospital gardens. There were three islanders with her—

an old woman and two children. The old woman was keening her distress while the children looked on in incomprehension. Ben hesitated, but then he walked close enough to listen.

Lily glanced up as he approached. He gave a slight shake of his head. The hope that had flared in her eyes faded, and she turned again to the old woman, pulling her into her arms and hugging her close.

'Hush. Kira died instantly, Mary. You know that.'

'My only sister.'

Lily didn't speak again. She simply held her, not hurrying, waiting until the woman had sobbed the worst of her grief out, waiting until she raised her head of her own accord, waiting until she was ready to talk.

'Do you want help to look after the children?' she asked her at last. 'I can find someone if you need to be alone.'

The old woman glared and pulled away as if Lily had said something obscene. She put out her arms and the children, a girl of about five and a boy of about three, scooted in and were hugged tight.

'They'll stay with me until their mother is well enough to care for them again. Or until their father can get here.'

'Here's Dr Blayden. He's here to help me with the injuries. He helped operate on your mother last night, kids. He's a hero, right when we need him.'

The kids looked up at him, doubtful, looking for a real-life hero. Ben smiled and crossed to the little group, squatting down beside them and delving in his pocket for sweets. He carried them everywhere, for just such an emergency as this.

'Tell me your names,' he said, folding the sweets into their hands before they had a chance to draw back.

'Nicki,' the little girl whispered, staring down at her lolly, while the boy huddled behind his grandmother, keeping his hand closed over the precious sweet. 'And my brother is Lanie.'

'Is your mother's name Louie?'

'Yes.'

'I did help fix her last night,' he told them.

'Nicki and Lanie were with their mother when the men came,' Lily said briefly, and Ben thought Lily knew what she was doing. Traumatised kids had to talk about what happened. 'Louie ran with them. She ran to her mother's.'

The bullet had pierced Louie's shoulder as she'd run. Ben winced. What sort of criminals shot at a mother, fleeing with her children?

'I think these men are very, very bad and very, very stupid,' he told the children. 'But our soldiers have them all in one place now and they can't hurt anyone. And your mother is getting better. You can visit her now if you like.'

'I was just coming to tell them that,' Lily said.

'She'll feel much better after she's seen you,' Ben said, and he smiled at the old lady. 'And after she's seen her mother.' He delved back into his pocket and brought out six more sweets. They were sold as Traffic Lights, round, flat shining discs, red, green and yellow. 'Choose one more each,' he told the children. 'And then I want you to choose two each to take to your mother. Can you do that?'

The children nodded and the old lady stood. Her face had cleared a little, some of the horror fading.

'My daughter truly will be well?'

'She truly will be well,' Ben said, and he and Lily stood and watched as the little family bade them farewell and went to do their hospital visiting.

Ben was left with Lily.

She looked a thousand per cent better than the night before, he thought. She'd showered and changed. She was wearing a tiny denim skirt, a T-shirt and leather sandals—hardly the attire of a doctor about to do her rounds—but he could see nothing amiss with it. Except that her legs were covered with scratches. A couple of them were deep and nasty.

'Let me see to your legs,' he said, and she gazed down as if wondering what he was talking about. Seeing the bloody scratches, she merely shrugged.

'They'll be fine. Trivial stuff.'

'Not so trivial if they get infected.'

'I have more to worry about than infected legs.'

'Maybe,' he said. 'But legs come first. You want to come voluntarily or do you want to be carried? I'm a lieutenant, you know. I have authority in this place.'

She managed a feeble smile. 'I'd rather be bribed with sweets,' she said, and he shoved a hand in his pocket and produced a handful.

'Eat one,' he said, and she shook her head.

'When did you last eat?'

'I can't remember.'

'Then eat a sweet,' he told her. 'I'll bathe those legs and then you're going to be fed.'

'But—'

'Don't argue, Dr Cyprano. As of last night your deputy head of council gave us authority in this place. I'm therefore representing the occupying force and what I say goes. You eat.'

She opened her mouth to protest. He'd been unwrapping a sweet while he'd talked and he popped it in.

'No protests.'

'No, sir,' she told him with a mouth full of red sweet. 'Or, yes, sir. I don't know which.'

He dressed her legs. She stayed silent throughout, which suited his mood. There were things that had to be said but he didn't know where to start. Bathing her scratches, applying antiseptic and dressing the worst of them gave him time to think. It was as if he was getting used to her all over again.

She lay passively on an examination trolley while he worked. She stared straight ahead, seemingly oblivious when he had to scrub, though he must have hurt her. Then he took her to the mess tent, waved away anyone who would have talked to them, sat her down and watched as she mechanically ate the pasta he brought her, as she drank coffee, and as she pushed her mug away and rose and said, 'Thank you very much, I need to go now.'

'I'm coming with you.'

Unless there were new developments Ben wasn't needed now in the hospital. The uprising had been quelled so fast that maybe they could have managed with less manpower. But the fact that they'd come fast and hard had maybe averted a greater tragedy, he thought.

But for now there were enough medics to cope with medical needs. There was no more organisation for Ben to do. He could stay by Lily's side. For she intended to go back to the roadblock in front of the compound. He knew that without asking. That was where negotiations were taking place. If he had been Lily, that was where he'd want to be.

And it was where he wanted to be. For it was his son held hostage. The concept was so overpowering he didn't know what to do with it, but all he knew was that he needed to go with her.

The roadblock was half a mile from the hospital, across the beach road. It was mid-afternoon and the heat was getting to him. Lily was lightly dressed but Ben was wearing fatigues, and he was feeling it.

'Walk on the beach,' he suggested, and Lily diverted her footsteps without saying a word.

Her silence was starting to scare him. This wasn't the Lily he remembered. She'd been bright, bubbly, fun and startlingly intelligent. Her professors had described her as smart as paint, and more than one had said it was a shame she wasn't staying in Australia to specialise. But Australia's loss would be Kapua's gain. They had all known that, and she'd never questioned her destiny.

He hadn't questioned her destiny either.

'Lily, we need to talk,' he said as they walked through the fringe of coconut palms to the beach beyond.

'What good is talking?' she whispered dully, and he heard how close to breaking point she really was.

'He'll be fine, Lily,' he said softly. 'The men and women doing the negotiating are the best. We flew them in as soon as we realised how serious the hostage situation was. They're never going to blast their way in. I've watched these people before and seen the way they work. They have all the patience in the world. It might take days but they'll get them out alive. They know their stuff.'

But Lily had only heard the one word. 'Days,' she choked. 'With those murderers? He's six years old. What he must be thinking… I should have taken him to Kira's myself. But the woman I was treating…she'd have bled to death. I couldn't. Dear God, I couldn't.'

'You had medical imperatives,' he said gently. He'd talked to the finance councillor by now—the woman was recovering in hospital—and he'd seen the wound Lily had somehow pulled together. Lily was right. If she'd taken the time to take care of her son before she'd treated her, the woman would be dead. 'You saved her life, Lily.'

'But I should have kept Benjy with me,' she whispered. 'He's my son. I'm all he has.'

'Doesn't he have Jacques?' he asked, and she looked blindly up at him, uncomprehending. 'Your fiancé's in there as well, isn't he?'

She steadied a little at that. 'Jacques,' she said, and then more strongly, 'Jacques. Maybe that's why he's there. Maybe he went to Jacques.' But then she shook her head. 'But he'd have had to come past the hospital to reach Jacques.'

'Jacques is in administration?'

'He's in charge of finance,' she told him. 'Oh, we have a finance councillor but Louise isn't exactly smart. She does what Jacques says. Except for selling oil. Louise dug her heels in over that. So did we all.' She fell silent. She was trembling, Ben saw, even though the day was hot. She was walking in the damp sand near the water's edge. Here the water was a turquoise blue, clear to the bottom. Ben could see fish feeding on weed drifting in and out in the shallows. The beach was wide and golden. This place was indeed a tropical paradise. That such tragedy had come to it…

Lily must have been thinking the same. A tremor ran though her, and Ben took her hand.

'He'll be OK, Lily.'

'I'm sorry,' she whispered.

'There's no—'

'I mean I'm sorry I didn't tell you about Benjy.'

He didn't answer. He couldn't.

'He's such a…such a…' She took a deep breath. 'He's very much like you. Ben, if anything happens to him and you haven't met him…' She hiccuped on a sob and then seemed to regroup. 'I thought I had the right,' she told him. 'I thought… It was me who was pregnant, not you, and I knew you'd be appalled. But seeing you here… He's your son, Ben, and I should have made the effort. Even if you didn't want him.'

'Why would I not want him?'

'What were we, Ben?' she demanded, suddenly angry. 'Babies ourselves. We were young for med school. We were young for life. You were so lit up about joining the army. You were off to save the world. Armies are used for peacekeeping, you told me, but it was excitement that was in your heart. Action. Drama. Sure, you didn't want to fight, but you did want to go wherever there was action. And me…all I wanted to do was come home. My mother had sold everything she owned to send me to med school, and the islanders helped because everyone here needed a doctor. I was as excited as you were—but I was excited at coming home to help my people.'

'Did it work out?' he asked, and she took a deep breath. There wasn't a trace of colour on her face. She looked sick.

'I guess it did,' she said slowly. 'But there was a cost. My mother died just after I got back. She had cancer. She'd known for two years but she hadn't told me because she hadn't wanted to interrupt my studies.'

'Oh, Lily…'

'You see, when I found I was pregnant I was just as shocked as you would have been. We were so careful but, then, our lecturers used to say the only sure-fire contraception is a brick wall. We're proof of that. So what could I do? You'd made it clear you never wanted a family. I couldn't burden you with one, against your wishes.' She steadied then, forcing her voice to sound neutral. 'I had to come home. As it is, I've made a life for both of us here. Every islander loves Benjy. Every islander is his uncle or his aunt or his cousin, by traditional ties if not by blood.'

'And he has Jacques?'

'He has Jacques,' she agreed, though it took her time to respond. Her voice was uncertain now, as if he'd touched a nerve.

'They don't get on?'

'Why would you ask me that?'

'It is my business if he's my son.'

'He's not your son. I won't burden you with him. He's—'

'Lily, I want him to be my son.' The words surprised them both. They stopped, and a wave, higher than usual, washed in over their feet. Lily's sandalled toes were washed clean. Ben was wearing tough army boots. The water receded and they hardly looked damp.

It was dumb to be looking at boots, Ben thought. The whole thing was dumb. Maybe Lily was right. Maybe he should back off right now.

But he had a son. By Lily.

And she looked distraught.

He reached out and touched her face. There was a fine coat of dust over everything, courtesy of setting up the field hospital on land where the grass had withered during the dry season. Dust was on Lily's face, streaked now by tears, and he tracked a tear with his finger.

I wonder what this place is like in the rainy season, he thought inconsequentially.

Lily didn't move. She submitted to his touch without comment.

'I think I loved you, Lily,' he said, and she managed a ghost of a smile.

'Benjy was conceived in love,' she whispered. 'I've always believed that.'

'It's the truth.'

'Just lucky we're older, eh?' she said, but her voice was strained to breaking point. She brushed his hand from her face, turned determinedly northward again and started walking. 'Just lucky we've found sense.'

'And you've found Jacques.'

'As you say. Do you have anyone?'

'No.'

'You're still running from relationships?'

'I don't run.'

'No.' She hesitated, and then glanced sideways at him. Cautious. 'You're angry?'

'Maybe I am.'

'Because I didn't tell you about Benjy?

'Yeah. But maybe you're right,' he said bleakly. 'Maybe seven years ago I wouldn't have wanted to know. I was dumb.'

'We were both dumb.'

'Mmm.' He kicked some more sand and tried to think of other things besides how close this woman was, and how bereft she looked, and how he wanted to…

He couldn't want. She had a life here and a son and a fiancé and he was here with a job to do.

He should be working. He should go back to the hospital and organise paperwork for the evacuations. He could help treat the minor wounds of islanders still cautiously presenting.

His team were doing that. He wouldn't be needed again unless there was a blast-out in the hostage situation.

A blast-out. Benjy. His son.

Think of something else, he thought fiercely. They were nearing the headland where the compound lay and the strain on Lily's face was well nigh unbearable. She was staring ahead as if she was willing herself to see through walls. He had to distract her.

'Lily, there's a couple of things bothering me.'

'I don't have time to—'

'Not about us,' he said gently. 'About this situation. Can you help?'

She took a deep breath and steadied. 'Of course.'

'You told me seven years ago that this island was like a huge family. Everyone knew everyone and no one locked their doors. Is that right?'

'Yes, but—'

'But what?' he asked. 'The insurgents were forced to leave the hospital alone, and we've been wondering why. We've been told there's been a drug problem on the island, so you've trained orderlies to act as security guards. Is that right?'

'Yes, but—'

'Do you know these drug users? Are they locals?'

'No,' she said slowly, and he knew she was having trouble concentrating, but she was determined to try. 'We've had three break-ins over the last two months. None before. Down south there's a surf camp. The surf here is fantastic and devotees come to train, but for the last couple of months there's been guys there who are worrying. They just lie around and drink, and the break-ins started at the same time they arrived. They've had three-month visas. Our local policeman couldn't find evidence to deport them, so he trained and armed our orderlies and we let it be known.' She gave a rueful smile. 'Our orderlies are the most peaceable of men, but it acted like a deterrent. The break-ins stopped.'

'So where are these men now?'

'Maybe I heard they were to go to one of the outer islands. I'm not sure.'

'You never thought to get a profile on any of them?'

'I'm a doctor. I didn't think anything.'

'But you—'

'It's not my responsibility,' she flashed. 'Ben, if you knew how hard I work… There's no other doctor on any of these islands. Kapua's the biggest in the chain but there's twenty inhabited islands. The health service is me. No one wants to fly to Australia for treatment. Hardly anyone will leave their own island. Pregnant mothers are supposed to fly out to Fiji to give birth but hardly any do. Elderly islanders won't leave, no matter how sick they are. I fly by the seat of my pants, doing what comes next, and policing isn't on my list. Sure, our policeman should have investigated more, and maybe if I'd thought of it I would have reminded him, but I didn't. I was just grateful the break-ins stopped.'

'I'm sorry,' he said, startled by her anger, and she stooped and picked up a shell and tossed it into the sea with such savagery that she came very near to knocking out a seagull. The gull rose with a startled shriek and Lily stared at it for a moment and then sighed.

'Sorry, bird,' she said. And then, 'Sorry, Ben. It's just… during med school everyone—including you—assumed I was coming home to an idyllic island existence. But this place… We need a full medical service, with helicopter evacuation, with at least two doctors and a set-up where I can do operations that involve more than me cutting frantically while I'm instructing Pieter in the niceties of anaesthesia.' She broke off, turned her face to the council compound again and winced.

He tugged her against him. For a moment she resisted, staying rigid in his grasp, but he on kept holding her, willing some of his strength into her.

'I promise we'll keep your son safe,' he said softly. 'I swear.'

But what sort of dumb promise was that? How could he make it good?

But she finally gave in and let herself lean against him. His arms held her and he smelt the citrus fragrance of her hair. Memories flooded back of the Lily of seven years ago and he thought, She's the same Lily, my Lily. And with that thought came self-knowledge. If there was a choice… If he could walk into the compound and say let the boy go, take him instead, he'd do just that.

For Lily.

But it wasn't just for Lily. For things had changed. The child in the compound wasn't just Lily's son. He was his own son.

He had family.

The thought was incredible. His world had changed, he thought, dazed. It had shifted on its axis, leaving everything he knew unaligned.

And suddenly, desperately, he wanted to kiss this woman,

properly, as she needed to be kissed, as he ached to kiss her, taking her lips against his mouth, possessing the sweet core of her. Loving her…

But he knew that if he did that, she'd pull back. She was terrified for her son. She was taking strength from him and he wanted her to keep doing that. So hold yourself back, he told himself fiercely, though God only knew what effort that cost him.

But somehow he managed it, kissing her hair, but lightly, as one would have comforted a distressed child. He stood, holding her as she leaned against him. Warmth flowed between them. It was as if she was admitting finally that she needed help; she needed him.

But with that thought came an answering one. He needed her.

Lily.

He couldn't pull her tighter into him. He mustn't. What was happening here was too precious to be destroyed by stupid impulses, no matter how strong those impulses might be.

'Let's go,' he said gently, and somehow he put her away from him and smiled gently down into her strained-to-exhaustion face. 'Let's go and find our son.'

'Of course,' she said dully. 'If we can.'

'We will,' he said. 'We'll do this together. We're together until we find him.'

'Ben…'

He pulled her against him once more, but gently, as one would have comforted a friend. She was his friend. She was the mother of his child. He hugged her and then he linked his hand in hers and led her forward.

'You're not alone, Lily,' he told her. 'I'll be here for you for however long it takes.'

CHAPTER FOUR

THE days wore on, and the nights. Each night Ben lay in the dark and listened to the soft breathing of the woman in his arms. Imperceptibly his world changed.

Lily needed him, in a way he'd never been needed in his life.

This crisis didn't stop medical imperatives occurring elsewhere, and Lily had refused to stop working as the island's doctor. Ben and his team tried to take as much of the load from her as they could but the islanders made no secret of the fact that they trusted only Dr Lily.

'Just refuse to go,' Ben told her.

'I'll go crazy with nothing to do,' she'd say. 'Besides, there's a girl in labour on an outer island.' Or… 'There's an old man in severe pain. This is my normal workload, Ben. The islanders trust me but no one else. You're an outsider.'

He was an outsider, but he wasn't an outsider to Lily. He was father to an island child. A child he'd never met. The situation was surreal.

How Lily could work…

She could work only because she had him. He knew that by now, and so did everyone on the island. At the end of a long day she'd drag herself back to her bungalow behind the hospital and he'd make sure he was there waiting for her. She'd fall into his arms, exhausted with the fears and the frustrations and the pain of a day filled with medical need. He'd hug her close but carefully, rigidly—he'd take it no further. He mustn't. She'd run and she mustn't run. So he'd hold her and he'd tell her what, if anything, had changed in the hostage situation. Sometimes she'd cry and if she did he'd let her cry her fill. Then he'd cradle her to sleep as he'd cradled her tonight.

Seven years ago he'd lain with Lily as a man lay with the woman he loves. Their loving then had been exciting and fun and happy.

This time there was no love-making—or love-making in the sexual sense. She had no energy left for sex, and his desire for her had changed. He wanted her to sleep. He wanted her to drift into an unconsciousness where she didn't have to be terrified for her son.

This was a different sort of love-making, he thought. The girl he'd loved was gone. What was left was the mother of his son.

He loved her?

No, he told himself. In truth he didn't really understand it himself. He only knew that if the choice was an exciting return to the love-making of old or achieving a measure of peace for the woman he held in his arms, the choice was a no-brainer.

He hardly slept himself. That was no problem—he'd learned to exist on catnaps. He could survive. But the nights stretched on and he held on. He held his woman and his world…changed.

'I shouldn't be letting you do this,' Lily whispered to him in the dark. 'It's not fair.'

'I need this, too,' he told her. 'It's our son, Lily. Let's do this together.'

The end, when it came, was swift and deadly.

It was three in the morning. Lily was sleeping fitfully, nestled against him, her breasts moulded to his chest with only the flimsy fabric of her sleepwear between them. He'd been cradling her in his arms, murmuring softly to her at need, reassuring her when she'd wake at every unexpected noise.

And then he heard it. A low murmur at first, then building until it was a cacophony of sound heading towards them.

Helicopters. Big ones. He was out of bed, hauling on his pants and groping for his boots as Lily jerked into terrified wakefulness.

'What is it?'

'Choppers,' he said, his fingers clumsy in his haste. 'Not ours. Hell. We knew they had to have outside help. Lily, stay here.'

'In your dreams. Benjy—'

'I'll take care of him,' he said, and set his hands on her shoulders and propelled her back on the pillows. 'I swear I'll take care of him. Lily, please. Stay here.'

'I can't.'

'If you won't stay, I can't go,' he said. The helicopters were almost overhead and he knew what they'd be aiming for. But did they come with death to the islanders in mind? Surely not. 'Lily, promise me. Stay here until I bring Benjy to you.'

'I—'

'You must.' He had to go. There was no time to wait for promises. He kissed her, hard and fast and strong, taking strength from her as well as giving it. He grabbed the torch he'd left at the door, and he was gone.

Ben ran toward the compound. There were four helicopters—no, five—hovering overhead.

The moon was a mere sliver, its rays hardly reaching through the clouds. It had been steamy all day, and tonight it had rained. Maybe that's why they'd come tonight, he thought as he ran, keeping to the cover of the trees.

Why were they there?

And then the clouds parted for a moment and he topped a slight rise and saw.

The compound backed onto the beach. Despite the dim light, Ben could suddenly see the whole picture. While four choppers hovered, one helicopter was behind, protected, and it was landing on the beach.

Ben stood stock still. His job was to stay in the background and wait for casualties, assessing medical need, so he had to stay back now. Troops were running past, keeping to the shadows.

But the hostages…

A message rang out loudly. The sound system had been set up initially as a tsunami warning—a long, low siren—but technicians had tweaked it a couple of days ago, making it capable of transmitting voices, so in an emergency all could be warned of anything at all.

Now the warning was urgent. 'Take cover,' a voice boomed and Ben recognised their bass-voiced drill sergeant. 'Don't take aggressive action. I repeat, take cover.'

'Thank you,' Ben breathed, as he forced himself to wait some more. His team was good.

He realised now that the choppers were simply providing cover for an escape bid, giving the fifth chopper time to land and assist those leaving the compound.

He'd pulled further back into the shadows of the palms. The choppers had floodlights and they were searching the shadows.

A hand landed on his shoulder and he came as near to yelping as a grown man could.

'Ben.'

Lily! He grasped and held her. 'How the hell…? I told you to stay back.' She was dressed in windcheater and jeans—she must have moved as fast as he had.

'I can't.'

He tugged her back into the shadows, hauling her tight against him. 'How did you know where I was?'

'I followed you,' she whispered. But she wasn't concentrating on him. She was staring skyward, appalled. 'What's happening?'

'There's a chopper landing on the beach. The others are covering it. Whoever's in the compound will be going out the back way.' He grimaced and hauled her tighter.

'Why don't we stop them?'

'We could,' Ben said grimly, staring up. 'But there's four choppers directly over the compound. If we shoot, we risk a chopper coming straight down. They know that. See how they're clustered over the buildings. That's a defence in itself. Second…'

'Second?'

'We don't know who they are,' he said grimly. 'Those choppers are huge and expensive. We shoot them down, we find out who they are and we have to face the reality of maybe a neighbour being an armed aggressor. If they're here simply to get their people out of a bungled situation then our orders are to resolve a situation—not to start a conflict.'

'But Benjy,' she said wildly. 'If they take Benjy… How can you think politics when it's our child?'

Our child. The words pierced him, making him want to put away everything he'd ever been taught, making him want to run into the compound right now.

It'd help no one and he knew it. He tugged her harder against him. She was no fool, but where a child was concerned… His child…

'We have to wait,' he told her, and God only knew how hard it was to say it.

'But if they take him…'

'Why would they take him? Lily, we just have to believe they won't.'

* * *

And then it was over, as quickly as it had started. The chopper on the beach rose into the night sky to join its companions. They gathered together above the compound, a menacing, hulking threat, and then suddenly the five machines swept off together at full power, growing smaller and smaller until they disappeared.

They hadn't disappeared before Ben and Lily were running into the compound, hand in hand, stumbling through the darkness in shared terror.

Benjy….

The sound of the helicopters was still fading in the distance as Ben shone his torch into one room after another, while men shouted warnings from outside, saying not to enter until it had been checked. But neither of them were listening and Lily was clutching Ben's hand with a fierceness that urged him to move faster.

They found them. The hostages had been herded into one small bungalow at the end of the row. They were bound together, huddled against the furthest wall, their faces blank with terror.

All except one. One hostage was a child, and even as Ben swung the flashlight to find him Lily had her son in her arms, and she was holding him so tightly that it might be quite a while before anyone saw Benjy Cyprano again.

CHAPTER FIVE

MIRACULOUSLY there were no more deaths. The official decision not to oppose the rescue effort had been the saving of many, Ben thought gratefully as he worked through the night. The sound system's message and the noise of the choppers had made everyone seek refuge.

There were shock cases among the hostages, as well as gunshot wounds. The hostages were a trembling, stunned muddle of emotions, and Ben thought they'd need to bring in psychologists to counsel them.

As for Benjy… 'I'm taking him home,' Lily had said, solidly, loudly, as if she had been defying anyone to argue. Ben had been needed, so he'd reluctantly nodded to one of his men to accompany her—to see her home safely. She'd disappeared into the night and he hadn't seen her since.

Benjy was physically unharmed. For now that was all that mattered. He wanted desperately to go to them, but he couldn't.

Medical imperatives… He had a job to do.

It was almost midday the next day before he surfaced from the field hospital and could hand over the hospital to Sam.

'I'm going to Lily's,' he said, and Sam looked thoughtful.

'The whole army's relieved we got the kid out,' he said. Then he hesitated. 'You know, the islanders think the sun rises and sets around Lily. But there's talk. There's no sign of the boyfriend. It was assumed he was a hostage, but he's not.'

Ben knew that. The unknown Jacques. Lily's fiancé.

'Do you think he's an organiser?' Sam asked bluntly.

'I'm betting he is,' Ben said grimly.

'That's what we're thinking. The big boys will be wanting to talk to your Lily.'

'She's not my Lily.'

Sam raised his brows in mock enquiry. 'Not?'

'She's engaged.'

'To Jacques. Who's not here. I suspect she's not engaged any more, boyo.' He raised his brows. 'And the boy? There's rumours…'

'Scotch them.'

'Of course,' Sam said blithely, but Ben knew exactly where the rumours stemmed from and he knew there was nothing he could do about it.

He was wasting time. He had to see Lily.

Ben knocked and entered the little bungalow behind the hospital. There was no answer. He hesitated but he'd been in and out of this bungalow so many times over the last few days he felt he had the right. He pushed the door. It swung inward and he went right on in.

They were asleep.

For a moment the sight of them knocked him sideways. Lily's bedroom door was ajar. From the sitting room he could see them clearly, a woman and a child huddled together on a big bed, holding each other tightly even in sleep.

He went further in. They didn't stir.

Lily had been crying. He could see tear stains on her dusty face. The choppers, flying low, had sent up a swirl of dust and sand, and everyone who'd been near them had been coated. Lily was no exception.

She looked so young, he thought. She looked almost as young as the child in her arms.

And the boy? This was the first time he'd been able to see him clearly. Benjy.

Called after his father.

Ben stood stock still, taking in every detail. Benjy was six years old and skinny, his small face freckled and open. He was wearing stained shorts and a filthy T-shirt. His legs were bare and grubby. His small feet were callused as if his constant state was barefoot. Of course, he thought. This was an island child.

This was his child. His arms were twined around his mother's neck and his small nose was flattened against her breast.

He looked…like him.

There was a photo he had somewhere of himself at the same age, Ben thought, stunned into immobility. The likeness was unmistakable.

Benjy.

Safe with his mother.

He didn't cry. Hell, he never cried. Such a thing was unthinkable.

But the kid was…

'Ben.' With a start he realised Lily was awake. She was looking up at him with eyes that were uncertain. Almost as soon as she saw him her gaze went to her son, as if making sure his reality was not some hopeless dream. 'Ben,' she whispered again as the sleep faded from her eyes, and he wasn't sure who she was referring to.

'I'm glad he's safe.' It was inadequate but he couldn't think of anything else to say.

'Are there more casualties?'

'Five injured hostages, from the original attack, none critical. It's over, Lily.'

'They've gone?'

'Yes.'

'And...Jacques?'

'He's gone, too.'

'I see,' she whispered, and her lips touched Benjy's filthy hair. 'Do you need me?'

'No. I just came to make sure...'

'Benjy's fine. He's not hurt. He said...Jacques looked after him.'

Ben had guessed that much. However wicked Jacques was, there must have been a vestige of fondness for the boy. Otherwise he'd have been thrust out with the other rejected hostages. Or killed.

At least he hadn't taken him with him.

'I don't understand,' Lily whispered and neither did Ben. It might take weeks for this story to be pieced together, if indeed it ever could be.

'Let's leave it for now,' he said softly, and he stooped and kissed her softly on the forehead. He brushed tears from her eyes with his fingers, and then knelt and kissed her again. On the lips. She didn't move, just lay passive, not welcoming his kiss but not pushing him away either. Maybe she needed the contact as much as he did.

But he couldn't stay. Not now she had her son back. For that would be admitting something he couldn't begin to admit. A need of his own?

No.

'Just sleep,' he told her. 'We have two doctors and six paramedics on duty, and there's nothing for you to do but to care for your son.'

'Our son,' she whispered, and he felt his gut twist as he'd never felt it twist before.

'Our son,' he repeated, and he stood and stared down at them for a very long time.

Until Lily's eyes closed again.

She held her son now and not him.

He was no longer needed.

He left them. Somehow.

When she appeared at the hospital the next morning Ben told her sternly she was to spend the next few days with her son, that she wasn't to think of anything else, that he and Sam and Pieter had things under control. She looked at him blankly and left, but she didn't go home. On this island everyone knew everyone's whereabouts and Pieter told Ben what she was doing. She was working her way through the island homes, talking to each family about what had happened, and there was nothing Ben could do to stop her.

In medical school they'd been taught to stay emotionally detached. Emotional detachment on Kapua? The concept was ridiculous.

The concept of such involvement left Ben cold, but he couldn't remonstrate. He didn't understand why she needed to do this, but she did. And he had to take a back seat emotionally as well. She had enough emotional baggage already, without him adding more.

She'd need time to come to terms with Jacques's betrayal.

For it had been betrayal. It had been confirmed that Lily's fiancé had been in the group of insurgents who'd made the break away from the island.

'He was with them,' Ben had been told, and he'd had to say as much to Lily.

She hardly seemed to take it in. She desperately needed time.

So did he, he thought grimly as he worked on. How did you come to terms with fatherhood?

At least there was work enough to keep his mind busy elsewhere. Somehow the night of the hostage drama had changed the islanders' distrust of outside doctors. Whether it was Sam's big mouth or Pieter's he wasn't sure, but it was suddenly known everywhere that Ben was Benjy's father. And if he was Benjy's father then he had the right to protect Lily, to say, no, she couldn't come, her first priority had to be Benjy. Astonishingly the consensus now was that he had the right to treat the islanders.

How did Lily manage? he asked himself as the days wore on. He hadn't realised—had anyone?—what a medical centre Kapua had become. Lily was the island doctor not just for Kapua. She was island doctor for a score of smaller islands as well.

There was such need. In the three days after the hostage release he saw trauma as great as that caused by the uprising. Two men drowned on an outer island—they'd been fishing drunk and had ended up on rocks. Two boys survived the accident but they were now in hospital, one with a broken leg, one with multiple lacerations and shock. As well as that, he had viruses to deal with. He had infections. There was a manic depressive who'd refused to take her medication and was seeing aliens. There was a childbirth.

That was one where he'd really wanted Lily. The girl had gone into premature labour. The women caring for the expectant mother had rung the hospital to ask Lily to come, but they hadn't said what the need was. When they'd heard Lily wasn't available they'd simply hung up and tried to cope themselves. By the time they'd admitted defeat and called Ben, he'd had a premature baby of thirty weeks gestation on his hands.

It had still taken all his persuasive powers before mother and child had agreed to being flown to Fiji. 'Lily will fix my baby when she's back at work,' the girl had said, desperately trying to ignore the fact that her baby had major breathing difficulties. In the end Ben had simply said, 'Ruby, Lily can't help you. You go to Fiji on the next flight, or you have a dead baby.'

Ruby had conferred with the island women and had finally agreed that, yes, she and her baby could go, but there had been an unspoken undercurrent. If Lily had been there, she'd have fixed the baby herself. What did you expect of a male doctor interfering in women's business?

What Lily must have to cope with…

He ached to talk to her but he knew she had to have space. Somehow he let her be.

On the third evening he returned from an outer island late. An old lady with bone metastases had needed pain relief but she wasn't stirring from home, and it had taken him hours to get her settled and pain free. Finally, exhausted, he headed for the mess tent to face a congealed dinner. He carried his unappealing plate over to an empty table—and Lily walked in.

She was such a different Lily to the Lily he'd met and loved at med school, he thought. Oh, she was still dressed as she always was, as she had been then, in light pants and simple T-shirt. Her curls were washed and shining and her features were those of the Lily of old. She was smiling, with a trace of the laughter he remembered so well.

But the strain behind her eyes was dreadful.

She had her Benjy back, but there were still losses that must ache, he thought. Kira had been like a mother to Lily since her own mother had died. He'd gleaned that much from island gossip. Lily's grief for the old woman would be raw and deep.

There were few secrets on this island and wherever he went people talked of Lily. Even though he was taking away her load of acute medicine, he knew she was working with traumatised islanders, listening to them, being one of them, acting more effectively than any trauma counsellor his team could possibly provide.

'Hi,' she said, with that lovely trace of a French accent.

'Hi,' he said back, and attempted another mouthful of… What was this?

'I hear you've been out saving my world.' She sat and smiled across at him. 'Thank you, Ben,' she said, and his gut twisted, just like that. A simple thank you…

'I haven't saved everybody,' he said. 'I sent Ruby Mannering and her baby to Fiji. The women infer that if you'd been there no such trip would be necessary. And a couple of fishermen drowned on Lai. I know it's unlikely, but I have the distinct impression if you'd been around you could have brought them back from the dead.'

Her smile faded. 'I heard about them,' she admitted. 'Morons. And as for Ruby and the baby…' Her smile returned again, just a little. 'Sure, I would have sent her to Fiji and if I'd known she was pregnant I would have sent her earlier. But she didn't tell me she was pregnant and for once the island's grapevine let me down. I need to get over there and box some ears.'

'I can imagine you boxing ears.'

Her smile returned. 'You'd better believe it. If they want me to care for them then they have to tell me what's going on. I have enough problems without unexpected births.'

'You have enough problems anyway,' he said gently. 'This set-up is impossible.'

'It is what it is,' Ben,' she said. 'There's no point in questioning it.'

There was a moment's silence. So much to say. Ben attempted another bite of whatever lay on his plate—maybe lasagne?—and gave up. He pushed the plate aside and the mess sergeant came over to collect it.

'Not hungry?'

'No,' Ben lied. 'They fed me out on Lai.'

There was another silence. They were alone in the mess tent

now, apart from the two men behind the workbench. It was hot in there, and still.

'You want to go for a walk?' Lily suggested.

'Where's Benjy?'

'Asleep. Henri's dad, Jean, is staying at my house. Henri's getting on well, but Jean's having nightmares. Sam's sending Henri to Sydney in the next couple of days for reconstructive surgery but meanwhile Benjy and I are helping keep Jean's nightmares at bay.'

Here it was again. Lily, taking on the troubles of her world.

'But you're here,' he said, thinking she couldn't be keeping other people's nightmares at bay if she was out of the house.

'Jean's watching rugby on television,' Lily said, and that faint smile returned again. 'There are limits on neighbourliness. Come on. It's better outside and maybe we need to talk.'

So they left. It was cooler outside, the ocean breeze making the night lovely.

'Do you want to go to the beach?' he asked tentatively.

'Wait here for a minute.' She was gone for three or four minutes and when she returned she was carrying a basket. 'Dinner,' she said. 'I can see a lie when it rises up and bites me, and you saying you'd eaten on Lai was a great big lie, Dr Blayden.'

'It might have been,' he admitted cautiously, and she chuckled, a lovely, throaty chuckle that he'd almost forgotten but when he heard it again… How could he have forgotten?'

'Egg and bacon pie,' she told him. 'Sushi rolls. Chocolate éclairs.'

'You've been cooking!' He was astounded, and she chuckled once more.

'How little you know of this island. The currency here is food. I'm the islanders' doctor, therefore I have more food than I know what to do with. This week the island's cooks have been working overtime. There's not a family affected by this tragedy that doesn't have an overstocked pantry.'

'Great,' he said, because he couldn't think what else to say. He followed as she led him to the path down to the beach. There was enough light to see by, enough light for Lily to choose a spot on the sun-warmed sand, spread a rug and then plop down on her knees and unpack. As he didn't follow suit, she looked up at him.

'What?' she demanded.

And he thought, What indeed? He didn't have a clue.

The tide was far out. The sand was soft and warm and the moonlight made the setting weirdly intimate—a picnic rug in the night with this woman whom he'd known so well seven years ago but not known since.

He was still in his uniform, heavy khaki. He felt overdressed.

'You could take your boots off,' she suggested, as though she'd read his mind, and he smiled and sat and hauled his boots off, and that made it more intimate still.

'Eat,' she ordered, and that was at least something to do. Actually, it was more than something. Whoever was doing Lily's cooking knew their stuff.

'You don't need army rations while you're here,' she said. 'Help yourself to my fridge.'

'I'm not sure how much longer we'll be here.'

'Sam was saying. I talked to him today while you were away. But we have fifteen islanders still in hospital with injuries that need rehabilitation. Sam's thinking we'll have to airlift them out.'

'They'll hate it,' Ben said, who knew enough of the island mindset by now to realise such an airlift would create major problems. For patients like Henri who'd need further reconstructive surgery, the islanders would consider evacuation regrettable but reasonable. But if the patient was slowly recovering and all they needed was supervision and rehabilitation…

'I can't cope if we don't,' Lily said, and he heard a hint of despair behind the words.

'You won't have to. We'll work things out. Maybe some of our medical staff can stay.'

'Presupposing here's no crisis anywhere else in the region.'

'There is that. But, Lily—'

'You'll be wanting to talk about Jacques,' she said dully, changing the subject as if she couldn't bear talking about the last one. 'Everyone wants to talk about Jacques.'

'I don't especially.' He knew he sounded cautious. Hell, he was cautious. If she hadn't wanted to talk about evacuating the injured, how much more difficult would it be to talk about Jacques?

'I've been talking to your intelligence people,' she muttered bleakly. 'Intelligence…that's more than I have.'

He still wasn't sure where to go with this. 'Don't beat yourself up,' he tried, and she responded with anger.

'Easy for you to say. You didn't agree to marry someone who turns out to have betrayed the whole island.'

'He's a smart man, Lily. It wasn't just you he conned.'

For the essentials had been worked out by now. It must have been no accident that Jacques arrived on the island just after the council had decided not to sell their oil. Maybe they could be persuaded to change their minds. But no one had been persuaded, and Jacques's attempts to drum up political change had been met not just with apathy but with incomprehension. Then Jacques and whatever political power was behind him must have decided to take over by force. They must have thought no one would notice the distress of such a small island.

But the thugs sent to carry out the operation had been idle for too long, aching for a fight. Maybe Jacques had argued for more time, for better trained men. The hostages said that Jacques had been appalled at what had happened, knowing such bloodshed must have been bound to cause international response. But that didn't help Lily, who was staring out at the darkened sea, her face bleak and self-judging.

'You loved him?' he asked, and anger resurfaced.

'What do you think?'

'I guess you did if you agreed to marry him.'

'He was here for three years before I agreed.'

'That's a pretty long courtship.' He wasn't sure where she was taking this, but he didn't know where he was going either, so he may as well join her.

'He was great to Benjy,' she said, and some of the anger faded. 'He was smart and funny and kind. He transformed the island's financial situation. He worked so hard…'

'While he tried to persuade you to sell the oil.'

'That was the only thing we disagreed about. Six months ago, when he was given the final knock back, he just exploded, telling me the islanders were fools, they were sitting on a fortune and if they didn't want it, others did. He was just…vitriolic.'

'And then?'

'Then he just seemed to accept it,' Lily said. 'He stopped haranguing our politicians and just focused…well, on being nice again. On being…perfect.'

'So you agreed to marry him.'

'There wasn't anyone else,' she said. 'After you.'

He drew in his breath. It had to be talked about some time. It had to be now.

'Ours was a great friendship,' he said softly, and then watched as her anger returned.

'Is that how you think of it? As a friendship?'

'Don't you think that?'

'I loved you, Ben,' she snapped. 'I've never thought anything other than that. I broke my heart when we went our separate ways.'

There was a moment's silence while he thought that through.

For the life of him he couldn't think what to do with it. She'd loved him? Had he loved her? He'd been a kid, he thought, a useless kid just starting out on the adventure of life.

He hadn't known how to love a woman. He still didn't know.

'You should have told me about Benjy,' he said finally, and it sounded lame even to him.

'You wouldn't have wanted to know. You think back to what you wanted then—to be in the middle of every hot spot this world had to offer. Where did a child fit into that?'

'I would have…' He paused and she answered for him.

'What, Ben? Sent him a cheque at Christmas and a signed photo of his daddy doing brave and daring things all over the world?'

'That's not fair.'

She hesitated. For a moment he thought she was going to make some hot retort, but in the end she didn't.

'No, it's not fair,' she agreed at last. 'And you're right. I should have told you. Any number of times over the last seven years I've thought you should know, but…'

'Were you afraid I'd come?'

She shrugged. 'Maybe that was it. But I'm over it.'

She was over loving him? That was good. Wasn't it?

She'd loved Jacques.

'We're grown up now,' he agreed at last. 'We're sensible. We don't do the heart thing any more.'

'Did you ever do the heart thing?'

'Lily…'

'I know,' she whispered. 'It's not fair to ask if you loved me seven years ago. We were kids. But I did feel grown up in the way I felt about you.'

'As you felt…grown up about Jacques?'

'Even more grown up,' she said. 'And just as stupid. That was a decision of the head and look where that got me.' She rose and brushed sand from her pants, looking uncertainly back toward the hospital. 'I need to go.'

'I'd like to get to know Benjy before I leave.'

'Of course.'

It worried him, he decided, that she was being calmly courteous. This was a reasonable discussion, but he didn't feel reasonable. He felt like hitting something. 'Maybe I need to do that fast,' he told her. 'Most of the troops will be pulling out in the next few days.' Then, as he saw the flash of fear behind her eyes, he said, 'Lily, there's no need to fear anyone coming back. No one's naming names but we know who was behind this. Nothing can be said, no accusations can be made, but they'll be aware that the eyes of the world are on them now and they daren't try again. I suspect…maybe the islanders aren't as innocent as they thought you were.'

'How can we be innocent when so many of our number are dead?' she said, not attempting to hide her bitterness. 'And that they be allowed to get away with murder…' She faltered, and closed her eyes. Ben stepped forward, but her eyes flew open and she stepped away. 'Don't touch me.'

'I only—'

'I'm not the Lily you knew.'

'I can see that,' he said gravely. 'To have coped with the medical needs of this community for so long…'

'I'm fine,' she said. 'I'm fine because I have support from all the islanders. You know, when I came back here seven years ago there was a part of me that didn't want to come. But now…'

'You want to put up the barricades.'

'Jacques was an outsider and look what he caused. I should have known. So, yes, I want you all gone. I want my life normal—like it was before Jacques was here. How could I ever have been stupid enough to believe him? First you, then him. My choice of men…'

'You're putting me in the same category as Jacques?' he demanded, appalled, but no apology was forthcoming.

'Look at you,' she said scornfully. 'A grown man, chasing danger like it's some sort of adrenalin rush…'

'I don't need it.'

'Yes, you do,' she said, weariness replacing anger. 'I asked you to come and see my island when we finished med school and you know what you said? You said, "I've no intention of wasting time sleeping under coconut palms." As if my life has anything to do with sleeping. And now… You're on this island because it's what you term exciting. Someone else might stay behind and help me pick up the pieces but it won't be you. Sam told me…'

'Sam,' Ben said, and groaned inwardly, because Sam was the last person he'd want to be telling Lily what he was like now. 'What's Sam been saying?'

'Sam said you're a frontline doctor,' she said. 'You go in first. The heroic Lt Blayden. Where danger is, that's where you are.'

'So?' he said, cautious, unable to think of any way to avoid a criticism he didn't really understand.

'So maybe that's why I haven't told Benjy about you.'

'What have you told him about his father?'

'Not much,' she said, and flushed. 'Ben, this is crazy. I'm way out of my league. I've spent the last few days thinking Benjy might have been killed. That should make the rest of this discussion trivial, but it's not. It still matters.'

'I do want to get to know him.'

'So stay on,' she said, challenging. 'If a medic can stay here as long as the field hospital's needed, why can't that person be you?'

'My job means I don't stay in one place,' he said blankly.

'And my job is to protect Benjy,' she said, as if he'd ended the conversation. 'I need to get back to him.'

'I'll come with you.'

'I don't want you in my house.' She took a deep breath. 'I know. That sounds dumb—and mean. While Benjy was in danger I needed you—I needed anyone—and you sleeping in my house helped. But it doesn't help now. It only complicates things.'

'Why?'

'Because I don't need you any more,' she told him simply. 'I don't need you and I don't need Jacques. End of story. You've taught me a hard lesson, Ben Blayden, but maybe I'm finally learning. So go back to your quarters and move on.'

'And Benjy?'

'I can't figure that out. Maybe I will in the morning. I'm too tired now. It's too late at night and I'm not sleeping.'

'Lily—'

'Leave it,' she snapped. 'I don't want you being sympathetic. I don't want you to be anything at all. I just want everything to be as it was.'

'It can't be.'

'You think I don't know that?' she yelled, and her voice rose so high that a flock of native birds flew upward from the palms in sudden fright. She backed away from him, taking some of her anger out in movement. She glared at him, turned away and kicked out as the remains of a wave reached up to her toes. Water sprayed up around her, and then retreated. She was left alone on a patch of washed sand, shimmering in the moonlight.

Shimmering blue.

Electric blue.

Where a moment ago it had been dark and lifeless, suddenly a thousand lights had turned on around her feet.

She stood absolutely still and the lights slowly faded. But they were still there, a thousand, no, a million tiny blue lights shining from within the wash of white water surging in and out with the tide.

'Oh,' she whispered, deflected from her anger.

Light was everywhere. She gazed down at her feet and she wiggled her toes experimentally.

The lights went on around her.

'Oh.' It was scarcely a breath. It was a whisper of awe.

She bent and put a hand on the sand. Lifting it, she left a perfect handprint of light, shimmering blue. She stared down, awed, as the lights slowly went out again and her handprint became nothing but a darker patch in the wet sand. But still there were lights. Wherever the water washed, there was light.

'What is it?' she breathed. 'Oh, Ben…'

He was as awed as she was. But he did know what it was. He'd seen this once before, on the south coast of Australia, and it had blown him away then as it was doing again now.

'It's bioluminescence,' he told her. 'It's millions of tiny sea creatures called dinoflagellates. You rarely see them this close to shore. They're like fireflies, responding to movement with a tiny blue glow.'

'It's not magic?' She was turning round and round, very slowly, watching her feet glow around her.

'Almost.' In truth he was as awed as she was. 'Maybe it is. It surely looks magic.'

'Oh, Ben…'

He walked down the beach until he was beside her. As soon as he reached the soaked sand, his footprints lit up blue just like Lily's.

'This wasn't here when we came. We'd have noticed,' Lily breathed. 'How…?'

'They'll have come in on the tide.'

'They never have before.'

'It's rare as hen's teeth this close in.'

'It's…' She was still turning, slowly, with her hands held out, like a ballet dancer. She sank and dug her hands into the soaking sand. Lifting them high, the sand fell from her fingers in a shower of blue light.

She laughed, a laugh of pure delight, a laugh he hadn't heard for so long.

'It's magic,' she whispered. 'It's just magic.'

'It is.' He caught her as she rose and spun once more, and he tugged her against him. They stood side by side, their bodies touching, water washing over their feet, gazing out at a sea that was a wash of blue and shimmering silver, a magic show put on just for them. Just for this night.

They didn't speak. There was no need. The wonder of the night was before them—and it was also within them, Ben thought as he held her close and watched her wonder.

How could he have left this woman? She was so beautiful…

'Lily,' he said at last, uncertainly, and she took a deep breath, cast one last wondering look at the sea and then tugged away from him. Just a little, but enough.

'That was…awesome, Ben,' she managed. 'But I need to go.

'Lily—'

'Don't,' she said as he looked down at her in the moonlight, and they both knew what he meant. Don't take this further.

They were no longer lovers, he thought, and this was a night for lovers. This was a scene set for lovers.

She was right. They had to move on.

'Thank you for tonight, Ben,' she whispered, her voice suddenly ragged at the edges. She was forcing herself to break the moment. She was forcing herself to break away from him. 'Thank you for the last few days. But…I can't… I can't…'

She put her hand up to his face and she touched him, a fleeting gesture, maybe reassuring herself that he was real and not some figment of this magic night, this magic setting.

'I need to ground myself,' she faltered. 'I need to return to my islanders, my medicine and my son. I need…to go.'

'Do you?'

'Yes.'

'Lily—'

'No. No, please. You can't… And neither can I.'

She was right and he knew it. They both knew it. And she at least had the courage of her convictions.

This night was meant for them, he thought, but he could take it no further.

They both knew it. Before he could say another word she fled. She grabbed her sandals and her picnic basket as she ran up the beach, and then she disappeared into the night, behind the palms, back to her bungalow. Back to her life.

As she must.

As he must return to his life. For it was what he wanted. Wasn't it? He stared once more at the magic light show put on just for them.

'Find another audience, guys,' he said wearily. 'You misjudged this one.'

But how could she find sleep after that? She couldn't. The night was long and full of shadows, and Ben was no longer beside her.

She had Benjy back, she told herself. It should be enough. But Ben had lain with her in those nights of terror and she missed the warmth of him, the smell of him. She missed…Ben.

If she'd stayed at the beach…

Don't go there.

The night stretched on and Lily let her thoughts drift to the first time she'd met him. She'd been in her second year of university, studying furiously, her work taking up every available minute. Up three steps of a library ladder, she'd tugged out a tome that had been shoved in too tightly. The book had come out too fast, and all of a sudden she had toppled backward.

But Ben had been right underneath, ready to catch her. She'd landed in his arms; she looked up into his concerned eyes and she'd been smitten. He had been big and dark, with jet-black hair that curled randomly, flopping over his lovely brown eyes and making him look very, very sexy. He had been tall and big-boned and superbly muscled, and he'd had a smile to die for.

'Hey, the sky's falling!' he'd exclaimed, holding her close. 'But who's complaining if the sky looks like this?' He'd set her on her feet and he'd chuckled and brushed curls out of her eyes and picked up her books—and she'd fallen in love on the spot.

The years that followed were amazing. Ben took life as it came, seizing every opportunity with both hands. Oh, he was hard-working—his medicine was as important to him as it was to Lily—but from that day their mutual studies became fun. They studied together, they surfed, they went bushwalking, they drank coffee in late-night bars, they argued long into the night over anything and everything. It was a magical few years that almost blew her away with happiness.

But there was no long-term commitment. Ben's background was wealth and neglect—his parents were socialites who threw money at their son instead of affection. And there was more. Lily guessed at shadows he wouldn't talk of, and he wouldn't let her probe.

And Lily? Lily had been taught what love did and she'd thought she didn't want it. Her mother had abandoned the island and her people for a handsome Frenchman. When he walked out, Lily was four and mother and child were left destitute. Lily still had hazy memories of those days, which had culminated in her mother's attempted suicide when she was seven. French authorities contacted the islanders and Lily and her mother were brought home, to be accepted back with love but to know that the island was not to be lightly left. And to be taught by her mother that romantic love was catastrophic.

So she'd agreed with Ben that love was for others. She'd tried to mean it, too, but she'd failed. Her heart was irrevocably his, but there was no way she could tell him. She might love him, but she agreed there was no future for them. For when med school was complete she knew what she had to do.

And she'd done it, she told herself. She'd come home. And she'd borne Benjy—who looked like his daddy.

Benjy stirred now in his sleep and she kissed the top of his head. The resemblance was amazing.

'When Ben leaves again, I'll still have you,' she whispered, but it wasn't enough.

It had to be enough. For ever.

She had been right to leave the beach tonight, she told herself. She had to be right.

And Ben…

Back in his quarters, listening to Sam's not so gentle snoring, Ben was no closer to sleep than Lily.

What was wrong with him? He usually slept the moment his head hit the pillow.

Not now. He was thinking of Lily. Lily spinning slowly in her pool of phosphorescence. Lily.

Her face was right before him, the strain behind her eyes deep and real. The medical needs on this island were huge. She'd been working too hard before this had happened. And now… He'd leave her and she'd sink back into a life where duty overcame all.

She should have time off. That much was obvious. For her to calmly go on working with no time to adjust was asking for long-term trouble.

They had to get a medical team here on a longer-term basis, he thought. Well, maybe he could arrange that. In this current climate, no reasonable request would be refused. He could get doctors and paramedics here for at least the next few months.

That wouldn't stop Lily working.

But she had to stop working. He thought again of the strain behind her eyes. She'd collapse if she didn't stop.

She needed more nights like tonight, he thought. Oh, not with him, but nights where she could stop spinning because of work.

And then…

An idea came into his mind, so preposterous that for a moment he almost rejected it unexamined. She wouldn't.

But she needed it so much.

He thought of the island's political head. Gualberto Panjiamtu was a man in his seventies, who'd coped with being held hostage with dignity, and had emerged with his concern for his islanders paramount. Gualberto would understand that Lily's health was vital to all. Could he ask Gualberto to release Lily from her obligations for a while?

She'd never agree.

But ideas kept spinning, faster than Lily had spun on the beach.

He should sleep.

He didn't sleep. He lay and stared at the canvas overhead, and thought. About Lily.

CHAPTER SIX

LILY didn't see Ben all the next day. So much for Ben getting to know Benjy. Benjy stayed with her as she moved through the island, spending time with each of the traumatised islanders, trying to prevent long-term damage.

Normally whenever she visited island homes Benjy would dart off as soon as she arrived, blending with the familiarity of an extended family. But not now. He clung, listening in as the islanders talked through their terrors. He shouldn't be with her, Lily thought. He needed urgent attention himself, but what could she do? With Kira gone, Benjy clung to her as a lifeline and pushing him away would do more harm than allowing him to stay.

She should stay at home with him. But who else would do this? These were her people. She felt like she was being torn in two.

There was nothing to do except to work on through it, so she kept on doing what came next, and by her side Benjy was stoic.

She needed to get her life in order, she thought dully as she and Benjy walked home at dusk. But how? There were no answers.

As they approached her bungalow she saw her lights were on. Often the islanders would come to her house if they needed her. Surely not more work, she thought bleakly.

She was so tired.

'You can do this, Lily,' she murmured, and pushed her door wide.

There was indeed someone waiting for her.

It was Gualberto.

And Ben.

'Gualberto,' she said, setting Ben's presence aside as too confusing. Gualberto, as head of Kapua's council, was a stable presence, a surety in a world that was no longer sure. 'It's lovely that you're here,' she told him, and she meant it. 'How can I help you?'

'It's not for you to help me, Lily,' the old man said gravely. 'It's how I can help you. Ben tells me you need to rest.'

She flashed Ben a look of anger. He hadn't been near Benjy. So much for promises, and now to tell Gualberto she needed to rest… He was piling more problems on an elderly man who had enough to cope with. 'I don't,' she snapped.

'Hear us out, Lily,' Ben said, and she bit her lip.

'Go run a bath, Benjy,' she told her son, but Gualberto put out his hands and tugged her son onto the seat beside him.

'Benjy needs to hear what we've organised.'

'I hope you've organised nothing.'

'We've organised you a holiday, Lily,' the old man said, and he suddenly sounded severe. 'Sit down.'

This was so unusual a statement that she did sit. Benjy was on the chair by Gualberto. It was a four-chair table. That meant she had to sit by Ben.

She sat but she shifted her chair as far away from him as possible.

Gualberto smiled at the movement, as if he found it amusing. What was funny about it? Lily asked herself, and then decided she was too tired to care. She wanted them all to go away. She could sleep for a hundred years.

'There's a thing called burn-out,' Gualberto told her, and

his hand came across the table to grip hers. 'Ben tells me you have it.'

'Ben doesn't know me.' She tried to tug her hand away but she couldn't.

'Ben has organised for you to take a rest,' the old man said sternly. 'We've thought this thing through. We depend on you, and we've pushed this dependence too far.'

'I don't know what you mean.' This feeling of being out of control…she'd had it since that first morning when the finance councillor had stumbled, wounded, through her front door, and it was growing stronger rather than weakening. She felt as if her body was growing so light that any minute she could float free.

She felt terrified.

Maybe something of what she was feeling showed in her face, for the old man's sternness lessened. 'Lily, you're not to try any longer,' he said gently. 'After medical school you came home to work here, on this island, but as the outer islands have discovered we have a permanent doctor, they've been using you, too. Your workload has built to the stage where you can no longer cope. It's taken Dr Blayden to show us that.'

'He doesn't know—'

'I do, Lily.' Ben looked concerned, as he had no right to be on her behalf. 'Sam and I have been looking through the records of hospital admissions.'

'You had no right—'

'And we've talked to the island nurses. You're doing ten clinics a week, seven of them on outer islands. You're on call twenty-four hours a day, seven days a week. The hospital is nearly always full because the islanders refuse to go elsewhere—why should they when they have you to care for them? You're doing the work of three doctors.'

'Meanwhile, Kira's been caring for Benjy,' Gualberto said. 'And now Kira's dead.'

'Mama looks after me,' Benjy interjected, trying to keep up with what was happening, and Gualberto nodded in agreement.

'Of course she does. That's what mothers do. But your mama takes care of all the islanders as well.'

'She still has to look after me,' Benjy said.

Lily heard panic and rose and rounded the table and tugged him into her arms.

'Of course I do. Of course I will.'

'Some things go without saying,' Gualberto said heavily. 'But, Benjy, your mother's had a dreadful time, and we need to take care of her as she takes care of us.'

'I—I don't know what y-you mean,' Lily stammered, but Gualberto was pushing himself heavily to his feet. He'd had a dreadful time, too, these past days, and it showed.

'Lily, I can't heal anything,' he said. 'But I'll do my best. I know who Ben is and what he is to you.' He looked at Benjy and back at Ben, as if confirming the undeniable resemblance. 'There are many things you need to sort out, but one thing is already sorted. Ben is a good man. He *is* a good man, Lily,' he reiterated heavily. 'I know the men he works with and I know him myself. I've watched him work with our people in the time since he arrived and I tell this to you strongly—he is a good man, as Jacques never was. Maybe that's none of my business but I have accepted his proposal on your behalf.'

'Proposal?' She flashed a glance of pure astonishment at Ben.

'We haven't paid you as we ought,' the old man said heavily. 'When you returned after medical school we had a subsistence economy. You agreed to work for a tiny wage plus a share of the necessities we all share in. That seemed reasonable. But now… Ben asked me if you could afford to go away for a little and I had to tell him you couldn't.' He grimaced. 'Maybe we've been too afraid of what the oil money would do to us. Maybe we were too fearful of Jacques and his intentions. Regardless, what money we have is tied up in the short term.'

'That's nothing to do with—'

'It is something to do with you,' he went on, inexorable now he'd started. 'For there's no money to say to you go where you want. But there is an alternative.'

'I don't want an alternative.'

'Listen, Lily,' Ben said urgently and Lily subsided again. A little.

'Ben tells us that he owns a farm on the coast of New South Wales,' Gualberto said. 'This is what he proposes, and I agree. There's nothing there but a housekeeper and farm manager. Ben tells me there's a beach, horses to ride and nothing to do. Nothing, Lily. You will stay there for a month.'

'I can't.' She was staring wildly from Gualberto to Ben and back again. Were they out of their minds? To propose that she just leave…

And go to Ben's property?

'Ben will stay here to cope with medical necessities,' Gualberto said, interjecting before the next obvious objection was aired. 'Maybe he'll join you toward the end of your stay, but not before. He says you and Benjy need space to be by yourselves. We all agree.'

She opened her mouth but Ben was there before her.

'Think it through, Lily,' he said urgently, his eyes never leaving hers. 'I'll organise the medical set-up here. I'm due for leave and I'll take it as such, so even if there's a crisis I can't be called away. Officially Sam will stay on for a bit as well, and three of our nurses want to stay. With your people that's a full medical complement.'

'But…you can't just do that,' she faltered. 'You can't just walk in and say go to some farm I've never heard of.'

'Would you not like to get away, Lily?' Gualberto asked her, serious now, pushing for an answer. 'Truly, Lily? In your heart?'

'I don't... I don't...'

'You do,' Ben said. 'You're desperate for a break and you know it. Benjy needs time with you. Just say yes, my love.'

'I'm not your love,' she whispered, dazed.

'Of course not,' he said ruefully. 'I meant...Lily. Just say yes, Dr Cyprano.'

'A farm?' Benjy whispered. He'd been trying desperately to keep up and he thought he had it now. 'We can go to a farm, Mama.'

'Just say yes,' Ben repeated, and Gualberto smiled at them all and made to leave.

'I think the yes is already spoken,' he said gravely. 'Lily, for the next few weeks you're forbidden to practise medicine anywhere on this group of islands. We love you as our own but for the next few weeks you belong to yourself. Take your son and go. And now...' He smiled, a world-weary smile that still managed to hold a hint of real amusement. 'I'll move on to the next problem, but I believe I don't need to worry more about this one. I'll leave you in the capable hands of Dr Blayden.'

Ben stayed on. She asked him to leave but he simply shook his head and started making dinner.

'I can do this,' she told him, but he shook his head. She was sitting, stunned, at her kitchen table while this big man in army camouflage took over her life.

'I've found three casseroles in the refrigerator,' he told her. 'The one that looks best says it's red emperor in spicy coconut cream broth.' He grinned at Benjy, man to man. 'Red emperor'd be fish? I reckon that'd be guaranteed to put hairs on your chest. How about it?'

Benjy looked at Ben and then cautiously at his mother. Then he tugged the neck of his T-shirt forward and looked down at his hairless tummy.

He glanced again at Ben—who grinned some more and flipped a couple of buttons open, baring his chest to the waist. Definitely hairy.

'Like me,' he said. 'There's a heap of fish and coconut cream gone into this manly chest.'

'You're mad,' Lily said faintly, trying to block out the vision of a body any young boy would think was enviable. Though who was she kidding? It wasn't Benjy who thought it was fantastic. She so wanted to…

No. She wouldn't listen to her hormones, she told herself fiercely, while Benjy agreed that maybe he did want some of the casserole.

They ate together. Mostly they ate in silence, though occasionally Ben would direct a remark to Benjy, which Benjy would consider and answer with a monosyllabic reply. Ben didn't appear put out by the lack of conversation. He attacked the truly excellent casserole with relish, then cleared away while Lily sat, still stunned, seemingly unable to move.

Ben's farm, her mind was saying. No.

But… Get away, her heart was replying, and it sounded so desirable it was like a siren's song. Where were earmuffs when she needed them? And as well as that…

Ben's farm. That suddenly wasn't her mind talking. It was her heart.

Ben could be there at the end of their stay, just for a little. Benjy might get to know his father. At the end of the time she'd come back here and get on with the rest of her life, but Benjy might have established a relationship. Which he needed to have.

This was crazy. She couldn't leave. These were her people.

Benjy slumped in weariness almost before he finished his dinner. Trying her best to ignore Ben—she didn't know what else to do—she carried him through to bed. He was asleep before his head hit the pillow. She gazed down at his small face for a long moment and then turned to find Ben watching.

'You must let him have a break,' Ben said gently. 'You can't move forward from this as if nothing has happened.'

'You're a psychologist?'

'I've talked to psychologists.'

'What gives you the right—?'

'He's my son.'

She drew in her breath, but it was as if she didn't find any. Once more that disembodied feeling came over her, as if she was floating, out of control.

Maybe she swayed, she didn't know, but all of a sudden he was right before her, lifting her into his arms, holding her against him for a brief, hard moment, letting her feel the strength of his body against her—grounding her—and then lowering her gently onto the bed beside Benjy.

She didn't know how. She didn't know why. But it worked. The awful dizziness faded and she felt the pillow soft and cool against her face. For one crazy moment she considered giving in to this man—doing what he said—letting him take a control she no longer had.

It was a crazy thought, but right now she didn't have the capacity to fight it.

'Do you know how close to collapse you are?' Ben growled, and she thought about that, or tried to think, but things were a bit fuzzy. He was so…male, she thought inconsequentially. Nice.

Tomorrow she'd be sensible and tell him what he could do with his preposterous idea, she decided. Tonight… Tonight he was glaring down at her, concerned, and she thought how wonderful it was to have someone concerned about her. It was her whose job it was to be concerned about everyone on this island, and on every other island within boating distance. Now the tables were turned.

'I'm not close to collapse,' she managed, and Ben's gorgeous brown eyes crinkled into laughter, the laughter she'd always loved.

'Of course you're not,' he agreed. 'You could run a ten-mile race right now.'

'Maybe ten yards?' she said cautiously, and he chuckled.

'Maybe not even one foot from your pillow. You're going on this holiday, my lovely Lily. I've set it up for you. The islanders have agreed. There are people to take over your work… Lily, have you ever had time off with Benjy?'

How could she think about that when his eyes were on hers and the pillow was soft and Benjy was warm against her and Ben was…Ben was there?

'I don't—'

'That's what I've been told,' he said, and his smile faded. 'Don't fight me on this one, Lily. Tomorrow we're putting you on a helicopter out of here. We're taking two of our injured back to Sydney Central and then the pilot will take you to the farm. It's *en route* to base so there's no problem. Rosa and Doug, my farm managers, are expecting you. You're to spend the next few weeks healing our son and healing yourself.'

Our son.

Lily gazed at Ben for a long moment. *Our son.*

She should resent the words, she thought, but instead… It seemed as if she was handing over control. That was something she'd vowed never to do, but now it was happening it wasn't the void she'd feared. The lightness was with her again but instead of making her feel ill it suddenly felt like there might just be a sliver of joy in all this.

'No argument,' Ben told her.

How could she argue? She couldn't even raise her head from the pillow.

'You're so done in,' Ben said ruefully, and he knelt by the bed and touched her cheek with his forefinger. It was like a caress, a gesture of warmth and strength and caring. The feeling was an illusion, she thought, but for now she didn't care. She'd take her comfort where she could find it.

'No argument for tonight,' she whispered.

'That's great.' He sounded relieved.

She thought dreamily, Why was he relieved? As if she could ever argue with him.

But, of course, she could. She must. But not tonight.

'I'll argue tomorrow,' she whispered, and he smiled.

'It won't help. But you're welcome to try. Goodnight, my Lily,' he said, and he bent suddenly and kissed her, hard on the mouth, as she remembered being kissed all those years ago. She should push him away. She should…

But she didn't. The kiss lasted for as long as she wanted, a delicious, languorous indulgence in sensual pleasure that surely should have had her running back to her tightly controlled world. Men were dangerous. Ben was dangerous.

But not tonight. Tonight she let him kiss her. She even found the energy to put her arms around his neck, to hold his head in her hands, to deepen the kiss and to take what she needed.

Delicious, languorous pleasure.

She was almost asleep. It had to end, but when it did, when he finally pulled away, her eyes were closing on a lovely dream. Her world was right. Ben was there.

Which was a ridiculous thing to think, but think it she did and it pervaded her dreams. She snuggled against Benjy and she slept as she hadn't slept for a long, long time.

And kneeling beside her, Ben kept watch over Lily and her son—*his* son—until his pager crackled into life, until there were medical imperatives and he could watch no more.

CHAPTER SEVEN

SHE woke up and he was gone. For a moment the remnants of her dream stayed with her, making her smile, making her look expectantly to where Ben had been. But, of course, he wasn't there.

She glanced at her bedside clock—and found it wasn't there either. Startled, she checked her wristwatch—and yelped.

It was eight-thirty. There was a ward round to be done and…

And things were different. Benjy was awake. She focused on the rest of her bedroom. Benjy had pulled an ancient suitcase from the bottom of the wardrobe. He had a pile of clothes folded beside him and he was calmly assessing each item.

'Hi,' she said cautiously, and he turned and smiled at her. It was a great smile. It was a smile she hadn't seen for too long.

'Ben came round a while ago,' Benjy said. 'When he thought we were asleep he was going to go away again, but I heard him and we had toast together. He said I should start thinking about what I'll need to take to the farm.'

The farm idea hadn't been a dream, then. But it might as well be. The idea was crazy.

'We'll talk about it after I'm dressed,' she told him. 'Benjy, we need to—'

'Ben says Sam's doing house calls this morning,' Benjy told her. 'And the nice nurse with the funny-coloured hair. Yellow and green. Debbie. Ben said Sam and Debbie are going to sort out all our problems, no sweat.'

'Did he say that?' she said, starting for the bathroom. 'As if he knows.'

'He says we're leaving at ten and if we're not ready he's going to pick us up and toss us in the helicopter and take us regardless.' He stared down at two T-shirts. 'I don't know what regardless means. Mama, which one should I pack?'

'Neither.'

'Don't you want us to go?'

'Benjy, we can't.'

'There will be horses,' Benjy whispered. 'Ben said there will be horses and I can ride one.'

Drat the man. How dared he upset her son?

'Horses smell. And they kick. Did Ben take away my alarm clock?'

'Ben's horses wouldn't kick and I don't like your alarm clock.'

'Neither do I, sweetheart,' she told him. 'But it's all about who I am.'

'I want a holiday,' he said, suddenly stubborn. 'The children in my picture books have holidays. I want one.'

Lily's resolve faltered. She hesitated and there was a sharp rap on the outside door. It opened before she could respond, and Ben was there, dressed in his camouflage gear again, looking big and tough and dangerous. And smiling.

'Why are you wearing those clothes?' she said, trying to sound cross and not breathless. 'You look like you're heading into battle.'

'Believe it or not, I don't have anything else,' he told her. 'I didn't pop in an extra bag of casual gear.'

'I like it,' Benjy announced. 'I want to wear a uniform like that when I grow up.'

'No, you don't,' Lily told him, but her son looked suddenly mutinous. Uh-oh.

'What are you doing here?' she demanded, thinking maybe this was a dangerous conversation to pursue—though concentrating on Ben rather than Benjy seemed even riskier.

'I came to wake you up,' he said cheerfully. 'I didn't want you to sleep through your holiday.'

'You took my alarm clock.'

'Guilty, but it was an entirely altruistic action on my part, as here I am, replacing it. Wouldn't you rather wake up to me?'

'No,' she snapped, but his grin was making her think he had a point. He definitely had a point. 'Anyway, you make a lousy substitute. My clock was set for six.'

'A perfectly ridiculous time,' he told her. 'For the first day of your holiday.'

'Ben, I'm not—'

'Lily, you are,' he told her, and his smile faded. 'I meant what I said last night. If you could afford some other way of doing this—of getting away from the island a bit by yourself—and I thought you would, then maybe I wouldn't be this bossy. But all the islanders agree.'

'All…'

'Every single person I've talked to,' he said cheerfully. 'Bar none. The women want to pack for you but I figured you only needed spare knickers and togs.'

'Togs?'

'Swimsuit,' he said patiently. 'Honestly, Lily, you spent six years in Australia.'

'I know what togs are. Ben, I can't.'

He'd come to the bedroom door but no further, which was just as well. She'd woken some time in the night and had tugged off her pants and bra. She was now wearing a pair of very scanty knickers and a T-shirt that didn't come down quite far enough.

This man was the father of her child, she told herself, feeling desperate. He knew her so well that appearing before him in knickers and T-shirt shouldn't worry her.

It did. She wanted all the barricades she could get, and clothing was just the start of it.

'Lily, you can.' Still he didn't move. He's holding himself back, she thought. He's feeling the same as I am.

'Just in case you do want to take more than knickers and togs, Pieter's wife's here to help you pack,' he told her. He turned back and Mary was behind him. She came in now, cautiously, as if she was afraid what she might find, but when she saw Lily in her knickers and T-shirt she smiled, her broad islander face a tonic all on its own.

'You dress well to greet your visitors,' she said, and Lily glared at both of them.

'Mary, tell Ben he has no right ordering me around.'

'He does have a right,' Mary said softly. 'I'm here as back-up. I'm here to tell you we all agree. You were exhausted before this happened. All of us knew it. We just chose to ignore it because...well, maybe we needed you too much. But we don't need you now. You're to go, child. Take your Benjy and do what the good doctor says. You're not to come back before you've gained ten pounds and you've lost those dark shadows under yours eyes.'

'Mary—'

'Don't argue,' she said severely, and then rounded on Ben. 'What are you doing here?' she demanded. 'Lily needs to shower and pack and there's no room in that for you. Shoo.'

'Yes, ma'am,' Ben said, and he grinned and blew a kiss to Lily—and shooed.

An hour and a half later, Lily and her son were in the great army helicopter, heading for the mainland. She had to work during the journey. That was how Ben had squared it with the authorities—indeed, it suited them all well. A corporal with shrapnel in her knee and a supply sergeant who'd smashed a hip in the chaos of the night of the helicopters both needed constant medical attention, but they wanted to go home to Sydney.

So Benjy sat up front with the pilot, one half of him overjoyed to be right where he was and the other half of him thinking holiday, holiday, holiday, horses, horses, horses. Lily worked on in the rear. One part of her was still a doctor, checking her patients were comfortable, making sure there was no deterioration, talking to them about their condition and how they were looking forward to being reunited with their families. One tiny part of Lily was thinking holiday. But the biggest part was thinking Ben, Ben, Ben, and there was no way she could get the refrain from her head.

Ben watched the chopper disappear from view and it was as if he'd cut out a part from himself and sent it with them.

Lily and his son.

'You should be with them, mate.' It was Sam, coming up behind him and placing a hand on his shoulder. The sensation made Ben start and Sam grinned.

'You're not very awake, are you, lad? I could be the enemy.'

'There's no enemy here. Not any more.'

'No.' Sam eyed the retreating helicopter thoughtfully. 'So tell me again—why didn't you go with them?'

'I need to work here.'

'I'm working here.'

'So that makes two of us. Plus the nurses. It's what we need.'

'So let's see if I'm right,' Sam said thoughtfully. 'You've sent the lady to your family farm. You've also volunteered to take leave because you know the powers that be won't approve two doctors staying here, and the lady wouldn't have gone if she didn't know there were two of us to take over her work.'

'That's—'

'The truth,' Sam said. 'You've got it bad, mate.'

'I haven't got anything.'

'You're still in love with her.'

'She's gorgeous,' Ben snapped. 'Anyone would love her.'

'She used to be gorgeous,' Sam said bluntly. 'Now she's skinny. She's got too many freckles, her hair needs a decent cut and she looks like she hasn't slept for a month.'

'That's why she needs a holiday.'

'Yeah, but it doesn't say she's gorgeous.' He hesitated. 'You planning on following this through?'

'Like how?'

'The kid's yours,' Sam said. 'You marry her and you have an instant family. How does that seem?'

'It won't happen.'

'Why not?'

'I don't do family.'

'No,' Sam said thoughtfully. 'Of course you don't.'

'Look, can we leave this?' Ben said, exasperated. 'You're planning on operating on Larry Arnoo this afternoon?'

'Yeah,' Sam said, and grimaced. 'Larry should be on his way to Sydney, too. There's shrapnel too close to the spine to leave it there. If it hits a nerve he's stuffed. But there's no way he's going to Sydney. He's only agreed to have the operation here because he assumed Lily would do it.'

'As if she could.'

'Have you seen some of the work she's done on this island?' Sam demanded. 'She and Pieter—a nurse with no formal training whatsoever—have done operations in the past that would have made me quake. Because there's no one else to do them.'

'She's out of it now,' Ben growled. 'She has a month off, or more if I can manage it.'

'But you're not interested in marrying her?'

'Hell, Sam, I don't do marriage. And do you think she'd follow me where I go for the rest of her life? Or stay happily a home body while I'm away?'

'No chance.'

'Well, then,' Ben said heavily. 'That's it. We're back where we started. Long-term friends. But at least I won't leave her pregnant this time.'

'Not if you stay here and she stays there,' Sam agreed, and grinned. 'But that's not likely to be a long-term arrangement, now, is it?'

CHAPTER EIGHT

THE chopper crew set their patients down at Sydney Central. Benjy watched open-mouthed as Sydney appeared and disappeared underneath them. He didn't say another word until they reached Ben's property.

Neither did Lily. It had been seven years since she'd seen anything but the island, and there was a lot to see. They followed the coast north, until they came to a mountainous region where farms seemed few and far between.

'Here we are,' the pilot called cheerfully, and set the big machine down to land.

A woman seemed to be waiting. They saw her first, a dot beside a house set on coastal farmland. The dot grew bigger until it became the woman.

It must be one of Ben's managers.

In the tiny part of her mind that had dared to think ahead to what waited for them, Lily had imagined some sort of elderly family retainer, a plump and cuddly lady who made sponge cakes and beamed.

No such thing. Sure, Rosa was an older woman—in her sixties maybe?—but there the resemblance to her image stopped. She was thin and wiry, dressed in tight-fitting jeans, glossy boots and a crimson shirt with sleeves rolled up to the elbows. A defiant redhead, with auburn curls twisted into an elegant knot, she looked like some sort of retired Spanish dancer, Lily thought, tugging Benjy out from under the blades while the pilot tossed out their bags. She turned to say goodbye, but the chopper was already rising.

Her escape route was cut.

Benjy was right behind her, clinging as if the woman might bite. Lily took her son's small hand and propelled him forward, and then thought she was almost using her small son as a shield. She had that light-headed feeling of being out of control again.

Oh, for heaven's sake… This was nothing to worry about.

'Hi,' the woman called without a trace of a Spanish accent, and there was the second illusion dispelled. 'Welcome to Nurrumbeen.'

Nurrumbeen. All she knew of this place was what she'd seen as they'd circled before landing. It was a farm seemingly carved into the wilderness, rich grazing land encircled by sea on one side and rainforest on the other.

What on earth was she going to do here for a month? No people. No medicine. She wouldn't have minded the odd shop, she soundlessly told the absent Ben, and the thought of his possible reaction to such a whinge was enough to allow her to greet Rosa with a smile.

'We're Lily and Benjy. I hope you're expecting us.'

'We surely are.' Rosa shook Lily's hand with a grip as strong as a man's and then her eyes moved past her to Benjy. 'Benjy,' she whispered in a tone that said she either knew or she guessed Ben's involvement. There was intelligence in these black eyes. Not much would get past Rosa. 'You're both more welcome than I can say,' she said. 'Come into the house.'

The house was long and low, white-painted, with wide verandas all around and the all-pervasive scent of something that looked like honeysuckle running riot everywhere. They walked inside and there were so many questions in Lily's head that she felt as if she might burst. By her side, Benjy seemed awed into silence.

Ben should be here.

In all the time she'd spent with Ben during university, never once had he introduced her to his parents or taken her to any of the properties his parents owned. Neither had he talked about his family. 'We don't get on,' he'd said brusquely, and she'd never got past it. For her to come here now, with his son…

Without him…

There was a man inside, older than Rosa, small, wiry and greying. He was leaning heavily on a walking stick—and he was wearing an apron.

'This is my Doug,' Rosa said proudly, as if conjuring up something magical. 'We're here to look after you.'

'You're…Ben's parents' housekeepers?' Lily asked cautiously, and Lily and Doug both smiled.

'I'm Ben's housekeeper,' Doug said. 'But food first, questions later.' He sat them down in the big farmhouse kitchen and produced sandwiches, sponge cake and chocolate éclairs. Rosa poured tea for Lily and lemonade for Benjy and both Rosa and Doug beamed as they ate and drank, seeming to enjoy the fact that they were obviously disconcerted.

Ben *should* be here, Lily thought again. This is his house. Or…is this his parents' house?

'I'm not sure what the set-up is here,' she ventured, as Benjy wrapped himself around a chocolate éclair.

'Tell it like it is, Rosa.' Doug pushed another éclair forward and Lily couldn't resist. Yum.

'We're housekeeper and farm manager,' Rosa told her. 'Doug's the housekeeper—he makes the best sponge cake you've ever eaten.' She hesitated then, glancing at Doug and then nodding, as if coming to a decision to tell more.

'Doug was a farmhand here when he was young and I worked in the stables,' Rosa told them. 'Ben's parents were running the place as a horse stud but they spent very little time here. But we knew Ben when he was little. And his sister.'

A sister. Lily's eyes widened. She'd dated Ben for years. What else didn't she know? 'I didn't know Ben had a sister.'

'Bethany died when she was four,' Rosa said. 'But by then Ben was at boarding school. Anyway, when Ben was about twelve Doug had an appalling tractor accident.'

'It rolled on top of me,' Doug said, smiling at Benjy, as if trying to make light of what must have been dreadful. 'Damned wheel mount gave way on a slope. You ever thought how much a two-ton tractor can hurt? One day I'll show you the scars.'

'Wow,' whispered Benjy through cream.

'Anyway, Ben's parents wouldn't accept liability,' Rosa said, without rancour, stating facts. 'They said it was Doug's duty to maintain the tractor—the fact that there'd been no money to maintain it was carefully ignored and they doctored their bank accounts to make it seem like there was. There was a court case and we lost. The fight left us in debt for years. We left here. I worked in a racing stable and Doug…well, Doug stayed home and tried to keep himself occupied.'

'I learned how to cook,' Doug said.

'He did,' Rosa said affectionately. 'Then about six years ago Ben's father passed away. His mother had died earlier and it wasn't a month after his father's death before Ben came to find us.'

'He remembered us,' Doug said, smiling at a memory he obviously found good. 'His parents didn't come here often but until my accident they'd send Ben. He'd arrive on his own for holidays.'

'Like us,' Benjy announced, and Doug nodded.

'Exactly like you. Rosa taught him to ride a horse.'

'And he remembered us all those years later,' Rosa said softly. 'Until his parents died there was little he could do, but as soon as he could, he did.'

'What did he do?' Lily asked.

'He installed us back here,' Rosa said with quiet pride. 'There's a little house behind this one—it's beautiful. He's given us life tenancy. He sat and talked about what Doug and I could do and we said I loved the farm and Doug could keep a house clean. So that's what we are. Housekeeper and farm manager.'

'You should see me hoover,' Doug said, grinning, and Lily suddenly felt like grinning back. For the last week she'd been moving in a nightmare. This couple made her feel she was waking up. And Ben's care…

She'd fallen in love with him all those years ago. Suddenly she was remembering why.

'Does Ben come here often now?' she asked, and Rosa gave a definite nod.

'Whenever he can. We keep telling him he should bring friends here—girlfriends and the like—but he won't.'

'He's a bit of a loner, and he's not the marrying kind,' Doug added, but Rosa's eyes had moved to Benjy.

'Maybe he hasn't been until now,' she said. 'But things change.' Her gaze shifted to Lily. 'Do you and he—?'

'Leave the girl alone, love,' Doug said, starting to clear the table. 'No questions. You know what Ben said. She's worn to the bone. Just food and rest and plenty of both. Starting now. Rosa, take them to their bedrooms for a nap before they explore the farm.'

'Yes, sir.' Rosa clicked her riding boots together as she saluted her husband. Then she smiled and waited for Lily and Benjy to accompany her. 'Let's get you settled for a really long stay.'

* * *

They were at his farm.

Ben had several properties, left to him by parents who had valued everything in terms of money. Nurrumbeen was the only place he had any emotional tie to, and it was only his sense of obligation to Doug and Rosa that had created that tie.

He'd go there when he had the medicine on the island thoroughly sorted, he told himself.

But wanted to go there now.

Why?

Benjy was his kid, he thought as the days wore on. He had to learn to kick a football. He had to learn to ride a horse.

Rosa would teach him to ride.

Maybe it'd be fun to teach him himself.

But that meant involvement. The kid might even learn to need him.

He didn't do needing. He couldn't. It'd do his head in. He was a man who walked alone.

Until now, a little voice whispered insidiously in his head. You could stop and be a family.

And keep on doing the work I love?

You could change direction. You might even learn to love other things.

Which was a really scary thought. He thought back to his childhood. Every single thing he'd ever loved had been a fleeting attachment—to people like Rosa and Doug, people he had seen when his parents had allowed it and then who'd disappeared out of his life forever. Like his sister. Bethany. That's what love is, he thought bleakly. He knew enough now to shield himself from it.

If he loved, he lost.

Forget it. You have work to do here, he told himself severely. Stay here, stick to your medicine and get them out of your mind.

As if.

* * *

For the first three days Lily threw herself into her holiday as if she only had days to get to experience everything. She rode, she fished, she swam, she built the world's biggest sandcastle, she read late into the night, she rose at dawn to jog on the beach…

Rosa and Doug watched and said little. Benjy was drawn to them, she knew. They offered to take over his care and let her rest, but rest wasn't on her agenda. Neither was clinging to her son, but her legacy from the last few days was one of fear, and everywhere she went, Benjy went, too.

Benjy loved the horses. Rosa and Doug grazed beef cattle—that was the farm's main income—but Rosa had four mares and one stallion—just to give her pleasure—and they gave Benjy pleasure, too.

One of the mares was heavily pregnant and Benjy was fascinated. 'We can't go until Flicker's had her foal,' he told Lily, and Lily thought she wasn't sure how long she could stand being there.

She was still in overdrive, playing as hard as she'd worked on the island. The events of the past few days haunted her. The effects they'd had on Benjy haunted her as well, making her worried sick that there might be long-term repercussions. He hardly talked to her of the time in the compound. He hardly spoke of Kira. He never spoke of Jacques.

She'd betrayed her son by loving Jacques. Or…by thinking she'd loved Jacques?

She hardly slept.

'You're like a wound-up clockwork toy,' Rosa said on the third night. Doug was feeding the dogs, Benjy was supervising and Lily and Rosa were picking peas from the vegetable patch. 'Why don't you go for a walk by yourself after dinner? Let Doug read to the boy. It'd do them both good.' Her smile faded a little. 'I worry about Doug.'

'Why?'

'He has chest pain.'

Lily frowned. 'What sort of chest pain? Do you want me to talk to him? You know I'm a doctor.'

'No.' Rosa grimaced. 'He'd hate it that I said anything. He hardly admits it to me, and I'm sure it's worse than he lets me see.' She hesitated. 'But when Ben comes…maybe Ben will do something.'

'Rosa, if it really is chest pain, he needs urgent medical assessment.'

'If he goes to the doctor when Ben's not here and the doctor says he has to stop doing housework then we'll leave here,' Rosa said, sounding desperate. 'After Ben's been so good to us there's no way Doug would stay on if he can't work for his keep.' She hesitated. 'But maybe if it was Ben that was to do the telling… I know it sounds foolish but pride's one of the few things left to Doug.'

'Rosa, chest pain can mean—'

'There's nothing you can do or I can do,' Rosa said with finality. 'We wait for Ben. And as for now, you're to go for a walk. Ben says you should.'

'When did he tell you that?' she demanded, startled, and Rosa smiled.

'He rang us when you were at the beach. He worries about you.'

Then, as if on cue, the phone rang again. 'What's the bet this'll be Ben?' Doug called from the veranda. 'Rosa told him this morning that you wouldn't slow down, and he's worried.'

Suddenly she found she was shaking. Maybe Ben was right, she conceded. Maybe she was cracking up.

'It *is* Ben,' Doug called.

She walked up the steps to the kitchen. Rosa and Benjy followed. So much for privacy. They were all watching her. She turned her back on the lot of them. Rosa, Doug and Benjy were gazing at her as if she was their evening's entertainment.

She *was* cracking up.

'Hi,' she said, and took a deep breath and tried again. 'Hi.' That was better. Her voice didn't squeak this time.

'Rosa says you're running on overdrive,' Ben said.

Lily thought, Great, cut to the chase, why don't you?

'I'm fine,' she told him. 'I need to come home.'

'The island's OK without you,' he said softly, as if he understood where her head was, which was crazy for how could he know? 'Sam and Pieter and I have the medicine here under control. You're not coming home until you're well.'

'I am well.'

'You're not well. I want you to do something for me.'

'Not unless I can come home.'

He chuckled, that deep throaty chuckle that had once made her smile but now suddenly made her want to weep. 'It's not going to happen, sweetheart,' he said.

'Don't call me—'

'Lily,' he corrected himself. 'If I've figured out the time difference right, you should be just about to have dinner.'

'How did—?'

'Doug's meals are like clockwork.'

'How often do you come here?'

'We're talking about you. Not me.'

'We shouldn't be.'

'Just shut up for a minute. If you go out straight after dinner—'

'I can't.'

'Let me speak,' he said, exasperated. 'There's a track from the house to the ridge up on Blair Peak. It's a full moon here so it's a full moon there as well. We're under the same moon Lily. Remember that. Anyway, I want you to put some decent boots on and take yourself up to the peak.'

'Tonight?'

'Tonight,' he said. 'Sit up at the peak for as long as you need. Then walk straight down to the beach and wander back with your toes in the water.' She heard his smile again. 'Take your boots off first.'

'Is this some sort of order?'

'It's a medical prescription.'

'Benjy can't—'

'This is not for Benjy,' he said. 'It's for you.'

'It's dumb.'

'It's a medical prescription, Lily,' he repeated, his voice softening. 'Trust me.'

'Why should I?'

'For no reason other than I'm asking,' he said. 'Lily, do this. For you.'

'I can't.'

'Yes, you can, my love. Or, at least, you can try.'

'Don't tell me what to do.'

'OK. I'm not telling. I'm suggesting. You can be angry while you do it, but I still think you should do it.'

And the phone went dead.

She replaced the receiver on its cradle, and turned slowly to face the rest of them. They were all looking at her, expectant, waiting for news. *You can, my love...* He had no right to call her that.

But he had.

'He said I should go up to Blair Peak,' Lily said, noticing in some abstract way that her hand was no longer shaking.

'That's a fine idea,' Rosa approved. 'Wear boots.'

'That's what Ben said.'

'The snakes don't move so much at night,' Doug added. 'But you should err on the side of caution.'

'Snakes,' she whispered, and suddenly her mind was sharp again. 'Are you out of your minds?'

'Nope,' Rosa said cheerfully, dumping peas on the table and starting to pod. 'It's a tiny risk and with boots it's negligible. And so worth it. Ben's right, dear. You have to go.'

'I don't have to do anything.'

'If you want to get well, you need to go,' Doug told her. 'It's better than all the medicine in the world.'

'Go, Mama,' Benjy said. 'You want to be better.'

She stared down at her small son, confounded. 'I'm not sick.'

'No, but you want to be better,' Benjy said. 'It might stop your hands from shaking.'

'So it might,' she whispered. Just how much had her small son noticed?

'There you are, then,' Rosa said, and beamed. 'Benjy, do you want your mama to read you a bedtime story first, or do you want her to go straight after dinner?'

So she went. She hadn't the least idea why she was going, but there were four bulldozers forcing her to go, Rosa and Doug and Benjy—and Ben.

What right did Ben have to propel her to do anything? she demanded of herself, trying to be angry. Trying to be anything but deeply in love with him. But how could she be angry? He'd never been anything but honest with her. And now he'd been the means of sending her to this place, and already Benjy was looking better, the terrors of the past few days becoming something they could face down together.

Regardless, the desire to be angry was still there. The track was easy to follow in the moonlight, but it was steep. She was puffing with effort and kicking stones in front of her as she climbed. Anger was a much simpler emotion to concentrate on than anything else. Anything else was just too darned complicated.

'Just pity the snake that gets in my way,' she said out loud, and then she thought, Lucky it's not Ben who's here, the toad. Pushing her around…

It wasn't working. She tried a bit harder to justify it—and couldn't—and suddenly it was Jacques who was before her.

She'd hardly been able to think of him until now, but suddenly it was Jacques she wanted to kick.

Jacques had seemed caring and compassionate and loving. He'd wooed her for years and she'd finally let herself agree to marry him.

'And you were a criminal,' she said into the darkness. 'You rotten, deceiving toe-rag. You bottom-feeding maw worm.'

She tested out her vocabulary a bit more. That led to frustration. She didn't have the words to match her anger.

Nancy Sinatra's song came into mind, an oldy but a goody—'These Boots Are Made For Walking'. She hummed a few bars and then broke out in song, setting up a squawk in the undergrowth as night creatures were startled out of their peaceful activities.

'Sorry, guys,' she told them, but she sang some more, and suddenly she wasn't thinking about Jacques any more. She was thinking about Ben.

'Well, I don't need you either, you macho army medic.'

Anger faded. She did need Ben.

But he didn't need her.

But then she reached the top, a rocky outcrop at the height of the ridge. Here, for about twenty yards in either direction, no trees grew. She could almost see her island from here, she thought, and she found herself scanning the horizon, looking for home.

There was a rustling in the bushes at the edge of her rock ledge. She turned and a pair of tiny wallabies had broken cover, maybe for no other reason than to look at her. They gazed at her for a long moment. Finally they decided she was harmless and started to crop the mosses at the edges of the rock.

The sky was vast and endless. The moonlight shimmered

over the water. Behind her was the mountain range dividing the coast from the hinterland. It looked as if the whole world was spread out before her.

She felt tiny. Insignificant. She turned to the two wallabies, awed and wanting to share. 'Does this spot put you in your place?' she asked them. They gazed at her, not answering but taking in every detail of what was obviously a very interesting specimen.

'Yes, but a specimen of what?' she whispered.

Ben had sent her up there. 'I'm under the same moon,' he'd said. She let his words drift, and they felt OK. Her island was under the same moon she was under right now. Ben was out there somewhere, caring for her island.

The awful feeling of being bereft, without anchor, without purpose slowly melted.

'Trouble is, he's been under the same moon since the first time I met him,' she whispered. 'I can't get him out of my mind.'

Do you need to?

Maybe we can be friends, she thought, and for a moment felt so bleak that she winced.

But the night wasn't going anywhere. It seemed like she couldn't go down the ridge until she'd thought this through, and the wallabies were waiting for answers.

'He's a good man,' she told them, and they looked as if they might agree. 'He sent me up here.'

It was a bit of a one-way conversation. She needed a bit of feedback, she decided, so she turned back to conversation with herself.

You should have sorted this out seven years ago, she told herself. You know you should. You should have told Ben about Benjy. You should have taught Benjy to care for Ben, and you should have given Ben access. Other parents do that. And maybe you could have even grown to be friends.

It would be good to be Ben's friend.

You don't want to be Ben's friend.

Yes, I do, she told the night, fiercely answering her own accusation. Ben walks alone but that doesn't make him any less of a person. He's a wonderful man and he'll make a wonderful father. Just get things in perspective.

Like how?

Like telling yourself to be sensible. Like admitting you find Ben seriously gorgeous—heck, you know that already. You've had his baby. There's no harm in admitting how sexy you think he is. And if he wants to be part of Benjy's life, you'll see him lots.

That was a good thought. It was even a great thought.

And you can stop feeling guilty, too, she told herself. It wasn't that you were looking for a replacement for Ben that made you accept Jacques. If Ben hadn't been in the back of your mind you probably would have married Jacques a long time ago, and where would that have left you?

Her eyes widened at that. 'So Ben saved me from marrying Jacques,' she whispered. 'Good old Ben. Maybe I should tell him.'

She grinned. She thought about it a little longer, and it felt…OK. 'I'm giving myself my own psychotherapy here,' she told the wallabies. 'Courtesy of Ben.'

She rose, stretched and gazed out to sea. Ben was over there. Just over the horizon.

'I love him,' she told the silence. 'Now I just have to learn to like him.'

You can do that.

'Yes, I can,' she told the wallabies, and she grinned at them both and turned to take the track down the ridge. 'I might have to come up here a few times and talk to you guys again but, hey, you're cheap. Now, if you don't mind, I have a holiday to start.'

How the hell had she done all this?

Ben had told Lily he had the medical needs of the island

totally sorted—which wasn't quite true. He and Sam were both working full time and they never reached the end of the queue.

'Do you think these people have been saving their dramas for the last forty years, just waiting for us to arrive?' Sam asked a week after Lily had left. 'I thought medicine in a war zone was hard. This is ridiculous.'

'There is a financial issue,' Ben said thoughtfully. He'd talked to Gualberto at length now, and he had a clear idea of the problems Lily was facing. 'When Lily first started here there was no money for decent medical facilities. No one's looked at the broader picture since they found oil.'

'Lily won't have had time to look. She'll have been too busy to think past the next case of coral poisoning.' Sam lifted his day sheet, summarising his daily patients, and winced. 'Do you have any idea—?'

'How many times islanders cut themselves on coral and get infected? Yes,' Ben said. 'I saw six cases yesterday myself.'

'Maybe we could bomb the hell out of the coral,' Sam said morosely. 'That'd fix it.'

'There speaks a surgeon. If it hurts, chop it out.'

'You got any better ideas?'

'I have, actually,' Ben said. 'Use some of the oil money. Set up a first-rate health system, with a state-of-the-art hospital and medical bases on all outlying islands. We could advertise to medics from Australia initially but we need to organise more of the island kids into medical training. Lily was an exception—there's been none since. We need island kids thinking about medicine and ancillary services as careers. We also need a helicopter service devoted to medical needs, and staff to run it.'

'So...' Sam was regarding his friend in awe. 'A complete medical service for all the islands. This sounds serious. You're seriously thinking of setting this up?'

'Not me. But I can advise.'

'You wouldn't be tempted to stay?'

'It's not what I do.'

'You need to establish some sort of relationship with Benjy.'

'I'll see him at the farm when I leave here.'

'For a few days, on your way to the next disaster.'

'That's what I do.'

'Yeah,' Sam said, still thoughtful. 'So it is. I forgot.'

'Just as well I haven't,' Ben said, but as he walked away his friend's eyes stayed on him.

Thoughtful.

Life had slowed to a crawl. The biggest excitement was the impending arrival of Flicker's foal and after three weeks at the farm Lily was having trouble even sharing that.

She slept long and deeply, untroubled by dreams or nightmares. Benjy slept in the big bed beside her and after the first few days his dreams also seemed to disappear. He had needed this, Lily conceded. Ben had been right.

'We didn't need Jacques,' he confided to Lily, and Lily agreed.

'He wasn't a good man, Benjy.'

'I shouldn't have gone to him,' Benjy whispered. It was late at night and he was cuddled against her before sleep—a time when demons could be faced together and dispersed as unimportant.

'When Kira was killed I was really scared,' he whispered. 'I was running toward the beach and I heard shooting. Men were running up the road toward me so I ducked into the trees until they were past. Then I saw what had happened on the beach. I started running back to you but then I saw Jacques yelling at the men, really angry, and they weren't shooting at him so I came out of the trees and he said come with him.'

He snuggled even closer, trembling. 'But I shouldn't have, Mama.' He hesitated and then he added, 'Ben's nicer than Jacques.'

It wouldn't take a lot to be nicer than Jacques, Lily thought bitterly, but she made herself answer mildly. 'He is.'

'Is Ben our friend?'

'Yes.'

'Is he a better friend than Jacques?'

'He is,' Lily repeated, trying to figure what else to say. How to tell a child that Ben was much more than a friend? How to tell a child that a stranger was his father?

'He likes me better than Jacques did,' Benjy murmured.

'I went to university with Ben,' she told him. 'He's been my friend for a long time.'

'But he hasn't visited us before.'

'He's been busy, Benjy. He looks after everybody when there's trouble.'

'You look after everyone when they're in trouble.'

'No, but...' She hesitated. 'Benjy, on the island...when those men came...they were friends of Jacques and they wanted our oil. Jacques didn't know they were going to shoot anyone but they did. I think Jacques wanted to be rich. Ben doesn't want to be rich. He just wants to stop people hurting.'

'Like you.'

'A bit like me, but Ben travels all around the world. We stay on the island.'

'But you like it here,' Benjy reasoned. 'There might be lots of other places that are cool.'

'One place at a time,' she whispered, floundering.

'Doesn't Ben go to one place at a time?'

'I guess so.'

'Then he could still be our friend. We could visit him.'

'He goes to dangerous places.'

'Then he could keep visiting us,' Benjy persisted. 'We could tell him our place is dangerous and he would come then. It is dangerous.'

'It was only dangerous once. It's safe now. You know that.'

'Then he won't come and visit?'

'I don't know, sweetheart,' she said helplessly. 'Let's just wait and see.'

'She's only agreed to take four weeks off. If you leave it any longer, you won't have any time with her at all.'

'Maybe that'd be for the best,' Ben said for the tenth time or more.

'But what about Benjy? He's your kid,' Sam said, letting his exasperation show. 'Doesn't he deserve a father?'

Sam talked so much that occasionally he said something sensible. Ben had almost managed to turn off. But that comment… It hit a nerve.

Benjy deserved a father? He hadn't thought of it like that.

Until now he'd thought of this from his own point of view and from Lily's. Not from Benjy's.

'You can get by without one,' he said, trying to sound confident.

'Says you,' Sam said mockingly. 'Says the man whose parents tossed you into boarding school at five and paid people to look after you on holidays. You survived, so Benjy should, too? Is that what you think?'

'Where the hell do you get your information?'

'I'm a doctor,' Sam said smugly. 'We learn by listening in medical school. Plus I looked up your army notes. When you applied to this unit they gave you a psych test. As a medical officer I just happened to look…'

'You could get struck off for that.'

'I never look at anything that's not available from other sources if I had time to look,' Sam said virtuously. 'I'm just being time-efficient. But the psych test said you were a loner and listed your background as evidence. Hence you get the frontline work, while good old Sam, who has his Christmas with thirty or so relatives, gets to stay home till you clear up the villains.'

'So quit asking questions,' Ben growled. 'Use those sources of yours to find out what you want.'

'Med school taught me to get patient profiles from a variety of sources,' Sam said, still virtuous. 'The best source of all is the patient.'

'I'm not your patient.' His patience at an end, Ben's voice was practically a roar. They were in the staff quarters of the field hospital. The walls were canvas. There was a startled murmur from outside and Sam grinned.

'Great,' he said. 'That's started a bunch of rumours. Doctor cracks under pressure. You need a break. A nice family holiday?'

'Will you cut it out?'

'I'm playing family counsellor,' Sam said. 'It's my new role, starting now. Go make friends with your son and get yourself reattached to Lily.'

'You're single,' Ben snapped. 'Go find yourself a family.'

'Ah, but there's the rub,' Sam told him. 'You're not happily single. Me, I'm meeting ladies, shortening my list, figuring out where I fit in before I settle down. But you… You're running in fear, my friend. And I also got to know Benjy. He's a great kid and he deserves more than you're prepared to give. So I reckon you should reconsider. You're not needed here any more. You've set up the bones of the new medical service. We can do the rest. There's a chopper leaving in the morning. You should be on it.'

'Butt out.'

'Not until you're on the chopper.' Sam eyed him, consideringly. 'There's levels of brave, Lt Blayden,' Sam said softly. 'Off you go and face the next level.'

* * *

'Do you think Ben will come while you're here?' Rosa asked, and Benjy looked worried.

'We want him to come, don't we, Mama?'

'Mmm.' Lily tried to be noncommittal. They were walking back to the house, leading Flicker. The mare was growing heavier every day with the weight of her foal. She loved the lush pasture by the river but she couldn't be trusted to graze there by herself.

'Her normal paddock's on the far side of the river,' Rosa had explained. 'With the dry weather, the river's dropped and the ground on this side is marshy. If we left her be she'd end up stuck in mud.'

Lily wasn't sure if that was true, or it was an explanation designed so she and Benjy had to spend a couple of hours each morning supervising Flicker's grazing, but, contrivance or not, it was working. There was a lot to be said for supervising a pregnant mare and doing nothing else. This place was the Ben Blayden cure for post-traumatic stress.

Or the Ben Blayden heart cure?

No. His prescription hadn't worked for that.

'He's very busy,' she told Benjy. 'He's probably needed somewhere else by now.'

'There's time if you make time,' Rosa said darkly. She shook her head. 'He's so unhappy. Since he was a little boy he's been looking for a family.'

'Rosa…'

'I know.' Rosa smiled down at Benjy. 'I have big ideas for your mama and our Ben. But big ideas are not necessarily bad ideas. I just wish that he'd come.'

And two hours later he did. They were washing for lunch when they heard the helicopter, and Benjy was out of the house in a flash.

'It's got to be him,' he told Lily as she joined him on the veranda. 'It has to be.'

And it was.

CHAPTER NINE

BEN stepped out from under the rotor blades and looked across at the house. She was there.

Lily was standing on the veranda, dressed simply in shorts and a singlet top. Even from here she looked different.

And Benjy… Benjy was racing to meet him, a nugget of a kid, all arms and legs, his grin the same as Lily's, multiplied by ten.

His grin was Lily's grin before she'd taken on the worries of the world.

'Ben, Ben, Ben!' Ben was forced to drop his holdall as Benjy catapulted himself into his arms. Before he knew what was happening he was hugging his son and being hugged, and looking over the mop of curls to where Lily was smiling a welcome of her own. His gut twisted so sharply it was physical pain.

'Ben's here,' Benjy called, deeply satisfied, and wriggled in Ben's arms to face his mother.

'Really,' Lily said. 'I thought it was the milkman.'

'Silly,' Benjy said reprovingly. 'It's our Ben.'

'You never said that about Jacques.' Lily halted on the third step down from the veranda. Ben had reached the base of the steps. He needed to climb three steps to reach her but he hesitated, aware that this moment was important.

'I didn't like Jacques,' Benjy said, and buried his face in Ben's shoulder. 'He kept saying I had to be a man.'

'You're a kid,' Lily said.

'I know,' Benjy said, and peeped his mother a smile. The smile was pure mischief, Ben thought. He'd never seen Benjy like this, as free as kids were supposed to be free.

Their stay here had done them both worlds of good. He could read it in their faces.

Maybe they'd want to leave almost straight away.

Well, that was OK. He'd only dropped in to check on his way to the next mission. On his way to the next danger.

'I can ride a horse,' Benjy told him, wriggling until Ben set him on his feet. 'But not Flicker 'cos she's going to have a baby. Rosa says I can help choose a name for her foal.'

'And what about your mama?' Ben said, smiling up at Lily. 'Can she help choose?'

'Mama chose my name,' Benjy said. 'It's not fair that she chooses the horse's name, too.' He skipped up the steps to Lily. 'Why did you call me Ben's name?' he asked.

'Because…' Lily said, and faltered. She looked at Ben, in her eyes a question. Now or never, her gaze said, and he had to make an instant decision.

OK. He could do this. Maybe this wasn't the best time, but was there ever a good time for something so momentous? He nodded.

'Benjy, I've told you about Ben,' Lily said softly. 'I told you all about the good things he does and the brave doctor he is. What I should have told you, Benjy, is that Ben is your father.'

Ben's small mouth dropped open. He stared at his mother like she'd lost her mind. Then, very slowly, he turned on the steps to stare at Ben.

'You're my dad?'

'Yes,' Ben said, feeling…odd. 'I am.'

'Henri said Jacques would be my father.'

'No,' Lily said. 'Ben is.'

'You mean he gave you the tadpole that went into your egg,' Benjy demanded, and Ben almost choked, but he didn't because, funny or not, this was a really serious moment.

'That's it,' Lily said, sounding relieved.

'I knew I had to have a father somewhere,' Benjy said. He looked Ben up and down, head to toe. 'You're sure?'

'We're sure,' Ben said softly. 'We should have told you before, but I've been off adventuring and your mama didn't want to tell you by herself.'

Benjy considered that for all of ten seconds. He looked at it dispassionately—and decided it was acceptable. More than acceptable. His grin came back with a vengeance. 'Cool! Can I ring up Henri in hospital and tell him?'

'Sure,' Lily said. 'We'll ring tonight.'

'Can I tell Flicker now?'

'Of course.'

'Cool,' he said again, and breathed a great sigh of satisfaction. Then he bounced down the steps and headed horsewards to spread the news.

'I guess I've done what I came to do,' Ben managed. Benjy's departure had created a silence that was lasting too long. He didn't know how to break it and his words now sounded flippant. And sort of…final?

That was how she took it, anyway. 'You should have held the helicopter,' she said stiffly. 'Maybe if you radio fast they'll come back and collect you.'

That was so ridiculous that he didn't respond and she didn't press it.

'Tadpole, huh?' he ventured, and the tension eased a little. She managed a smile.

'Fathers are supposed to give their sons sex education. Not

mothers.' Her smile grew rueful. 'Actually, I didn't give him the tadpole bit. I suspect that was from Henri or another of his mates on the island.'

'Maybe it's time I took a hand.'

'If you have a better sex spiel than tadpoles, be my guest.'

Her agreement took him unawares. Here he was, meeting his son as his son for the first time, and Lily was handing over responsibility for sex education. It was his responsibility?

Maybe it was.

He wasn't going to be there.

'There's no need to panic,' Lily said, and he sensed a fraction of withdrawal of friendliness. 'I can do it myself.'

'I'd like to help.'

'I don't want help,' she said. 'Parenting's not about help. You either do it or you don't. You parent on your own terms.'

'That sounds ominous.'

'I read it in a book,' she confided, and suddenly she smiled again, abandoning tension. 'In truth I know nothing about the rules from here on in. You and Benjy will have to work it out for yourselves. But meanwhile Rosa and Doug will be aching to see you. They'll be trying to give us private time but just about busting a corpuscle to see you.'

'Busting a corpuscle?'

'It's a medical term,' she said wisely. 'I'm surprised you haven't heard of it. It involves mess into the middle of next week.'

He'd forgotten that. He'd forgotten Lily happy. He grinned at her; she grinned back and then she stood aside so he could come up the steps and past her into the house.

'Welcome home,' she murmured as he passed, and it was all he could do not to turn and kiss her. Maybe she would have welcomed it, he thought, but it behoved a man to act cautiously.

Nevertheless, as he passed her he was extremely glad that he hadn't asked the helicopter to wait.

* * *

They had a great dinner. Doug had pulled out all stops to create a feast. Roast beef with all the trimmings, followed by an apple pie that made Ben's eyes light up with pleasure the minute he saw it.

'I remember this pie.' He glanced at Doug and frowned. 'Hang on. When I was a kid here, you and Rosa worked outside. How did you know I loved this? How did you get the recipe?'

'Mrs Amson was the cook here then,' Doug said placidly. 'When you offered us the job I rang her and asked her for recipes.'

'For anything you liked,' Rosa said softly. 'It seemed the least we could do when you were handing us our lives back.'

Ben coloured. Lily stared across the table, fascinated. The normally in-control doctor who handled crisis after crisis with aplomb was seriously discombobulated.

'Why are you staring at Ben?' Benjy asked, her and Lily answered without thinking.

'He's discombobulated.'

Benjy thought about that for a minute and then giggled. 'That sounds like his arms and legs have come off.'

'Just his cool,' she said, and smiled across the table at Ben. 'I like to see a man discombobulated for good reason.'

'What's good reason?' Benjy asked, still intrigued.

'Because he does good things for people,' Rosa said, rising and starting to clear away. 'Except no one's supposed to thank him. He doesn't like people hugging him, our Ben, so all we can do is make him apple pie.'

'We could hug him,' Benjy said.

'So we could,' Lily agreed. 'He's been very good to us, our Ben.'

'He is our Ben,' Benjy agreed. He turned to Doug. 'He's my dad.'

'I thought that must be it,' Doug said gravely. 'And dads should be hugged.'

'I don't know whether he wants to be hugged.'

'You'll have to ask him.'

'Ask me tomorrow,' Ben said, getting up from the table in such a hurry that his chair crashed to the floor behind him. 'I need to take a walk.'

'We can come with you,' Benjy offered. 'Do you want to meet Flicker?'

'Tomorrow,' Ben said, backing out the door as if propelled. 'For now I need some space to myself.'

'He always needs space to himself.' Rosa and Lily were washing up. Benjy had asked Doug if he could do bedtime reading duty and Ben was nowhere to be seen. 'It'll take an indomitable lady to break down those barriers.'

'I'm not sure I'm that lady,' Lily said. She hesitated but by now she was sure Rosa had figured out everything there was to know about her, and she surely knew Ben as well. 'I'm not sure there'll ever be a lady for Ben.'

'He's looking like a man in love tonight.'

'He's looking like a man who's afraid.'

'If he asked you to marry him…'

'He won't,' Lily whispered. 'And even if he did, I can't leave the island.'

'Can't you?' Rosa dried her hands on the dishcloth and turned to face her. 'Is there really no one who could take your job?'

'There's no money to pay anyone.'

'Of course there is,' she said briskly. 'Doug and I have been reading the newspapers. Kapua has as much oil wealth as it wants. They can easily pay medical staff enough to encourage them to come. It's not like Kapua's a desert either. It sounds lovely.'

'It is lovely,' Lily whispered. 'It's home.'

'Home's where the heart is,' Rosa retorted. 'Look at me. I've been following Doug for years, working where he's needed to be.'

'But that's different.'

'Why is it different?'

'Because Ben wouldn't want us where he is. Nothing's changed since medical school. Like leaving the table now. The conversation was too close to the bone. He's cultivated armour and no one's getting through.'

'You love him,' Rosa said gently, and Lily nodded.

'I always have.'

'Then…'

'Then nothing,' she said. 'His armour's thirty years deep. No one's getting through. We'll stay in touch now for Benjy's sake, but we won't do more than that. And me? I have to rebuild some armour of my own.'

Which was why she should be in bed. Which was why she should be anywhere but where she was at midnight, which was sitting on the back veranda, waiting for Ben to come home.

He did come home, walking steadily across the paddocks in the moonlight. He was still wearing the army camouflages he'd been wearing when he'd arrived. Maybe he had no casual clothes here, she thought. These must be the only clothes he took with him as he travelled the world.

Or maybe there was a reason he still wore them. This was army camouflage, a reminder that he was still on duty somehow. A reminder that his armour had to stay.

He didn't see her as he strode up through the garden to the veranda. She was sitting on an ancient settee to one side of the front door.

'Have you been up to the peak?' she asked gently as he reached the top of the stairs, and he froze. There was a moment's stillness while he collected his thoughts. When he turned to her he was smiling but she wasn't sure the smile was real.

'You guessed.'

'It's a great place,' she told him. 'It made me stop.'

'Stop?'

'Let go,' she said gently. 'I spent the first few days here doing what I normally do—trying to cram in as much as I possibly could. Blair's Peak sort of took that out of me. I've slowed down so much now that I'm practically going backwards.'

'I'm glad. It's what you needed.'

'How about you?' she asked. 'Has it slowed you down?'

'Unlike you, I don't need to be slowed down. I'm not a workaholic.'

'Sam said you're an adrenalin junkie. Which is just as bad as me.'

'Sam doesn't know what he's talking about.'

'He's your friend.'

'I don't have friends.'

There was a silence at that. It stretched out into the night sky. Permeating everything.

'We were friends,' she said at last.

'And now I find you've borne me a son without telling me. So much for friendship.'

'You think it might have been something more, then?' she demanded. He was standing before her, dressed for battle, and that was suddenly how she was feeling. Like she was geared up for battle as well. She hesitated, but the look on his face said he wasn't even going to consider their relationship. OK, then, try another track. 'Do you love Rosa and Doug?' she asked, and his brows snapped down in confusion.

'What sort of question is that?'

'Just answer it. Do you?'

'As much as I love anyone.'

'That's what I thought. Do you know Doug has angina? Or worse. Rosa's terrified but she can't persuade him to go near a doctor.'

'Why didn't she say?'

'How can she say anything when your visits are so rare they make special dinners? They'd never dream of interrupting one of your visits with medical necessity.'

'That's crazy.'

'It is,' she retorted. 'It's because they love you.'

'Hell, Lily…'

'I'm tired,' she said, pushing herself to her feet. 'I wanted you to know about Doug, so if you leave tomorrow you'll at least know there's trouble here. He won't take advice from me. It sounds like angina but it could be more serious. I can't tell that unless I examine him and how can I?'

'I'll talk to him.'

'Which will solve the problem this time. But after that?'

'Hell, Lily, I'm not responsible for these people.'

'Then you should be,' she snapped. 'They love you. Just like…' She caught herself, drawing herself back, closing her mouth with a gasp. 'No. That's it. Leave it.'

'Lily—'

'Leave it!'

'Fine,' he said cautiously, and she made to push past him to go indoors. But his hand caught her shoulder and he turned her so she was facing him.

'Lily, you don't need to go back to the island.'

'Of course I need to go back to the island.'

'You don't,' he said heavily. 'Sam and I have worked it through with Gualberto. We've set up an embryonic medical service that should be up and running within weeks.'

'An embryonic medical service…'

'Gualberto's agreed,' he told her, eager to move to a neutral, impersonal topic. 'It's time for the island to stop sitting on all its resources. We had a massive meeting last week. The consensus is that they'll not exploit their oil for individual wealth but they'll spend real money on education and medicine. Which is where you come in.'

'I come in where?'

'Everyone knows you're overworked. The plan is to get at least two fully trained doctors plus interns working on the island—but that's just for starters. We see a medical service that eventually serves all outlying islands, with you or someone like you as administrator, but with every specialty represented. We see a much bigger hospital. You need connections to Australian teaching schools so Kapua can become part of their remote training roster for young doctors. You need a helicopter service for outlying islands, and the oil money is more than enough to fund it for generations to come. It'll be huge, Lily.'

She stared at him, dumbfounded, and ran her tongue over lips that were suddenly dry. 'You've set all this up already.'

'Yes. Gualberto—'

'Gualberto never thought of this by himself.'

'No. Sam and I—'

'Have been on the island for little more than a month,' she said blankly. 'What do you know about what we need?'

'We know what you need. Lily, this leaves you free to spend time away from the island.'

'Why would I spend time away from the island?'

'You could spend time with me,' he said, suddenly uncertain. 'Maybe we could spend a couple of weeks here a year. While I get to know Benjy.'

'You'll be a father two weeks a year?'

'I can hardly do more.'

'No,' she said bleakly. 'Of course you can't.'

'Lily, I don't do family.'

'Why the hell not?'

'I told you—'

'So many years ago. When we were kids. I'd hoped you'd change by now.'

He stared at her in the moonlight. 'What more do want of me, Lily?' he asked. 'You tell me.'

'I don't know,' she said wearily. 'But I'm scared. Benjy knows you're his dad, so now there's two of us. Two of us spending months of every year not knowing where you are. What you're doing. If Benjy get as attached to you as I am, how can I put him through that?'

'You're attached…'

'Of course I'm attached.' She sighed, 'You know I am. I tried so hard to fall in love with Jacques—with anyone—but all I ever wanted was you. You've been in my heart every minute since the day I met you. But I'm not letting you destroy my life. I'm not letting you mess with Benjy's life. Come here two weeks every year and fall in love with you all over again… How can I do that and survive?'

'Lily, it's what I am. It's non-negotiable. I didn't ask to be Benjy's father.'

'But that's non-negotiable, too.' She gulped for breath and regrouped. 'I didn't ask to be Benjy's mother, but I am. I didn't ask to fall in love with you, but I did. Ben, you've spent your entire life finding yourself a place where you didn't have to get attached. You swing into a crisis situation, save lives, do good but you never visit them again. You never need to hear feedback from patients two years after the event. You don't need to attach yourself to a community in any shape or form. Sam says you even hold yourself aloof from the crisis response team.'

'I can't help what I am.'

'No, and neither can I,' she said. 'But seeing you for two weeks every year… It'd destroy me, Ben. So somehow you need to work out a relationship with Benjy that doesn't include me, and don't ask me how you can do that because I don't know.

I'll support whatever you want but I can't continue to be near you. I just…can't.'

'Lily…'

'What?' She sighed again and looked up into his face. Which was a mistake.

Because, regardless of anything else, this was Ben. Her Ben. The Ben she'd carried in her heart for all these years.

He wasn't hers. She'd known that then and she knew it now. The scars of his childhood were too deeply etched. There was no place she could reach him.

'I'm sorry, Ben,' she whispered, and she reached up and touched his lips fleetingly with hers.

Which was a further mistake.

She backed away but as she did so she saw his eyes widen, flare.

'Lily,' he said, and it was the way he'd always said it. Like it was a caress.

'Lily.' It was a plea.

She didn't move. She didn't move and she didn't see him move, but she had or he had or whatever, and suddenly she was being held tightly in his arms, crushed against his chest, kissed and kissed some more.

This was dumb. This was crazy, letting herself be kissed in the moonlight, letting herself be kissed as she'd been kissed all those years ago.

For it was the same, exactly as she remembered. It was a searing, molten kiss that felt like two forces were being hauled together and fused into one. It was a white-hot heat that made her heart twist with longing and desire and love.

Ben.

She couldn't pull away. Where was the strength for that? Nowhere.

How could she ever have thought she could love Jacques? She'd tried so hard and she'd failed and she knew it was no character flaw in Jacques that had prevented it—though, heaven knew, it should have been. It was because she considered herself irrevocably married to this man.

Her heart.

But here was no happy ending. Ben had been raised to never give his heart. How could such a man change? How could such a man admit a need?

He couldn't, but she did. Oh, she did, she thought as her body melted into his. She kissed him back with a fierceness that matched his own. She loved him with every fibre of her being, willing him to soften, willing him to love her as she loved him.

His hands were tugging her against him. He felt wonderful—a big man, superbly muscled, strengthened by years of military training, moving from emergency to emergency, running…

He was still running, she thought in that tiny fragment of her mind that was available for such thought—which wasn't much, admittedly, but it was enough to tinge this kiss with sadness, to tinge it with the inevitability of parting.

He was so right for her. She was so right for him. Her breasts moulded against his chest as if she was somehow meant to be there. They'd been made in one cast and then split somehow, and now, for this tiny fragment of time, the two halves of the whole had come together.

There had to be a way. There had to.

The kiss extended for as long as a kiss could without moving to the next step—the seemingly inevitable step for a man and a woman who'd loved before and who'd been apart for seven long years. She couldn't take that step, she thought. She mustn't. There was no such thing as a one hundred per cent effective birth control and to take another pregnancy back to the island…

'No,' she managed as he drew back a little, and she saw a trace of confusion cross his face.

'No?'

Heaven knew where she found the strength to say it, but it had to be said. 'No further, Ben. We can't.'

'But—'

'I don't want another child.' But that was a lie, she thought. She'd love another child. Another piece of Ben to carry forward into her life without him.

'Hey, we're not about to…'

'We might have been about to,' she whispered. 'But we can't.'

'That doesn't make sense.'

'I think it does,' she said, and pulled further away. Just a little. Just as much as she could bear to. 'Ben, I love you.'

'Maybe I do—'

'Don't say it,' she said, suddenly urgent. 'Because you don't. You never have. You just love the part of me that you're prepared to accept.'

'What does that mean?' He seemed genuinely baffled and she shook her head. Nothing had changed, she thought bitterly. This was the same problem they'd had seven years ago. Oh, maybe it had been clearer then. The islanders had paid for her medical training and there was no way she could refuse to return. But there were two reasons she couldn't be near with Ben. One was her obligation to her island home. And the other was that Ben didn't want her.

Ben didn't want her.

'Maybe we could work something out,' he said, his voice husky with passion and desire. 'Lily, OK, I don't do family, but maybe… What I feel for you… There'll never be another woman I feel this way about. So maybe we could do something. Marriage or something. Maybe I could come to the island whenever I'm on leave.'

She stared at him, stunned. 'You're talking marriage?'

'I don't know.' He ran his fingers through his hair in a gesture of pure bewilderment. 'But we have to do something—to make this work.'

'For Benjy?'

'How can I be a father to him if you're not there? And if we were married, would that make you feel better about me being there—sometimes?'

'You're asking me to marry you because of Benjy?'

'I want you, too, Lily.'

'Two weeks a year?'

'However long I can spare. I'll try—'

'You can't just…try.'

But then she looked into his eyes and saw his confusion and she felt her heart twist. He was trying. He was trying so hard…

This was her Ben. If she said yes he'd sweep her into bed right now, she thought, and that was what she wanted more than anything else in the world. All she had to do was say yes and he'd marry her and Benjy would have a father and then…

And then he'd leave for the next crisis.

'Would you think of us while you were away?' she asked, and the look of surprise she saw in his eyes answered her question before he spoke.

'Of course I would,' he said, but she didn't believe him.

'Did you remember I was on Kapua?'

'Yes.'

'Sam said you didn't.'

'Sam—'

'Sam talks too much,' she whispered. 'But he answered my questions. He knows you well, Sam. And so do Doug and Rosa. They say you never stay long enough anywhere to be involved. You run like you're terrified of what happens if you lose your heart.'

'Psychoanalysis by Rosa and Doug.'

'And by Sam and by Lily,' she whispered. 'What did they do to you, those parents of yours, to make you so fearful?' She hesitated. 'Ben, what happened to Bethany?'

'Bethany…'

'Your sister. All the time we spent together, you never told me you had a sister.'

'She died when I was six. It's old news.'

'Did you love her?'

'Hell, Lily, I was tiny.'

'Did you love her?'

'That is none of your business. And it's nothing to do with what I am now. I'm a grown man.'

'Yes, you are.' She took a deep breath. 'And I'm a grown woman. A woman who thought about you every day that we were apart. Who'd die a little if you died. And who feels sick that you lost someone you loved and you won't talk about it. But you won't. You've closed off. God knows if it's because of your sister. I don't. You won't let me near enough to find out. But, Ben, if any of us went missing…Doug or Rosa or me or Benjy or Sam or anyone else who cares for you…would you miss us?'

'Of course.'

'Be truthful, Ben.'

He paused. She stepped back a little. The veranda light was on and she could see his face clearly. What she saw there answered her question without him finding the words.

'You'll never let yourself get that close,' she whispered. 'Will you?'

'Lily, I'm saying I think I love you.' He sounded exasperated rather than passionate, she thought. He sounded… confused? 'I'm offering marriage.'

She shook her head. 'How can you say you think you love me? Don't you know?'

'How can I know?'

'I'll tell you,' she said, anger coming to her aid. 'Love's great, but it's opening yourself again to that chasm of loss. It's lots else besides, but it's definitely not putting a signature on a piece of paper and a deal to spend a few days each year together.'

'I can't—'

'Of course you can't,' she said, anger fading and a bleak acceptance taking its place. 'Of course you can't. I should never have agreed to come here. I'm putting more pressure on you than you can bear. Even by telling you that Benjy is your son…'

'You should have.'

'If I had, maybe the pressure would have been on you for the last seven years and maybe you would have fallen properly in love. Or maybe you would have cracked under the strain. I don't know. But I do know that I need to back off now. I need to let you be.

'I'm going to bed now, Ben,' she said, and somehow she kept her voice resolute. 'I'm going to bed alone and I'll stay that way. Because no marriage at all is better than the one you're offering. I have to stay sane, for Benjy's sake if not my own.'

'Lily—'

'If I were you, I'd take another walk up to Blair Peak,' she told him. 'I think you need it more than I do. Oh, and, Ben…'

'Yes?' It was a clipped response. He was angry, she thought, and she knew it was confusion that was causing the anger. He thought he was doing the right thing—the noble thing. And she was rejecting that absolutely.

How hurtful was that?

Practicalities. When in doubt, talk medicine.

'Ben, Rosa's really worried about Doug,' she told him, and somehow her voice was steady. And it worked. She'd deflected him, she thought, seeing the relief in his eyes. Medicine was the great escape. 'Don't worry about me,' she said. 'Don't worry about Benjy. We'll be fine. Worry instead about Doug, who isn't fine.'

She saw the confusion fade still more. She saw him clutch at medical need as if he was clutching a lifeline.

'How long has he had pain?'

'Rosa says for months, but he's admitting little and he won't see a doctor. Rosa says he's been waiting for you.'

'For me?' he demanded, startled. 'Why the hell? I'm not his doctor.'

'No,' she said softly. 'There's an attachment there that I don't think you're admitting either.' She hesitated. 'Rosa's scared it's worse than Doug's letting on. She thinks Doug might want to talk to you about caring for Rosa if…'

'He'd know I would.'

'You would what?'

'Look after Rosa. But I need to find out what's wrong.'

'You'll look after Rosa how? If anything happened to Doug, she could hardly stay here.'

'This is a dumb conversation. Nothing's happening to Doug.'

'He's showing every sign of worrying himself into a coronary. Sure, he needs an examination and maybe treatment but the best thing you could do is what you're incapable of doing.'

'Which is?'

'Giving yourself,' she whispered. 'Telling Rosa you'll be here for her.'

'I'll look after her.'

'The same way you'd be husband and father to us? No,' she said sadly. 'That's no use to anyone. Oh, Ben.'

And she turned before he could say another word. She walked into the house and let the screen door slam behind her.

He did indeed walk up to Blair's Peak but the answers weren't there. She was asking too much of him, he told the night, but he knew that was a falsehood.

He was afraid.

She'd accused him of not loving. Of not throwing his heart into the ring and letting fate take a hand.

She was right.

Why?

He needed a shrink, he decided, but he sat up on the peak and he knew the answers were already his.

For the first time in more than twenty years he let himself think about Bethany.

At six he'd been sent to boarding school. Lots of kids were sent to boarding school at six. They survived, and he'd hardly seen anything of his parents anyway. He could hardly say he'd missed them.

But there'd been his kid sister. Bethany had been four years old to his six. His little sister. Even now the memories of her were warm and strong. With an assortment of nursery staff caring for them, Bethany had been his constant.

She'd suffered from asthma.

He still remembered the terror of her attacks. The feeling of helplessness as she'd gasped for breath. His six-year-old self telling untrained nursery staff what to do.

And then his father leaving him at boarding school. 'Who'll look after Bethany?' he'd demanded, and he could remember his desperation, the fear.

'She'll be looked after,' his father had said brusquely. 'You look after yourself.'

There had been nothing else to do. He'd looked after himself but Bethany had died before the year had ended. The school matron had told him of her death, her face crumpling with sympathy, moving to hug him, but he'd wanted none of it.

His parents hadn't come near him.

He looked after himself.

Any shrink in the world would tell him that was holding him back now. He knew it himself. But to break through…

He couldn't. He just…couldn't.

Even Blair Peak had no answers.

CHAPTER TEN

BREAKFAST the next morning was a strained affair. Once again Doug had gone to enormous trouble, frying home-cured bacon, making pancakes, setting the big kitchen table with fine china, old and fragile. Lily looked across at Doug's strained face. It was better than looking at the silent Ben, she thought, and there was enough tension on Doug's face to make her concerned. Why had he used the best china? The kitchen was equipped with a dishwasher but china like this would have to be hand-washed.

She concentrated on this small domestic problem rather than let herself think about Ben. Ben was eating silently, while Benjy was watching him with a certain degree of speculation. The knowledge that Ben was his father was clearly of immense importance to Benjy, and he was cautiously reassessing the man before him for parental qualities.

All in all, it didn't make for a casual breakfast.

Think about Doug, she told herself. Doug's eyes were as strained as Lily felt, and she wondered just how bad his chest pain was.

'Rosa and Benjy could take Flicker down to the river this morning,' she suggested. 'Ben and I will do the washing-up. You need to take a rest, Doug,' she told him with a sideways warning glance to Ben. 'You look as tired as I felt three weeks ago.'

But the elderly man was having none of it. 'Don't be daft, girl,' he said. 'You've lots of catching up to do, and if I know Ben he'll be flying out of here before we know it.'

'No, he won't,' Lily started, but then she looked uncertainly at Ben. 'Will you?'

'The chopper's not coming back till tomorrow,' Ben said. 'But if I need to, I can delay it.'

'That's what you call plenty of time,' Doug said derisively. 'To get to know your son. If that's all the time you have, there's no way I'm taking up any of it.'

'Doug, I'm really worried about your chest pain,' Lily said bluntly. If he really was hiding pain…

'I'm having no more pain now than I've been having for months. I read about it on the internet. It'll be angina. My mother had it for years and she died when she was ninety seven.' He managed a shaky grin. 'She was hit by a bus then, so that leaves me twenty odd years of angina before I meet my bus.'

'If it is angina,' Ben growled. 'We don't know. You need to be examined.'

'You can listen to my chest this afternoon,' Doug said, so much like he was conferring a benevolent favour that they all laughed. But even so… Lily's eyes met Ben's and she saw her concern reflected there.

Ben really did care, she thought. He tried desperately not to, but he couldn't hide it completely. Just as Doug couldn't hide the fact that he hurt.

Rosa rose and started clearing away plates, looking relieved. 'This afternoon you'll be examined, then,' she told Doug. 'You've agreed before witnesses so there's no wriggling out of it now. Meanwhile, I'll do the housework while Ben and Benjy and Lily take Flicker to the river. You rest. That's my final word, Doug, so no arguments.'

Doug opened his mouth to argue—but then thought better

of it and gave a sheepish grin. 'I can almost understand your reluctance to tie the knot,' he told Ben. 'See what you let yourself in for? Women!' He flung up his hands in surrender. 'Fine. I'll have an idle morning, as long as you three spend the morning together. Promise?'

'We promise,' Lily said. 'Don't we, Ben?'

'I'd rather examine you now,' Ben said, but Doug shook his head.

'That's an excuse not to spend time with Lily and Benjy, and you know it. I've had this discomfort for months and it's going nowhere. Stop your fussing and enjoy the day.'

So Ben, Lily and Benjy led the pregnant mare to the river. The day was fabulous, but Lily wasn't concentrating on the day. How could she ever break through this man's barriers? she wondered. And why wouldn't he talk about his sister? His silence hurt, but if it hurt her, how much more would it be hurting him?

'He's never talked about Bethany,' Rosa had told her. 'So I don't see how you can make him start now.'

They walked slowly. The mare was so heavy with foal that Ben was concerned. 'Are we sure we should be taking her out of the home paddock?'

'Rosa says a bit of exercise does her good,' Benjy told him. 'And she says the grass by the river is horse caviar.' He thought about that and frowned. 'I don't know what caviar is.'

'Fish eggs,' Ben told him, and Benjy wrinkled his nose in disbelief.

'So the grass tastes like fish eggs?'

'There's no accounting for taste,' Ben told him, and grinned. Benjy was leading the mare, with Ben by his side. Lily was walking behind, watching her son. And his father. The likeness was uncanny, she thought. The sun was glinting on two dark heads. Ben had only brought a small holdall with him, but he must leave clothes here for he'd finally ditched his uniform. This morning he was wearing chinos and an open-necked shirt with the sleeves rolled up. He looked wonderful, Lily thought, and the longing she had for him, the longing that had stayed with her for all those years, surged right back, as strong as ever.

She blinked back tears. She was right, she told herself fiercely. She couldn't marry this man. She couldn't break down the barriers. By herself she could block out this pain, but with the marriage he was suggesting it would stay with her all the time. She and Benjy would have a few short days with him, but then he'd be off, over and over, intent on his life of drama. Putting her and Benjy out of his mind. Not letting himself need…

There was the crux of the problem, she thought. She needed Ben, but he didn't need her. And he surely didn't need Benjy. He'd taught himself fiercely not to need, and who could blame him?

'Why do you like fighting?' Benjy asked him now, and she stilled and listened. They were trudging slowly toward the river, keeping pace with Flicker's slow amble. Ben and Benjy were at Flicker's head and Lily was behind, but Ben may as well have been talking to her.

'I don't like fighting,' he said. 'But when fighting happens, people are often wounded. That's what happened on your island. My job is to fix people after fighting. Or sometimes I go to where other bad things have happened, like tsunamis and earthquakes.'

'My mama fixes people,' Benjy said, following a line of reasoning yet to be disclosed.

'She does.'

'Are your people hurt worse than Mama's people?'

'I guess not. It depends.'

'And do you get to see the people when they're better? Mama says that's the best thing about doctoring. She sees people when they're sick and then one day when they're better they come to our house and sit on our porch and tell Mama how better they're feeling. Or the ladies come and show us their babies. Sometimes Mama even cries when she hugs the babies. Do you cry when you hug babies?'

'That's not what I do.'

'I guess mamas wouldn't come close to you with babies when you're wearing your scary uniform.'

'Maybe they wouldn't.' Ben sounded strained to breaking point, Lily thought. He wasn't enjoying this one bit. If the helicopter landed right now, would he climb aboard?

'I like you better without your uniform,' Benjy told him, giving a little skip of contentment, as if his line of questioning had achieved the results he'd wanted. 'But I need a picture of you in your uniform. Henri will think it's cool, but it's better like you are now. You're more like a real dad now.'

'Thanks.'

'Can you kick a football?'

'Yes.'

'Can you swim?'

'Yes.'

'Will you swim a race with me at the river?'

'I didn't bring my gear.'

'You can swim in your boxers,' Benjy told him. 'I swim in my boxers.' Then a thought occurred to him. 'Doug wears flappy white jocks that make me giggle when Rosa hangs them on the clothesline. But Henri's dad wears boxers. You don't wear flappy white things, do you?'

'Um…no.'

'Ace,' Benjy said, satisfied. 'Mama can hold Flicker and we'll go swimming.'

'Doesn't your mama go swimming?'

'Someone has to look after Flicker. She's the mama.'

'That's not very fair.'

'I'm happy to watch,' Lily volunteered from behind them. 'After all, Benjy can go swimming with his mama every day. How often can he go swimming with his dad?'

So she sat on the grassy bank, watching her son and his father swim, while Flicker grazed contentedly beside her.

Benjy swam like a little fish. Island kids practically swam before they could walk and Lily took it as a given, but she saw now that Ben was astounded by his small son's skill. This was no splashing-in-the-shallows swim. This was an exercise in Benjy showing his dad exactly what sort of kid he had. He weaved and ducked around Ben's legs, surfacing when least expected, doing handstands so his small feet were all that was seen above the water, challenging Ben to a race…

But Ben was a fine swimmer, too. They raced from one tree fallen by the river bank to another three hundred yards upstream. Lily watched as Ben started to race. She saw him check his pace and she knew he was holding back so Benjy could win.

She grinned—and she saw the exact moment when Ben realised Benjy had been checking his pace as well, but only so he could put on a burst of speed at the end. Benjy's small body surged ahead and suddenly Ben was left behind. His raw strength wasn't enough to compensate for the lead he'd given Benjy. Benjy surfaced, glowing, laughing at Ben and then calling triumphantly to his mother.

'He thought he had to give me a head start,' he yelled to Lily. 'So I won.'

'More fool him. Race again,' Lily decreed, so they did. This time Ben didn't hold back. He used all his strength and all his skill—and he only just won.

'You beat me,' Benjy said, growing happier by the minute. 'Mama can't beat me. A daddy should be able to beat his kid.'

'Then stop getting better,' Ben growled, but, watching him, Lily saw his sudden flash of pride.

And then shock.

Up until then fatherhood had been some sort of abstract concept, she thought. Sure, he'd been shocked to learn of Benjy's existence and then he'd been concerned about him, but this was something else. This child was his son—this little boy who had so much life ahead of him, who had so much potential to be proud of. Swimming was one tiny thing but there'd be so much more as he grew. Little and big. Lily watched as myriad emotions washed across Ben's face and she wondered how he was going to handle this.

She thought how she'd felt as Kira had handed over her newborn son to her six years ago, and she saw those same emotions reflected now on Ben's face.

'Now we can make sand bombs,' Benjy announced. 'Can you make sand bombs? Don't worry if you can't 'cos I'll teach you.'

It was a day of wonders. Benjy had a father, a father he could be proud of, and he intended to milk it for all it was worth.

'If you're leaving tomorrow, we have to hurry up,' he told Ben. 'I can teach you to fish. I'm a really good fisherman. Can you teach me to shoot with guns?'

That was a discordant note, but it didn't spoil the day.

'I'm a doctor, mate,' Ben told his son. 'I might wear army fatigues but I don't shoot.'

'You'd shoot if you had to?'

'I won't have to.'

Benjy thought about that and found it was acceptable. 'OK then. Can you ride a horse?'

The only bad part of the day was the discussion that went on after Ben examined Doug. Doug managed to hold Ben off until late afternoon, but finally Ben told him if he didn't submit then he, Rosa, Lily and Benjy would subdue him by force. Doug didn't smile, which was a measure of how frightened he really was, Lily thought, and when Ben came out of the bedroom after the examination his face confirmed those fears.

'Hell, Rosa, how long has he had this level of pain?'

'I don't know.' Rosa bit her lip, looking suddenly old. 'Six months that he's admitted to me. Maybe longer. He only admitted it to me when I found him in the kitchen one night looking grey and sick. He said it was indigestion but I didn't believe him.'

'But you didn't insist he see a doctor.'

Rosa swallowed. 'Maybe I was afraid to,' she whispered. 'My dad died of a heart attack. To admit Doug has a bad heart… I just kept hoping you'd come home.'

They thought of Ben almost as their son, Lily thought. There was such a depth of emotion in Rosa's voice. *I just kept hoping you'd come home.*

And Ben heard it. She watched his face and there were was an echo there of the emotions he'd felt that morning. He had a son, and now he had something akin to parents.

And a wife?

He couldn't accept any of those things. She saw the tiny flare of panic behind his eyes and she thought there was no way he'd take this further. Parents, son, wife? The whole domestic catastrophe?

No.

'There's definite arrhythmia,' he told Rosa, and Lily knew that once again he was seeking some sort of refuge in medicine. His voice was brusque and strained. 'There's something badly wrong. His blood pressure's high as well. I'm guessing he's had some sort of infarct—a heart attack. Maybe that's what it was the night you said he was in such pain. He's telling me the pain's not so bad now, but he's still uncomfortable, which means the pain before must have been awful.'

'Dear God,' Rosa whispered, colour draining from her face. She clutched at Lily. 'You think…'

'Ben's not saying he's going to die,' Lily told her, guiding her into a chair by the stove. Benjy had gone to his bedroom to sort story books he wanted Ben to read to him that night, and she thanked God for it. The sight of Rosa's face would have terrified him.

'Rosa, how old was your dad when he died?' Ben asked softly, and Lily nodded, silently agreeing with his line of questioning. Let's get to the heart of the terror here.

'Fifty-three,' Rosa whispered. 'Almost twenty years younger than Doug is now. He had pain, just like Doug, and there wasn't anything we could do about it. One day his heart stopped, just like that. So I thought…when Doug started getting the pain…well, what can doctors do? That's why I didn't insist. He's better staying here for whatever time he has left.'

'There's lots doctors can do,' Ben told her, and Lily thought he really was a good doctor. Tensions forgotten, he was facing down terror with confidence and reassurance. 'You must have heard of bypass surgery.'

'Yes, but—'

'No buts,' Ben told her. 'I'm listening to Doug's heart and I'm hearing a heart under strain. I'm not a specialist and it'll take tests to find out exactly what's wrong, but I'm suspecting he has minor blockages. One or more of the blood vessels running to or from the heart have probably narrowed, to the point where the blood supply is compromised. Forty years ago there was nothing we could do. Now bypass surgery is so common it's done routinely in every major hospital. Lily will concur.'

'I concur,' Lily murmured.

'So all we need to do is get Doug to one of those hospitals.'

'He'll never agree.'

'He has agreed,' Ben said. Then he added ruefully, 'Though not as soon as I'd like.'

'How soon would you like?'

'Now,' Ben said promptly. 'With pain like his, he's a walking time bomb. But he's refusing to leave until I leave.'

'But you're not leaving until…'

'Tomorrow,' Ben said. 'There's a Medivac helicopter in the area tomorrow. It was tentatively due to collect me, but I'll radio them to pick us both up.'

And that will be that, Lily thought. He'd found an excuse to run.

'You shouldn't go yet,' Rosa whispered.

'I need to go. I was only intending to stay for a couple of days and I need to accompany Doug.'

Of course you do, Lily thought bitterly. The medical imperative.

'Can I come, too?' Rosa asked, and then she bit her lip. 'But I can't leave the farm. Flicker…'

'I'll organise for someone to fly in and take over,' Ben told her. 'It'll be twenty-four hours at most. Then we'll fly you out to join Doug.'

'It'll need to be someone who's good with horses.' Rosa was clearly torn. 'Flicker's due within the next week.'

'It'll be someone who's good with horses,' Ben assured her. 'You know I inherited three farms from my parents. I still keep them as working farms and I have excellent staff on each. I'll transfer someone here as soon as I can. When Doug's recovered we'll bring him back, and I'll leave someone here to help as long as you need.'

'Thank you,' Rosa whispered, her eyes suddenly brimming with tears. 'I think… Can I go and see Doug now?'

'Of course,' Ben told her. 'But he stays in bed and rests until we leave. If he doesn't then I call in a Medivac team right now.'

'That's fine by me,' Rosa whispered, and fled.

Which left the two of them, facing off over the kitchen table.

She should shut up, Lily thought dully. She should say nothing. There was nothing to be gained by conflict.

But she was going to have to tell Benjy that Ben was definitely leaving. The thought of his disappointment made her cringe.

'So there's no doctor on the Medivac chopper?'

'Sorry?'

'You know very well what I mean. I assume the chopper will be bringing someone back to this district from the city. Is that what you meant when you said it'd be in the area tomorrow?'

'Yes.'

'Since when has the Medivac service carried patients without a medical team?'

'I didn't ask.'

'You didn't ask whether there'd be a doctor on board?' She raised her brows in disbelief. 'Maybe we can ask now.'

'Doug wants me to go with him. He's terrified.'

'And so are you.'

'What are you talking about?'

'You're falling in love with your son,' she said softly. 'For you that's even more terrifying than falling in love with me. So you're running. The trouble is… I'll back off. I'm not sure Benjy will.'

'He'll be back on your island and I won't see him.'

It was a gut response. He said it and then realised what he'd said. It was an acknowledgement of fear. An acknowledgement that he was putting as much distance as possible between himself and his embryonic family.

'Coward,' Lily whispered.

'I'm not a coward.'

'Rosa told me about Bethany. How many years have I known you, Ben, yet you never told me about your sister? You've been running since then?'

'Rosa had no right. And I'm not running.'

'You know you are.'

'It's you who's refusing to marry me.'

'That's a joke. You don't know what marriage is. It's surely not waiting for you to drop in for a few days each year.'

'Lily—'

'Leave it,' she said dully. 'But don't pretend to be hurt because I won't marry you. You're not asking me to marry you. You don't know what the word means.'

They ate a desultory dinner—steak, cooked by Lily and not even close to the wonderful food Doug had prepared—and then Lily and Benjy went for a walk to say goodnight to Flicker, Rosa went to sit with Doug and Ben was left to his own devices.

He'd expected to spend that evening with Benjy. He'd thought maybe they could do something together—some sort of bonding thing, he thought, like taking a cricket bat and hitting a few balls. He only had tonight. He should be angry that Benjy had elected to go with his mother and talk to a horse rather than spend time with him.

But Benjy had watched him over the dining table and had made his own decision. Benjy had lost Kira only a few weeks ago. That pain would be still be raw. Maybe he wasn't going to put himself in the position where it hurt again.

Or maybe it already hurt. Ben had been there when Lily had told Benjy that Ben would be leaving in the morning. He'd seen his face shut down.

He knew that look. He'd perfected it himself.

So…

So stay, he told himself as he walked out onto the veranda. In front of the house was the home paddock. Benjy and Lily would be there with Flicker. He could join them.

But his feet turned the other way. He walked down to the beach, found a likely looking sand-hill and sat and watched the moon over the water.

Out there was Kapua. Home to Lily and Benjy.

He could get there twice a year, he thought, or maybe even more if he made the visits brief. Whenever he had a decent leave, he could spend a few days with Benjy.

But he had a night free now and Benjy had elected to go with his mother. As Lily had elected to stay with Benjy.

'We're all protecting ourselves,' he told the night.

He thought about the plan they'd made for the medical services for Kapua and the outlying islands. Lily could take over the role of medical director but there was another major position to be advertised. Director of Remote Medical Services—a doctor who'd be based in Kapua but who would take care of the outlying islands. He and Sam had listed the requirements for such a position. Emergency medicine. An ability to work alone. Experience in tropical medicine. And preference would be given to someone with a pilot's licence—someone who in an emergency could take control of a helicopter.

'Hey, I know someone who fits this,' Sam had said. 'Do you?'

Ben had ignored him. He'd had to. Because if he ever took a job like that, then every night he'd come home to Lily and Benjy.

So? Lily was quite simply the loveliest woman he'd ever met. Would ever meet. The way he felt about her was non-negotiable. And Benjy was great. Benjy was his son.

So why the terror? Why the ice-cold feeling that gripped his guts whenever he thought about taking things further?

Committing, not to a marriage but to a relationship where Benjy and Lily were permitted to need him.

Maybe he should just jump in at the deep end. Try it out and see.

But if he failed…

He'd looked at Lily's face tonight over the dinner table, and he'd looked at Benjy's, and he'd seen the same wooden look of pain. He'd hurt them already. How much more would he hurt them if he committed?

He wanted Lily to commit.

No, he didn't. He saw it now, more clearly than he'd seen it at any time in his life. Lily was prepared to throw her heart into the ring, and maybe so was Benjy, but didn't they understand that he could crush it? If he wasn't capable…

'Coward,' he told himself, but it didn't help a thing.

Lily lay in the dark and stared at the ceiling. She was under no illusions. Tomorrow Ben would leave. She'd see him next when he made a flying visit to Kapua to see his son.

So what was different? She'd lived with loneliness for seven long years.

But now she didn't even have Kira.

She hadn't wept for the old woman. She'd stood at the graveside and her face had stayed wooden. She'd felt wooden.

But now…

She wanted Kira and the pain she felt for the wonderful woman who'd been part of her life for so long was suddenly so acute she couldn't bear it. And it was mixed up with the way she felt about Ben. She'd loved and she'd lost.

She'd never admitted to herself that she hoped Ben might resurface in her life. She'd even finally agreed to marry Jacques. But maybe that thought had always been there—that tiny flare of hope.

And now it was dead. As Kira was dead.

Life went on. As a doctor she'd seen grief from many angles and she knew that grief could finally be set aside.

But not tonight. The house was asleep. Her son was asleep. She wasn't needed. There was no one to see her.

Dr Lily Cyprano buried her head in her pillow and she wept.

Breakfast the next morning was dreadful. None of them seemed to have appetites. Doug had refused to stay in bed but he was grim-faced and silent. He looked strained and ill, Lily thought, and even though it meant Ben would leave, she was relieved for Doug's sake. Doug needed specialist medical intervention urgently. She even found it in herself to be grateful Ben was going with him. That must give some reassurance to Rosa. Rosa trusted Ben implicitly.

Maybe she did, too.

'When will everyone be coming back?' Benjy asked in a small voice, pushing his toast away uneaten.

'Doug will be back here in a couple of weeks,' Lily told him. 'After the doctors have fixed him up.'

'What about my dad?'

They all waited for Ben to answer that, but he didn't. He concentrated on buttering his toast and Lily stopped thinking she trusted him implicitly and instead allowed anger to surge. She glowered across the table at Ben. Low life, she told herself, but it didn't work. She couldn't produce anger.

He wasn't someone she could be angry with, she thought miserably. He was just Ben. A man so wounded by life that he could never make a recovery.

'We'll be gone by the time Ben gets back,' she told Benjy gently. 'But he's promised to visit us on Kapua.'

That was something, but not enough. Benjy sniffed and

sniffed again, heroically holding back the tears Lily had shed the night before.

'Come out with me to see how Flicker is this morning,' Rosa suggested, rising from her own uneaten breakfast and casting an uncertain look at her husband. 'You're ready?'

'Bring on the chopper,' Doug said morosely. 'You've packed everything I could possibly need.'

'While you cleaned the kitchen,' she snapped. 'He got up at dawn and scrubbed out the cupboards,' she told Ben and Lily. 'Of all the obstinate, pig-headed…'

'Go out with the boy,' Doug said. 'Please, Rosa. You're making me nervous.'

'Fine,' Rosa muttered. There was still half an hour before the helicopter was due and she looked strained to the point of collapse.

'I'll check on the chopper time,' Ben said, and Lily knew he wanted the chopper to be there now. Just for Doug? Or was he running, too?

Of course he was running.

'Lily, I need to run through what has to be done here while we're away,' Doug told her, dragging his eyes from his wife's strained face. 'If you're to stay here until Ben sends help then I need to make a list.'

'Fine,' Lily told him. Rosa and Benjy went out one door. Ben went out the other. She stared at the closed door for a moment—and then turned back to Doug.

Doug had turned to the bench to find a pad and pencil. He lifted the pencil a couple of inches from the pad.

'Oh,' he said, in a tiny, startled voice, and he dropped the pencil.

'Doug?'

Nothing. She saw his eyes focus inward.

'Doug!'

By the time Lily reached him he was sliding lifelessly onto the floor.

'Ben,' Lily was screaming even as she broke Doug's fall. She lowered him to the floor, taking his weight. He'd slumped between a chair and the bench. She shoved the chair out of the way with her feet. It crashed into another and splintered.

She didn't notice.

Doug wasn't breathing. She had her fingers on his neck, frantically trying to find a pulse.

None.

'Ben,' she screamed again. She'd been three weeks away from medicine but she was all doctor now. She hauled Doug onto his back, ripping his shirt open.

'Ben!'

He'd heard. The door slammed open and Ben was with her, shoving the mess of furniture out of the way so savagely that the chair leg Lily had broken splintered off and skittered over the linoleum.

'Check his airway,' Lily snapped, and Ben was already doing it, feeling in Doug's mouth, turning his face to the side as Lily thumped down on his chest.

Ben stooped and breathed into Doug's mouth, then straightened. 'Let me,' he told Lily, and she knew at once what he meant. CPR needed strength and he had more of it than she did.

'Do we have any oxygen?' she demanded.

'No.' His hands were already striking Doug's chest, over and over, trying desperately to put pressure on his heart as Lily gave the next breath. 'Come on, Doug. Don't you dare die. Come on, Doug. Please. Come on.' His eyes didn't leave Doug's face as the CPR continued, strong and sure and as rhythmic as Lily could possibly want. 'Please.'

Please. Lily couldn't talk but she could pray, over and over. Please. She breathed and she waited and she breathed and she prayed and she breathed and prayed some more. There was a roaring overhead and it was the backdrop to her prayer, building in volume as she breathed and Ben swore and pushed downward over and over.

Please…

The door swung inward. 'Doug, it's the helicopter…'

It was Rosa. She took one step inside the door and stopped dead as she saw what was in front of her. Her hands flew to her face, her colour draining. 'Oh, God.'

'Rosa, is that the Medivac chopper?' Ben's voice was curt and hard, slicing across her terror.

'Doug—'

'Rosa, tell me.' His order was almost brutal. 'Is that the Medivac chopper? Yes or no?'

'Yes,' she whispered. Her face was as ashen as Doug's and she clutched for the table for support.

But Ben would have none of it. Terror was an indulgence they had no time for. 'Then run,' he told her. 'We need oxygen and a defibrillator. They'll have them on board. Run, Rosa. We'll save him yet.'

Rosa gave a gasp of sheer dread—and turned and ran.

There was no choice but to continue. Lily kept on breathing. She'd never done artificial respiration without an airway, but there was no hesitation. Doug felt like family.

It had to work.

Please.

Then…

At first she thought she was imagining it. It was the air she was breathing in for him that was making his chest rise.

But no. She drew back as Ben kept applying pressure, and she saw it again. Chest movement she wasn't causing.

'Ben,' she screamed and he drew back, just a little.

And she was right. Doug's chest rose imperceptibly, all by

itlsef. A weak shudder ran through his body and his eyes flickered.

Then Rosa waas back, bursting through the door with a man and a woman behind her. They were dressed in the uniforms of the Australian Medivac Service. Rosa must have been coherent enough to make herself heard, for the woman was carrying a medical bag and the man was carrying a defibrillator.

But maybe, blessedly, a defibrillator wouldn't be needed.

'Oxygen,' ben snpped, not taking his eyes off Doug. 'We have a pulse.'

Dear God…

One of the newcomers—the woman—was hauling open her medical bag. lily grabbed an oxygen mask and was fitting it to Doug's face before the girl could make a demur.

The man was carrying an oxygen cylinder as well as the defibrillator. he set it on the floor and Ben fitted it swiftly to the tube attached to Doug's mask. he watched Doug's chest every minute. As did they all. They had no attached monitor—all they could go by was the rise and fall of Doug's chest.

But it rose and it fell.

'Let's get an IV line up,' Ben snapped. The two newcomers ad obviously realised by now that Ben was a doctor—or maybe they already knew—and they'd merged seamlessly into a highly skilled team. There were now four medics and the right equipment, and suddenly Doug had a chance.

More than a chance. his eyes flickered open again and this time they stayed open.

'Don't try to talk,' Lily said urgently. 'Doug, you've had a heart attack, but you're OK. You'll be fine if you stay still.'

'Rosa.' He didn't say the word but Lily saw his lips move and knew what he wanted. She shifted a little so he could see his wife and Rosa could see him.

'She's here,' Lily said, and she felt like bursting into

tears—but, of course, she didn't because she was a doctor and doctors didn't weep over their patients, no matter how much they felt like it.

But she looked across Doug's body at Ben, and she saw exactly the same emotion on Ben's face as she was feeling herself.

Doctors didn't cry. No matter how much they wanted to.

And after all Ben's conniving, the choosing of who would leave the farm today was now decided differently.

The two Medivac officers were Dr Claire Tynall and Harry Hooper, a nurse trained in intensive care. Claire and Harry took over Doug's care with smooth efficiency, fitting a heart monitor, adjusting the oxygen supply, transferring Doug to a stretcher that could be raised onto wheels so he could be could be transferred easily to the chopper. There was space for one more person in the helicopter and it wasn't going to be Ben.

'I need to go with him,' Rosa sobbed, and Ben agreed.

'Of course you do. Lily, could you pack her some essentials while we get Doug into the chopper?'

So Lily did a fast grab from Rosa and Doug's residence while they loaded him. Doug was at risk of arresting again. They had to get him to a major cardiac unit fast.

'I hope this is all you need,' Lily told Rosa as she ran to the helicopter to find Doug and Rosa already aboard.

'Buy whatever else you need and put it down to me,' Ben said gruffly. 'I'll be with you as soon as I can.' Then, as Rosa's face crumpled in distress, he climbed up into the chopper and gave Rosa a swift hug.

That was it. Ben climbed down again. The door slammed shut. The chopper rose into the morning sky. It hung above their head for an instant, then headed inland.

Ben and Lily were left standing side by side, staring after it.

'It's OK, Lily,' Ben said, as if reassuring himself. 'We did good.' He reached out and touched her hand.

'We did, didn't we?' she said, and her voice broke. She pulled away—just a little but enough. It was suddenly enormously important that she didn't touch him. She was very close to complete disintegration. She'd seen deaths from cardiac arrest many times in her professional life, but today… Well, things had changed. She'd stayed independent, too, she thought, but Ben had come back to her and now her independence was a thing of the past.

But she had to find it again. She had to.

'He'll be OK,' Ben muttered, as the sound of he helicopter faded to nothing. He shoved his hands deep into his pockets and Lily thought he looked as strained as Rosa had.

He loved these people.

'He will be,' she said softly, in the voice she might have used for a frightened family member after a trauma. He looked… bewildered?

'I… Yes.'

He was more than bewildered. He was in shock, she thought, but she had to move on.

'I need to find Benjy,' she managed. 'Are you OK?'

'Of course I'm OK,' he said, and he seemed to give himself a mental shake. 'Why wouldn't I be?'

'Because someone you love almost died?'

'I don't…'

'Love? Yes, you do,' she whispered. She held his gaze for a moment, watching what looked like a struggle behind his eyes. Had he not realised how important Doug and Rosa were to him? They were desperately important, she thought, maybe in the same way Kira had been important to her.

The aching void of loss slammed home again, as it had hit home time and time again since Kira's death. But at least Kira had died knowing she was loved, Lily thought. At least she'd told the old lady that she was loved, and so had Benjy.

Had Ben ever told Rosa and Doug they were loved? Had he admitted it to himself?

'You'll see them soon,' she said softly, and he flinched.

'Sure.' He shook his head, somehow hauling himself back under some sort of control. 'I'll…I'll get someone here to take over the farm as soon as I can.'

Because you want to see Doug and Rosa, or because you want to leave us? Lily wondered, but she didn't say it. She had to do a bit of self-protection here, too.

'I…I need to find Benjy,' she repeated. She needed to give her little boy a hug—mostly because she needed a hug herself.

The totally in-control Ben Blayden seemed somehow now right out of his comfort zone. He was staring ahead like he was looking into an abyss. And maybe he was even considering jumping. 'OK,' he managed. 'Let's find…let's find our son.'

Our son? Lily thought. Our son? But he was already moving away. Questions had to wait.

CHAPTER ELEVEN

FINDING Benjy was easier said than done.

Despite the emotional nuances between Lily and Ben, almost as soon as she thought about Benjy Lily was aware of a wave of unease. Where was he?

As she hurried back to the house she forced herself to rewind the events of the last half-hour. Rosa and Benjy had gone out to talk to Flicker, but then Rosa had hurried back to tell them the helicopter was there. Benjy may well have stayed with Flicker.

But he must have seen the helicopter land, she thought. Wouldn't he have come back to the house by now?

Ben was by her side but before she reached the house she'd started to run, leaving him behind. 'Can you check the front of the house?' she called. She ran up the veranda steps, just inside the back door. 'Benjy?'

No Benjy.

OK, he must still be with Flicker. She walked back out onto the veranda, expecting to see Benjy on his favourite perch, on the end of the water trough where he talked to Flicker. In these last weeks Flicker had become Benjy's new best friend; someone to talk to when adults didn't cut it.

But the trough was bare. He *must* be in the house, Lily

thought, retracing her steps. Had he come in while they'd been trying to save Doug? What had he seen? Benjy had suffered too much trauma for one small boy.

She reached the back door again and started to call, but then she turned again to stare down at the home paddock.

She'd almost missed it. Her eyes had swept the paddock, looking for Benjy. But now… She did another long perusal. There were no other animals in the home paddock.

The other four horses were grazing in the pasture on the far side of the river. It was only Flicker who was kept this side, as Rosa wanted her close for foaling. But the gate at the far side of the paddock was open, and Flicker was gone.

She catapulted down the back steps. Ben came around the corner of the house and she almost ran into him.

'Whoa,' he said, reaching out and steadying her. 'He's not out the front. Isn't he here?'

'N-no,' she stammered. 'Neither is Flicker. The gate's open.'

Ben stilled. Without releasing Lily, he turned to check the paddock.

Nothing.

'Would he have tried to take her to the river?'

'Maybe he would,' Lily whispered. 'He was so upset about you going. If he and Rosa were getting Flicker ready for her daily walk and Rosa came back inside…'

'Let's go.'

Side by side they ran, down the track leading to the pasture where they normally brought the mare to graze. They reached the rocky outcrop at the bend to the horse pasture and stopped dead as they saw the deserted river bank before them.

No horse. No small boy.

'She's a strong horse,' Lily whispered. 'At the fork in the track even Rosa sometimes has a battle turning her this way. Rosa says she wants to join the other horses.'

'Closer to the sea,' Ben said, and they were already moving. 'Hell, it's marsh down there. If the horse gets stuck…'

And it seemed that was just what had happened.

For most of its length this river was deep and fast, surging from the mountains to form a swift-running channel, but at its mouth it broadened and shallowed.

On the far side of the river was a rocky incline, delineating the edge, but not this side. Because it was summer and the water from the mountain catchment was less, the width of river had narrowed. There was now thirty or forty yards of river-flat on this side, normally under water but now dry. Or almost dry.

On the far side of the river Lily saw the other four horses belonging to the property. They were staring over the river toward a clump of rocks. For a moment she couldn't see what they were staring at. And then, appallingly, she did.

Flicker was there, half-hidden by the rocks. Lily hadn't seen her because she'd been searching for something of horse height and Flicker was now a lot lower than horse height. The mare had taken herself halfway across the flat, trying to reach her companions. And then she'd sunk. She was up to her withers in mud, struggling to free herself from what looked to be an impossible situation.

Her world stilled. Where was Benjy? Dear God, where was Benjy?

But Ben was there before her. 'Benjy.' Ben was yelling his son's name, breaking into a run across the mud, regardless of whether it was safe or not. 'Benjy!'

'I'm here.' It was a terrified wail from behind the horse. 'Dad, I'm here. Help me.'

She was running almost as fast as Ben. The ground gave a little under her feet, but she was moving too fast to sink. It was firm enough to hold her—just—but it was a miracle Flicker had got this far out.

Ben reached the horse before she did. By the time she reached them he was around the other side of Flicker. And there was Benjy. He was still clutching the halter as if he alone could stop the mare sinking, but the mare's struggles had made the ground at her head a quagmire. It looked a glutinous mess that had hauled Benjy into it as well as the mare. He'd sunk to his chest, and the mare's struggles were driving them both deeper.

But Ben had him. He sat on the ground behind Benjy, with his legs on either side of his son. His arms came around Benjy's chest, and he leaned backward.

'Don't struggle,' he told Benjy. 'Just go limp in my arms. Let me do the work.' He looked at the mare. 'Hush,' he told her, and crazily the mare stopped struggling for a little. She looked wild-eyed and as terrified as Benjy but maybe Ben's bedside manner was not bad for horses either.

But Lily had eyes only for Benjy. She sat as Ben was doing—the mud only sucked you in if there was a big weight on a small surface so she presented the mud with her backside. And prayed it was big enough. She was desperate to help but Ben had Benjy fast in his arms, fighting for the mud to give up its prize.

And it did. Slowly, gradually, Benjy was eased outward. Then, wonderfully, as his torso came free, the rest of him came in a rush and Ben sprawled backward, his arms full of mud and boy.

Lily reached for him but Ben wasn't relinquishing him. They lay in the mud, a tangle of legs and arms and mud and pure emotion. Ben's small shoulders were shaking with sobs and his face was a blotched and crumpled mess. He lay on Ben's chest while Lily reached out and ran her fingers through his hair and felt her heart go cold at the thought of what might have been.

'She kept pulling,' Benjy sobbed at them, still cradled against his father. 'I tried to take her to the nice grass but she wouldn't come. And she keeps sinking more.'

'Oh, Benjy. It'll be OK.'

'It's not OK,' Benjy managed, hiccuping on a sob. His small body might be crumpled against Ben, gathering comfort, but he was made of stern stuff, and he'd only slumped a little and now he was pulling away. 'She's stuck and we have to help her.' He bit his lip, trying valiantly not to cry any more.

Enough. This was her baby. Lily sat up and tugged him away from Ben, into her arms. 'Sweetheart, let's think about you first. We'll look after Flicker but we need to check you. Are you hurt? Were you kicked?'

'N-no. Just stuck.'

'So nothing hurts now.'

'My dad pulled me out of the mud,' Benjy whispered. 'So I'm OK.'

'It's what your dad does best,' Lily whispered back, holding him close. 'He's very, very good at making people OK. Just lucky we had him here, hey?'

There was a moment's silence. Lily very carefully didn't look at Ben—but it was a struggle.

'Tell us what happened,' Ben managed at last. He was sitting up too now, taking in the full mess the mare was in. Or maybe he was trying not to look at his son. He'd been rocked to the core, Lily thought, and she knew it because she was feeling exactly the same. The only difference was that she'd known she loved her son to bits.

Ben looked like a thunderbolt had hit him.

But Flicker needed them. Ben's question was waiting to be answered and finally Benjy took a deep breath and told them.

'Flicker was acting funny when Rosa and me came out this morning. She kept going back and forth by the gate, over and over. Rosa said maybe something's happening, but then the helicopter came and she said stay with Flicker and she went inside. And no one came and no one came and Flicker was going back and forth and back and forth and I thought I'd start taking her down to the river like she wants. 'Cos you'd know where I'd be. But she was still acting funny. She was whinnying and looking behind her all the time. And then she came the wrong way. She pulled and pulled and I couldn't stop her coming here. Then she got stuck and every time she fought I went deeper and I couldn't get out of the mud.' His words ended on a frightened whisper. Lily hugged him close and looked at Ben, who was watching them as if…

As if nothing.

'What can we do?' This was no time for wondering what Ben was thinking, she decided. She didn't have a clue. When had she ever?

'Let's check.' Ben edged forward, lying by the mare's flanks, keeping out of range of the churned mud at her head. She was still for the moment, but quivering in obvious fear. And pain? He ran his hand down her side and he frowned.

'Maybe she's in labour,' he said, and Lily winced and held Benjy tighter still. Mare stuck in mud. In labour?

'Throw us another complication, why don't you?' she demanded, and Ben managed a smile.

'Sorry. But let's assume the worst. We need equipment.'

What sort of equipment? Maybe putting the mare down was the kindest option, she thought bleakly. Oh, but Benjy…

'It's not time for that yet,' Ben said, his smile fading, and she knew he'd seen the bleakness of her thoughts. 'Benjy, I want you and your mother to stay here while I fetch what I need. I want you to stay calm and stay away from the churned-up mud, and I want you to try and keep Flicker calm as well. No more struggling. I'll be as fast as I can.'

He hesitated, then he moved back to where they sat and touched Benjy lightly on the cheek. Then, with the same muddy finger, he touched Lily. It was a feather touch and why the touch of a mud-caked finger should warm her—why it reassured her that all was well—she didn't know. But it did.

'Great beside manner,' she managed, and he smiled again.

'The doctor will make it all better,' he said. 'Just keep on believing that, you two. But the doctor had better move. I'll be back as soon as I can be. Stay calm.'

It was all very well staying calm and controlled when Ben was close, but the moment he disappeared it got a lot harder. But she was a doctor, too, Lily decided. So conjure up your own bedside manner, she told herself. Right!

'We have to stay calm,' she told Benjy sternly, and they both turned to looked at the mare. Her eyes were wild and fearful, and while they watched, Lily saw a ripple pass over her glossy hide. A muscle contraction? Labour?

Lily had been in some tricky delivery situations before but none surpassed this.

'Ben will know what to do,' she murmured, more to herself than to Benjy or Flicker. 'He's gone to get what we need.' What did they need? A crane? Did farms have cranes? She knew the answer to that would be no.

She reached out across the mud and touched the mare's nose, but Flicker snorted and flung back her head in alarm. 'It's OK, girl,' Lily told her, but maybe the mare heard the lack of certainty in her voice.

'I sang her a Kira song before you came,' Benjy whispered. 'She went down so far I thought she might go all the way. I was scared I'd be pulled down, too, and I didn't know what else to do so I just held onto her and sang.'

'That was a really sensible thing to do,' Lily said, swallowing hard at the thought of the bravery he'd shown. She thought of what sensible things she could do and she came up with only one suggestion. 'Do you think we could both sing?'

'OK,' Benjy said doubtfully. 'I will if you will.'

So they did, and it was dumb but it seemed to work. They sat on the soft ground in front of the mare—but not so close as to alarm her or be sucked down as well. Lily held Benjy on her knee and they sang together the songs Kira had taught both of them, soft island songs, meant to pacify a child before sleep. They were songs that were meant to murmur that all was right with the world and it was safe.

All wasn't right with her world, Lily thought, but Ben had saved her son and he'd save the horse as well—she knew it. So she held Benjy tight and she sang until finally Ben reappeared, driving the farm truck. He parked it just in front of where the ground became soft. While Lily and Benjy finished the song they'd started, he climbed from the cab and started unloading gear.

Planks. Lots and lots of wooden planks, each about six feet long. Spades. What looked like tarpaulins.

'Let's help,' Lily said, but Flicker tossed back her head, her eyes fearful again. 'Benjy, you keep singing while I go to help Ben. She's your friend.'

'OK,' Benjy said. 'But I'm scared.'

'Ben's here now. Flicker will be fine. The best person to be here in an emergency is an emergency doctor. You'll see.'

By the time she reached him, Ben had almost finished unloading. He smiled at Lily as she approached, the same way he might smile at a terrified patient.

'We'll get her out.'

'You're as worried as I am,' she accused, and he gave a rueful smile.

'I might be.'

'And if we can't get her out?'

'I've called the local vet for back-up.'

'And the local vet would be how local?'

'He's half an hour's drive away.'

'So he'll be here in half an hour?'

'Not quite. He'll be here half an hour after he delivers a heifer of her first calf.'

'Oh, great.'

'I brought the rifle,' he muttered, and Lily gulped. Um, that was never a back-up plan in her sort of medicine.

'It's only if she breaks anything or starts to struggle deeper,' he said.

'She can't deliver a foal where she is.'

'We don't know she's in labour.'

'I'm sure she's having contractions.'

'Right.' His lips compressed. 'So we get her out before she has her baby.'

'How?'

'Dig,' he said, and handed over a spade. 'We're in this together.'

They were.

They laid planks around the mare, giving themselves a solid place to work. Right. The next thing was to stop the mare sinking further. Ben knelt on one side of the mare and shoved a tarpaulin under her belly, talking softly to her all the time. Lily knelt on the other side.

Flicker's belly was resting on mud, sinking a little beneath the surface. Ben worked his way in from one side; Lily burrowed from the other; Flicker stayed still and they were able to drag the tarp through.

There were three more contractions as they worked.

'Now what?' Lily demanded, struggling to her feet again, a heap of mud coming with her.

'Now we dig,' Ben said. 'Benjy, you keep singing. You're exactly what Flicker needs. Lily, we're working down from about six feet in front of her, digging what will act as a ramp outward from her hooves. We'll be sliding planks in as we dig and then we'll cover them with canvas. She should be able to get purchase.'

'Really?'

'Got any other suggestions?'

'Nope,' Lily said, and started to dig.

They worked for half an hour, digging forward steadily. Lily wasn't half the digger Ben was, but every few minutes they swapped so the trench they were creating was even. Fifteen minutes into the digging, Lily had blisters on blisters but she would die rather than admit it. The thought of the rifle in the back of the truck was the best of spurs.

And all the time Benjy sang, in a high, quavery voice that held the occasional sob. Every time he paused, the horse became agitated again, rolling her eyes, pulling back. Her legs had no purchase in the mud and she'd almost ceased trying to get herself out, but Lily was worrying now about shock.

How did you tell if a horse was in shock?

'Can we contact the vet and see if we can give her a sedative?' she asked as she dug.

'I'm imagining a sedative will cross the placenta, the same as in human babies. Wouldn't you say?'

'Yes, but—'

'I already asked the vet,' Ben said grimly. 'No sedative. Let's just dig.'

So dig they did, forming a sloping hole downward, until they had what was essentially a ramp from close to the mare's front legs. They left about a foot of mud between the hole and the mare's legs, deciding they'd break through in one hit at the end, fearing she might lash out.

Finally the hole was dug. Swiftly they lined it with boards and covered the boards with canvas, shoving the canvas under the boards at the ends and the sides so as soon as the horse was on it, her weight would hold it in place.

'Now we just have to break through,' Ben muttered. 'Lily, hold her halter, talk to her, see if you can distract her.'

Ben didn't want to get kicked, Lily thought, and she was in complete agreement. Neither did he want her to surge forward when only one leg was free.

'OK, Benjy, we're into distraction.'

The mare was in obvious pain now. Labour must be advancing. Her eyes were panicked, and Lily thought it was more than being stuck that was panicking her.

She had to distract the mare from pain—and from Ben.

She knelt on the mud to the side of the mare and tugged Flicker's halter, making her look sideways rather than straight ahead.

'No struggling,' she said sternly. 'Benjy, tell your friend Ben's trying to help. Flicker, look at us.' She jerked the halter. 'Look at us.'

Ben was in the hole. He was scraping at the last of the mud, trying to break through. Nearly there. The last barrier of mud was collapsing down on itself, freeing the mare's legs.

Flicker appeared not to notice. Her eyes were looking inward. There was a foal in there, battling to come out.

'OK,' Ben muttered, and hauled himself up and onto the far side of the hole from Lily. He reached out and grabbed the other side of Flicker's halter. 'Let's get you out, gorgeous. Lily, pull.'

Lily staggered to her feet.

'Stand aside,' Ben ordered Benjy.

'Shall I sing?' Ben's face was a picture of bewilderment, fear and the beginnings of excitement.

'No,' Ben said. 'Get behind her and shout. As loud as you can.'

'Only her front feet are free,' Benjy said doubtfully, staring at Flicker's still trapped hindquarters, and Ben grimaced.

'I know,' he told Benjy. 'But she's a strong horse. It should be enough.'

It had to be enough, Lily thought, for to dig under the abdomen to free the back legs was impossible. It'd be impossible even if they had time. Which they didn't.

So Lily and Ben pulled and Benjy shouted. For a long moment Lily thought the mare simply wasn't going to try. There'd be so many sensations hammering the mare now that being stuck in mud would be the least of them. But Lily pulled as if she really believed the mare would come free and Ben pulled, too. Flicker suddenly hauled a foreleg upward, the mud squelching as it released its grip. One hoof hit the canvas-covered wood and found purchase. Encouraged, she tried the second hoof and it, too, found purchase.

'Now for the big pull,' Ben murmured. 'Come on, my beauty.'

'Please,' Lily muttered. 'Please.'

And then it happened. The mare gave one last despairing whinny, found purchase with both hooves and hauled herself forward, with a movement so sudden that Lily sprawled backward in the mud. Ben didn't stop. The mare was lurching out onto the boards, and Ben was tugging the mare forward, further, further, leading her as fast as he could over the soft ground so she couldn't sink again. While Lily lay in the mud and tried to regain her breath, man and horse made it to the pasture.

Safe.

Lily lay on the mud and watched them, and smiled and smiled. Benjy came up to her, worried about why she hadn't risen, and she tugged him down and held him tight and grinned.

'Wasn't that the best?'

'You're covered in mud. Just like me.'

'And I love it. Just like I love you.'

'Oi!' On dry ground Ben was holding the mare's head and looking back at them in bemusement. 'Benjy, could you remind your mother that she's a doctor. We have a baby to deliver, guys, so if you're finished wallowing in the mud, maybe you could help.'

* * *

What they needed was a nice easy delivery but, of course, that wasn't going to happen. Flicker was exhausted and distressed to begin with and she hardly had the strength to push.

But Ben had thought past getting the mare out of the mud. He'd filled a couple of huge Thermos flasks with hot water and he'd tossed buckets and rags and rope into the back of the truck.

'Practically a whole birthing unit,' Lily noted. 'But no incubator?'

'The sun's incubator enough,' Ben growled. 'If we can get it out.' He glanced at Benjy, who was starting to look distressed again. 'I meant if we can get it out quickly. Benjy, do you think you can keep these buckets full of clean water? If you took one over to the river and half filled it, then we'd have it ready. We'll top it up with hot water from the Thermos. That way we can have as much warm, soapy water as we need. Stay on the firmer ground where there are rocks to walk on. Don't go anywhere near where we've been digging.'

'Sure,' Benjy said, desperate to be doing something to help.

Lily was the same. She stood in the sun, the mud drying hard on her body, and felt like she needed direction.

It was Flicker doing the work.

'Hold her head,' Ben ordered, so she did. Ben cleaned the mare down a little, washing away the worst of the mud. The mare submitted to his ministrations with uneasy patience. She kept looking behind her as if she couldn't figure what was hurting. And then what must have been a deeper contraction hit. She whinnied a little and sank to her knees, then rolled onto her side.

'Where's the vet?' Lily demanded nervously, as Benjy lugged over his fourth bucketful of water.

'Why do we need a vet?' Ben asked.

'How long do horse labours last?'

'I have no idea. But let's not panic yet.'

'I can't think of anything else to do.'

'There speaks a thoroughly competent doctor.'

'You went to the same medical school,' she snapped. 'So what are you doing that is useful? Any minute you'll tell me to go help Benjy.'

'It's better than you both pacing the waiting room,' he retorted. 'Maybe you could go buy some cigars.'

'Or maybe I can just pace,' she muttered. 'Hurry up, Flicker.'

'I'd reckon she's doing the best she can.'

'How would you know?'

'And how would you?' They glared at each other and Ben put his head on one side and surveyed her, a strange smile behind his eyes.

'You're beautiful when you're panicking.'

'Shut up and deliver a foal.'

'There's no—'

But his words were cut short. The mare gave a mighty heave. A gush of water flowed, followed seconds later by a tiny hoof.

'Two hooves?' Lily murmured. 'Come on.'

Another contraction. No second hoof.

Another contraction.

No hoof.

'There has to be,' Ben muttered, worried, and Lily guessed what he wanted before he said it. She emptied a Thermos into the closest bucket, then swished soap round in it, handing the cake to Ben. It couldn't be harder than a human baby. Could it?

Ben was already soaping his arm. He felt around the tiny hoof and then had to pause until another contraction had passed.

Now.

But it wasn't now.

'My hand's too big,' he gasped. 'I'm not as sure of what I'm looking for as I am in human birth. You try.'

She was already soaping. She knelt, then figured she was

still too high so she lay full length on the ground and waited for the next contraction to pass.

'Ease back, Flicker,' Ben told the mare. 'Breathe for a bit.'

'I bet she skipped prenatal classes,' Lily muttered. 'Irresponsible ladies…'

And then the contraction was past. Lily soaped her hand some more, then carefully slid her fingers past the one tiny hoof.

Where…? Come on….

Her fingers found another hoof.

Fantastic. There had to be a nose, she thought, and then wondered if it was a front hoof or a back hoof. Did horses come out forward or backward? Was that a nose she was feeling? Whatever, she shoved her fingers as far back as she could, hooked the tiny hoof and hauled it toward her.

Another contraction hit. Her hand was still trapped. She gasped in pain, the sensation that of a vice against her hand. 'Yike,' she muttered. 'Yike, yike, yike…'

'Benjy,' Ben was yelling, calling to Benjy to leave his final bucket of water and come back. 'We think the foal's coming.'

'I know what's coming,' she muttered. 'She's delivering my arm. Don't you dare call Benjy.'

'Why—'

'My language,' she yelled, as another contraction rolled through. 'Block your ears.'

The hoof had slithered through her fingers and wasn't forward enough, but now she had it again. This time she tugged with more certainty. Heaven knew if it was right but it had to come in her direction so why not aim it that way? She just had it where she wanted it when the next contraction hit.

Her hand lifted free. The second hoof appeared like magic. With a nose.

And then…and then a foal slithered slowly out into a brand-new world.

* * *

It had been a huge physical effort, as well as an emotional one. Ben looked on as Benjy examined the perfect little foal. The little boy burst into tears and was gathered into his mother's arms and held.

Ben cleared the foal's nose and lifted the tiny creature round to his mother's head so Flicker could nuzzle her baby then lie there in exhausted contentment.

Lily had been lying full length during the foal's birth and she'd now rolled sideways to give Ben room to work. But she was going nowhere. She hugged Benjy to her as he sobbed and sobbed, and Ben thought this was much more than a foal being born. This was a culmination of all that had gone before—a month of hell.

Or more than that.

He looked down at Lily, bloodstained, filthy, smiling through her tears, holding her son against her breast, cradling him to her, whispering nothings.

He loved her.

He loved them all, he thought. Flicker and foal. Rosa and Doug.

Benjy. His son.

And Lily.

He always had, he thought, and it was such a massive, light-bulb moment that he felt his world shift in some momentous way that he didn't understand.

But his world hadn't moved from its axis. It was as if it had settled back onto an axis that he hadn't known had been missing.

He thought back to something Benjy had said.

My dad pulled me out of the mud, Benjy had whispered. *So I'm OK.*

His son had needed him and he'd been there. If Benjy needed him again, how could he not be close?

If Lily needed him… It was exactly the same.

And more. He thought then that it was more than him being needed. Because what he felt for them both was a need itself.

He needed them both. They might need him but he needed them so desperately that he could never again walk away.

He hadn't been there for Bethany, he thought, thinking suddenly of his baby sister. It hadn't been his fault. He hadn't been permitted to be there. But he'd loved her and now suddenly the grief for her loss settled, as if something had been explained that had been tormenting him for years.

He'd loved Bethany. It was OK to grieve for her. She wasn't…nothing.

And with that thought the guilt he'd been carrying for years suddenly, inexplicably, eased.

Today he'd been there for his son. He'd been there for Lily and he would be again, for ever and ever, as long as they both lived.

He needed them. This was his family.

You are my north and my south.

Who'd said that? He'd heard it at a funeral, he remembered. It had been the wife of a sergeant killed in East Timor. The woman had stood dry-eyed and empty, talking to her lost love.

You are my north and my south.

He'd hardly listened. He remembered hearing the words and then consciously deciding that he needed to think about what he was doing the next day. He couldn't let himself dwell on it.

Because love like that was terrible.

Only it wasn't. He'd only thought it was terrible.

Today Benjy had called him Dad.

Sure, it might end, he thought as he looked down at his woman and his son. The thought of that was empty, bleak as hell, yet what he'd been doing until now was just as bleak.

To do without that love because one day it might end—

that was dumb. He could see it now with a clarity that almost blew him away.

'It's not just you,' he said to Lily, breaking in on the conversation to himself halfway through. 'It's more than just you.'

Lily looked up at him, smiling past her son's rumpled curls. 'It's not just me?'

'I do love Doug and Rosa.'

'How about that?' she whispered, and smiled at him.

It was enough. He sank to his knees and stooped to kiss her. But she had her arms full of child and his kiss went awry, as it had to in these crazy circumstances, but, then, he knew his intention.

And maybe she did, too. For she was still smiling, her eyes full of unshed tears but the beginnings of joy not far behind.

'I need you,' he told her. 'Lily, I've always needed you. I've just been too stupid to see. But what happened today… We're a family. I know I don't deserve a second chance but I'm asking you for one. I want to marry you. I want to adjust our lives so we can be together. But I never want to be apart again.'

'Oh, Ben…'

'Will you come and live on our island?' Benjy asked, absorbing Ben's words and heading straight to what mattered most.

'Yes,' he said, and watched as Lily's eyes filled with tears.

'Ben, we can't ask you…'

'You're not asking. I'm telling. I'm coming home.' He bent forward and kissed her on the nose, and then, more surely, he kissed her on the mouth. When they finally broke away they were all smiling and Benjy's was the biggest smile of all.

'Kisses are yucky but I liked that,' he said.

'Great,' Ben told him. 'It's good that you like it because I intend to kiss your mother just like that every day for the rest of our lives. Once first thing in the morning, once just before we go to sleep and a hundred times in between.'

'We have a happy ending,' Lily whispered.

'I don't believe in endings.'

'No?'

'No.'

'I think this morning…' he told her as he gathered woman and child into his arms and held them tight. 'I think this morning is a happy beginning. Benjy, do you know what a phosphorescent tide is?'

'No,' said Benjy, puzzled.

'It's when the lights go on in the sea,' he said. 'In shallow water it might happen once in a lifetime. Your mother and I saw it but you missed out. So I've decided. I need to come back to your island so we can watch out together for phosphorescent tides. I have a feeling that when we're around, the concept of once in a lifetime is ridiculous. We've been given a second chance, and from now, from right at this minute, we're going to take any chance we're given.'

CHAPTER TWELVE

THE first anniversary of the insurrection on the island could well have been a day of sadness, but the islanders of Kapua had never looked on death as a final farewell. Funerals were a time of celebration, of affirmation of the power of life. They were a thanksgiving for the joy of life itself.

But the shock of the attempted coup had thrown the islanders off course. The funerals twelve months ago had been blurred with horror. Now, a year later, the islanders wanted to do it better. They'd come to terms with their losses in their own way, and they wished to right a wrong—to celebrate the lives of those they'd lost and to turn mourning into a peaceful acceptance and a deep thankfulness for lives well lived. Those killed by Jacques's accomplices had been loved, and that love would live for ever in the hearts of those left behind. And of those to come.

That was the gist of the words spoken by the island's pastor on this day of remembrance. Everyone on the island was there. The soft sea breeze blew gently across the graveyard, and the scent of frangipani mixed with the salt from the sea.

Lily stayed in the background, with Benjy by her side. On the other side of Benjy, holding his hand, letting the child lean against him, stood his father. Her husband.

Ben and Benjy. Her family.

She listened to the pastor's words, and let the peace of acceptance drift into her heart. 'Thank you for loving me,' she told Kira, and she glanced across at her husband and she smiled. 'And thank you for bringing Ben back home to me.'

For Ben was truly home now. He was an accepted islander. Lily's husband. Benjy's father. The islanders had accepted him into their hearts with nothing but pleasure.

And why would they not have? In less than a year Ben had transformed the medical set-up on the island. There were remote clinics on each of the outer islands, with rapid transfer available to the main base on Kapua. And the base at Kapua was wonderful. The tiny hospital had been extended to double its size. Lily was based there now, as were two interns on rotation from Sydney. And Sam… That had been a coup in itself. For when the time had come for Sam to leave he'd looked long and hard at the island—and at Pieter's pretty teacher daughter—and he'd decided that maybe Kapua wasn't such a bad place to put down roots.

So there were now five doctors on the island, and maybe there'd be even more when the new wing of the hospital opened. The obstetric wing.

It was magic, Lily thought as she continued to listen. From an island with basic medical facilities, they were moving fast to be state of the art.

Her island home had become even more of a paradise.

Not that they stayed there all the time now. In the few days after Doug's heart attack, when Lily and Ben and Benjy had been marooned, caring for a newborn foal but with little else to do but talk, and nothing to talk about but their future, they'd worked it out. Doug and Rosa would be grandparents to Benjy. They'd been practically all the parents that Ben had known and grandparents couldn't be left out of the equation of this embryonic family. Therefore four times a year they'd spend at least a week at the farm, and four times a year Doug and Rosa would be flown out to the island to spend as long as they wanted there.

They were there now. After his double bypass Doug looked and felt wonderful. Doug and Pieter had struck up a fast friendship, and Doug and Gualberto were as thick as thieves. Many more of the islanders would end up as visitors back at the farm, Lily thought happily. Her world had been extended and was about to be extended even more.

But first… There were ghosts to be laid to rest. First loves to be acknowledged.

The pastor had finished speaking now. Flowers had been laid on each grave, and the islanders were drifting away. There'd be a celebration on the beach tonight, but for now individual families needed time to themselves to assimilate all they'd felt that day.

Rosa and Doug were moving from the graveyard, too, but before they left Rosa reached into her capacious bag and produced a box. She smiled across at Lily, in her eyes a question, and Lily left her husband and son to take the box from her.

'What is it?' Ben asked as she returned.

She looked up at this wonderful man she loved with all her heart, and she thought, Was this the right thing to do? She'd done it without asking. She and Rosa had done it without talking to him about it because they knew this would hurt. They wanted the hurt to be brief but they also knew that unfinished business must be completed before moving forward.

'It's Bethany's ashes,' she said, and she saw his face become blank with shock.

'Bethany…'

'Rosa said you weren't permitted to go to her funeral. She said as far as she knew your parents hadn't ever told you where she was. Doug remembered a fight when you were about eight—you asking what had happened and your father saying to leave it, the dead were best forgotten.'

'Doug and Rosa always thought it was wrong,' she whispered. 'Only they never knew what to do—how to broach it with you. But after we married, Rosa talked to me about it. She knew that Bethany had been cremated. She knew her ashes had been left in a memorial wall at a huge Sydney cemetery. She'd always hated the thought. So…' She faltered a little then, looking at the blankness on his face, hoping she'd done right.

'We wrote to the accountant who was the executor of your parents' estate,' she whispered. 'We asked if we needed your permission but he said you'd never been involved—that as far as he knew you didn't even know where Bethany's ashes were. But he was happy to sign a release form. Because we thought… Rosa and Doug and I thought that you should bring Bethany home. We thought maybe you could scatter her ashes here. Or maybe you could scatter them at the farm. Wherever. But we thought we'd like to help you to do that.' She faltered. 'Ben, If you want us to take the ashes back to Sydney then we will. But Rosa and Doug and I thought…we thought this might be right.'

The blankness faded as Ben stared down at the box, thinking through what they'd done. His gaze lifted, meeting hers. Beside him, Benjy stood watchful. Lily had explained to Benjy who Bethany was. Kira's death had made Benjy more mature than his years. He knew enough now to be silent, and he knew this moment was important. He held Ben's hand and Lily thought that this was right. Ben was holding his son as he thought about a little sister he'd loved a long time ago yet had never said farewell to.

'I love you,' Ben whispered.

'I know,' Lily replied, trying to hold back tears. 'But Bethany was your first love. Benjy and I would like to be with you while you say goodbye, but if you don't want us…'

'Of course I want you.' He tugged Benjy closer and hugged him. 'You know that. You know how much.'

She did. The world settled a little. This was the right thing to do, Lily thought, feeling a sense of peace and absolution sweep over her.

She held out the box to him, then gestured to Benjy. Benjy came to her as Ben took his sister's ashes in both his hands.

'If you want to do it here, now, the pastor is waiting,' Lily told him. 'And Rosa and Doug are just through the trees. They loved Bethany, too. They'd also like the chance to say goodbye.'

'Yes,' he said softly, and then more firmly, 'Yes. This is a good time to do this. The best.'

So this memorial service became the memorial service for one other. The pastor came forward quietly and said a prayer and a blessing, and Ben opened the box and scattered his sister's ashes over the wildflowers of the churchyard; over the graves of those who had gone before; over the calm and lovely headland of this, their island home.

And when it was over, they turned and walked together, Ben and Lily, with Benjy walking behind between Rosa and Doug. A family going home.

'It was the best thing,' Ben told her, holding her close. 'To let me say goodbye…'

'It's a lovely name, Bethany,' Lily whispered. Her hand was warm in his, secure, loved. 'Do you think we should consider using it again?'

'For…'

'For a new little life,' she whispered, and she smiled and held his hand tighter. 'Today we've said goodbye to some of our family, my darling Ben, but in a seven months' time…time to say hello.'

That night, in the waves around Kapua, the tiny phosphorescent creatures came again.

The lights went on in their sea.

Miracles happened.

A BRIDE BY SUMMER

BY
SANDRA STEFFEN

Sandra Steffen has always been a storyteller. She began nurturing this hidden talent by concocting adventures for her brothers and sisters, even though the boys were more interested in her ability to hit a baseball over the barn—an automatic home run. She didn't begin her pursuit of publication until she was a young wife and mother of four sons. Since her thrilling debut as a published author in 1992, more than thirty-five of her novels have graced bookshelves across the country.

This winner of a RITA® Award, a Wish Award and a national Readers' Choice Award enjoys traveling with her husband. Usually their destinations are settings for her upcoming books. They are empty nesters these days. Who knew it could be so much fun? Please visit her at www.sandrasteffen.com.

For my beloved brothers, Ron and Dave.
Every girl should have a big brother.
I was lucky enough, and so blessed, to have two.

Chapter One

Reed Sullivan wasn't an easy man to read.

Not that the two women waiting in line behind him at the drugstore in Orchard Hill weren't trying. In the security camera on the wall he saw one nudge the other before motioning to the small carton he'd pushed across the counter. The pharmacy tech held any outward display of curiosity to a discreet lift of her eyebrows as she dropped his purchase into a white paper bag.

Apparently men didn't buy paternity test kits here every day.

He didn't begrudge any of them their curiosity. Most of the time he appreciated that particular trait inherent in most women almost as much as he enjoyed the way they could change the atmosphere in a room just by entering it. He had a deep respect for women, enjoyed spending time with them, was intrigued by them and appreciated them on so many levels. He did not leave birth control to chance. And yet here he was, making a purchase he'd never imagined he would need to make.

He paid with cash, pocketed his change and left the store, by all outward appearances as cool, calm and confident as he'd been when he'd entered. Out in the parking lot, a bead of sweat trickled down his neck and under the collar of his shirt.

Reed understood profit margins and the challenges of zoning issues. Those things always made sense in the end. This was different. Nothing about this situation made sense. Gnawing worry had jolted him awake at 4:00 a.m. It didn't require great insight to understand the cause. It all centered around the innocent baby he and his brothers had discovered on their doorstep ten days ago.

The very idea that someone would abandon a baby in such a way in this day and age was ludicrous. And yet there the baby had been, unbelievably tiny and undeniably alone. Reed, Marsh and Noah were all confirmed bachelors and hadn't known the first thing about caring for a baby, but they'd picked the crying infant up and discovered a note.

> Our precious son, Joseph Daniel Sullivan. I call him Joey. He's my life. I beg you take good care of him until I can return for him.

Our precious son? *Whose* precious son?

The handwritten note hadn't been addressed. Or signed.

Reed wasn't prone to self-doubt, but now he wondered if they *should* have performed a paternity test immediately. He should have insisted. What had he been thinking?

He hadn't been thinking. None of them had.

They'd spent the first week fumbling with formula and feedings, diaper changes and sleep deprivation while doing everything in their power to determine what the infant in their charge needed and wanted.

Joey had a lusty cry he wasn't afraid to use, and yet before his first night with them was over, he'd looked with burgeoning trust at the three men suddenly thrust into this new and foreign role. He didn't seem to mind their ineptitude.

Until that night, Reed and his brothers hadn't considered the possibility that one of them might have become a father without their knowledge. To make matters worse, they had no way of knowing which of the women from their respective pasts might have been desperate enough to leave Joey in such a manner. The million-dollar question remained.

Which of them was Joey's father?

Reed placed the small paper bag containing the paternity test kit on the passenger seat and started his car. As he pulled out of his parking space, the impulse to squeal his tires was strong. He quelled it because he was the middle brother, the one who thought before he reacted, who kept his wits about him and his head out of the clouds, the one with nerves of steel and the willpower to match.

Minutes later he was on Old Orchard Highway, a few miles from home. The sunroof was open, the morning breeze already fragrant and warm. The radio was off, the hum of his car's engine little balm for the uncertainties plaguing him today.

That first night, he, Marsh and Noah had put their heads together and had come up with a schedule for Joey's care, as well as a plan to try to locate his mother. It hadn't taken Noah long to find the woman from his past. A daredevil test pilot, he'd realized soon after coming face-to-face with Lacey Bell again that covert moves weren't her style. Joey wasn't Lacey's baby, and therefore Noah had been certain he wasn't his, either. That hadn't kept him from pulling out all the stops to rekindle the love affair of his life. Noah and Lacey had eloped two nights ago.

Paternity came down to Marsh or Reed.

They'd hired a private investigator to follow clues and leads regarding the whereabouts of the women who seemed to have disappeared into thin air. Under ordinary circumstances, he and Marsh didn't talk about their sex lives. If not for Joey's arrival, Reed wouldn't have known that Marsh had spent an idyllic week with a woman named Julia Monroe while on vacation last year or that she'd seemed to disappear into thin air as soon as the week was over.

Like his brothers, Reed liked to keep his private life private. There was only one woman, and one night, he couldn't account for. She was a waitress he'd met on a layover in Dallas during a business trip last year. She'd told him her name was Cookie—now he wished he'd asked a few questions. Could she have left Joey on his doorstep a year later?

He and Marsh had hired a P.I. with an impressive success rate. But so far every lead Sam Lafferty had followed had turned into a dead end. At least, once Reed and Marsh determined which of them was the baby's father, Sam could focus on finding one woman instead of two.

The test kit slid to the edge of the seat as Reed approached a banked curve in the highway. Behind him a red car that had been a speck in his rearview mirror a few seconds ago was closing in on him fast. The sports car came so close to his bumper he braced for a rear-end collision. All at once, the car swerved across the double yellow line and began to pass.

Up ahead an eighteen-wheeler was barreling around a curve straight toward them. An air horn blasted and tires screeched. The driver of the Corvette cranked the wheel to the right, thrusting his car back into Reed's lane. With no other place to go, Reed took the shoulder of the highway. He braked, but it was too late. His tires broke loose. And he started to spin.

Around and around he went, on the highway and off, from one shoulder to the other. Gravel churned and dust rose. He somehow missed an oncoming vehicle but clipped a highway sign with one of his mirrors. When he finally came to a complete stop, his engine was racing and so was his heart rate. He gripped the steering wheel, his foot pressed hard on the brake.

The dust was settling when he noticed that another car had stopped a short distance ahead of him on the opposite side of the road. The door opened. The next thing he knew, a slender, sandal-ensconced foot touched the ground.

Ruby O'Toole hit the pavement running.

She raced across the highway toward a silver Mustang sitting at an odd angle along the side of the road. The driver was looking at her through the windshield, his eyes narrowed and his jaw set. She stood back as he got out, and watched as he opened his fists and unclenched his fingers, straightened his arms and rotated his broad shoulders, as if checking to see if everything was still operational.

"Are you okay?" she asked.

He didn't answer, making her wonder if he was in shock.

"I'm calling 911. I've seen a lot of accidents and you could have whiplash."

"I don't need an ambulance." His voice was steady and deep, but the way he put a hand on the back of his neck made her wonder if he was more shaken than he was admitting.

"It's best to err on the side of caution," she insisted. "Adrenaline and shock can mask an injury like whiplash or a spinal column misalignment."

With a grimace, he said, "My back is fine. And I don't have whiplash." In his early thirties, he had short, sandy-blond hair and wore a gray dress shirt, the sleeves rolled partway up his forearms.

"You just never know," she argued. "The stiffness wouldn't necessarily set in until later."

He circled his car, his face impassive as he ran his hand over the Mustang's hood.

"Trust me. I'm fine."

"If you say so, but if I were you, I'd be stomping my feet and shaking my fist and swearing at that jerk who ran you off the road. You could have been killed! The creep had no right to drive like some bat out of hell. Jerks like him think they own the road and everything in their path." Catching him looking at her, she said,

"Some women cry at emergencies. I get mad. I have a temper. And don't tell me it goes with my hair."

"I won't."

She thought he might smile. When he didn't, she heard herself say, "It's what my boyfriend used to say. My ex-boyfriend. Peter. Cheater Peter." She had to clamp her mouth shut to keep from continuing. What was wrong with her?

"That explains the ex," he said in a deep, smooth voice that gave little away. As he examined his loosened mirror, he asked, "Are you an EMT?"

She'd been in the process of smoothing her hands down her shorts and straightening her tank top, and had to stop for a moment to wonder at his question. "Oh," she said. "You mean because I said I've seen a lot of accidents. No, my most recent career jag was driving a tow truck for my dad's wrecker service near Traverse City."

She didn't bother telling him that prior to working for her dad she'd spent three years with a trendsetting marketing firm in L.A. This stranger didn't need to hear how much trouble she'd had deciding what she wanted to do with her life. Reverting to small talk, she asked, "Do you live in Orchard Hill?"

"A mile from here." The breeze ruffled his blond hair and toyed with the collar of his shirt.

"I just moved here two days ago," she said. "In all likelihood, my mother is rearranging the furniture in my new apartment as I speak, while my father adds to his ever-growing list of all the reasons buying a tavern in this college town is a mistake. So, did your life pass before your eyes?"

* * *

Reed did a double take and looked at the talkative woman who'd stopped to make certain he wasn't hurt. She wore shorts that fit her to perfection and a white tank top that made her arms and shoulders appear golden. A silver charm shaped like a feather hung from a delicate chain around her neck. Her hair, long and red and curly, fluttered freely in the wind. When he found himself looking into her green eyes, he wished he'd have started there.

His gaze locked with hers, and the air went oddly still. In the ensuing silence, he wondered where the birds and the summer breeze and the traffic had gone.

Her throat convulsed slightly, as if she was having trouble breathing, too. "You're not much of a talker, are you?" she finally asked.

"Normally," he said, "I'm the one asking the questions."

She took a backward step and said, "Are you a lawyer?"

"Why, do I look like a lawyer?"

She shrugged one shoulder. "It's just that lawyers tend to ask a lot of questions."

"I'm not a lawyer."

"A journalist, then?"

"No."

"A Virgo?" she asked with a small smile.

He had to think about that one because astrology was hardly something he put stock in. "My birthday's November sixth."

"Ah, a Scorpio. You water signs are deep. And moody. Obviously." She shook herself slightly and said, "If you're sure you aren't hurt, I'll be going."

The smile she gave him went straight to places that made a man stop thinking and start imagining. It was intimate and dangerous, not to mention off-limits, given his present situation.

She glanced back at him as she opened her car door, and said, "Two-X-Z-zero-three."

"Pardon me?"

"The Corvette's license plate number." She started her car, and through the open window said, "It's two-X-Z-zero-three. I happened to notice it when the jerk flew by me at the city limit sign."

"You *happened* to notice it."

"I have a photographic memory for those kinds of details." With that, she drove away.

Reed got back behind the wheel of his car, too. When the coast was clear, he made a U-turn and continued toward home. He drove more slowly than usual, the entire episode replaying in his mind, from the uncanny near miss, to the chance encounter with the modern-day Florence Nightingale along the side of the highway. He wondered if he'd ever met anyone with a photographic memory.

The woman had asked if his life had passed before his eyes as he'd spun out of control. He hadn't seen the images of either of his brothers or his sister, or of their parents, killed so tragically years ago, or the first girl he'd kissed, or even the most recent woman. He hadn't seen his oldest friend or his newest business associate. The image in his mind as he'd spun to what might have been his death had been Joey's.

Sobered further by the realization, he pulled into his driveway and parked in his usual spot beside Marsh's

SUV. He cut the engine then felt around on the floor until he located the test kit.

For a moment, he sat there looking at the sprawling white house where he'd grown up. Beyond the 120-year-old Victorian sat the original stone cider house his great-great-grandfather had built with his own hands. Ten years ago Reed and his brothers and younger sister had converted the sprawling old barn into a bakery, where they sold donuts and baked goods, and fresh apple cider by the cup or by the gallon. There was a gift shop, too, and sheds, where their signs and equipment were stored. Behind them was the meadow where thousands of customers parked each fall. From here Reed could see the edge of the orchards, the heart and soul of the entire operation.

He hadn't planned to move back to Orchard Hill after college, but life had a way of altering plans. Reed wasn't a man who wasted a lot of time or energy wondering what he'd missed. Bringing the family business into the current century was one of his proudest achievements. His brother Marsh knew every tree on the property, every graft and every branch that needed to be pruned. Reed knew all about business plans, spreadsheets, tax laws, health inspections and zoning. He'd been the one to have visions of expansion.

Already he could picture Joey following in his footsteps one day. What was shocking was that he *wanted* Joey to follow in his footsteps. Until they'd discovered that little kid on their doorstep ten days ago, Reed hadn't realized how much he wanted to pass on the legacy of Sullivans Orchard and his business acumen to another generation.

He would be proud if Joey was his son.

With that thought front and center in his mind, he went up the sidewalk and through the unlocked screen door.

Chapter Two

Even on days when Reed swore everything was changing, there were a few things that always remained the same. Today it was the scent of strong coffee on the morning air.

He followed the unmistakable aroma into the kitchen and found his older brother at the counter across the room, pouring steaming brew into a large mug. Reed's gaze settled on Joey, nestled securely on Marsh's left arm, his eyes wide and his wispy hair sticking up in every direction.

Baby bottles filled the sink, and spilled formula pooled on the counter nearby. A load of clean baby clothes was piled in the middle of the table. It was hard to believe that two weeks ago the only items on the counter had been take-out menus, a cell phone or two and car keys.

"Did you get it?" Marsh asked without turning around.

"In the first pharmacy I tried." Reed kept his voice gentle because Joey had locked his eyes on him over Marsh's shoulder.

A toothless smile engaged Joey's entire face and brought out every fierce protective instinct Reed possessed. Everyone they'd consulted agreed that Joey appeared to be approximately three months old. The sum of the baby's age and the length of a normal pregnancy corresponded with the timing of the business trip Reed had taken to Texas last year.

"I heard from Noah," he said, sharing news from their younger brother with Marsh. Noah never had been one for long letters or phone calls, and his text was no different. Two words, hot damn, spoke volumes. "I'd say he and Lacey are pretty happy."

Joey smiled again, evidently happy, too. Already that little kid always assumed everybody was talking to him.

Reed tossed the discreet paper bag onto the table and continued toward his brother. "I'll take him. It looks as though you could use two hands for that coffee."

Joey didn't seem to mind the transition from one set of strong arms to the other. He was trusting in that way. Reed wondered if that trait came from his mother.

Paternity-wise, they weren't going to be able to make so much as an educated guess without the test, for Marsh and Reed were too closely related and nearly identical in height, bone structure and build. They were polar opposites in most other ways, however. Dark where Reed was fair, brown-eyed to Reed's blue-gray, whisker stubble where Reed was clean-shaven, Marsh was two and a half years older. Today he wore his usual faded jeans, scuffed work boots and a holey T-shirt Reed hadn't seen in years.

It reminded Reed that practically every item of clothing they owned was dirty. They needed help around here with laundry and dishes and especially with Joey's care, which was why they were interviewing someone later this morning. Luckily, Joey seemed oblivious to the havoc his arrival had brought. Tipping the scales at eleven and a half pounds, he was a handsome, sturdy baby with hair as dark as Marsh's and eyes that were gray-blue like Reed's.

"Hi, buddy," Reed said with more emotion than he'd known he was capable of feeling for a child so small. He carried the baby to the table and took a seat. "Is this formula still good?" he asked his brother.

Marsh looked at his watch, nodded, and Reed offered the baby the last ounce in the bottle. As Joey drank, he looked up at him and wrapped his entire hand around Reed's little finger. Reed was growing accustomed to the way his heart swelled, crowding his chest.

He'd read a tome's worth of information and suggestions about how to care for infants these past ten days. Maybe the way Joey grasped the finger of whoever was feeding him was reflexive. Reed was of the opinion that it had more to do with being a Sullivan, which among other things meant he wanted what he wanted when he wanted it.

Marsh was leaning against the counter across the room, ankles crossed as he somberly sipped his coffee. "How many times do you think we waited out the night sitting around that table?"

"During Noah's rebellious years—which was most

of them—and last year with Madeline? Too many to count," Reed said.

It reminded them both that they weren't novices when it came to handling tough situations. After their parents were killed in an icy pileup on the interstate thirteen years ago, twenty-three-year-old Marsh had suddenly become the head of the family. Reed had nearly doubled his class load at Purdue, and as soon as he graduated a year later, he'd come home to help. Noah had been a hell-raising seventeen-year-old then. Their sister, Madeline, had been fourteen and was struggling to adjust to a world that had changed overnight. It was hard to believe Noah and Madeline were both married now.

"This feels different, doesn't it?" Reed said, looking into Joey's sleepy little face.

"Different in every way," Marsh agreed.

Marsh tore the paternity test kit package open, read the directions and then handed them to Reed, who carefully moved Joey to the crook of his left arm, then read them, too. They filled out the forms with their pertinent information and followed the instructions to the letter before sealing everything in the accompanying airtight sleeves.

"What do you think Dad would say if he were here?" Reed asked as he closed the mailing carton.

"After the shock wore off, he probably wouldn't say much," Marsh answered quietly. "Mom would be the one we'd have to worry about."

Reed and Marsh shared a smile that took them back to when they were teenagers. Reed said, "She'd expect us to do the right thing. They both would."

"We are doing the right thing, or at least as close

to the right thing as we can under the circumstances," Marsh said. "Have you decided what you're going to do if Joey is yours?"

Reed eyed the baby now sleeping in his arms. If Joey was his son, it meant Joey's mother was the curvy blonde waitress named Cookie who'd accidentally spilled chili in his lap during a layover in Dallas last year. She'd blushed and apologized and somehow, when her shift was over, they'd wound up back at her place.

"If it turns out Joey's mine, and Sam locates Cookie and she has a legitimate reason for leaving him, I'd like to get to know her better." He wished he'd asked more questions that night. She'd mentioned an ex-husband, somewhere, and a local play she'd been auditioning for. He didn't recall ever hearing her last name. Now he wished he had asked. After all, if she was the mother of his son, she deserved better. She deserved the chance to explain. "What about you? What will you do if the test proves Joey is yours?"

Marsh took his time considering his reply. "The week I spent with Julia on the Outer Banks last year was pretty damn idyllic. I thought I knew her as well as a man could know a woman. I thought we had something. If Joey is our son, she would have had to have a very good reason for all of this. The Julia I knew wouldn't have left Joey unless she had no other choice. I have a hundred questions, but it does no good to imagine what might have happened to her or what might be happening to her now. I only know that if Julia is Joey's mother and I am his father, she will return for him, and when that happens I'd like to try to work things out, as a family."

It wasn't surprising that they wanted the same thing, for Reed and Marsh were both family men at heart. They grew silent, each lost in his own thoughts. The only sound in the room was Joey's hum as he slept in Reed's arms and the tick of the clock on the old stove.

"Why don't you put Joey in his crib for his morning nap," Marsh suggested. "The agency is sending another woman out for an interview later. You should have plenty of time to overnight the paternity kit and be back before then. Unless you want me to mail it."

"You had the late shift with Joey," Reed said. "I'll take the kit to the post office."

After laying Joey in his crib in the home office they'd converted into a nursery last week, he returned to the kitchen, where Marsh was still somberly sipping coffee. Keys in one hand and the sealed test kit in the other, Reed headed for the door.

"Hey, Reed?" Marsh stood across the room, his jeans riding low, his stance wide, his brown eyes hooded. "May the best man win."

Again, that grin took Reed back to when they were kids and everything was a competition. He shook his head, but he couldn't help grinning a little, too.

Getting in his car with its loosened side mirror, he wondered if Marsh was picturing Julia right now. Reed could only wonder what might have prompted Joey's mother—whoever she was—to leave him with only a vague note and a loose promise to return for him.

He was at the end of the driveway when it occurred to him that he couldn't seem to bring Cookie into sharp focus in his memory. Her bleached-blond hair kept switching to red.

* * *

"How was your drive?" Ruby's closest friend, Amanda Moore, asked the minute Ruby got back. "Tell me you got completely lost."

Ruby shook her head. "Sorry to disappoint you, but no."

"Not even slightly turned around?" Because Amanda had been lost when she'd met her fiancé, Todd, she was convinced that the key to finding happiness was that sensation she'd experienced when she'd made a wrong turn but somehow wound up in the right place.

But as Ruby had told her a hundred times, she didn't get lost. Ever. Her innate sense of direction was intricately linked to her keen memory for all things visual. Both had gotten her out of countless scrapes over the years.

"The reunion is in just over two weeks." Amanda was tapping away on her notebook at the end of the bar in Ruby's new tavern. "That doesn't leave us very much time to find you a date."

"You're my best friend, and I would give you a kidney or the shirt off my back," Ruby declared from behind the bar. "But I told you. I'm not taking a date. From now on I'm flying solo. I mean it, Amanda." Her laptop was open, too. Next to it was the box she'd started filling with cameras from the former owner's collection. "I don't even *want* to attend the class reunion."

"You have to, Ruby."

"Peter's going to be there."

"I know," Amanda said gently. "That's why I think you should bring a date. As former class officers, we're not only the planning committee, but we're the welcoming committee, too. Don't even think about trying to get out of it. You promised, and you never break your promises."

With a sigh, Ruby returned to compiling the menu of drinks that would be indigenous to her saloon. So far her list included alcoholic beverages with names such as Howl at the Moon and Fountain of Youth and Dynamite. Since she thought best when she was moving, she wandered to the pool tables in the back of the room.

Amanda tucked her chin-length brown hair behind one ear and followed. "Number one," she said, fine-tuning a line on the small screen. "This goes without saying because it's always number one with you. Nonetheless, number one." She cleared her throat for emphasis. "He must be tall. T-a-l-l. Tall, with a capital *T.* Number two. It would be nice if he spoke in complete sentences."

Ruby rolled her eyes. While she was looking up at the ceiling, a loud scrape sounded from above. Evidently her mother was still rearranging her furniture, even though Ruby had told her that the layout was fine the way it was.

Nobody listened to her, she thought as she shook out the plush sleeping bag she'd found near the pool tables and refolded it. It was a strange place to leave a sleeping bag, but at the closing yesterday, the previous owner, Lacey Bell Sullivan, had asked Ruby to keep the bedroll here for safekeeping for a few days while Lacey's brand-new husband whisked her away on their honeymoon. Lacey had vaguely mentioned that someone might come by to pick it up. Ruby believed there was something Lacey wasn't telling her, but Amanda was right. To Ruby, a promise was a promise.

Amanda was rattling off number five, apparently unconcerned that Ruby had missed numbers three and four entirely. “No bodybuilding Mr. America wannabes. And your date should be sensitive but not too sensitive. You don’t want to be apologizing all the time.”

Ruby smiled in spite of herself.

While Amanda recited the remaining must-have qualities from her list, Ruby took another look around. It was hard to believe this building was hers. The main room of the saloon was large and L-shaped, stretching from Division Street all the way to the alley out back. The tables and chairs were mismatched and the lighting questionable. There was a jukebox on one wall and two pool tables in need of a little restoration in the back. The ornately carved bar, where drinks would be served and stories swapped, was the crowning jewel of the entire room.

The ceilings were low and two of the walls were exposed brick. The hardwood floors were worn and the restrooms needed a little updating, but the building was structurally sound and included an apartment with a separate entrance.

Lacey Bell Sullivan had moved to Orchard Hill with her father when she was twelve. She’d inherited the building when he died. Business had fallen off, but she believed with all her heart that what the tavern really needed was a breath of fresh air. A new life.

Ruby thrilled at the thought.

“Rainbow of Optimism,” she said under her breath as she hurried back to her laptop and added another drink title to her menu.

Amanda hopped back onto her barstool, the pert

bounce of her hairstyle matching her personality. "What are you working on?"

"I'm giving Bell's a new identity so it will appeal to a lively, energetic, fun-loving crowd. Right now I'm compiling a menu featuring one-of-a-kind drinks."

Amanda turned the screen around in order to read the menu. "These are fun, Ruby. Fountain of Youth and Dynamite are self-explanatory. What's this two-X-Z-zero-three?"

"Oh, that doesn't belong on the list. It's just the license plate number of a Corvette I saw run a sweet Mustang off the road earlier. I stopped to make sure the driver of the Mustang was okay. What do you think of Happy Hops?"

"Was this driver a guy?"

"We're talking about the title of a drink," Ruby insisted. "Is Happy Hops too trite?"

"Was this handsome stranger under, say, thirty-five?" Amanda asked.

"I didn't say he was handsome."

"I knew it," Amanda quipped.

Another scrape sounded overhead. Holding up one hand, Ruby said, "You and my parents are making me sincerely wish I had hired a moving company."

Just then Ruby's father came bounding into the room waving a sheet of yellow lined paper. A brute of a man with a shock of red hair and a booming voice, he said, "The smoke alarm doesn't work. The bathroom faucet drips. Only one burner works on the stove, and that refrigerator is as old as I am. Did you count the steps leading to the apartment? Do you really want to have to climb twenty steps at the end of a long day?"

"Walter, would you stop?" The only person who

called Red O'Toole Walter was his wife. Ruby's mother now joined them downstairs. The freckles scattered across Scarlet O'Toole's nose gave her a perpetually young appearance, which was at odds with the streaks of gray in her short red hair.

"It isn't too late for her to get out of this," Red said to his wife.

Scarlet wasn't paying attention. She was listening to Amanda, who was telling her about the near accident Ruby had witnessed and the driver she'd stopped to help earlier.

"Was he tall?" Scarlet quizzed her daughter's best friend.

"I asked her that, too," Amanda replied. "That particular detail has not been forthcoming. Yet."

Ruby dropped her face into her hands.

"She needs to come home with us," her father insisted, as if that was that.

"She signed the papers," her mother said dismissively.

"I don't like the idea of our little girl serving up hard liquor to a bunch of rowdy m-e-n."

Ruby didn't bother reminding them that she was standing right here.

"Driving a tow truck you were okay with." Ruby's mother had a way of wrinkling up her nose when she was making a rhetorical statement. She demonstrated the tactic, and then said, "She's only a three-and-a-half-hour drive away."

Ruby backed away from the trio—not that any of them noticed—and traipsed to her laptop, where she added another one-of-a-kind drink title to the top of her menu. Kerfuffle. If her life thus far was any indication, this one was going to be a big seller.

"It's time for you to go," she said loudly enough to be heard over the din.

All three turned to face her.

"What?" her mother asked.

"But I'm not finished—" her father grumbled.

"You're kicking us out?" Amanda groused.

Ruby stood her ground. "Thanks for all your help these past two days. I mean that from the bottom of my heart."

"You're asking us to leave?" her six-foot-three-inch father asked incredulously.

"I'm begging you," she said.

"See what you've done?" Scarlet said to Red.

"So I'm worried that my little girl is a barkeeper."

Red O'Toole's little girl was twenty-eight years old and stood almost five foot eleven. But she smiled at him as she rounded the bar to give him a daughterly kiss on the cheek and a heartfelt hug. "The smoke alarm probably just needs a new battery. One burner and a microwave is all I need. I can deal with the leaky faucet, and those steps will be a good workout."

Heaving a sigh that seemed to originate from the vicinity of his knees, her father said, "Isn't there some legal provision that allows you three days to change your mind?"

"Even if there was a provision like that, I wouldn't back out of this," she said gently but firmly. "I like this town and I especially like this bar. I feel a connection to this place. I can't explain it, but I want to make it a success. It's going to be a challenge, but I can do this. I know I can."

"Don't worry, dear, you still have me," Scarlet said to Red. "And Rusty. If you want to worry about one of your children, worry about him. Our daughter's right. We should be getting back to Gale. She's going to have plenty to do putting her furniture back the way she had it. Isn't that right, honey?"

Ruby pulled a face, for her mother knew her well.

"Are you coming, Amanda?" Scarlet asked.

"I rode with Ruby, remember?" Amanda said. "I either have to catch a ride home with you two or take a bus. But nobody's going anywhere until she answers my question." She spun around again and faced Ruby. "Details would be good."

"Details about what?" Ruby's innocent expression didn't fool anybody.

"What was the guy driving that sweet Mustang like?" Amanda asked, sounding like the kindergarten teacher she was.

Even Ruby's father waited for Ruby's reply.

"What was he like?" Ruby echoed, seriously considering the question. "Let's see. He didn't slam his car door or kick the no-passing sign even though it took out one of his mirrors."

She saw the looks passing between her mother and her best friend. There was nothing she could do about what they were thinking.

"Patient isn't on my list," Amanda said, "but it should be. What else?"

With a sigh of surrender, Ruby said, "He was blond and well dressed and understandably irritated but polite."

"And?" Amanda stood up straight, as if doing so would make her less dwarfed by the three tall redheads.

"And that's all," Ruby stated.

"That's all?" Amanda echoed.

"Isn't that what she said?" her father asked gruffly.

"But, honey," Ruby's mother implored.

"Was he tall?" Amanda and Scarlet asked in unison.

Ruby opened her mouth, closed it, skewed her mouth to one side and finally shrugged. "I didn't notice."

"You didn't notice?" her mother asked gently.

"But height is *always* what you notice first," Amanda insisted.

"I told you. I'm not interested in finding a man. Maybe I'll get a dog. Perhaps a rescue with a heart-breaking past and soulful eyes."

"You're bound to run into him again, you know," Scarlet said, and very nearly smiled.

"Since you didn't hear me, I'll say it again. I'm finished with men. All men. For good."

There were hugs all around and a few tears, but those were mostly from her father. Ruby promised her mother she would call. She promised her father she would keep her doors locked. When Amanda reminded her that the reunion was in two weeks' time, Ruby reluctantly reconfirmed her promise that she would be there, too.

Finally, she stood in the hot sun in the back alley, waving as her parents and best friend drove away. Alone at last, she returned to the tavern and looked around the dimly lighted room. She had a lot to do, from remodeling to advertising to hiring waitstaff. Already she could see the new Bell's in her imagination. There would be soft lighting and lively music and laminated menus featuring one-of-a-kind drinks and people talking and laughing and maybe even falling in love. Not her, of course. But friends would gather here, and some of them would become her friends, and all of them would be part of her new life.

Happiness bubbled out of her. No matter what her father claimed, buying a boarded-up tavern in Orchard Hill wasn't a mistake.

She happened to catch her reflection in the beveled mirror behind the bar. Chestnut-red wouldn't have been her first choice in hair color and she'd never particularly liked her natural curls. Her face was too narrow and her lips too full, in her opinion, but her eyes were wide and green, and for the first time in a long time, there was a spark of excitement in them.

She hadn't made a mistake, not this time. Buying this tavern on a whim was the first thing she'd done in too long that was brave and a little wild, like the girl she used to be. She hugged herself, thinking how much she'd missed that.

Once again, the near accident she'd witnessed replayed through her mind.

Had the driver of the Mustang been tall?

Normally she had only to blink to bring the particulars into focus. In this instance her snapshot memory didn't include that detail.

Thinking about her history and her recent decision regarding singlehood, she decided to take that as a good sign, and left it at that.

Chapter Three

Two hours after her parents and Amanda left, Ruby stood tapping her foot on the sidewalk at the corner of Jefferson and Division Streets. She wasn't thinking about the quote she'd requested from the electrician or the baffling little mystery regarding the sleeping bag folded neatly on one of the pool tables in her tavern. She wasn't even thinking about the broodingly attractive man she'd encountered on Orchard Highway earlier. Well, she wasn't thinking about him very much.

She was thinking that if the walk sign didn't light soon, she was going to take her chances with the oncoming traffic, because she was starving.

At long last, the light changed and the window-shoppers ahead of her started across, Ruby close behind them. There was a spring in her step as she completed the last little jaunt to the restaurant at the top of the hill.

Inside, it was standing room only. People huddled together in small groups while they waited for a table.

Ruby made her way toward a handwritten chalk menu on the adjacent wall and began pondering her options. The door opened and closed several times as more people crowded into the foyer. Ruby was contemplating the lunch specials when someone jostled her from behind.

"Sorry about that," a tall man with a very small baby said, visibly trying to give her a little room.

Ruby rarely got caught staring, but there was something oddly familiar about the man. He had dark hair and an angular jaw and brown eyes. Upon closer inspection, she was certain she'd never seen him before.

He eased sideways to make room for someone trying to leave, and Ruby found herself smiling at the baby.

With a wave of his little arms, the little boy smiled back at her. "He likes you," the father said.

"It's this hair." She twirled a long lock and watched the baby's smile grow.

"You aren't by any chance looking for a job, are you?" the man asked.

Voices rose and silverware clattered and someone's cell phone rang. Through the din she wondered if she'd heard correctly.

"Provided you have never been arrested, don't lie, steal, cheat on your taxes or have a library book overdue, that is," he added.

She took a step back. "Um, that is, I mean—"

"Forgive me." Unlike the baby, this man didn't appear to be someone who smiled easily. In his mid-thirties, he looked tired and earnest and completely sincere. "It's just that Joey didn't take one look at you and start screaming."

She took a deep breath of warm, fragrant air and noticed that someone else was entering through the heavy front door. The crowd parted, making room for the newcomer. Suddenly she was standing face-to-face with the man she'd encountered along Old Orchard Highway earlier.

He looked surprised, too, but he recovered quickly and said, "Hello, again." He gave her one of those swift, thorough glances men have perfected over the ages. His eyes looked gray in this light, his face lean and chiseled. "I see you've met my brother Marsh."

Did he say brother?

She glanced from one to the other. But of course. No wonder the man holding the baby looked familiar. These two were brothers.

"I'm Reed Sullivan, by the way."

Upon hearing the name Sullivan, she said, "Ruby O'Toole. Do you by any chance know Lacey Bell Sullivan?"

"We've known Lacey forever," Marsh said. "Two days ago she married our younger brother, Noah."

"How do you know our new sister-in-law?" This time it was Reed who spoke.

And she found her gaze locked with his. "I bought Bell's Tavern from Lacey. I'm a little surprised to run into you again so soon," she said. "I mean, one chance encounter is one thing."

"Is that what this is?" Reed asked. "A chance encounter?"

His hair was five shades of blond in this light, his

skin tan. There were lines beside his eyes, and something intriguing in them.

Something came over her, settling deeper, slowly tugging at her insides. She couldn't think of anything to say, and that was unusual for her. Reed's gaze remained steady on hers, and it occurred to her that he wasn't talking anymore, either.

He was looking at her with eyes that saw God only knew what. It made these chance encounters feel heaven-sent, and that made her heart speed up and her thoughts warm.

In some far corner of her mind, she knew she had to say something, do something. She could have mentioned that she'd met their sister, Madeline, a few months ago, but that made this feel even more like destiny, and that simply wouldn't do. Someone mentioned the weather, and she was pretty sure Reed said something about the Tigers.

Normally, the weather and baseball were safe topics. They would have been safe today, but Reed smiled, and Ruby lost all sensation in her toes. Moments ago, the noise in the room had been almost deafening. Suddenly, voices faded and the clatter of silverware ceased.

Ruby's breath caught just below the little hollow at the base of her throat and a sound only she could hear echoed deep inside her chest. Part sigh, part low croon, it slowly swept across her senses.

In some far corner of her mind, she was aware that Marsh said something. He spoke again. After the third time, Reed looked dazedly at his brother.

"Our table's ready," Marsh explained.

It took Ruby a moment to gather her wits, but she

finally found her voice. "It was nice meeting you," she said to Marsh.

Her gaze locked with Reed's again. She wasn't sure what had just happened between them, but something had. She'd heard about moments like this; she'd even read about them, but she'd never experienced one quite like it herself. Until today.

After giving him a brief nod, she wended her way through the crowded room toward the counter to order her lunch to go. Initially she'd planned to wait for a table. Instead, she fixed her eyes straight ahead while her take-out order was being filled. All the while, her heart seemed intent upon fluttering up into her throat.

It was a relief when she walked out into the bright sunshine, the white paper bag that contained her lunch in her hand, her oversize purse hanging from her shoulder. Dazedly donning a pair of sunglasses, she hurried down the sidewalk. She'd reached the corner before the haze began to clear in her mind. Up ahead, two young girls were having their picture taken in front of the fountain on the courthouse square and several veterans were gathered around the flagpole.

Ruby skidded to a stop and looked around. *Where was she?*

She glanced to the right and to the left, behind her at the distance she'd come, then ahead where the sun glinted off the bronze sculpture on the courthouse lawn. With rising dismay, she shook her head.

She was going the wrong way.

"Care to tell me what you're doing?" Marsh asked Reed after the waitress cleared their places.

Decorated in classic Americana diner style, the Hill

had its original black-and-white tile floors, booths with chrome legs and benches covered in red vinyl. Other than the menu, which had been adapted to modern tastes and trends, very little had changed. The Sullivans had been coming here for years. This was the first time they'd brought a baby with them, however.

Reed double-checked the buckles on Joey's car seat. The baby's head was up, his feet were down and the straps weren't twisted. Ten days ago he hadn't known the correct way to fasten an infant safely into a car seat. That first week had been one helluva crash course for all three of them, but now Reed could buckle Joey into this contraption with his eyes closed. He could prepare a bottle when he was half asleep, too. Even diaper changing was getting easier.

Sliding to the end of his side of the booth, he said, "I'm buckling Joey into this car seat. What does it look like I'm doing?"

"You noticed nothing unusual here today?" Marsh countered in a quiet voice strong enough to penetrate steel.

"If you have a point, make it. I don't have time to play Twenty Questions," Reed declared.

"You don't seem concerned that the judge joined us for lunch," Marsh said, digging into his pocket for the tip.

Ivan Sullivan was one of those men few people liked but most couldn't help respecting.

After discovering Joey on their doorstep ten days ago, Marsh, Reed and Noah had paid their great-uncle a visit at the courthouse. An abandoned minor child was no laughing matter, and no one had been laughing as the brothers fell into rank in the judge's chambers. The note clearly stated that Joey was a Sullivan, and they'd had every intention of caring for him themselves while they unraveled this puzzle. In order for Joey to remain under their care, they were to keep the judge apprised of Joey's progress in detailed, weekly in-person reports.

Reed glanced over the heads of other diners and watched his great-uncle cut a path to the door. The way the aging judge tapped his cane on the floor with his every step only added to his haughtiness. Today's interrogation had been impromptu, but it was completely in keeping with his character. Surely, Marsh agreed.

His older brother left the tip on the table and Reed picked up the car seat with Joey strapped securely inside. Showing up in public with the baby had been the private investigator's suggestion. Arguably the most successful P.I. in the state, Sam Lafferty was banking on the possibility that seeing Marsh and Reed with Joey would stir up a little gossip and perhaps jar someone's memory of having seen an unknown woman with a small baby in the area.

"We're doing our best to care for Joey," Reed insisted. "The judge knows that. We leveled with him today."

"We?" Marsh countered. "He asked what steps we're taking to locate Joey's mother and why we haven't hired a permanent nanny and how much Joey weighs and where he sleeps. You, who can outtalk most politicians, barely said boo."

"I wouldn't go that far," Reed argued.

"That a fact?"

Reed narrowed his eyes at his brother's tone. And waited.

"You ordered the salmon," Marsh said offhandedly.

"That was salmon?" Reed asked.

Marsh slanted him a look not unlike the judge's. "You had meat loaf. It arrived with a loaded baked potato just the way I ordered it. Shelly mixed up our plates. You dug into my lunch the moment she set it in front of you."

With his sinking feeling growing stronger, Reed raked his fingers through his hair, for surely the shrewdest judge in the county had noticed Reed's faux pas. If he and Marsh were going to keep Joey out of the system, neither of them had better display so much as a hint of poor behavior.

They walked outside together and stood shoulder to shoulder beneath the red-and-white awning shading the restaurant's facade.

Grasping the handle of the car seat firmly in his right hand, Reed let the seat dangle close to the ground, simulating a rocking motion that was lulling Joey to sleep. "I owe you," he said. "You don't even like salmon."

"It's nothing you wouldn't have done for me, but that was some reaction you had to the redhead who bought Lacey's place."

A city crew was working on a burst water main at the bottom of the hill on Division Street, and traffic was being rerouted. Unbidden, Reed's thoughts took a little detour, too, over long legs and creamy skin and amazing hair and green eyes that had locked with his.

"Holy hell," he muttered under his breath.

He didn't get any argument from Marsh.

A horn honked at a delivery truck parked in the left-turn lane and three boys with shaggy hair and black

T-shirts raced by on skateboards. A meter reader was marking tires and three old men were talking in front of the post office. It was just another ordinary summer day in Orchard Hill, and yet nothing had felt ordinary to Reed and Marsh in the past ten days. Joey's arrival had changed their lives, and neither of them could shake the feeling that something monumental was coming.

Their phones rang moments apart, startling them both.

Reed fished his phone out of his pocket, and over the booming bass of a passing car's radio, he said, "Yes, Sam, I'm here. Slow down."

When it came to investigative work, Sam Lafferty didn't mince words. Reed listened carefully to the latest report while keeping his end of the conversation to simple yes-and-no answers.

Marsh's call ended first. After a few minutes, Reed slipped his phone back into his pocket, too. Waiting until two dog walkers were out of hearing range, he said, "Sam located another woman named Julia Monroe."

He had Marsh's undivided attention.

"According to Sam, she's five feet tall, has curly blond hair, a doting husband and a six-month-old baby daughter who looks just like her."

Joey's eyelashes fluttered as he slept. Reed wondered if he was dreaming of his mother. He didn't know if that was possible, but lately a great deal had happened that he'd never imagined was possible.

"The Julia I know is five-six and has dark hair."

Marsh's voice sounded strained and his disappointment over yet another dead end was almost palpable. He wanted a resolution to this as much as Reed did.

"Sam is following every lead he has on both Cookie and Julia," Reed said. "He'll locate Joey's mother. Or she'll return for him, as she said in her note. We need to be prepared either way, to do what's best for Joey *either way,* and we're working on that. We are. You know it and I know it. Who was your call from?"

"It was Lacey," Marsh answered. "She and Noah stopped in Vegas and decided to spend the rest of their honeymoon there. She wants one of us to pick up those old cameras her dad used to display on the shelves behind the bar at Bell's."

"Why don't you take Joey home," Reed said. "I'll get the cameras and be right behind you."

"Are you sure that's a good idea?"

Obviously Marsh was thinking of Reed's reaction to Bell's new owner. But Reed was determined to stay levelheaded as he awaited the eventual outcome of the paternity test they'd performed that very morning. If the results of that test indicated that Joey was Reed's son, Reed's life would include Joey's mother in one capacity or another. Until they knew for sure, he had no intention of getting involved with anyone.

"Maybe I should collect those cameras," Marsh said.

"I'll go," Reed said. "Don't worry, I have this under control."

The last time Reed had been summoned to the alley behind Bell's Tavern, he'd had every intention of calmly talking Noah out of a fight. He'd wound up with a sore fist and a bruised jaw. When it was over, he and Noah had brushed the alley dust off their shoes and walked away, leaving the three troublemakers sitting in the dirt.

The alley was paved now, the steps leading to the second-story apartment freshly painted. Determined to maintain a far greater degree of restraint this afternoon, he parked beside Ruby O'Toole's sky-blue Chevy. He would knock on her door, politely ask for Lacey's cameras and then leave. If he felt so much as a stirring of red-hot anything, he would douse it before it spread.

Cool, calm and collected, he started up the stairs. At the top, he knocked briskly. In a matter of seconds the lock scraped and the door was thrown open, and Ruby O'Toole was squinting against the bright sunlight, hard-rock music blasting behind her.

"Isn't that Metallica?" he asked.

"Are you taking a survey?"

Reed had the strongest inclination to laugh out loud, and it was the last thing he'd expected. Ruby wasn't laughing, however, so he curbed his good humor, as well.

She'd put her hair up since lunch. Several curls had already pulled free. The hem of her white tank had crept up at her waist and a strap had slipped off one shoulder, revealing a faint trail of freckles that drew his gaze. The ridges of her collarbones looked delicate, her skin golden. He couldn't help noticing the little hollow at the base of her neck, where a vein was pulsing.

"I'm in the middle of something here," she said huffily as a curl fluttered freely to the side of her neck. "So, if you don't mind—"

Subtle she wasn't.

"You're busy," he said. "I'll come back at a better time."

She was shaking her head before he'd uttered the last word. "Oh no you don't. Uh-uh." Gritting her teeth, she said, "That isn't what I meant."

Two motorcycles chugged into the alley, the riders conversing over their revving engines. Stifling irritation that seemed to be directed toward him, she opened the door a little farther and said, "You might as well come in."

She didn't add *Enter at your own risk,* but she might as well have. Again, he had the strongest inclination to smile. His curiosity piqued, he followed her inside.

He closed the door but remained near it as he looked around. The living room had dark paneled walls and high ceilings and worn oak floors. A doorway on the left led to the kitchen. On the right was a shadowy hallway.

Ruby veered around half of a large sectional sitting at an odd angle in the center of the room and didn't stop until she reached a low table on the far wall. Her back to him, she quickly reached down for the volume button on an old stereo. No seeing man could have kept his eyes off the seat of those tight little shorts.

She spun around and caught him looking. While she narrowed her eyes, he reminded himself he had a legitimate reason for being here.

He'd come to—

It had to do with—

Discretion. Yes, that was it. And valor, and honor and responsibility and, huh, other important things, he was sure.

Apparently experiencing a little technical difficulty with the neurons in his brain, he took a moment to reacclimatize. It wasn't easy, but he forced his gaze away and once again looked around the room. An old trunk had been pushed against the wall, a carpet rolled up in front of it. There was an overstuffed chair and a floor lamp, too, and a few dozen boxes stacked two and three high. The fact that she'd been unpacking and arranging heavy furniture explained the sheen of perspiration on her face. He wasn't sure what to make of her irritation.

"Is something wrong, Ruby?" he asked.

Wrong? What could possibly be wrong?

Ruby didn't know whether to huff or, gosh darn it, swoon. She'd never really cared for her name, and yet Reed Sullivan made it sound like a treasure. He had one of those clear, deep voices perfectly suited for late-night radio shows and the dark. She almost wished he would keep talking.

He couldn't seem to keep his eyes off her. Unfortunately, she couldn't keep hers off him, either.

He wore dark pants and a dove-gray shirt, and it must have been hours since he'd shaved. He'd politely kept his distance, and yet the shadow of beard stubble on his jaw suggested a vein of the uncivilized. Her imagination took a little stroll that made the possibilities seem endless. The fact was, she liked the way he looked in that shirt and she was fairly certain she would like the way he looked with the buttons undone, too.

Whoa. She had to put a stop to this.

She'd made a promise to herself. She'd listed her goals when Amanda and her parents had been here hours ago. They had to do with pride and determination and succeeding and nothing to do with the way the air heated and her senses heightened every time she came within ten feet of Reed Sullivan.

She gave herself a firm mental shake and reminded herself that she really needed to focus. "Here's the thing," she said sternly.

There was a slight narrowing of his eyes, but he remained near the door, watching her, waiting for her to continue. His brows were straight and slightly darker than his hair, his face all angles and planes, his lips parted just enough to reveal the even edges of his teeth. She wondered what his mouth would feel like against her lips, her throat, her—

Grinding her molars together, she straightened her spine. She supposed she couldn't legitimately fault him for the color of his eyes or the way his pants rode low at his waist.

She blinked and refocused.

While the fan whirred behind her, she said, "I've been known to make bad choices, but I've never gotten thoroughly lost and I'm not about to start now. Do you understand?"

"This has something to do with getting lost?" he asked.

"I went the wrong way today, but I was not lost."

"I see."

He was being polite again, and patient, which only increased her frustration. Holding out her hand in a halting gesture, she said, "Yes, you're tall, with a capital *T.* And you have a slightly sinful smile you don't overuse. All that aside, you're just another good-looking guy in a fine broadcloth shirt. No offense."

"None taken." There went that sinful smile he didn't overuse. And there went the feeling in her toes.

She sighed. "It's true that I have fly-by-the-seat-of-my-pants tendencies. My father expects my new business venture to fail, and my cheating ex-boyfriend believes I'll come crawling back, and maybe I have made rash decisions in the past, but I never get lost. It has to do with my photographic memory. Technically it's called eidetic imagery."

He assumed a thoughtful pose, his left arm folded across his ribs, his chin resting on his fist.

Ruby's clothes were beginning to feel constricting, her bottom lip the slightest bit pouty and her pulse fluttery. And her toes, well, blast her toes.

While twenty-year-old heavy-metal music played in the background far more softly than Aerosmith ever intended, Reed rested his hands confidently on his hips and said, "In essence, you're saying you got lost today and it had something to do with me."

"Not lost," she countered. "Slightly turned around. I don't want— I just don't think— I shouldn't." She shook her head, straightened her spine. "I won't."

The old stereo shut off. Without music, the whir of the fan was a lonesome hum in the too-warm room.

"I'm spontaneous," she said, trying to explain. "Unfortunately, I bore easily. Believe me, it's a curse. I had a dream job in L.A. that I hated, and now I'm here, and I don't want to go back to my dad's towing service. I bought this tavern and I need to focus on getting it open and running and keeping it that way, not on some guy who, it turns out, is *tall*."

"With a capital *T*." He met her steadfast gaze. "Isn't that how you put it?"

The air heated and her thoughts slowed. It was all she could do not to smile.

Time passed slowly. Or perhaps it stopped altogether. She found herself staring into his blue-gray eyes, and doing so changed everything, until there was only this moment in time.

She swallowed. Breathed.

Yes, he was tall, she thought, and he didn't scream expletives after he'd been run off the road, and the color of his eyes was as dense and changeable as storm clouds. It was unfortunate that staring into them had wiped out the feeling in her toes, but it wasn't his fault.

"Ruby?" Reed said.

"Yes?"

"I stopped by to pick up Lacey's cameras."

She blinked. For a second there she thought he said he'd stopped by to pick up Lacey's cameras.

Ohmygod. That's what he said.

She hadn't blushed since she was thirteen years old and she really hoped she didn't start again now. Since the floor failed to open up and swallow her whole, she whirled around, stuck her stupid tingly toes into the nearest pair of flip-flops, grabbed the key ring off the peg in the kitchen and started for the door.

She darted past him, down the stairs and around the barrel of purple-and-yellow petunias blooming at the bottom. Every concise little thud the heels of his Italian loafers made on the stairs let her know he was following her.

She unlocked the tavern's back door, and as the heavy steel monstrosity swung in on creaking hinges, she said, "You could have stopped me."

Surprisingly, his voice came from little more than two feet behind her. "Only a fool would stop a beautiful woman when she's insinuating she's profoundly attracted to him, too."

Ruby must have turned around, because she and

Reed stood face-to-face, nearly toe to toe, his head tilted down slightly, hers tilted up. Holding her breath, she found herself wondering why it seemed that the smallest words in the English language were always the most poignant and powerful.

Too, Reed had said.

She was profoundly attracted to him, *too.*

That meant he was profoundly attracted to her, *also.*

They were profoundly attracted to each other.

Lord help her, she was reacting to this profound attraction again, to his nearness and the implications and nearly every wild and wonderful possibility that came with it. His gaze roamed over her entire face as if he liked what he saw. As the clock on the courthouse chimed the quarter hour and a horn honked in the distance, Ruby's heart fluttered into her throat, her toes tingling crazily and her thoughts spinning like moons around a newly discovered planet.

She and Reed seemed to realize in unison how close they were and how easy it would be to lean in those last few inches until their lips touched. If that happened, it would undoubtedly be incredible and there was no telling where it would lead. Fine. There was a very good chance it would lead to sex, wild, fast, ready, middle-of-the-day sex that spiraled into a crescendo of adrenaline and exploding electricity not unlike the music she'd been listening to before she was so rudely—okay, not that rudely—interrupted.

They stilled. Taking a shaky breath, she drew back, and so did he, one centimeter at a time.

He was the first to find his voice. "As tempting as it is to take a little detour here, I'm not going to."

"You're not?"

He shook his head. "You have my word."

"Oh. Um. Good." Since his word was something she doubted he gave lightly, she led the way through a narrow hallway, past the storage room and restrooms, and into the cavernous tavern in need of paint and a good scrubbing and a brand-new image. Flipping on light switches as she went, she continued until she reached the ornately carved bar where she'd left the box she'd started filling with Lacey's cameras.

"Here's the thing," Reed declared, using her exact terminology.

It occurred to Ruby that he was not a man of almosts. He wasn't almost tall or almost handsome or almost proud. He was all those things and more. He'd drawn a line in the sand and apparently he intended to make certain she knew exactly how far, how deep and how wide the line ran.

"The baby you saw my brother carrying before lunch?" he said.

"Joey?" she asked, standing on tiptoe to reach the last three cameras on the top shelf.

"Joey, yes. You assumed Marsh is his father."

She stood mute, waiting for him to continue.

"Unless I'm mistaken, you alluded to that at the restaurant," he said.

Half the lights in the room were burned out and the bulbs in the other half were so dim and the fixtures so grimy, light didn't begin to reach into the corners. Murky shadows pooled beneath the small tables and mismatched chairs. The billiards tables in the back were idle, the shape of the neatly folded bedroll barely discernible from here.

Carefully tucking Bubble Wrap around another

camera, Ruby finally said, "Are you telling me Marsh isn't Joey's father?"

"It's possible he is." Reed's voice was deep, reverent almost, and extraordinarily serious. "But it's also possible I am."

Surely Ruby's dismay was written all over her face all over again. But she didn't have it in her to care how she looked.

The baby she'd seen before lunch was possibly Reed's? Had she heard him correctly?

"Oh, my God."

He nodded as if he couldn't have said it better himself.

She slid the cumbersome box of cameras aside. Resting one elbow comfortably on the bar's worn surface, she gestured fluidly with her other hand and said, "Have a seat, cowboy. This is one story I've got to hear."

Chapter Four

For years, Bell's Tavern had been considered the black sheep of drinking establishments in Orchard Hill. It was where someone just passing through town went to drink too much and whine to strangers, where regulars and first-timers alike drowned their sorrows and cheated at cards, among other things. Its saving grace had also been its most redeeming quality.

What happened at Bell's Tavern stayed at Bell's Tavern.

It seemed oddly fitting that Reed was about to reveal details of a nearly unbelievable situation to the new owner right here at Bell's, where countless others had undoubtedly done the same thing. Choosing a stool, he sidled up to the bar and made himself comfortable.

The carton containing his sister-in-law's cameras sat on the counter near Ruby's right elbow. As she tucked an old movie projector from the fifties into the box, another curl pulled free of the clip high on the back of her head and softly fluttered to the side of her face. Her skin looked smooth, her lips full and lush, her eyes green and keenly observant.

A warm breeze wafted through the open back door, but other than the muffled sounds of midafternoon meandering in with it, Bell's was quiet and still. And Reed's voice was quiet as he began.

"My brothers and I discovered Joey on our doorstep ten days ago. We heard a noise none of us could identify and rushed out to the front porch. There the baby was, strapped into his car seat, wailing his little head off."

"He was by himself? But he's so small," she said.

Reed released a deep breath. "I know. Who leaves a baby on a doorstep in this day and age? Noah is an airplane test pilot and always buzzes the orchard when he's returning from out of town. From the cab of his plane an hour before we discovered Joey, he saw a woman walking across our front lawn. Despite the fact that it was eighty degrees out that day, she was wearing a dark hooded sweatshirt. We think she was hiding Joey underneath it."

"And you believe this woman was Joey's mother?"

"Who else could she have been?"

When Reed was growing up, his dad always said Marsh and Noah had been born looking up, Marsh to the apple trees and Noah to the sky, while Reed looked at the horizon and the future. That night the three of them had stood dazedly looking down, completely baffled and dumbfounded by the sudden appearance of the baby crying so forlornly at their feet.

"Joey was wearing a blue shirt and only one sock. Days later Noah discovered the other one under the weeping willow tree near the road. We theorize that his mother hid there until we'd taken him safely inside."

Ruby covered her mouth with one hand as if imagining that. If it was true, Joey's mother wasn't someone who'd carelessly and heartlessly dumped her innocent baby off and driven away without a backward glance. Instead, she'd hidden behind a tree where she could see the porch but no one could see her, and had remained there until she was certain Joey was safe.

Reed remembered looking out across their property that evening, past the meadow that would serve as a parking lot that would be teeming with cars in the fall, to the apple trees, gnarled and green, and the neatly mown two-track path between each row. The shed where the parking signs were stored along with the four-wheelers and all the other equipment they used for hayrides and tours every autumn had been closed up tight.

He'd peered at the stand of pines and the huge willow at the edge of the property, but he'd seen nothing out of the ordinary. Certainly no one had moved.

He could only imagine how still she must have held, and he couldn't even fathom how difficult it must have been to leave Joey in such a way. What he didn't know was why. Why had she left him? Why hadn't he or Marsh been told one of them was going to be a father? Why had she waited? Why had it come to this? Why?

"When I picked the baby up, a note fluttered to the porch floor. It said, 'Our precious son, Joseph Daniel Sullivan. He's my life. I beg you take good care of him until I can return for him.'"

Ruby seemed to be waiting for him to continue. When he didn't, she asked, "That's it? That's all the note said?"

Reed nodded. "Nearly word for word. It wasn't addressed or signed. So we don't know which of us is Joey's father." He paused for a moment before clarifying. "It's not what you're thinking."

Tucking another loose curl behind one ear, she said, "You know what I'm thinking?"

"Are you thinking that sounded perverse and oddly twisted?" he asked.

She smiled, and some of the tension that had been building inside him eased. Without explanation, she ducked down behind the bar, disappearing from view. He heard a refrigerator door open below. When she popped back up, she had a bottle of chilled water in each hand.

He accepted the beverage she offered him, and while she opened hers and tipped it up, he thought about that first night with Joey. In five minutes' time, life as he'd known it had gone from orderly to pandemonium.

"Joey was crying and Noah and Marsh were trying to free him from the car seat and I was desperately digging through the bags he'd arrived with until I found feeding supplies. After a few clumsy attempts we managed to prepare a bottle, and while Noah fed Joey, I did a little research online. Judging by his size, the way he made eye contact, supported his own head and kicked his feet and flailed his arms, he was likely three months old, give or take a week or two. We did the math, and reality sank in like a lead balloon. One of the three women from our respective pasts had some explaining to do."

"That's putting it mildly," she said.

He lifted the plastic bottle partway to his mouth and added, "Why would a woman go through a pregnancy alone, physically, financially and emotionally, only to desert a baby as strong and smart and damn close to perfect in every way three months later?"

Ruby shrugged understandingly, and Reed thought she might have missed her calling until now. "Is Lacey the woman from Noah's past?" she asked.

"Yes, she is," Reed said. "She took herself out of the equation almost immediately. Once you've gotten to know Lacey better you'll believe me when I say she wasn't subtle about it, either."

"So," Ruby said gently. "Paternity comes down to you and Marsh."

Reed nodded before taking a long drink of his water. "When you happened upon my near miss this morning, I was on my way home from the drugstore with a paternity test kit. Marsh and I have been interviewing potential nannies all week, but until we find one we both approve of, we're taking turns caring for Joey. Marsh needs to work in the orchard this afternoon, so Joey's going to help me balance the books in the new business system." With that, he pulled the carton of cameras toward him and stood up.

She stepped out from behind the bar and followed, switching lights off along the way. "You two are looking for a nanny for the baby. That's why Marsh practically offered me a job earlier."

"He what?" Reed stopped so abruptly she slammed into him, every lush inch of her front pressing against every solid inch of his back.

Her hands landed on his waist like a pair of fluttery

birds, her breath warm and moist on his shoulder. She was svelte and soft and slender, and if his hands hadn't been busy carrying the cumbersome carton containing Lacey's cameras, there was no telling where he might have put them.

The contact was over quickly, and yet her imprint remained. Heat surged under his skin and need churned in its wake. Heat and need. Man and woman. Hunger and allure.

This was not good.

It felt good, damn good. That wasn't good, either.

"Sorry about that," he said, his voice huskier than it had been moments earlier. "I guess I shouldn't stop in front of you without warning."

An awkward silence stretched like evening shadows. Her cheeks were pink and she didn't seem to know where to look. Reed couldn't stop looking. A vein was pulsing wildly in the little hollow at the base of her neck. One strap of her tank top had slipped off her shoulder again, baring a faint sprinkling of golden freckles he wanted to touch, with his fingertips, and with his lips.

Not good. Not good at all.

Attempting to move his thoughts out of dangerous territory—again—he cleared his throat and said, "You must have made quite an impression on Marsh in order for him to have offered you the position without consulting me."

"At the time," Ruby said on her way once again toward the open door, "I thought it was strange when he asked me if I've ever been arrested or cheated on my taxes or had an overdue library book."

That sounded like his older brother, Reed thought. "Did you accept his offer?"

She made a sound men were hard-pressed to replicate. It was a breathy vibration females learned at a young age. He couldn't see her expression, but he imagined she was rolling her eyes as she said, "Accepting job offers from complete strangers in crowded restaurants is on my bucket list along with picking up hitchhikers, hiking in the woods with serial killers and amputating my toe for fun."

Reed walked outside smiling.

At the threshold of the tavern's back door, she quietly asked, "What about Joey's mother?"

That, he thought, was the million-dollar question. He hoisted the carton of cameras a little higher in his arms and said, "She's either someone I met during a layover in Dallas last year or an artist Marsh fell for on vacation earlier in the same month. Unfortunately, it could take up to four weeks for the paternity test results to be processed and mailed back to us."

"And if she returns in the meantime, as her note implied? What then?" she asked.

"We'd know which of us is his father, wouldn't we?"

"Why did that sound as if you have a plan?" she asked.

Reed was accustomed to feeling unsettled. Feeling understood was new and far too pleasant.

Not good. Not good at all.

"I couldn't hand Joey back to his mother and pretend this never happened. I couldn't forget he exists, and I doubt Marsh could, either."

"You'd fight for custody?" Ruby asked.

Shifting slightly beneath the blazing afternoon sun,

he opened the trunk of the Mustang he was driving until the mirror on his other car was repaired. "If I'm Joey's father, and if Cookie had a good reason for leaving him with no explanation—and it would have to be a very good reason—it's highly likely she'll be in my life. I don't know how this is going to end or what's going to happen between now and then."

Shading her eyes with one hand, she said, "Now isn't a good time for me to lose my direction and it isn't a good time for you to change yours."

"I appreciate the recap."

She pulled a face, but she couldn't help smiling at his wry humor. "Good luck, Reed. I hope you find what you're looking for."

"I prefer not to rely on luck." He closed the trunk and strode to his door. "We've hired the most successful P.I. in the state. And by the way—" he turned back toward the bar and pointed "—we're keeping our eyes open for the young woman Lacey and Noah saw climbing out the tavern's window."

"What?" Ruby yelped. "What woman? What window?" Her voice rose in pitch and volume with every query.

She swung around and looked where he was pointing. Until this instant she hadn't given the window in the loft space above the tavern more than a passing thought. A pipe that had once served as a downspout ran alongside the window all the way to the roof. The pipe had been cut off at some point in time and capped six feet above the ground. The bottom of the window itself was at least fifteen feet up. "You're telling me a woman was seen climbing down the downspout outside my window?"

"Technically it wasn't your window at the time."

She didn't need to tell him this wasn't funny. He wasn't laughing. In fact, he looked dead serious.

"Who was she? What was she doing here? And why would she have been climbing through a second-story window of a derelict building regardless of who owned it at the time?"

Reed reached inside his car and snagged a pair of sunglasses off the dash. Slipping them on, he said, "I suppose because there's no other access to the loft anymore."

She shot him a look that had maimed lesser men.

"Seriously," he said. "Lacey and Noah didn't recognize her, but evidently a few days earlier, Lacey had discovered a sleeping bag under one of the pool tables at Bell's."

A sleeping bag? A gong was going off in Ruby's skull. "But why?" she asked. "What does that have to do with—"

"Apparently someone had been sleeping downstairs in the tavern."

The temperature on the thermometer across the alley registered eighty-seven degrees. That meant Ruby's goose bumps had another origin.

"Lacey called the police," Reed explained. "During a thorough inspection, the officer discovered a water bottle with a pink lipstick stain on the rim under one of the pool tables where the bedroll had been. It's possible whoever stowed the items there was a college student or a runaway. The police have no reason to believe she's still in the area."

"Then she's long gone?" Ruby didn't think she'd ever met a man who held so still, and it occurred to her, as her hand fell away from her eyes, that his stillness was a prelude, like the calm before the storm.

"That's their theory," he said.

"But not necessarily yours," Ruby said, calming down.

"She was sleeping here," she said, thinking out loud. "And the sleeping bag is still here. I'm more interested in your theory than theirs."

"Honestly? I think she'll be back, if not to retrieve the sleeping bag, then for whatever she came to Orchard Hill to do."

"Could she have been Joey's mother?" Ruby asked.

"The women my brother and I were involved with are in their early thirties," he replied. "Lacey thought this girl was closer to seventeen or eighteen, and had light brown hair down to her waist. I don't believe in coincidence, either, and the fact is, Lacey discovered that sleeping bag the same night my brothers and I discovered Joey on our doorstep."

Her unease evaporated like dew in morning sunshine. What did she have to be afraid of, really, except a teenage girl with waist-length hair and a penchant for trespassing?

Ruby had taken self-defense classes in college, although admittedly her best training had begun in childhood. Growing up with a tyrannical twin brother had taught her to recover quickly from surprise attacks around corners, and of course, the sweet art of retaliation.

Operating one of her father's tow trucks hadn't been without risk, either. Now, in purchasing Bell's, she had inadvertently inherited a mystery, and a very puzzling one at that. But she wouldn't let that scare her and get in the way of her plans.

Reed slid behind his steering wheel and started his car. "I appreciate you boxing up Lacey's cameras. Knowing her, she'll stop over and thank you in person when she and Noah get home from their honeymoon next week." With that, he drove away, one arm resting on his lowered window. There was a hint of reluctance in his wave.

Ruby retraced her footsteps inside, where she made a wide sweep of the tavern's interior. At the billiards table where the plush sleeping bag was folded neatly, she went perfectly still, listening for phantom footsteps overhead.

A fly must have followed her in and was buzzing from one light fixture to another. Otherwise, the room was utterly quiet. There were no suspicious creaks, no hollow thuds or discordant scrapes of a window being opened or closed, no footsteps of any kind. In fact, the only other sound in the tavern was the slow release of the breath she'd been holding.

She took one last look at the bedroll on the pool table and locked the back door. As she started up her stairs, she reminded herself that the police didn't expect the young woman to return.

The former owner did, though. And so did Reed Sullivan.

At four-thirty on Friday, Ruby was settled comfortably in a booth at the Hill with a glass of ice-cold lemonade near her left hand, her iPad and phone in front of her and an order of appetizers due any minute from the kitchen.

She'd been in all-systems-go mode since early yesterday. So far she'd hired a father/son duo to refinish the floors and paint the tavern's ceilings, scheduled the electrician, taken applications from two college students with experience waiting tables and arranged to interview a bartender from Lansing. She'd spoken with dozens of people. Many were men. Some were tall. Her toes hadn't tingled once.

Absently sipping her lemonade, she reminded herself that she wasn't going to think about her tingling toes. She wasn't going to think about Reed Sullivan's puzzling situation or how lean and fit he'd felt during those brief moments when her body had been pressed against his. She especially wasn't going to think about that.

She had plenty to occupy her mind, as well as every moment of her time: namely, preparing for Bell's grand reopening three weeks from tonight. Thanks to the little inheritance her grandmother had left her, she'd been able to pay cash for the building. Ruby was a saver from way back—her mother claimed all the O'Tooles still had their first nickel, and she had the money for the renovations and a year's expenses in her savings account. That didn't mean she planned to burn through it. The sooner she had the tavern up and running the better.

She'd missed lunch, and right now, those appetizers she'd ordered were vying for her attention, too. She took another sip through her straw and looked around. Other than a large group seated around a long table in the back of the room, she and a handful of others had the restaurant to themselves. It was the ideal atmosphere to work through dinner.

She drained her lemonade and reviewed the order form she was filling out from a local winery. Prices were high, and although there was a column for unforeseen costs written into the budget, she knew she had to expect hidden expenses.

She *wasn't* expecting a woman with dark hair and a dozen bangles on her wrist to slip uninvited into her booth. Tall and slender, the woman hunkered down slightly in her seat directly opposite Ruby as if trying to make herself as small as possible. Her dress was black and sleeveless, her violet eyes expertly made up, her fingernails as polished as the rest of her. "If you don't move an inch," she said, "dinner is on me."

Ruby had to fight the temptation to look over her shoulder. *"That,"* she said, "is the second-best offer I've had today. Ex-boyfriend?"

"God, no. I'm a wedding planner and that group in the back is here for the rehearsal dinner. I'm finished for the day, but a few minutes ago I was going over a last-minute detail with the bride. Her brother squeezed my, ah, shall we say, derriere? Luckily, his fiancée wasn't looking. This time. My client has been dreaming of her perfect wedding day her whole life, so I think I'll wait until after the cake is cut tomorrow to make a scene. But enough about me. What was your best offer of the day?"

Ruby slanted the woman a secretive smile and said nothing. After a moment the brunette smiled, too.

"I'm Chelsea Reynolds."

"Ruby O'Toole."

"I know. You bought Lacey Bell's tavern. Three nights ago she and Noah Sullivan eloped before flying off into the wild blue yonder. You drive a sky-blue

Chevy and yesterday you were seen talking to the other two Sullivan brothers in the lobby here."

Being careful not to lean forward as she reeled from sheer surprise, and thereby give Chelsea's position away, Ruby said, "What did I have for breakfast?"

Two perfectly shaped eyebrows rose like crescent moons as Chelsea said, "If you give me a minute, I could find out."

Ruby found herself laughing out loud.

With an answering smile, Chelsea said, "I heard Marsh and Reed brought the baby to lunch with them yesterday. Everybody's talking about it. First, Noah elopes, and now, either Marsh or Reed is a father? Women all over Orchard Hill are crying in their beer, which will be good for your business. And if Marsh or Reed wind up planning a wedding, it'll be good for my business. By the way, thanks for allowing me a little cooling-off time-out at your table."

"You're welcome," Ruby said.

"Why did you?" Chelsea asked.

Watching a bead of condensation trail down the side of her glass, Ruby said, "A few months ago I ducked behind the produce stand at Meijer when my ex-boyfriend came into the store."

"Did he see you?" Chelsea asked.

"I'm afraid so," Ruby said. "Evidently being among the last to know he was a lying two-timing flea-ridden hound dog wasn't humiliating enough."

Chelsea stopped brushing invisible lint from the front of her dress and sneered. "If he shows up in Orchard Hill, let me know. I have extremely sharp kneecaps, or, if need be, a fantabulous pair of pointy-toed Jimmy Choo knockoffs."

Ruby would have to keep that in mind, although she wasn't worried Peter would show his face in Orchard Hill. He was just conceited enough to believe she would come crawling back to him. She really had thought she loved him. Now she dreaded seeing him at the class reunion, and hoped he didn't embarrass her further.

"Jimmy Choo knockoffs?" she said. "Be still my heart."

"I know," Chelsea agreed. "It's all about being in the right place at the right time."

The stuffed mushrooms and mozzarella sticks arrived piping hot and smelling like heaven, and while Chelsea and Ruby compared dating horror stories, another place setting was brought out, another order for dinner placed, and cheating men and fitting retaliations discussed and diabolically plotted. For the next hour and a half, Ruby left her iPad off, silenced her cell phone and simply enjoyed Chelsea Reynolds's wry humor and quick wit.

"Tell me about the new Bell's," Chelsea said as she dipped her breadstick in marinara sauce.

And Ruby launched into her favorite topic these days: her vision for her tavern. "Think upscale pub meets back-alley brewery. There will be cards in the back, billiards tournaments the first Friday of every month, fun, noise and laughter. And, of course, dancing on weekends."

Spearing a wedge of tomato in her salad, Chelsea said, "There's nothing like hot and loud to work up a thirst and keep the drink orders coming."

"There is that," Ruby agreed. "It's so much more than a business venture to me. I want Bell's to be a place people come to have fun, a place where someone goes to celebrate finally turning twenty-one or where coworkers meet at the end of a long week. I'd like it to be a stop for soon-to-be brides having one last hurrah with the girls before marrying the man of their dreams. Who knows? Couples might even meet for the first time there, and maybe fall in love. I hope people have a good time at my new place regardless of why they stop in, and when they need it, a chance to sulk or brood."

Sometime after their entrée dishes were cleared away and their desserts ordered, Chelsea reached into her bag and brought out a sketch pad. Animated and invigorated by the opportunity to talk about her tavern, Ruby was only vaguely aware of the jangle of bracelets as Chelsea made wide sweeps across the paper with her pencil.

They talked about the renovations she was making and the one-of-a-kind drinks she planned to offer. Chelsea loved Kerfuffle and Dynamite and Starstruck. She suggested Cheater Beater, which was similar to Ruby's brother's suggestion, Ball Buster, both of which Ruby thought she'd pass on. But Chelsea was easy to talk to, and just as easy to listen to.

Finally, there was a lull in the conversation, and they both pushed their half-eaten desserts away. Chelsea tore the top sheet of paper from her sketch pad and with a flourish held it out to Ruby.

Taking it, Ruby could only stare in wonder at the whimsical sketch. "You're an artist?"

"I'm not trained professionally, but I can't help myself sometimes. This is your personal little welcome to Orchard Hill."

The waitress arrived with the check and foam boxes

for leftovers, and soon Ruby and Chelsea wended their way through the crowd now filling the restaurant's lobby. Outside, Chelsea unlocked a shiny black Audi, and Ruby veered into the first alleyway she came to. She had her oversize bag on one shoulder, an amazing sketch advertising Bell's grand reopening tucked away neatly inside. She also had an invitation to dinner tomorrow night circling the back of her mind, and a new friend. Not one of those had been on her to-do list, which proved once again that sometimes the best things in life simply happened.

She strode east, then north and east again through the alleys that crisscrossed the business district of Orchard Hill. Smiling at dog walkers, kids on bikes and couples out for an evening stroll, she didn't give the route she took more than a passing thought. She didn't need to. Her sense of direction was once again in perfect working order. Obviously yesterday had been a fluke.

Feeling hopeful about the future and happy about today, she rounded the final corner and instantly saw a girl coming toward her.

They both veered slightly, effortlessly averting an awkward collision, Ruby's red hair swishing around her shoulders and the girl's waist-length hair swishing around hers. Ruby smiled, but the girl only gave her a curt nod in return. Without so much as slowing down, she continued on her way.

Ruby stared after her, her heart thudding. The sight of a teenage girl with long hair and a T-shirt emblazoned with the words Beethoven Rocks was no cause for alarm, and yet Ruby was seriously considering following her. It had nothing to do with the girl's hair or her clothing or even her dancer's gait, and everything to do with the pink-and-green bedroll tucked beneath her arm.

She didn't look back. Ruby watched to make sure. After the girl had disappeared around the first corner she came to, Ruby ran to the tavern's back door, unlocked it and threw it wide open.

She knew what she would find, but she turned on lights and hurried to the pool table, anyway. The sleeping bag was gone, just as she'd expected.

Ruby thought about everything Reed had told her about his situation and its possible connection to the girl Lacey and Noah had seen climbing from the window outside Ruby's back door. She could only imagine how shocking it must have been to discover a baby on their doorstep, and to realize that one of them was little Joey's father. Reed had most likely barely scratched the surface when he'd mentioned what they were doing to care for Joey and the steps they were taking to locate the baby's mother.

He'd been right about one thing. The girl certainly wasn't a figment of anyone's imagination. Ruby had seen her with her own two eyes. She appeared to be in her late teens and she was definitely still in Orchard Hill. Apparently she was still letting herself in and out of the tavern without the use of a key, too.

Was her presence here in Orchard Hill connected to little Joey Sullivan's, as Reed suspected? How could it be, and if so, what possible connection could there be between a girl letting herself in and out of Ruby's bar and one little baby boy?

It was a puzzle, and yet, Ruby felt strongly that Reed was right. It seemed unlikely that these puzzling coincidences weren't somehow related in some profound way. How remained a mystery, and yet, reaching into her shoulder bag for her car keys, she knew what she had to do.

Chapter Five

"You two are killin' me here. You know that, right?" the P.I. asked as he rummaged through a coffee-stained file folder.

Reed and Marsh both shrugged. Sam Lafferty had arrived at their door fifteen minutes ago in faded jeans and an impossibly wrinkled shirt. His red-rimmed eyes and gruff attitude hadn't fooled either of them. Sam may have been short on sleep and long on dead ends, but he had the stealth of a leopard on the scent of an antelope.

Wherever Joey's mother was, *whoever* Joey's mother was, he would find her. That knowledge—no, that *faith*—made it a little easier to sleep at night for both Sullivan brothers.

"I have another photo here I want you to look at,"

Sam said. "Where the hell did it go? I saw it a minute ago. I'm sure of it."

Reed felt the man's sense of urgency. Times ten.

They'd begun this evening's meeting seated around the iron-and-glass patio table outside. It hadn't taken Joey long to drink his bottle and it hadn't taken Reed long to grow restless. Putting the baby to his shoulder for a burp, he'd risen to his feet. Now all three men stood in a semicircle in the dappled shade near the back door.

It was that time of the day when sounds seemed to carry for miles. Insects buzzed and a television perpetually tuned to the weather droned faintly through the open window. An airplane rumbled above the clouds and every once in a while another car could be heard pulling away from the stop sign on the corner. Much, much closer, Joey made mewling sounds against Reed's shoulder.

Reed had a keen business sense, always had, and yet he could set his clock by the length and angle of the shadows in the orchard. All four of the Sullivan siblings could. On this, the first official day of summer, sunset was still another two and a half hours away. Even then, darkness would creep slowly from one horizon to the other, gathering in doorways and around corners before saturating the very air between the earth and the sky.

Not long ago Reed had had that kind of patience. Now he wanted action. He wanted answers. And he wanted both right now.

"Here it is," Sam said, handing over the print he'd been looking for. "Take a look at this one, Reed."

Sam had been searching for Joey's mother for ten days now. To Reed, it felt like much longer. The P.I.

had conducted dozens of internet searches and personal searches, had sat through tedious hours of surveillance and had followed leads to North Carolina, Tennessee and Texas. He'd been kicked, punched and threatened, but insisted it was all in a day's work. He'd spoken with the owners of the little shops and coffeehouses Marsh and Julia had visited on the Outer Banks last year, and he'd also made a pass through every little restaurant within a five-mile radius of the Dallas airport where Reed had met a waitress named Cookie a few weeks later.

Sam had called in favors and had forwarded to Reed and Marsh pictures of women who might potentially be Joey's mother doing everything from shopping to running a red light. "Does the stacked little blonde in that photo look at all familiar?" he asked.

Keeping one hand on Joey's back, Reed studied the image carefully. The woman in the photograph had shoulder-length blond hair and plenty of it. Texas hair, Cookie had called it.

"It was taken at a crosswalk on a busy street in downtown Dallas yesterday," Sam explained. "Until seven months ago, she worked at a restaurant near the airport."

Reed continued to study the image. In the photo, her head was turned slightly away from the camera, showcasing her profile. Could this be her?

He'd racked his brain trying to remember every detail about their brief encounter last year. "The woman I knew was blonde and nice-looking. She had a great body, but I don't remember her being quite this chesty."

"Have you ever seen a woman who's been breastfeeding? If you haven't, you need to," Sam insisted.

"Trust me, if Cookie had a baby, she'd likely be even more stacked. Does it look like her, otherwise?"

Even in heels, the woman in the photo was shorter than the people she was with, just like the flustered waitress who'd accidentally spilled chili in Reed's lap last year. This woman's height was right, her hair was right, the clothes were right, the city was right. "I suppose it could be her," he said.

"Shoot me some odds," Sam grumbled.

"It's possible. I don't know beyond that," Reed said. "What else do you know about the woman in this photo?"

"She's twenty-nine, works as a sales clerk at a department store and recently began a new job moonlighting at a restaurant that just opened up downtown. Her name is Bobby Jean Pritchard, but according to my source, her friends call her Corky. Occasionally she goes by Cookie. God knows, Texans like their nicknames. Why don't you tell Uncle Sam here what pet name she had for you."

The sound Reed made through his clenched teeth was as uncouth as he would allow himself to be with the baby in his arms. Sam chuckled. Marsh's curiosity must have finally gotten the better of him, for he took the photo when Reed was finished and looked, too.

Reed had told Sam all the pertinent information he could recall from his encounter with Cookie last year. She'd waited on him at a little café near the airport. When the bowl of chili he'd ordered slid off her tray and landed upside down on his table, thick red globs dropping onto his lap, her eyes had widened in genuine horror. She'd apologized over and over and started dabbing up chili with paper napkins. He'd stopped her before she'd done any real damage.

She said her name was Cookie, that she was single and had been born and raised in Dallas. She'd had what sounded like a genuine Texas accent and wore a ring on her little finger, more than one bracelet, big hoop earrings and clothes that were tight in all the right places.

Attractive and a little pushy, she was the one who'd suggested they go someplace more private when her shift was over. Reed certainly hadn't objected. They'd taken his rental car to her place. It seemed to him that her apartment building had been only a mile or two from the restaurant. This was one instance when an eidetic memory would have come in handy, for the apartment complex had looked like hundreds of other apartment complexes. She'd had the usual furniture, a small television, a few framed photographs, potted plants on a low table and shoes scattered about.

Had Joey been conceived in a nondescript apartment beneath a noisy window air conditioner? The idea chafed. They'd used protection, but every man alive knew that only abstinence had an unwritten guarantee.

Joey wiggled at Reed's shoulder the way he always did when he needed to burp but couldn't. Patting his little back as if it was second nature, Reed couldn't help thinking that the encounter that produced this amazing little kid should have been more memorable. But berating himself wasn't doing any good. It wouldn't be the first time a child had been born as a result of a one-night stand and it probably wouldn't be the last. That didn't ease his sore conscience, however.

He and Cookie had both been adults, and they'd both known what they were doing. Neither of them had done a lot of talking after they'd reached her place. Now he wished he would have at least thought to ask her real name. It was a shame he hadn't saved the heart-shaped note she'd tucked into his pants pocket hours later, for on it she'd written her phone number in bright pink ink.

Joey finally burped, and it was unbelievably loud for someone so small. Even Sam, who insisted he didn't know one end of a baby from the other, couldn't help smiling.

"What else can you tell us?" Reed asked the P.I.

"Before I left Dallas," Sam said, closing the file folder on the table, "I had a guy I know run the note you found the night you discovered the baby. He lifted five partial sets of fingerprints. Four came from men with big hands." He held up his bear paw. "Mine, and since all three of you Sullivan brothers handled the note, it stands to reason your prints would be on it, too. The fifth set was smaller, definitely female."

"And?" Reed and Marsh prodded in unison.

"Her prints aren't on file with the police. It appears our girl doesn't have a record, which is good for her but another dead end for us. I had another friend analyze the handwriting, the ink and the paper."

Reed and Marsh were so intent upon what Sam was telling them that they paid little attention to the light blue car slowly coming up their driveway. Maybe they'd get lucky and this new information would be the breakthrough they'd been waiting for. Hopefully it would lead them to the woman who'd left Joey on their doorstep seemingly out of the blue less than two weeks ago.

"Was Julia Monroe right- or left-handed?" Sam asked Marsh, his gaze flickering to the driveway.

"Right-handed."

Sam looked at Reed next. "What about Cookie?"

Reed recalled the way Cookie had slowly torn his receipt from her order pad that night, and later scribbled her phone number on a small piece of paper. "She was right-handed, too," he said. "What did the handwriting analysis reveal?"

"Plain white stationery, blue ink, a steady, flowing script written in a woman's right hand. Now, which one of you is holding out on me?"

"What are you talking about?" Marsh groused.

"The question you should be asking isn't what," Sam insisted. "It's who. As in, who's the redhead?"

Reed finally took a good look at the sky-blue Chevy pulling to a stop behind Sam's dusty Ford. The next thing he knew, the driver's-side door was opening and Ruby O'Toole was getting out.

There were three men standing near the sprawling white house when Ruby parked behind a dented SUV with a Michigan license plate. All three were tall, and all three watched her so intently as she approached she had to fight the temptation to smooth her skirt and fiddle with her bracelet.

Reed was holding Joey and talking with Marsh and a man she didn't recognize. Judging by their squared shoulders and serious expressions, she'd interrupted something important.

"You were right, Reed," she said, getting directly to the point the instant she reached the patio. "That girl with the long hair is still in Orchard Hill."

"How do you know?" Reed asked.

"I saw her."

His brow furrowed as he said, "When?"

"A little while ago in the alley outside my place. She returned for the bedroll, just like you thought she would."

The slight breeze sifted through Reed's short blond hair, and a shadow darkened his jaw. Joey wiggled, his head bobbing as he looked at something over Reed's shoulder.

"Are you two talking about the girl who was sleeping in the tavern?" Marsh cut in.

Ruby started. Oh. Right. There were others present.

"Yes," she said to the darker-haired Sullivan. "I came face-to-face with her while I was walking home from dinner not more than half an hour ago."

"You're sure it was her?" Marsh asked.

"I'm pretty sure, yes."

As if trying to piece together her impromptu encounter with the mysterious girl, Reed said, "You mentioned that she returned for the bedroll. Did you actually see the sleeping bag?"

"It was tucked under her arm. I was pretty sure it was the same one. The moment she was out of sight, I ran to the tavern and checked. The bedroll Lacey asked me to leave out was gone. You told me you thought this girl's presence in Orchard Hill was somehow related to Joey's, so I drove right over."

His tired smile caught her unawares, stirring something in that secret place beneath her breastbone where forgotten dreams lay waiting. Although the patio was shaded, heat lingered in the flagstones beneath the soles of her sandals. Surely that was where this warmth originated.

"Reed," the man she hadn't met said. "Maybe you

could do the honors. And somebody bring me up to date here."

Reed's eyes widened for a moment, but when he spoke, it was with efficient practicality. "This is Sam Lafferty, Ruby, the P.I. helping us locate Joey's mother. Sam, Ruby O'Toole."

She and Sam Lafferty forewent a formal handshake as they sized each other up. So he was a private investigator, she thought. She might have guessed that from his appearance, although he could just as easily have been a bouncer or an undercover cop or a fugitive, for that matter.

Close to six-four in his scuffed boots, he stood with his feet apart, muscles flexed, hips slightly forward in the cocksure manner of a man who was confident in his sex appeal and wanted everyone to know it. She'd known men like that. In fact, she'd fancied herself having a future with one, but that was before she'd discovered Peter had been cheating on her.

Never again.

To his credit, Sam Lafferty's gaze didn't slip below her shoulders. She cut him a little slack for good behavior and followed his gaze to the table where a thick file lay near an empty baby bottle.

"Walk us through the encounter," he said. "From the beginning, if you wouldn't mind."

"Of course," she replied. "I've been exploring the alleyways that run behind the businesses lining Division Street, familiarizing myself with the stores and shops while testing my sense of direction, you might say." She happened to glance at Reed. Once again, it wasn't easy to look away. "I rounded a corner and came face-to-face with the girl."

"Can you describe her?" the P.I. asked.

"She was around five foot six, had an oval face, blue eyes and brown hair down to her waist. I didn't see any piercings, but there was a butterfly tattoo on the inside of her right wrist. Her bag was Coach and her sandals had cork heels. And she had the sleeping bag under her left arm."

"How long did this encounter last?" Sam Lafferty asked.

She pondered a moment, considering. "She didn't stick around long. We were probably walking toward one another no more than five or six seconds."

"That's a lot of detail to recall after only five or six seconds," he pointed out.

It was Reed who explained, "Ruby has an eidetic memory." At Sam's raised eyebrows, he said, "Do a Google search. Better yet, she'd probably recite your license plate number if you asked nice."

She rattled off the number effortlessly, her gaze never straying from the unkempt P.I.'s.

Sam's surprise was almost comical. He recovered quickly, though, and said, "How old would you say this girl was?"

"Late teens most likely. I seriously think twenty would be a stretch. She wasn't at all what I would expect someone who sleeps in derelict buildings and climbs out of second-story windows to look like. She seemed polished. Poised. She must have nerves of steel because she didn't glance over her shoulder as she hurried away, although I sensed she knew I was watching her. There's one more thing."

She turned to Reed and Marsh. "She was wearing

a silver chain around her neck and a monogrammed charm. I'm pretty sure two of the initials were J and S."

"Joseph Sullivan," Reed said.

She found herself looking at the baby. His little T-shirt was bunched slightly beneath Reed's hand, exposing the top of his diaper and the unbelievably soft-looking skin on his lower back. His feet were bare, his dark wispy hair standing adorably on end. It was hard to imagine anyone abandoning a child so innocent, so small and healthy in every way.

Silence stretched and the mood became even more somber. The clues were stacking up, and they all indicated that the girl with the long hair was indeed connected in some profound way to Joey and this case, although at this point the actual nature of the connection was pure speculation. Was she a family member, someone who was somehow related to Joey's mother and consequently Joey, too? Or was she a close friend? What did she know? Why was she here in Orchard Hill? And where was the baby's mother?

Questions abounded. Eventually they would be answered. They had to be. But when?

Since Ruby had relayed everything she'd come here to say, she backed up a step, preparing to leave. "You three undoubtedly have important matters to discuss."

"Thank you," Marsh said, his voice deep and moving. "For taking the time to drive out here and for going to the trouble to try to help. Would you care for something to drink before you head back? A Pepsi or a cold beer? I don't know about you, but I could use a nice neat scotch."

She laughed unconsciously. "Thanks, but I'm meeting someone later. I'll have something then." With a nod at all three, she began the short walk to her car.

Reed didn't stop to analyze his actions as he fell into step beside Ruby. He simply matched his stride to hers. His shoulder was close to hers, their elbows nearly touching. Their shadows glided ahead of them over the grass, her skirt airy and her long red hair curly and free.

This late in the day, the shade from the maple tree his great-grandfather had planted the day after he returned from World War One stretched across the driveway. Joey had been fitful earlier, but now he was completely relaxed, his little head turned so that his cheek rested on Reed's shoulder, his body completely supported in Reed's arms.

Being careful not to jostle the baby, Reed stopped in the fringe of dappled shade, reached around Ruby and opened her door. "That's twice you've gone above and beyond the call of duty and twice all I have to offer is my gratitude."

"Gratitude-smatitude," she replied, wrinkling her nose.

There was something appealing about her irreverence. It wasn't the first time he'd noticed. "You're uncommonly kind, Ruby."

Her smile was wide and genuine, her bottom teeth just crowded enough to make it unlike anyone else's. He took a deep breath, and caught a hint of flowery perfume. He hadn't been expecting that any more than he was expecting her to reach her hand toward him. He thought she meant to touch him, but she laid her hand gently on Joey's back, instead.

"He looks safe and secure in your arms, Reed, as if he knows he's home."

The simple observation touched him most of all.

She got in the car, adjusted her skirt and fastened her seat belt. "Good night. And good luck," she said.

As she was driving away, he wondered who she was having drinks with later. Not that it mattered. It didn't, not in the least. He was curious, that was all.

Very curious.

Marsh and Sam were looking at him when he returned to the patio. Reed wanted to wipe the smug expressions off both their faces.

"My Sunday school teacher had it all wrong," Sam exclaimed.

"Leave it alone, Sam," Marsh warned.

"You went to Sunday school?" Reed asked.

"You're missing my point," the big man with the attitude to match declared.

"Maybe you should make your point," Reed said, his voice so gravelly Joey stirred in his arms. "Are you on the clock?"

"Prickly, aren't you?" Sam quipped. "It's no skin off my nose what you do, or who, for that matter. It's just that it occurred to me that maybe the Garden of Eden was an orchard not a jungle. Apples and temptation seem to go hand in hand." He cast a pointed look at the apple trees nearby. "Reed, I'd lay nine to one odds that your life is about to get even more complicated. For the record, that observation was a freebie. The kid's asleep. Do you want to put him in bed before or after I tell you what lead I'm following next?"

Reed gritted his teeth. Remorse didn't sit well with

him. Tightening his arms protectively around the baby, he said, "What's next? Fire away."

And without further ado, Sam did.

The stars were out.

Reed had watched them flicker into view one by one. Normally he wasn't much of a stargazer, but he'd been out here for a while. Brooding. Berating himself.

He could see the lights in Orchard Hill from here. A mile and a half away, the tallest building downtown was four stories high. When September rolled around, the football field would be lit up like a space station every Friday night. The brightest streetlights lined the business district; the rest of the city stretched out beneath the softer glow of streetlamps on every corner. It was a far cry from an urban skyline.

Reed put the plastic bottle to his lips and let the cool water run down his throat. Why was he sitting here in the dark? Why had he let Sam get to him? Why seemed to be the question tonight.

He leaned back in his chair and stared at the lights in the distance. At last count, there were twenty-five thousand people living in Orchard Hill. Technically twenty-five thousand was a high number, but compared to Chicago or Baltimore or Seattle, this was a small town. Once upon a time, he'd been certain he would spend his entire adult life in one of those cities. He'd certainly never planned to come back to the family orchard. To visit, sure, but not to live.

The Orchard O's varsity basketball team had taken state's his senior year. As the starting center, he'd been offered a sports scholarship from a big-ten college downstate. Reed didn't have the passion or the desire or, truth be told, the talent to be a professional athlete, and he'd known it. He'd had something else in mind, and Purdue came through with an academic scholarship. The following September he had been on his way toward an eventual MBA and an urban lifestyle that included a different restaurant every night and elevators to the twenty-eighth floor.

Then Marsh's phone call had come one cold February afternoon. His voice as hollow as an echo, he'd said there had been an accident. Either Marsh had stopped speaking in complete sentences after that, or Reed only heard every other word. An icy pileup on the interstate. Twenty miles from home. Their parents. Killed instantly. Both of them. Gone. Just gone.

Reed had returned to Purdue after the funeral, and he'd remained on the dean's list and the debate team and in all the right clubs for promising young professionals. He could have stayed the course he'd set because Marsh, then nearly twenty-three years old, had stepped into the role of head of the family, becoming guardian to Noah and Madeline, both just weeks away from their sixteenth and thirteenth birthdays respectively.

But Reed's course had been changed instantly and irrevocably by a force no mortal could fully comprehend. He'd doubled his class load and hurriedly finished his degree. He'd followed a new course, for he'd discovered a need for something deeper than a concrete skyline and an elevator to the twenty-eighth floor.

He'd come home and never regretted it. For Reed, it had become a point of pride. In the years since, he'd rarely thought about that old urban dream. He certainly never considered moving to Seattle or Baltimore anymore. Instead of living in some loft or high-rise, he'd moved back to the sprawling white house where he'd grown up. Together, he and Marsh had finished raising Noah and Madeline. With hard work, careful planning, educated risks and a little luck, they'd expanded the family orchard into the business it was today. Reed wasn't rich, but his life counted. That thirst for something that was missing had never quite been quenched, though.

Until the night Joey arrived.

He scrubbed a hand over his eyes. Earlier he'd done some work in his office off the living room after Sam left. Unable to concentrate, he'd brought his laptop out here only to close it before the first stars appeared. He'd heard Joey crying briefly earlier. By now Marsh had most likely tucked him into the crib they'd assembled together a few days after they'd discovered him on this very porch.

The screen door creaked open. Relying on moonlight and the light spilling through the living room window, Marsh joined him on the porch, a bottle of water in his hand. Two weeks ago they would have both been having a beer about now.

"Joey asleep?" Reed asked.

"Yeah." Marsh sat down, his forearms resting on his thighs, the bottle held loosely in both hands. Reed knew that pose. Whatever he had on his mind was important. Looking at the sky, Reed thought it was possible the stars would burn out while he waited for Marsh to speak. Thankfully he didn't have to wait quite that long.

Finally, he began. "Twice now I've seen the way

you reacted when you came within ten feet of Ruby O'Toole."

Silence.

Marsh unscrewed the cap and tipped the bottle up, then lowered it again. "I noticed you didn't deny it."

Reed didn't waste his breath telling Marsh he was making too much of this.

"I know how you feel." Marsh's voice was barely more than a dusky whisper, but full of conviction. "It's like holding Great-granddad's divining rods too close to a power line. The buzz paralyzes you, but not quite everywhere."

Reed could have done without the analogy, even though it described the sensation fairly accurately. "Was that how it was when you met Julia?" he asked.

Marsh made a reluctant sound that meant yes. "I know you want Joey to be your son. And you know I'm hoping he's mine. We haven't talked about it, but we're handling it. We always do. That said, in a perfect world, he would wind up mine, not because I'd be a better father than you. He'd be mine because that would mean his mother is the woman I fell in love with at first sight last summer."

Reed couldn't fault Marsh for the insinuation that it would be better somehow if Joey were the product of something more meaningful than a one-night stand. He'd thought the same thing. That didn't change anything, however.

"I thought Julia felt the same way about me, and yet once the week was over, she never returned my calls. I tried for weeks. I assumed she didn't want to talk to me. What else could I think? Still, if I were in charge of a perfect world, Joey would be mine," Marsh said after taking another swig of his water. "And Mom and Dad would be the ones sitting on this porch and Madeline wouldn't have had to go through the hell she went through last year, and those kids from Lakewood wouldn't have drowned in Lake Michigan last month and nobody would die until they were good and ready. But then Madeline wouldn't be happily married and expecting her first child and, hell, I suppose the world would get pretty overpopulated my way."

"You're saying maybe it's best that we can't see the big picture?" Reed asked.

"I wouldn't go that far."

Reed was tempted to smile.

"The fact is," Marsh said, "Joey could just as easily be yours as mine. I can't think of anyone, barring myself, who would be better for the job. Either way, we'll both do the right thing because that's who we are."

Reed felt a deep stirring of affection for his brother. They were so different, yet profoundly the same.

"But, Reed? If Cookie, or whatever her name is, is his mother, Ruby O'Toole might just be your Achilles' heel, and by association, mine."

"I'm not some rutting teenager, Marsh. I can handle this. Contrary to what Joey's very existence might indicate, I'm not a prisoner to my hormones."

"Reed? This involves more than hormones. I saw it with my own two eyes. She lights you up. We both know there's a lot at stake here."

Reed took a careful breath. Marsh wasn't telling him anything he didn't know. Monday morning they had another appointment with their great-uncle, Judge Ivan-the-Terrible Sullivan. It wouldn't take much for that contrary old buzzard to decide Joey would be better off in foster care than with a couple of single brothers who didn't even know which of them was his father. The employment agency was sending two more nannies for them to interview on Monday afternoon. They desperately needed help with Joey's care, but so far no one they'd interviewed had come close to being good enough. Until a nanny could be found their time was divided between Joey's care and work. The trees were loaded with apples. They needed to be sprayed and the heaviest branches braced. After last year's devastating spring frost, they needed a good yield, a prosperous year.

"There's a lot riding on our shoulders," Marsh insisted.

"You mean on our actions," Reed said.

"And on our *re*actions. Ruby O'Toole is a stunner, Reed."

Mile-long legs, sparkling green eyes and a generous smile flashed unbidden into Reed's mind. "She's uncommonly kind."

"I believe you. It's part of the package that lights you up. I'm speaking from experience when I say that kind of electricity isn't easy to resist."

"There's nothing improper between us. I'm resisting just fine."

Marsh raised his bottle. Instead of drinking, he said, "What we resist persists."

Reed nearly groaned. Their baby sister had gone all Zen last year. Not Marsh, too.

"It's like floodwater," Marsh explained. "It always finds the point of entry it seeks."

"Ruby has her own reasons for keeping things light, Marsh."

"And yet, the zing."

Of the three Sullivan brothers, Marsh was the gruffest and the quietest. At times like this, he was also very, very wise. "What do you suggest?"

"Honestly? I'm hoping you'll remember it's your turn to go for takeout."

The last thing Reed expected to do was laugh, but it rumbled out of him, rusty and real. He and Marsh were two single men who weren't afraid of the washer and dryer, vacuum cleaners, disinfectants and mops. Madeline had liked to cook when she was growing up. When Noah was home between sky events, he'd picked up the slack and fired up the grill. When it was just Marsh and Reed, they invariably ordered out.

"You're saying you're hungry?" Reed asked.

"Is this a day that ends in *y?*"

Feeling lighter somehow, Reed stood up. "A loaded pizza from Murphy's okay with you?"

"Now you're talking."

He recapped his bottle of water and carried it with him to the steps. At the bottom, he said, "Marsh?"

"Yeah?"

"Even if Sam locates Cookie first, even if the results of that paternity test name me as Joey's father, I hope you find Julia. She has to be out there somewhere."

Reed left his brother sitting in the dark with his bottle of purified water, and headed for his Mustang. He had the pizza ordered before he reached the end of the driveway. And he thought about Marsh's maxim.

What we resist persists.

Not only was his older brother wise. In this instance,

he was probably right. By the time Reed passed the city limits sign, he knew what he had to do about Ruby O'Toole and this zing.

Chapter Six

Kissing was in the air tonight.

Ruby glanced delicately at the couple stealing kisses at a nearby table. She needn't have been discreet. They were going at it pretty heavy and wouldn't have noticed if cymbals clanged and lightning struck.

Not that lightning would. It was a beautiful night, the stars faint above the soft glow of outdoor lights, the air mild even now.

She'd chosen this table here in the courtyard at Murphy's because of its clear view of Bell's. Situated on a diagonal across the street, her place was dark tonight, the curbside parking wide-open. That wouldn't be the case for long.

Her two companions were no strangers to Murphy's. In fact, they hadn't been strangers anyplace they'd gone tonight.

"Abby," Chelsea Reynolds said. "I'll give you ten dollars if you go inside and kiss that biker with the red bandanna on his head before he plays 'Shut Up and Kiss Me' one more time. You would be doing humanity a favor if you put him out of all our misery."

Abby Fitzpatrick pushed her short wispy hair behind her ears and said, "If you want the misery to stop, kiss him yourself. He's a little scary for my taste."

"You have taste?" Chelsea asked.

Abby stuck out her tongue at Chelsea, and Ruby thought there was never a dull moment with these two. Longtime friends, they'd arrived at Ruby's hours ago. Petite and blonde, Abby wore tight jeans and amazing heels, the effects of which were wasted since most of the guys she'd encountered hadn't been able to peel their eyes off her chest. Abby was a reporter and office manager at the local newspaper. As lively as a sailor on weekend leave, she believed in having fun.

With her dark hair and violet eyes, Chelsea was lean and lithe, and had forgone jeans entirely for a short black skirt and silk tank. She'd received a lot of looks, too, but her admirers were cautious about it. It was as if the men in Orchard Hill knew any open ogling would bring them pain of one sort or another.

It had been Abby's idea to check out the competition tonight. Located on the third block of Division Street, Drake's had mouthwatering bar burgers, but their service was slow and the majority of their clientele was in the over-fifty category. Like Murphy's, the Whiskey Barrel had found a unique niche. It was on one of the side streets off Division, and was the only place in town with karaoke on Friday nights. Ruby had lost count of how many songs people had sung about kissing. What could she say? Kissing was in the air tonight. Even Chelsea had sung along to "Seven Little Girls Sitting in the Back Seat." Although Murphy's had a full-service bar inside, it was more of a beer-and-pizza place. It was also the most crowded and might just be her biggest competitor. But Ruby was a firm believer in an abundant universe, and wasn't worried about the competition.

From her peripheral vision, she saw a guy wearing cargo shorts and a polo shirt approaching the table. "Hey, Abby," he said, "are you going to introduce me to this tall gorgeous splash of water you brought with you?"

"Why would I do that, Warren?" Abby asked. "She hasn't done anything to me."

Evidently accustomed to Abby's wry humor, he focused on Ruby and cranked up the wattage in his smile. "I haven't gone by Warren since middle school. I'm Ren Colby. Can I buy you a drink?"

It wasn't a bad smile. He wasn't bad-looking, all things considered. Dark hair, decent shoulders, definitely not tall, though. "Thanks, but I'm the designated driver tonight." She jangled the crushed ice in her Diet Coke. "Why don't you stop by Bell's grand reopening in three weeks? If you bring your friends I'll buy *you* a drink."

"I'll do that." He sauntered away, taller suddenly.

Abby shook her head in amazement. "My, you are good. Chelsea's right. You *are* worthy of us. Do you see that guy by the brick wall underneath the speakers?"

"The one with the ponytail or the pirate tattoo?" Ruby asked.

"Ponytail. He wore black-rimmed glasses long before they came back in vogue. I got stuck in an elevator with him once. Long story. He kisses like a cocker spaniel."

"Too much tongue?"

"Would you two mind?" Chelsea grumbled, dropping her pizza crust onto her plate. "I'm trying to eat here."

"Jeez, Chelsea," Abby admonished. "You're a grouch tonight. We really need to find you a man. How about that guy by the door?"

"You can have him," Chelsea said. "You can have them all. Or have you already?"

"Very funny." Abby turned to Ruby. "Don't listen to her. I might kiss and tell, but I don't let just anybody past first base." She stuck out her chest a little. "Gotta protect the girls here, you know? For the record, I haven't kissed every guy here. I haven't kissed Reed."

"Who?" Ruby asked, perhaps just a teensy bit too quickly.

"Reed Sullivan," Abby replied. "He's over by the pizza window. He just got here."

Ruby couldn't help looking over her shoulder. The take-out window was separated from the "drinking" section by thick rope draped between heavy posts. Reed stood on the other side of the divider looking much as he had when she'd driven away earlier, tall and lean and lost in thought. The old-fashioned gaslights turned his hair the color of beach sand and bleached the blue of his shirt nearly white.

Abby sighed. "My sister says no one French-kisses like Reed. The choirboys really are the ones you have to watch. I'm going to the restroom. Anybody care to come along?"

A new song blasted from the speakers and Chelsea made some sort of reply. Ruby had stopped listening. She felt the bump of bass from a passing car, but the courtyard and the world beyond had fallen strangely silent. Her heart beating like a drumroll, she watched Abby and Chelsea stroll leisurely toward the door, which was perhaps ten feet from the window where Reed was now paying for his pizza. Abby must have called to him, because he glanced over his shoulder at them. Their backs were to the street now, and evidently they didn't notice the scooter that was jumping the curb, the single headlight barreling right toward them.

Ruby held her breath, and the next thing she knew, Reed was vaulting over the ropes and hurtling through the air toward the pair directly in the scooter's path. A split second later, Abby and Chelsea were airborne, too.

Ruby reached them moments after they landed on the ground, an iron post crashing down beside them. It fell short, missing them all by mere inches. The scooter and the driver were on the ground, too, exactly where Abby and Chelsea had been standing seconds ago.

"Are you hurt?" Ruby asked the heap of people.

Like hands on a clock, they'd landed pointing in slightly different directions. Abby was faceup on top, legs spread-eagled, her right hand caught under Chelsea, who was facedown sandwiched between the other two. Reed was on the bottom.

"Are you guys okay?" somebody else called.

Ren Colby had come up beside Ruby. In fact, she noticed that a small crowd had gathered.

Miraculously, all three of her friends were unhurt.

Abby's bosom was heaving and Chelsea's skirt was hiked up to her hips, presenting the onlookers with a memorable view. The two of them managed to scoot off Reed and onto the ground. Sitting up, they straightened their clothes, shook out their fingers and rotated their shoulders. Apparently finding everything in working order, they took the hands the men gathering around them extended and stood up.

Reed found his feet on his own. The last one up, he brushed the dirt off his palms and then from the seat of his pants. Ruby swore Abby looked as if she wanted to help.

"You saved my life," the petite blonde said breathlessly. "There must be some way I can repay you."

"Worst-case scenario," Reed said levelly, "you would have been run over by a scooter, not a bus, Abby. You okay?"

Something bloomed inside Ruby. Glancing at Chelsea and Abby, she doubted she was the only one who appreciated his modesty almost as much as his bravery.

The owner of the bar himself cut through the little crowd that had gathered. It was unclear to Ruby if Murphy was his first name or last. In his early sixties, he was a robust man with a square face, a thick mustache and a deep booming voice. "What the hell happened?"

While Ren Colby and a few others filled him in, the boy responsible said, "The throttle stuck. I just got this scooter and I couldn't— I tried, but I guess I musta panicked. I didn't mean for— My dad's gonna kill me."

It was Reed who went to him. Ruby watched as he helped him stand the scooter up and ran his hand over the dented fender and broken spokes on the front wheel. With his bobbling Adam's apple and shaggy hair, the boy reminded her of one of the younger Jonas Brothers. She couldn't hear what Reed said, but it must have been the right thing because the teenager got his phone out of his pocket and made a call.

"Everyone here okay?" Murphy asked.

Reed scooped the crushed pizza box off the ground where they'd all landed and opened the lid. "The biggest casualty is my pizza."

"We'll get you another," Murphy exclaimed, slapping Reed on the back hard enough to cause him to wince. "On the house." He turned to Abby and Chelsea next. "You two gonna sue me?"

"For a bad pizza?" Abby quipped. "Like it's the first time that's happened."

"How're your mom and dad, Abigail?" Murphy said. "How about yours, Chelsea? Reed, you need anything besides another pizza?"

With that, the crowd began to sift back to their tables inside and out. And Ruby thought she was going to like being a part of this town.

Abby and Chelsea continued to the restrooms as they'd initially intended. Ruby stayed outside and took everything in. She noticed that Ren Colby was trying his luck with someone who'd just arrived, and the biker in the red bandanna was leaving with a hardy-looking gal wearing combat boots and a leather vest similar to his. The couple making out earlier hadn't even come up for air.

Ruby wasn't certain why she looked at Reed last. Maybe she'd felt him staring back at her. It occurred to her that she'd been wrong.

Lightning could strike tonight.

* * *

Reed felt a burning inside.

His shoulder was going to be sore as the devil tomorrow, but it wasn't that. Stepping over the rope lying on the ground, he walked directly to Ruby.

His first instinct was to move in close so she would feel the heat emanating from him and he would feel the sultriness swirling around her. He fought it, though. Resisted.

"Do you have a minute?" he asked.

He didn't catch her answer, but she led the way to a table where a leather bag hung from the back of a chair. A Prince song was playing, and a car idled at the light on the corner, its window down, the radio so loud Reed felt the bass anyplace his skin was exposed to the air. People were talking at the tables he passed. He barely heard, his eyes practically glued to Ruby. It had less to do with the fact that the fit of her jeans should be outlawed and everything to do with the fact that he was glad it wasn't.

They'd barely gotten settled in their chairs before Abby and Chelsea joined them. Close friends of his sister's, they asked about Joey and Marsh and Noah and Lacey, and relayed their daily interactions with Madeline via every social media network known to modern man. They talked and joked and laughed the way they had a hundred times before, seemingly oblivious to the tension coiling tighter inside Reed with every passing minute.

Finally they talked about leaving. Something about some story Abby was covering and a wedding Chelsea was working tomorrow. Instead of going with them, Ruby told them she'd call them in the morning. As they walked across the street and disappeared into the alley beside Bell's, the tension in Reed began to uncoil.

Ruby darted him a look after they'd gone. "You really are one of the good guys, aren't you?"

He didn't know if she was referring to his leap over that rope earlier or something else. And he didn't ask. It was beside the point.

Her skin was creamy, her cheeks touched with pink, her lips shiny. The old-fashioned gaslights in the courtyard threw shadows through her eyelashes every time she blinked and deepened the green of her top and the chestnut color of her hair, but it was her eyes—those green, green eyes—he focused on. "I hadn't planned to get into this tonight."

"Into what?" she asked plaintively.

He propped both elbows on the table and said, "A little while ago Marsh reminded me of everything riding on my actions, and my *re*actions. More precisely, on my reaction to being within twenty yards of you."

Cupping her chin thoughtfully in one hand, she said, "What *is* riding on your actions or your reactions? Are you talking about Joey?"

That she'd homed in on the heart of the issue gave him pause. The scratchy song waffling from the speakers ended. Without it, the night was quieter, almost still. He lowered his voice accordingly. "We have another appointment with the judge first thing Monday morning. He's usually fair, but he's an ornery old cuss and has the power to force us to put Joey in foster care. I can't let that happen."

"Reed?" she interrupted.

"Yes?"

"You want Joey to be yours, don't you?"

"I don't see the relevance in—"

But she interrupted him. "Why?"

"What do you mean why?" he asked.

He'd been told the sharpness in his voice could be off-putting. It didn't deter her in the least.

"A lot of guys would be secretly hoping to be let off the hook. Most guys I know would be terrified to find themselves the single parent of a baby."

"If I told you I'm not like most guys, it would sound like a line."

She looked at him without blinking. "Try giving me a straight answer," she said point-blank. "All I'm asking is why? Why does he mean so much to you? Why do you want him to be yours?"

"If I took the time to analyze *that,* I would have to take the time to analyze why I'm glad you were out with Chelsea and Abby tonight."

Her chin came up as if she'd caught something between the eyes. "Oh," she said. And then, "O-o-o-h."

She took a sip of her watered-down drink, and he took a moment to consider the best way to explain. "I assured my brother that you and I have talked about this, and are in complete agreement that neither of us has any intention of pursuing, er, anything."

"Because you're looking for a needle in a haystack and I'm not looking at all."

"Yes," he said, although he couldn't seem to stop looking. "Ruby?"

She put her glass down. Waited.

"Resisting this isn't working."

"But of course it is," she argued.

"When I just now saw you looking at me from the other side of that downed rope, I wouldn't have remembered my name if someone had asked. I don't remember how I got from there to here. That zing overruled my resistance. Marsh brought the reason to my attention earlier. What we resist persists."

She sat up a little straighter, her eyes on his. "I wouldn't have pegged your brother as a philosopher, but I'm listening."

Absently rubbing his right shoulder, Reed said, "You probably noticed we seem to keep running into each other. You've been in Orchard Hill a matter of days. How many times have we found ourselves in the same place at the same time? What does tonight make? Four times? Five?"

"Five, but—"

"So you're counting, too. Ruby, would you just stop and consider this? What if Marsh has a point? What if it's true?"

"Okay," she said a little too quickly. "For argument's sake, let's say there's something to your brother's assessment, and it's possible that the more we resist, the more this—" she motioned from her to him and back again "—persists. What do you suggest we do about it?"

"We disarm and disable the attraction," he said.

"How?"

"We stop resisting." He caught her looking at his mouth. And then she leaned down and did something to her foot under the table.

"Of course," she sputtered. "That sounds easy enough. Why didn't you say so? But how, pray tell, do you propose we do that?"

Because he couldn't help noticing how full her lower lip looked when she was being sarcastic, he said, "We delve directly past kissing. All the way."

She opened her mouth to speak, closed it and tried again. "All the way?"

"Allow me to rephrase." Leaning closer so no one around them would hear, he said, "How often do we go out with somebody only to wind up just friends in the end? A woman who looks as good as you do knows the drill. You meet someone, go out, take it to the next level and maybe you take it slow or maybe it's one fell swoop. Either way, eventually you start to notice tiny annoyances. Pretty soon they're big red flags."

She shrugged, nodded, silently agreeing he had a point.

And he continued, "What if you and I skip dating, skip the frenzy, skip the marathon and go directly to the finish line?"

Ruby found herself holding her breath. Okay, enough.

Gongs were going off inside her skull. She had to stop for a sec. She had to think. Breathing would be good. Slipping her shoe off, she absently rubbed her right big toe on her left calf and thought about the road to relationships Reed was describing.

"What exactly constitutes the finish line for you?" she asked.

He groaned quietly. "Contrary to how that sounded, I'm talking about friendship."

Oh. Well. Huh.

Leaning back in her chair, she thought about the frenzy of a new romance, the buildup and the expectations and the elation, the strategizing and all the energy expended for something that ultimately fizzled out or went sour. Reed had made a strong argument for the pro side of the just-friends debate. On the one hand it sounded absurd. Absurdity aside, she believed in the pull of the moon and the power of Venus in retrograde. She believed destiny was the mapmaker but it was the choices people made that determined their path. She also believed that sometimes there was a moment, just one moment, that changed everything. Reed had a word for that moment. *Zing.*

Something else he'd said had struck a chord in her. He'd admitted that he didn't remember walking over to her. She'd experienced a similar sensation when she'd first seen him tonight. It was as if someone had pushed the mute button on the big picture. Sound ceased and everyone in the courtyard at Murphy's disappeared.

Except him.

He was right about something else, too. They *did* keep running into one another, and each time the connection *was* stronger. Could it be that resisting only intensified the magnetic pull?

"I expected you to have more to say," he pointed out.

"Do you really believe we can be friends?" she asked.

"I don't see how we can help being friends, Ruby."

"Are you proposing that we stop resisting and go directly to BFFs?"

He shook his head the way men did when dealing with certain types of women, maybe all types of women, and then said, "A person can never have too many friends, right?"

An argument broke out at a nearby table and a waitress counting the minutes until her shift was over delivered Reed's pizza. While she trudged on over to investigate the ruckus, Reed asked, "Do you have any thoughts or questions about anything, Ruby?"

She spent a moment in quiet deliberation. "Actually, I do have one."

"Fire away."

"Did you really French-kiss Abby's sister?"

He didn't even try to hide his surprise. His golden eyebrows shot up and his storm-cloud eyes widened. "Abby told you about that?"

"She said you choirboys are the ones we have to watch out for."

"That right? I was never in the choir."

Reed Sullivan had classic bone structure and a mouth made for rakish grins. He accepted the responsibility of caring for an abandoned baby and he saved people from speeding freight trains, or scooters, whatever the case may be. If he said he'd never been a choirboy, she believed him.

"You were saying about Abby's sister," she prodded.

"Bailey and I were doing homework and had no idea her bratty kid sister was hiding in the closet. I'd made my move before I heard Abby snicker. She extorted money from both Bailey and me and promised it would be our little secret. Then Abby demonstrated what she'd seen in front of her class during show-and-tell the very next day. It was the only time I was ever called to the principal's office."

"How old were you?" she asked.

"I don't know. Fifth or sixth grade, I guess."

"That old?" she said as an Elton John song began to play.

"I was a late bloomer." His smile started in his eyes, spreading pleasantly across the rest of his face.

He was a wise guy, she thought, a tall polished wise guy with a dash of heroism and a vein of the uncivilized running through him. Scooting her chair back when he did, they both got up.

"What exactly do you do with your friends who happen to be women?" she asked. "My turn to rephrase. What constitutes friendship in your book? I guess I'm a little fuzzy on the next step."

"It can be whatever you want. Do you need fifty bucks until payday? Someone to let your dog out? Do you have any furniture that needs moving or help with heavy lifting in general?"

She raised her right arm and made a muscle. "Have you seen these guns? I don't have a dog and I still have the first dollar I ever earned."

"You can't think of anything you need help with?" He was serious.

"Not off the top of my head. I guess I'll have to think about it and let you know."

She looked up slightly. He looked down slightly. And they both smiled.

"Friends," he said.

"Friends," she agreed.

They shook on it, a handshake between friends. Then they parted company, Reed with his fresh hot pizza in his right hand and Ruby with her oversize bag on her shoulder. Neither of them mentioned the vibration they couldn't quite brush away.

Sawing. Drilling. Pounding. Crashing.

It was Monday, and the renovations at the tavern were well under way. The drop ceiling was lying in hundreds, if not thousands, of pieces on the floor. A carpenter in a tool belt was manning a vicious-looking saw, and two others were swinging hammers. More clanking and banging was coming from the restrooms, where the plumber was working on leaky pipes.

Ruby stood in the midst of it all, looking up at the dust sifting down from the rafters. The two guys on the ladders were responsible for the demolition. The tall one in charge looked down at her from his perch. "You need to put a hard hat on if you're going to stay. There's an extra one in the back of the truck. And watch out for upturned boards with nails sticking out."

In other words, she needed to get out of the way.

The electrician would come as soon as the demo work was complete, tomorrow most likely. And then the carpenters would return and the painters would work their magic. Finally the floors would be refinished. If everything went according to plan, the upgrades would run like clockwork.

Ruby's phone made the sound it always made when a text came in. Fishing it out of her back pocket, she carefully stepped around the debris without running a nail through the sole of her tennis shoes, which would have meant a trip to the emergency room and probably a tetanus shot, too, and strolled to the hallway leading to the restrooms.

It was from Amanda. And like the twenty-five previous texts from Ruby's best friend back home, it ended with C U @ the reunion.

They'd been at this for days. The first time, Ruby had replied, I'm coming down with a cold. Probably pneumonia. Or a tumor.

I'll be sure and pick up some vitamin C U @ the reunion.

Another time she'd typed, What's that? Reception's bad here.

Error. Excuse only valid on actual calls. C U @ the reunion.

Around the fifteenth text, Ruby had typed, You kids have fun.

We're going to. C U @ the reunion. PS Found a date yet?

Ten minutes ago, Ruby had texted, Are you a stalker? Do I know you?

Wondering what witticism Amanda would send next, Ruby veered around a pile of lumber in the hallway. A loud clank and mild swearing carried through the open door of one of the restrooms.

She read the latest text from Amanda as she went. Luv U. C U @ the reunion.

Ruby typed, Now you're playing dirty.

It's why you luv me, 2. C U @ the reunion.

Ruby did love her BFF. She'd always been lucky in the friend department. Her old friends in Gale had been supportive through the whole Cheater Peter debacle. Ruby didn't take infidelity lightly. She didn't take friendship lightly, either. She and her college roommate did a destination get-together once a year; she kept in touch with her friends in L.A., too. The new friends she'd made in Orchard Hill were turning out to be the kind with lasting-friendship potential, as well.

On Facebook, she'd *liked* the story Abby covered about ghost sightings at a local inn. And while she'd been waiting for Chelsea at the restaurant yesterday, Ruby had sent Reed the picture she snapped of the bulletin board where a note from a licensed day-care provider had been tacked. She'd seen him driving by a few hours before and returned his friendly wave.

Friends, she thought. A girl really couldn't have too many of them.

She reached the end of the hallway and noticed that the doors of the restrooms had been propped open. The bathrooms here had cracked tile floors and rust-stained sinks and corroded faucets. Those were their good features. The lights were on in both poorly lit spaces, but the clanking was coming from the ladies' room. She strode to the doorway with the intention of checking the plumber's progress, only to spin around.

It was too late. The image had been lasered onto the insides of her eyelids. Rubbing them didn't blur the picture she now carried of said plumber's, er, well, there was no pretty word for that part of an overweight man's anatomy.

Criminy. Humans had the capability to send messages around the world at the speed of light via computers that fit in the palms of their hands. And yet no one had been successful in designing a belt that could hold up a plumber's jeans.

She was still grimacing when her phone chirruped. It wasn't a text this time but an actual call.

It was Reed.

"Quick," she said, stepping into the alley outside. "Say something to erase what I just mistakenly witnessed in the ladies' room here at Bell's."

"I thought you had an eidetic memory," he said.

"I didn't say your job was going to be easy."

He laughed, but it sounded tense.

"I hear Joey crying," she said, squinting in the sudden brightness outdoors. "That's good, right? It's not good that he's crying, but the fact that he's crying at your place means your meeting with the judge went well." When Reed said nothing, she added, "Did it go well?"

"We've been granted another week's reprieve. So far the judge hasn't decided Joey would be better off in foster care than with Marsh and me. When it comes to deciding what's best for minor children, the court system is holding all the cards."

Ruby had heard horror stories about small children being literally ripped out of their parents' arms by a well-meaning social worker. No wonder he and Marsh were worried.

He must have picked Joey up because now it sounded as if the baby was crying directly in Ruby's ear. "It's one o'clock," she said, wondering how Reed could possibly hear her, or anything else, for that matter. "I thought you and Marsh were interviewing a potential nanny at one."

"Marsh went to Tennessee with Sam. The woman from the agency isn't here yet. Tardiness. Strike one."

"What's wrong with Joey?" she asked.

"What? Hold on." He must have moved his phone to his other ear. "What did you say?"

"I was just wondering why Joey's crying." *Her* ear was ringing. She could only imagine what all that wailing was doing to Reed's.

"Good question. He ate. He burped. He isn't wet.

He does this sometimes. Not often, thank God. Wait. I think someone drove in."

The crying continued. Gosh, the kid sure had a set of lungs.

"False alarm," Reed said. "No one's here."

Ruby imagined Reed walking the baby from room to room, jiggling him, patting him, doing everything he could to soothe him. "Have you tried singing to him?" she asked.

"What do you think started all this?"

She smiled, and imagined him smiling, too. "Did you call for any particular reason?" she asked.

"I'm killing time. I wondered if you've thought of anything you'd like help with."

"Not yet," she answered.

The *waaa-waaa-waaaaing* continued. "The woman you're interviewing still isn't there?"

"No."

"How long will Joey keep this up?"

"I'll have to ask him."

Men, she thought. But this time she was sure she'd heard a smile in his voice. "Let me know what he says, okay?"

"I'll do that."

Joking aside, Reed and Marsh desperately needed to hire someone to help with Joey's care, and in order to do that they needed to make a good impression. "You know, Reed," she said, filling a plastic can with the hose and watering the parched petunias in the barrel at the bottom of her stairs. "It might be divine providence that that woman's late. If Joey is screaming like a banshee when she drives up, she might run the other way."

"I feel better, thanks."

Laughing, she set the empty watering can inside the door and looked at the dust settling on the ladder leaning up against the wall and the lumber stacked underneath it. Reed and Marsh needed the help of professionals as much as she did. Feeling in the way here, she had an idea.

"Reed?"

Silence. Well, not total silence. Joey was still screaming.

"Reed? Can you hear me?"

But his attention was on Joey. "It's okay, buddy. I've got you. Don't worry. Everything's going to be all right."

Something went soft inside her and she heard herself say, "I'll be right there."

Chapter Seven

Ruby lifted Joey a little higher against her chest and tried not to grimace. Those muscles she'd bragged about Friday night were getting quite a workout and her trainer weighed less than thirteen pounds. She might never be able to straighten her elbow again, but it was a small price to pay.

Checking their reflection in the mirror outside Reed's den, she saw that Joey's eyes were only half open and his cheek was scrunched where it lay against her shoulder. His little bow lips were puckered and a dark spot was forming on her shirt beneath them. He was almost asleep. Mission nearly accomplished.

She padded quietly from room to room in the sprawling hundred-year-old house, listening to the clear concise tones of Reed's voice. He was in the process of conducting another interview in the kitchen.

Good grief, she thought, halfway around the dining room table. Had he really just asked Nanny McPhee's double if she'd ever been spanked?

Ruby had arrived three minutes ahead of the first interviewee. Operating under the assumption that Ruby had never seen a baby, let alone held one, Reed had asked a gazillion questions about her capabilities. She supposed she shouldn't have been surprised that being his *friend* didn't exempt her from careful scrutiny where Joey was concerned. She'd been only too happy to put his mind at ease, but all right already. Time was a-wasting.

"Reed," she'd insisted loud enough to be heard over the baby's earsplitting wails. "I bought my first car with babysitting money. It was this sweet cobalt-blue SHO—well, it had one green door and an orange fender, but everything else was blue. Do you know how many babysitting jobs it takes to save enough money to buy a car?"

Seeing his eyes narrow speculatively, she'd added, "That was rhetorical. Suffice it to say I was in great demand. I love babies. I love politicians who love babies. Some of my best friends used to be babies. I'm good with them. They like me. They do."

Joey had cried on.

Gesturing to his little head and then to his equally little bottom, she'd said, "This is the end you feed and this is the end you diaper. See? I'm practically an expert."

She'd held out her hands in silent expectation. And still Reed had been reluctant to hand him over.

"I'll guard him with my life. I promise."

Magic words, evidently. The doorbell had rung

while Reed was transferring the fitful baby to her arms. By the time she'd completed her second circuit through the sprawling house with its decidedly masculine furnishings, Joey's cries had lost their vehemence and the interview for a nanny had begun.

The first candidate of the day had been youngish and slender and not very tall. Wearing navy slacks and a white blouse befitting nannyhood, she had been as perky as Mary Poppins herself. While Ruby had walked and swayed and softly patted Joey, the young woman had recited an impressive work history for someone her age.

Apparently the baby knew something Ruby didn't. He grabbed a fistful of her hair and, still fussing, settled in for the ride.

Reed had seemed impressed with the young woman's credentials, too. In fact, he'd sounded very friendly in the interview, warm and understanding and cordial, as if he was going to be a wonderful boss. Things were going *super,* which apparently was Nanny Number One's favorite word.

A few questions about where she'd received her education led to more about where she liked to hang out and who she hung with, her favorite movies and her favorite sports team. The personal questions had turned out to be her downfall, for she developed collywobbles of the mouth, and soon she was telling Reed about her mother and soon-to-be ex-stepfather and how her boyfriend wanted to move in with her but she just wasn't sure because she might get a dog instead, and besides he was allergic.

Ruby closed her eyes on the young woman's behalf. Oh, boy. Too much information.

By the time the next woman had arrived, Joey was doing that little hiccuppy thing babies did when their crying jag was over but the memory of it remained. Notoriously too nosy for her own good, Ruby had peeked out the window and watched as a heavyset woman ambled up the sidewalk. Looking very much like a headmistress or perhaps a monk, she had short frizzing gray hair and a square face and wore a loose-fitting gunmetal-gray sack dress.

She'd told Reed she'd worked for the same family for fifteen years and was looking for another good fit. The spanking question had given the woman pause. Ruby imagined Reed must have been smiling benignly at her from across the kitchen table, because the grandmother of two confided that "her mama had done a little spanking in her day."

"Obviously she raised you to be a woman of strong character," Reed said.

"Why, thank you. It's so nice to discover somebody your age on the same page in that department. The apple doesn't fall far from the tree, believe you me. It's like I tell my daughter. Sometimes a little swat placed just so really gets their attention, doesn't it?"

Ruby could hardly believe her ears. Who knew collywobbles of the mouth was viral?

Reed was good, she thought. Sneaky good. If she hadn't been holding the baby, she would have taken notes. Wondering if he'd learned those tactics in Basic Interviewing 101 or if he'd developed the skills on his own, she made a mental note to remember them tomorrow when she met with one of the applicants for the bartending position at Bell's.

It wasn't long before Joey was humming in his sleep

and Reed was seeing the second woman to the door. Joey remained nannyless. No surprises there.

Reed stared out the window over the sink as the abrasive old bat flounced out the door. Squeezing the bridge of his nose, he closed his eyes. Joey's last crying jag had left his right ear ringing and that second interview had left a bad taste in his mouth.

Both women had been highly recommended by the agency, and he'd had high hopes that one of them would live up to her reputation. He could have overlooked the older one's chin hairs and even the grating sound of her voice, but her philosophy on discipline was not acceptable to him and it wouldn't be to Marsh, either.

The first interview had gone better. He'd been willing to give her a chance despite her tardiness. A flat tire was a plausible, understandable excuse. The fact that she'd handled it and hadn't canceled the interview was even commendable. He could have excused her drama-queen prattle, too. If only she hadn't failed the most important criterion of all. She hadn't asked to meet Joey.

He couldn't allow someone so disinterested to care for his—for Joey. He wouldn't.

The pad of footsteps sounded behind him. "Are Mary Poppins and Nanny McPhee both gone?" Ruby asked.

He let out a breath and turned around.

Ruby had arrived an hour ago in the nick of time in faded jeans, a Red Wings T-shirt and tennis shoes. Her curly hair was even more mussed now, her head tipped a bit to the left. Joey was sound asleep at her shoulder, his favorite position in the world.

Missing a sock again, the baby didn't look as if he had a care in the world. Now, why on earth did Reed suddenly feel as if an invisible fist had him by the vocal cords? He cleared his throat, swallowed. "You really do know a thing or two about babies," he finally said.

"Told you."

She did this little thing with her nose, wrinkling it slightly in a show of pained tolerance. It shouldn't have sent an electrical current through him.

He was becoming accustomed to Ruby's Florence Nightingale generosity, her uncommon kindness and good nature. She probably offered the same open helpfulness to all her friends.

Friends.

Cliché or not, friendship really was the means and the solution here. Win-win. His own words replayed through his mind. *Skip the frenzy, skip the marathon and go directly to the finish line.* Running metaphors, he thought. Not his most profound work, but it was the best he'd been able to come up with on the fly.

Crossing the room in four long strides, he said, "Here, I'll take him before your arm goes completely numb. It's amazing how heavy he can get when he's asleep."

Transferring a sleeping baby was never smooth. In this instance, it resulted in a yelp from Ruby. "Wait," she said. "He's tangled in my hair."

They stopped halfway through the switch, four hands holding one small baby. Joey's head was turned in his sleep, his arm extended, his fingers squeezed tight around a thick lock of curly hair.

"Sure," she said quietly, "*now* he's out like a light. Do you think you could get him to loosen the stranglehold he has on my hair or should we just yank that section out?"

Reed found himself smiling. Carefully shifting Joey back to her, he went to work untangling chestnut strands of spun silk from one unbelievably small and strong fist.

He and Ruby stood close together, her slender hand resting along Joey's back, her head tipped slightly in order to give Reed better access to the hair spilling over her shoulder. It was almost a relief when she started talking.

"My brother's little girl used to get her hands tangled up in her own hair. The more upset she got, the more she pulled, and the harder she pulled, the more she cried," she said.

"You have brothers, too?" He worked as quickly as possible, focused on the task.

"Just one. Rusty, well, his name is Connor but everyone calls him Rusty. He's my twin brother, actually. We're not identical."

He laughed because obviously a brother and sister could not be identical. "One unidentical twin brother and one niece? How old is she?"

"Kamryn is five. For an entire year we all believed she was Rusty's baby. No one knew the truth except his fiancée, who turned out to be a slut in disguise. His ex-fiancée now. I'm not sure if she's still a slut, but she probably is. We all really miss her. Kamryn, not the heartless ex."

Reed's fingers stilled for a moment, his gaze going to hers. She looked back at him, her eyes wide and green and guileless as she said, "Collywobbles of the mouth *is* contagious. I knew it."

He laughed. And he swore the house sighed. Perhaps that was his vocal cords unfurling. Ruby's affability, her easygoing outgoing loquaciousness was almost contagious, too.

Almost.

"It's nice that you don't hold grudges," he said.

"That's what I always say."

"So no husband or kids of your own yet?" he asked.

She tapped her foot. "No kids, no husband, not even an ex-husband. I know, right? I'll be thirty in a little over a year. I was almost engaged once, but alas, we were too young. I told him we needed to finish high school, or at the very least the ninth grade. Now he's a priest. Tell me he didn't take the breakup hard. I mean, seriously, a commitment to a lifetime of celibacy speaks for itself, don't you think?"

Reed didn't know when he'd met a woman with a drier sense of humor, but decided it might be best to bypass any discussions about celibacy for the time being. "There, you're untangled." He took Joey back into his arms, tucked Joey's arm to his side and smoothed the hair he'd just freed off Ruby's shoulder away from the sleeping child.

His fingers stilled. He hadn't meant the contact to be anything more than…anything, really. And yet it felt like…something. She must have felt it, too, for her eyes darted to his and just as quickly away.

They both recovered with about as much subtlety as the refrigerator clanking on. Taking a giant step backward, she gingerly rubbed her scalp and said, "I told Marty, Father Marty now, that if he happens to reconsider the whole priesthood thingy before I leave my childbearing years completely behind, we can still have our little Madison and Montana. Probably not the best thing to tell a man at his ordainment."

Reed laughed again. The momentary awkwardness between them gone, he said, "You're something else, you know that?"

"That's what all my friends say." He noticed she was smiling, too.

Her phone made the same sound his made when a text was coming in. She disappeared into the next room for a moment and came back with her phone and her keys.

"Did you think of anything yet?" he asked, his arms tightening around Joey.

Absently checking her message, she said, "Have I thought of anything about what?"

"Have you thought of anything I can do to help *you* for a change?"

"Oh, that. Not yet," she answered on her way to the door. "I need to get back to Bell's. Work on the renovations has begun. If you're in the neighborhood in the next couple of days, stop by."

"I'll do that," he said. He walked her to the door, held it with his free hand. "Thanks again, Ruby."

She did that thing with her nose once more. "That's what friends are for, pal."

He watched her go, and saw her dash off a text on her way to her car. The last thing he heard through the screen before she got in her vehicle was her rich, luscious, sultry laugh.

Ruby reread Amanda's latest text while she put her seat belt on. Ran into Jason. Asked about you. Bet he'd be your date for the reunion. C U @ said event.

Jason Horning had had a crush on Ruby since kindergarten. She'd been a head taller than him then, too.

I'd rather go with Father Marty, she typed back.

Not acceptable. I'll think of something. C U @ the reunion.

Can't talk, Ruby typed. Trapped under something heavy.

She'd barely started her car before the next text arrived. a. Person b. Place c. Animal or d. Thing? If it's a. spare no details. C U @ the reunion.

Ruby shook her head and backed around Reed's Mustang. Her best friend in Gale had a one-track mind. It was only one of the reasons they got along so well.

Friends, she thought, adjusting her rearview mirror—now, why on earth did she turn it so she could see her own eyes?

She'd called Reed pal.

Pal. Buddy. Comrade. Chum. Amigo. Bro. All were synonyms for friend, which was what he was, what she was, what they were. Friends.

She checked for traffic and pulled onto the paved road. Friendship was…peaceful. It may not have been as invigorating as *the frenzy,* but it was nice, pleasant, enjoyable, even. Safe. Being friends beat resisting, hands down.

She neared the four-way stop on the corner of Old Orchard Highway and Orchard Road, both named by early Dutch settlers who reputedly squandered nothing, not when naming roads and city streets or even their children, for that matter, who quietly and unobtrusively went their entire lives without middle names. An old woman eating by herself at the Hill had shared that particular gem of folklore only yesterday. Ruby enjoyed hearing about legendary people and myths and memories. She always had. She had one of those faces people talked to, she thought as she coasted to a halt at the corner. It was a good barkeeper's face.

A friendly face. Waiting her turn, she glanced in the mirror—nobody was behind her—and met her own gaze once again. Choosing the friendship route with Reed was turning out to be exactly what they both seemed to need. A few minutes ago she'd been standing statue-still a foot away from him, his breath warm on her cheek and his fingers gentle in her hair. Her toe had been on its best behavior.

Friendship definitely cured the zing. Her hand went to the tendrils he'd touched. Well, for the most part, anyway.

Two days later, Ruby stood in the middle of her tavern and viewed the renovation's progress, although lack of progress would be a more fitting description. Work had come to a screeching halt yesterday—some problem with the authenticity of a temporary permit, which had turned out to be a perfectly legitimate piece of paper. By the time she'd gotten that verified in writing from the correct city servant *twenty-six* hours later, the drywall hangers had started their next remodel and wouldn't be able to squeeze Bell's back into their schedule until Friday, *at the earliest.*

Ruby had many fine qualities. This she knew for a fact. She was kind, helpful, nonjudgmental, socially tolerant, accepting and generally quite friendly, not to mention a lot of fun.

Patient, she wasn't.

She stomped around the cavernous room where the jukebox and tables and chairs had been. The billiards tables were covered with tarps, as were the old, ornately carved bar and all seven attached stools, which was good. Once the renovations were completed and the protective plastic was removed, a little tung oil and elbow grease would bring out the bar's best features, mars, scratches, scars and all. The plumber had finished his work in both restrooms. Again, that was a good thing. The mountain of broken pieces of the yellowed, disgusting drop ceiling had been shoveled into buckets and carried out to a rented Dumpster. The positives were adding up.

Friday at the earliest? Were they kidding?

All right, she told herself, her hands in her back pockets, the curls around her face springing free of the knot high on the back of her head. This wasn't the end of the world. As long as the drywall crew returned when they said they would, Bell's would still be ready to open on time. It wasn't best-case scenario, but it was doable, and doable was fine.

Fine wasn't elation, but, she decided as she turned out the lights and locked the door, there was nothing she could do about it. Friday at the earliest.

Oh, brother.

Wandering around her new apartment hours later, she was still clenching. She'd gone over the beer, wine and liquor order with a fine-tooth comb and would place it first thing in the morning. She'd come across an advertisement online for a restaurant liquidation sale, and chose her top-ten favorite one-of-a-kind drink titles. She even began designing the simple menu. She'd invited Abby and Chelsea to see a movie playing at the newly reopened theater downtown. But Chelsea was in Grand Rapids at a bridal show and Abby was meeting somebody she met online. Ruby hadn't felt like going alone.

Her mother had called, and her brother and Amanda, too. Even though she didn't ask for their opinions, her mom said she was PMSing and Amanda said "this too shall pass" and her brother suggested she should either get drunk or laid or both.

She should have known better than to complain. Hormones, idioms, booze and sex. They'd certainly covered everything. Unfortunately, it didn't make her feel any less like chewing glass.

Finally, she'd taken a shower and changed into yoga pants and a tank top she'd washed so many times it was as soft as a second skin. Feeling refreshed and comfortable, if not happy-snappy, she thought about grabbing a bite to eat and considered going to bed without it. She looked at her phone. Gosh, it was only nine o'clock. Seriously?

For lack of a better idea, she wandered onto the stoop for a little fresh air. Though shadowy here in the alley, it *was* still broad daylight. Was she stuck in a time warp?

Interestingly, a silver Mustang was pulling to a stop down below. Reed got out and looked up at her, his feet apart, brown chinos slightly wrinkled, the sleeves of his white shirt rolled halfway up his forearms.

She waited until the clock on the courthouse completed its ninth chime to say, "That's two minutes slow."

"Has been for years," he called up. "Elementary-school teachers have incorporated it into basic math lessons. If the courthouse clock is two minutes slow and the clock strikes seven, what time will it be in fifteen minutes?"

Another interesting tidbit of area folklore, she thought. "What are you doing here?"

"I'm taking you up on your invitation to show me the renovations at Bell's."

"They're at a standstill until Friday at the earliest." She couldn't control her little sneer. "I was just thinking I missed dinner. You're welcome to join me."

"Do you cook?"

"Not well."

"What are you having?" Obviously he was picking up on her less than jovial mood.

"Triple fudge ice cream. It's called Death by Chocolate, which has to be better than Death by Friday at the Earliest."

She could see him trying not to grin as he started up the stairs. Leaving him to find his own way in, she headed to the kitchen for the bowls and spoons.

Reed took the steps two at a time and strolled through the door Ruby had left open. The last time he'd been here, music had been playing and the room had been in wild disarray. Tonight her small apartment was quiet, the sectional in its rightful place opposite the TV, the rug rolled out flat. There was a large conch shell on the trunk she was using as a coffee table and a green-and-blue watercolor on one wall.

Ruby was drying her hands when he entered the minuscule kitchen. "Rough day?" he asked, eyeing the tub of Death by Chocolate ice cream.

She answered without looking up from the carton she was opening. "More like a missed window of opportunity." She paused, as if pondering something. With a mild shake of her head, she reached for a bright yellow ice-cream scoop and got busy.

The antiquated fluorescent lights overhead flickered the way old fluorescent lights often did, and every ten seconds the oscillating fan on the table stirred the air in their direction. Ruby wore knit pants and a faded tank top that had been washed so thin the lace of her bra showed through. Beneath that lace, her breasts rose and fell with her every breath. Concentrating on her task, she spooned ice cream into the first of two flowered bowls. One scoop, two.

"Strawberry jam or grape?" he asked hurriedly, forcing his gaze elsewhere.

"Strawberry jam or grape what?" she grumbled, adding another scoop.

"It's a getting-to-know-you question." It happened to be more than that, a lot more, for with it he was trying to distract his wayward thoughts and the way he was reacting to Ruby.

Seeing her skewing her mouth to one side in serious contemplation, he said, "There's no right or wrong answer." When it became apparent she wasn't going to reply, he studied her expression even more closely. "Okay, let's try another one. You were listening to vintage music when I stopped by to get Lacey's cameras the other day. Which do you prefer, Guns N' Roses or Leonard Cohen?"

"That's another tough one," she said.

He eyed the bowl that was getting so full he didn't see how it could hold any more. She found room, though.

"Give it a whirl," he said. "Choose one."

Pulling a face, she set an open jar of fudge topping in the microwave and started filling the second bowl. "Music is one of the reasons I bought a bar," she finally said. "Did I tell you I want to have live music on Saturday nights? And that old jukebox in the back still works, a bonus if there ever was one. Music is kind of my thing. You name it, I like it—rap, country, heavy metal, classical, anything old most of all. Billy Joel, ACDC, the Rolling Stones, Elvis, Waylan Jennings, Mozart, the Pointer Sisters."

"Fair enough," he said. "What's your favorite color?"

Noticing her inner struggle again, he was beginning to see a pattern. "Cats or dogs?" he asked.

Silence.

"Sunrise or sunset?"

Sticking a spoon into the mound of ice cream, she held the bowl out to him.

"Trains or airplanes?" He took a step closer.

She crossed her eyes.

"Summer or winter?" Another step brought him within reach of her.

"Did I mention I have trouble making up my mind?" she asked.

"Day or night?"

"Reed?" The fan whirred. The fluorescent lights flickered. And she raised her gaze to his.

"Yes, Ruby?"

"What are you doing?"

"That ice cream's for me, right?"

"Of course." The microwave dinged, and she said, "Would you care for some hot fudge?"

"There isn't room in my bowl," he answered.

He wasn't surprised that struck her as funny. Tipping her head back, she started to laugh. She had a marvelous laugh. He'd noticed that before. Rich and sultry, it floated out of her like the lyrics of a song, making him glad he'd stopped by.

She returned the nearly empty carton to the freezer, and added hot fudge to the chocolate concoction in her bowl. He watched her take her first bite and saw the rapture on her face. Sampling his, he was struck anew by the differences between men and women. There was only one activity that brought men that much pleasure.

"You don't have Joey with you," she said after she'd taken the edge off whatever was fueling her ice-cream marathon. "That must mean Marsh is back. How did his trip to Tennessee go?"

It was Reed's turn to shrug.

With a wrinkling of her nose, she said, "Don't expect me to answer questions if you won't."

"You didn't answer any questions." Watching her turn a spoonful of ice cream upside down in her mouth, he considered telling her about Sam's newest discovery. It was the biggest lead they'd had yet. Nothing had been verified and certainly nothing had been proven, but Sam was getting closer to finding the woman behind Joey's sudden appearance on their doorstep. Reed felt it in the pit of his stomach. Her identity still hovered slightly out of reach like a word on the tip of his tongue, as vital as the air he breathed.

For some reason, when he opened his mouth, that

wasn't what he said. "Your first car was a blue SHO with one green door. Mine was my dad's old Charger. He handed me the keys the day I accepted the scholarship from Purdue. Told me if I was going to college on my own brainpower-induced nickel, the least he could do was give me wheels to get there. He knew I had my eye on a future in some sprawling city like Houston or Seattle or maybe Miami, but for those next four years, he wanted me to have a way home.

"Every time I pulled into the driveway for a weekend at the orchard, he'd invariably lay his hand on the hood of that car and say, 'She's yours now, son. You keep her in gas and oil changes, and she'll get you where you need to go.'"

The windows in Ruby's upstairs apartment were open, but Division Street was quiet this time of the night in the middle of the week. Other than the whir of the fan and the hum of the fluorescent lighting, her kitchen had grown quiet, too. She ate her ice cream slowly, and didn't ask why he was telling her this or what his father's gift meant to him. Maybe that was why he continued.

"It was ten below zero the day I got Marsh's call. I knew by the way he said my name it was bad. Then he told me about the accident. How Mom and Dad were dead. But Noah was okay. Madeline, too."

Reed stared into the spinning blades of the fan, but it wasn't the blur of metal he saw. "The temperature was ten below zero and yet that car started the first time I turned the key. There are two hundred seventeen miles between West Lafayette and our driveway. I don't remember one thing about the drive that night, but Dad was right. The Charger he entrusted to me took me where I needed to go. It brought me home."

Surfacing, he found himself standing across the small room from Ruby. Her ankles were crossed, her lower back resting against the counter, her spoon in one hand, her empty bowl in the other. It was hotter than blazes in here, and the humidity had made her hair curlier and her skin dewy. He wondered if she knew she was naturally beautiful, gorgeous really.

Her spoon and bowl clattered as she set them in the sink near the bright yellow ice-cream scooper. Hooking her thumbs on the counter on either side of her waist, she said, "Whatever happened to that Charger?"

She didn't ask how he'd managed to draw a breath after he'd heard the news. She didn't ask how he'd made it home during the worst blizzard of the decade, or how it'd felt when he got there.

No. Not Ruby. She asked the one question he could answer.

"Noah wrapped it around a tree two years later. He and Lacey are getting back from their honeymoon this weekend. If you see him, make sure you mention how lucky he is to be alive. Not because of the wreck, although it was a miracle he survived that. He's lucky I didn't strangle him with my bare hands."

"I haven't actually met Lacey's husband yet. I'm sure that will get us off to a great start."

He nodded in total agreement.

Later, he wouldn't recall whether they'd shared a smile then. They changed the subject, and conversation ultimately turned to her plans for Bell's, the varieties of apples grown in Reed's family orchard and a new secret graft Marsh was working on. She told him about the going-out-of-business sale at a restaurant in Sparta and the barware she hoped to purchase there.

Taking his forgotten bowl from him, she said, "I take it you're not the Death by Chocolate type."

He let his gaze flick over her once more, at her wildly curly hair and her slender shoulders and the outline of lace under her shirt. "If you mean am I a girl, no."

She gave him one of her deep, sultry chuckles while he glanced at a new text buzzing in from Marsh. "My brother's wondering where I am. You'd think he hadn't eaten in a week."

She asked, "Where are you going for takeout tonight?"

"What would you recommend?" He started for the door.

"You're on your own, pal. You saw what I had for dinner."

Reed thought she hadn't been fibbing when she said she had trouble making up her mind. There was a smile in his voice as he said, "Good night, Ruby."

Ruby followed Reed as far as her stoop and watched him start down the stairs. Darkness had fallen, and the air was starting to cool. She could hear the music at Murphy's through the alley and across the street. In the opposite direction someone was calling to a dog.

"Reed?"

The dog ran by, leash flying behind him as Reed turned around. "Yes?"

"Cats," she called. "And dogs. And goldfish. And armadillos. And ponies. Not snakes, though, or mice. *Maybe* gerbils but no rats."

He was laughing when he got in his car and drove

away. She went inside and stood resting her back along the length of her door.

They were opposites, the two of them. She was chatty. He wasn't. She was wearing the most comfortable clothes in the world. He wore a white shirt with a button-down collar and flat-front chinos. She'd complained about the delay in renovations, and he'd reminded her of Bell's potential.

She'd begun the evening in a funk. And so had he. Whatever had been bothering him when he'd arrived had still been on his mind when he left, but Ruby was beginning to understand why he wanted Joey to be his. It had to do with a tragic accident that tore a hole through an entire family, and one small baby who was somehow closing the gap.

As she stood at the kitchen sink rinsing out the bowls, she thought her mother and best friend and brother had been wrong. Her irascible mood had lifted and it hadn't been a shift in hormones or some trite saying or even the art of getting drunk or laid, or both, as Rusty had so eloquently put it.

It was conversation that went nowhere and silences that went everywhere. It was talking and not talking. It was comfortable and it wasn't. It was Reed. Yawning, she stretched her hands over her head and smiled for no particular reason.

Triple-fudge ice cream hadn't hurt.

Chapter Eight

Up and down Division Street, veterans, some of whom looked too young to shave and others so old they could barely shave themselves anymore, had teamed up with members of the city council and the high school marching band to collect for the upcoming Fourth of July fireworks display. They stood in incongruous teams of four or five on nearly every corner, the city officials accepting the donations, the patriots accepting praise and gratitude, and the band members playing their hearts out.

Ruby reached into her trunk for another cardboard box, and smiled at the somewhat discordant notes of "My Country 'tis of Thee." Scattered as they were over a seven-block area, the clarinet players tended to be a few notes behind the French horns and trombones, and the drums occasionally missed the fourth beat. She couldn't see the tuba player from here, but every so often she heard "thank you" in tuba notes. She smiled every time.

Today she *was* smiling. It was Saturday, and Saturdays were always good days. The weather was especially glorious. The drywall crew had come back to Bell's yesterday, and the renovations were on track once again. Everything she would need for Bell's reopening, from beer to wine to whiskey and seltzer water, had been ordered and was due to arrive in plenty of time for the Big Day.

Abby Fitzpatrick, reporter, photographer and advertising wizard for the *Orchard Hill News* had helped Ruby design the perfect ad, which would run in the paper this coming weekend and every day thereafter until the grand reopening. Ruby was practically giddy. To top it off, her first auction had been enormously successful.

Humming along to the "Battle Hymn of the Republic" now, she hefted another box laden with her new used barware into her arms. She spun around, and almost ran headlong into the man who'd planted himself between her and Bell's front door.

She let out a little yelp. "Reed!" Before she could drop the box filled with glassware, he took it out of her hands, and not gently, either.

"Where did you come from?" Glancing around, she didn't see his car. Somebody really needed to put bells on him.

Without a word, he turned on his heel and disappeared into her tavern. Ruby spared a look at the window-shoppers in front of the shoe store down the street and wondered what on earth Reed's problem could be. Reaching all the way to the back of her trunk, she pulled another box toward her and took it inside.

She found Reed in the tavern's kitchen, where he was pacing between the antiquated grill and the extra-deep and equally old metal sink. Every surface in the small room held boxes containing her new used bar-ware and the dozens of other items she'd picked up for a song at her first auction ever.

Reed stopped to glare at her in front of the stainless-steel exhaust fan. "You couldn't have gotten all this in your car."

That sounded like an accusation to her. "I did, actually. It's taken two trips to Sparta and back but—"

"We have a brand-new extended cab pickup sitting in the shed at the orchard," Reed cut in.

Eyeing all the cartons filled with dishes and glasses she needed to unpack and wash, and then arrange on the open shelves to the left of the sink, she bit her lip. She was starting to see where this was going.

"How many times have I given you the opportunity to ask for my help with something, with anything?" he asked.

Actually, she knew the answer, but simply said, "You have so much going on in your life."

"That's not the point."

The fit and style of Reed's clothes was worthy of *GQ*, the colors a combination of thunderclouds and smoke, like his eyes today. He'd worn a similar expression the first time she'd seen him. She didn't think failing to ask him for help was in the same category as being run off the road by some fool driving like a bat out of hell on Old Orchard Highway, but there it was, thunderclouds and smoke and a tightly clenched jaw. Suppressed anger, *GQ*-style.

"If it makes you feel any better, there are more boxes in the backseat," she said.

He obtusely failed to see the humor. She'd known men sporting similar expressions, as if pent-up steam was about to blast a hole through the tops of their heads. Her father and brother normally punctuated the display with a snort. Reed shot past her without making a sound.

He was on his way in with another armload by the time she reached the front door. "Friends ask friends for help when they need it," he said as he blew past her, glassware clanking as he went.

The volunteers were using the alley today, so after the sale she'd backed her loaded car into a parking space out front. Somebody had parked a little close on the driver's side, but the passenger side had plenty of room for her to open the door, which she did. Reed was there suddenly, reaching past her into the backseat, his shoulder brushing her arm, his hip nudging hers. Even though she backed up as far as the door would allow, there was only a matter of inches between them when he straightened.

In the tight space, she felt the heat radiating from him, and the tight coil he had on his temper. He didn't hold his pose for long. Turning on his heel, he shot past her yet again.

"Strawberry jam or grape?" she called.

He'd taken three steps before he exhaled, two more before he stopped. "Strawberry jam or grape what?" he asked, his back to her, ramrod straight, his shoulders rigid.

"It's a friendly getting-to-know-you question."

He faced her slowly, the box in his arms, a scowl on his face. "Grape."

As the marching band launched into "Home on the Range," she said, "I can see that about you. Cats or dogs?"

She could tell he was fighting a losing battle to stay angry. "If you must know, horses."

She grabbed a box of dishware, too. Falling into step beside him, she said, "Did you have horses when you were growing up?"

"A gelding named Stud."

"I'll bet he appreciated the vote of confidence." She knew she was out of hot water when one corner of Reed's mouth twitched. "Sunrise or sunset?" she asked.

Ever the gentleman, he waited for her to precede him through the door. He kept her guessing through two more trips to her car and back made in silence. After closing the trunk, he brushed the dust off his hands, and then took a pair of sunglasses from his pocket. She was in the process of swiping her hands on her gray T-shirt that covered all but the bottom few inches of her shorts when he said, "Sam has a new lead."

She stopped what she was doing and looked at him. She couldn't see his eyes through the dark lenses, but she felt him watching her. "That's good, right?"

"He has footage from a surveillance camera at a private airstrip outside Charleston. Even though the image was slightly grainy, one of the passengers bears an uncanny resemblance to the woman Marsh fell for on Roanoke Island last summer."

Shading her eyes with one hand, she asked, "Where was she going?"

"She was boarding a small private commuter plane for Detroit the same day we discovered Joey on our porch. That's some coincidence, isn't it?"

"Was there any evidence of Joey in that footage?" she asked.

He shook his head. "No baby, no diaper bag, no car seat, nothing but a small carry-on slung over her shoulder. I know. There's an enormous piece missing from the puzzle. Marsh thinks it was Julia, though."

The breeze ruffled the collar of Reed's shirt and stirred the leaves in the ornamental trees lining Division Street. She and Reed stood together in the dappled shade for a moment listening to the marching band play "Stars and Stripes Forever."

Marsh was searching high and low for a woman named Julia who may or may not have been seen boarding a plane for Detroit without a baby or any items a baby would need, and Reed was looking for a woman who may or may not have gotten pregnant as a result of a Fourth-of-July-rockets'-red-glare one-night stand. He hadn't actually used that terminology when he'd explained the situation to her, but she imagined a man like Reed would set off plenty of fireworks between a woman's sheets.

She wondered how Reed and Marsh stood so many unanswered questions. Their patience was humbling, for she'd nearly crawled out of her skin over a delay in Bell's renovations. The sooner the Sullivans received the results of the paternity test, the better.

"Sunset," he said out of the blue.

"Pardon me?" she said, not following the change in topic.

"You asked. I prefer sunset."

She glanced up at him and almost smiled at his take-it-or-leave-it attitude. “Summer or winter?”

Reed assumed his apparent favorite pose, feet apart, hands on his hips, head cocked slightly. “Fall.”

“That wasn’t one of the options. Have you always made your own rules?”

“Look who’s talking. You could have asked for a helping hand today. I would have loaned you a pickup or gone with you, for that matter.”

Slipping her hands into her back pockets, she said, “I can see that now, but it didn’t occur to me at the time. If it’s any consolation, I didn’t ask to borrow a vehicle from Abby or Chelsea, either.”

“The last I knew, Chelsea has never driven her Audi down a dirt road, and Abby’s car isn’t much bigger than she is. Logically, why would you have asked to borrow a ride from them?”

“We’re being logical?” Ruby quipped.

“You’re incorrigible,” he said.

He smiled, though. And so did she.

“Heavy metal or alternative?” she asked as he started away from her down the sidewalk. When he said nothing, she called, “If you can’t make up your mind, I understand. You can text me your answer. And it takes one to know one.”

She couldn’t quite bring herself to say pal. For some reason, that prickled the back of her mind and then stayed there.

He opened his door and got in his car, which was visible now that a panel truck had backed out of the space beside him. He didn’t wave as he drove away. He smiled, though. And then he was gone.

Another hot breeze wafted through town and one

patriotic song ended and another began. Ruby remained for a moment in the dappled shade in front of Bell's. Something had shifted between her and Reed today, and she couldn't put her finger on what had changed.

She looked down, wiggled her toes. All ten of them, with their bright pink polish, sat prettily at the ends of her narrow feet, nestled in her flip-flops, not buzzing, not tingling.

The area beneath her breastbone where forgotten dreams waited, though? There was plenty happening there.

That worried her most of all.

A few days later, Ruby sat across from Chelsea and Abby in her favorite booth at the Hill. Smelling of stroganoff, fried chicken, strong coffee and strawberry-rhubarb pie, the restaurant was as crowded and noisy as it always was on Fridays at one. Chelsea had gotten here early enough to order an appetizer tray and arrange the newspaper so it was open to the advertisement announcing Bell's grand reopening. It was the first thing Ruby saw when she arrived.

The ad was far more impressive than one would expect from a small-city daily. At first glance, the *Orchard Hill News* offices had looked like something out of an old Clark Gable movie. But Abby, reporter, photographer and miracle worker extraordinaire, had proven that the newspaper was far more than the culmination of steel desks and black phones.

Ruby had designed the ad herself; Abby had suggested a few minor changes. The end result was amazing. Printed on the third page of the local section, the ad was in full color and was undeniably eye-catching, if she did say so herself. There were three water rings on it now and a spot where an appetizer—Chelsea's treat—had dribbled. Ruby had another copy. Okay, three other copies.

The advertisement would run again on Sunday, and then smaller versions would appear each day prior to the Big Night, which was a mere week away. Ruby had butterflies.

She'd been stirring paint for the walls in the ladies' room this morning when Reed had called to ask her if she'd seen the paper yet. He read the ad on his iPad, but she'd put the lid back on the can and walked to the newsstand around the corner while he described it in detail and told her how effective it was. He was right. Nobody could miss it.

She hadn't actually *seen* him since he'd helped her carry the last few boxes of barware into Bell's on Monday, but they'd hit every circuit on the twenty-first century social media network motherboard.

He'd *liked* her online ad. He'd sent her information about a new winemaker in the area on LinkedIn. There had been Tweets and texts. One had read, Anything by Springsteen.

She'd answered, One of my favorites, too, but then so is "Twinkle, Twinkle Little Star," the only song I can still play after three years of piano lessons.

He'd called her to laugh in her ear. That little spot beneath her breastbone had vibrated at the sound of his voice.

A few days later she'd been the one laughing as he'd described the surprise home visit his great-uncle, Judge Ivan-the-Terrible Sullivan, had sprung on Reed and Marsh that day. They'd managed to pass inspection despite the fact that no nanny had been hired as of yet; Joey remained in their care.

"What about Jake Nichols?" Abby cut into Ruby's reverie.

"Who?" Ruby looked at the impossibly forward blonde on the opposite side of the table.

"Jake Nichols is the new veterinarian in town. He's nice-looking and close to six feet tall. He'd probably attend your reunion with you if you asked, as long as you aren't sensitive about the fact that he often smells a little like goats."

Ruby looked to Chelsea for help. "Goats?" Ruby mouthed.

"It's not what it sounds like," Chelsea replied.

Oh. Good? Now where was she? Oh, yes. About the reunion. "I told you," Ruby said to Abby as she speared the last stuffed mushroom on the platter, "I'm attending solo." She was sorry she'd brought up the subject of her class reunion. It was bad enough that Amanda was like a bloodhound on the trail of an escaped convict and wouldn't let the subject rest. Now Abby was on the scent, too.

She tucked a wisp of blond hair behind one ear and said, "Our class reunion was last summer. It was a major hookup fest, let me tell you."

"Oh, great" was all Ruby said. A hookup fest was all she needed.

"Forewarned is forearmed, I always say," Abby insisted.

"I've never heard you say that," Chelsea said.

"That's because no one ever listens to me. Most people don't take petite women seriously. It's true."

"So," Chelsea said, leaning closer to Ruby, pretty

much proving Abby's point. "What does your Peter look like?"

"He's not my Peter."

"He's every girl's *Peter,*" Abby countered. "That's the problem."

Ruby dropped her face into her paint-speckled hands.

"You did not just say that," Chelsea reprimanded.

Eye's sparkling with mischief, Abby mouthed, "Sorry."

Chelsea, ladylike no matter the subject matter, turned her violet eyes to Ruby and said, "You don't have to tell us, you know."

With a shrug, Ruby said, "He was covaledictorian, star quarterback, prom king, voted best looking, best dressed, best catch, best you name it."

"How good-looking are we talking?" Abby asked.

Ruby straightened her napkin in her lap and said, "If Jude Law and George Clooney had had a younger brother it would have been Peter Powelson."

"Oh, my," Abby said.

"Oh, dear," Chelsea agreed.

"Tell me about it," Ruby grumbled. "Six-two-and-a-half, thick unruly black hair, cobalt-blue eyes, a washboard stomach, long muscular legs, narrow hips, masculine swagger."

"You thought you'd make beautiful babies together," Abby said on a sigh.

"I was a complete idiot over him. I cried in public over him. And then I practically stalked him. I'm not proud, believe me. It was just— He just..."

"Let me guess," Chelsea said matter-of-factly. "He

told you you changed him in that deep man-place in his soul."

Abby tut-tutted supportively. "And he said it in a midnight-dark whiskey voice and your girl parts did somersaults. Whose wouldn't?"

"That's what I'm afraid of," Ruby said, mashing the innocent stuffed mushroom to smithereens on her own plate. "He wants me back. He's sorry. He insists he's changed. And he's told everyone I know back home that he's going to make his move at the reunion. What if my girl parts, er, you know? I may need a chastity belt."

"You need a date," Abby insisted.

"Yes, well," Ruby said, her gaze straying to the fabulous ad once again. "The reunion's tomorrow night. I'm not seeing anybody, so—"

"Oh," Abby said. "Hi, Marsh, Reed. So this is Joey, isn't it?"

Ruby's gaze swung to the two men who suddenly appeared at the end of her booth. Marsh wore a T-shirt. Reed's button-down was tucked neatly into black slacks. It occurred to her that she'd never seen him in faded jeans and a grimy T-shirt. She wondered what he wore when he relaxed. Did he ever relax?

Marsh held the baby carrier today. Perhaps because the little tyke was at her level, she found herself looking at Joey.

He was dressed in red and white and didn't seem to mind the din of voices and clatter of dishes and silverware. He had a dimple in his chin and an adorable cowlick he was probably going to hate someday. His eyelashes were long and dark—boys always got lashes to die for. He looked everywhere, focusing on nothing, as if in his own little world.

All at once, his gaze landed on Ruby. What followed was a three-and-a-half-month-old's equivalent of a double take. And then it happened. A moment's wonder lit his gray-blue eyes—eyes so like Reed's—his lips twitched and he smiled.

"Hello to you, too," she said.

As if he had a radar lock on her, his grin widened, all gums and round cheeks and sparkling innocence. No wonder Reed was hoping this baby was his. A nagging worry swirled inside Ruby, the tip touching down like the tail of a tornado deep in her chest.

"What are you two doing Saturday night?" Abby was still talking. And Marsh said something Ruby didn't catch.

"What about you, Reed? Are you up to making a former quarterback prom king sorry he ever cheated?"

Ruby did a double take of her own. With a dawning understanding, she said, "Abby." But her voice was still soft from Joey's smile.

She glanced up at the brothers. Marsh looked perplexed, but Reed waited patiently for Abby to continue.

"I'm asking because Ruby's attending her high school class reunion on Saturday, and her ex-boyfriend thinks she's going to let him waltz back into her life, as if he deserves her forgiveness, and, well, she needs a date."

"I do not need—" *Please,* she silently implored Abby. *Do not mention a chastity belt.*

"I might be available," Reed said. And Ruby swore there was a challenge in his voice.

"Great," Abby said. "That's great. Isn't it great, Ruby?"

Since the maiming look Ruby shot Abby had no

noticeable effects, Ruby turned her attention to Reed. "You really don't have to do this."

"That's true, I don't have to."

She tried to look away. Couldn't.

"Will you, though?" Abby asked.

"That depends." A stare-down ensued, and Reed was winning.

Marsh spoke to his brother and then to the three women before he and Joey followed the hostess to a vacant table. Reed stayed behind, holding his ground and Ruby's gaze.

"Well?" he said.

"Do you want me to invite you along, is that it?" she asked.

"*Are* you asking?" he asked.

Her breath caught at his serious expression. Was she? Should she? Did she dare? "I guess I am."

"All right, then," he said.

She thought he might voice some old platitude such as that's what friends are for, or say, "That wasn't so difficult, was it?" Instead, he cast another pointed look directly at her then followed the course Marsh had taken.

There was a noticeable hush at Ruby's table, a pregnant pause straight from an old-fashioned novel, a series of awkward silences that stacked one on top of the other until they teetered precariously, about to topple. Ruby found herself staring at Abby and Chelsea, who were staring back at her in waiting silence.

Finally, Abby whispered, "What was that?"

That, Ruby thought, glancing toward the table near the back of the room where Reed was pulling out a chair, was a polished modern man with a vein of the uncivilized coursing through him. That was the definition of dangerous.

"Apparently," she finally said, "that was my date for tomorrow night."

Ruby jumped out of bed and stubbed her toe. Hobbling now, she supposed that was one way to cure it of any future relentless buzzing. Although, it wasn't her toe that needed curing.

She groped for the bedside table and turned on the lamp. Now that she could see where she was going, she limped to her closet and began to flip through the clothes at the back. If she couldn't sleep, she reasoned, she might as well *do* something.

She already knew exactly what she was going to wear tomorrow night. She'd bought the dress before moving to Orchard Hill, so there would be no surprises, no guesswork. She'd unzipped the garment bag half an hour ago and taken a look. Hanging it on the hook on the back of the closet door, she lowered the zipper again.

The dress was perfect, that was all there was to it—flirty but not too flirty, feminine but not fussy, short but not too short. Perfect. The neckline dipped low in the front but not too low, and a little lower in the back, where she could get away with it. If she were wearing heels and fine jewelry, it might have been too dressy. But she'd found a shabby-chic necklace, a sash belt and the cutest sandals she'd ever seen. The end result was Caribbean casual, like water and air and the sea.

It wasn't over the top. It wasn't too much for a date to her class reunion. Not that it was a real date.

It wasn't.

There was no need to give the dress, the shoes or the jewelry another thought. There was no reason to give her escort for the evening another thought, either.

She crawled back into bed, the fan whirring, night sounds drifting through her screen. She and Reed had touched base earlier via a few strategic texts. She'd given him the banquet center's address and a wide window of time in which to arrive. Since she was part of the welcoming committee and planned to go early to help with last-minute details and he had a very tight schedule, she saw no reason to ask him to arrive when she did. Besides, she was spending the night with her parents, and he would return to Orchard Hill immediately after the reunion was over. Consequently, they were driving separately.

She could hardly believe she was doing this. Amanda was thrilled. Ruby felt…a little breathless. And there, just out of reach again, was that nagging doubt in the back of her mind.

It wasn't as though she was resisting and therefore the zing was persisting. It was— For heaven's sake, she didn't know what it was. She only knew it was midnight and she couldn't sleep for thinking about tomorrow night.

Just then, her phone alerted her to a new text coming in. It was probably Amanda, she thought. Rolling onto her side, she read the new message. Horror flicks or comedies?

She lay on her back again, and smiled. Reed was awake, too.

I live alone, she typed. What do you think?

I would have guessed old classics, he wrote back.

See you in the lobby at the bottom of the stairs at eight.

Smiling again, she turned out the light and settled into her pillows. Maybe she should rethink her shoes. She could always run out tomorrow and buy a pair of decadent heels. Even if Reed hadn't been several inches taller than her, it wouldn't have mattered. Movie stars towered over their escorts all the time. Ruby had never enjoyed leaning down for a good-night kiss. Not that she would kiss Reed. After all, this wasn't a real date. They were just two friends taking turns helping each other.

Liar.

There it was. What was bothering her. A little wish, a fleeting what-if.

What if Joey was Marsh's?

Marsh's, not Reed's.

Then Reed would be free. And there would be no need to resist, no need to pretend that her heart didn't stammer every time she saw him, no need to prepare herself for the possibility that some little blonde bombshell from his past could very well breeze back into his life any day.

She was horrible. No, she wasn't. Okay, maybe she was a little horrible, but in her own defense, it wasn't as if she had the power to change the ultimate outcome of that paternity test. The problem was, for all her good intentions, for all her lack of resisting, her feelings for Reed were deepening.

Whoever turned out to be Joey's father, it would be for the best. She believed that with her whole heart, even though that belief brought a little pang.

She pictured Joey's smile and the way his eyes had

crinkled at the corners. They were like Reed's that way. There it was, that nagging worry again.

Joey had Reed's eyes. Reed's, not Marsh's.

What if Reed really was his father?

Reed Sullivan may have had a vein of the uncivilized coursing through him, but ultimately he was one of those rare individuals who did the right thing no matter what. He would be a wonderful father. Should Cookie return, the fireworks that might have produced Joey could very well be rekindled. Families had been founded on less.

And she, Ruby, would always be a friend, a good friend, but a mere friend, nonetheless.

It would have to be enough. If only it felt like enough.

Ruby had come to Orchard Hill to start over. She was an independent woman and independent women did not need a man.

She was starting to care about Reed, though. Talk about classic.

He'd somehow known her favorite movies were the classics. Lying there listening to the sounds of Division Street in the wee hours of a Saturday morning, she wondered what movie they were most like, her and Reed.

There wasn't any her and Reed. There wasn't, but if there were, which one would it be?

Pride and Prejudice?

That was one of her all-time favorites, but no, she thought, staring at the crack of light shining around the shade at her window. Elizabeth and Mr. Darcy were too proper.

Titanic?

She drew the sheet up to her shoulders. Gosh, no. Too tragic.

Gone With the Wind?

Too epic. She would never be able to pull off a convincing faint. And what about those corsets? Oh, no, Ruby liked to breathe when at all possible.

Casablanca?

She felt dreamy just thinking about that one. She couldn't watch it without putting her hands over her heart. She hoped her life never mirrored it, though. If she ever had another love affair, it would have a happy ending.

She fell asleep thinking Happy Endings would be a good one-of-a-kind-drink title. And she dreamed of a long goodbye.

Chapter Nine

Long goodbyes were not the theme of the evening for the former classmates gathered in the banquet room of Gale, Michigan's, only country club. Boisterous hellos, slaps on the back, squeals of laughter and time-enhanced stories of famed stunts, pranks and adventures abounded.

Ninety-nine young adults had walked across the stage on graduation day ten years ago. There would have been an even one hundred if Cody Holbrook hadn't dropped out two weeks before commencement. Of those ninety-nine, an astounding seventy-one had RSVP'd that they were coming tonight.

By ten minutes before nine, thirty-six of them had asked Ruby, "Is he here yet?"

The he in question was Peter. Not Reed. *He* was stuck in traffic at the Pearl River Bridge, where a semi had reportedly rolled over, and besides, only Amanda, Ruby's absolute BFF, knew about him. Maybe she should have asked him to come earlier, or with her, but it was too late for that. He was driving separately, and he would be here. If not for the traffic jam, he would have been here on time. She was just going to have to be patient a little longer. Unfortunately, patience wasn't her strong suit.

Despite that and the fact that nearly everyone was waiting on pins and needles with bated breath for the highly anticipated promised *scene,* Ruby wasn't having a horrible time. Since she and Amanda were on the planning committee and the welcoming committee, they'd arrived early with name tags for husbands, wives and/or special guests and a Welcome Back Class of 2004 banner.

Most of the football team was in attendance, which explained the state of the hors d'oeuvres table. The once-beautiful arrangement looked as if it had been attacked by pirates or piranhas or both.

Dinner had been served at eight, and now the caterers were clearing the tables and a crowd was forming around the portable bar. Sean Halstead, who'd always been a gifted music fanatic, was supplying the sound track for the evening, and Ruby's brother, Rusty, was keeping an eye out should she decide to take him up on his offer to beat Peter up if he dared show his rakishly handsome face here tonight. Rusty had already blackened Peter's eye after Ruby caught him in bed with someone else, but Ruby forbade a repeat performance.

Secretly, she appreciated his loyalty. Rusty's. Not Peter's. *He* didn't have a loyal bone in his body. Obviously.

Everyone else she'd told, which was practically everybody she knew in Gale, L.A. and Chicago, agreed. It was bad enough that the other woman, a pretty sales rep from Chicago, had been married, but she'd been a *redhead,* too, although not a natural one. Unfortunately, the evidence of that was permanently burned into Ruby's memory.

"Ruby!"

She recognized the stereo of voices calling her name, and was smiling when she turned around. Identical twins Lisa and Livia Holden still dressed alike. Not even Ruby, who'd been on the cheerleading squad with them freshman year, could tell them apart. And she never forgot a face.

Hands up, hair down, smiles gleaming and identical, they yelled, "Give me a *V.* Give me an *I.* Give me a *C.*" And so on until the victory cheer was done.

"Is he here yet?" Lisa, or maybe it was Livia, asked in a normal tone of voice when they were done.

"I wouldn't know." It was Ruby's stock blasé reply. She would have used a similar bland tone if someone had asked if she happened to know who Tom Cruise was dating these days or if she believed aliens had anything to do with building the ancient pyramids. It wasn't that she didn't care at all. She just didn't care very much. Luckily Father Marty was in Rome or she might have had to confess that.

Catherine Ericson, the shyest girl in the class, joined her and Amanda after the twins wandered off to cheer for someone else. "Hey, Ruby," she said.

Ruby and Catherine had been in the drama club together junior year. Catherine's acne had cleared up since then and she'd taken off some weight. She looked quite pretty, but then, she'd always been pretty underneath. Evidently her painful shyness hadn't improved, and she still blushed scarlet. Despite that, she still managed to squeak out *the* question on everyone's mind.

"Is he here yet?"

Bother.

Just then, a hush fell from one end of the room to the other. It didn't require great insight to know what it meant.

He was about to arrive. Peter. Not Reed. She hadn't heard from *him* since a little after nine.

While all eyes were turned toward the door where everyone's favorite tall, dark, handsome and so misunderstood former football star was making his grand entrance, Ruby slipped onto the patio to watch the sun set over the ninth green. Amanda, Evie Carlyle and Violet VanWagner, her closest high school friends and the best posse a girl could ask for, came, too.

It was a warm summer evening. Most of the golfers had headed to the clubhouse, but two remained on the ninth green. One of them missed an easy putt. The cumulus clouds on the horizon concealed all but the faintest shades of coral and lavender tingeing the western sky. Even with the wind whipping Ruby's hair into her eyes, it was still better than witnessing the entire parting of the Red Sea taking place inside.

Ruby, Amanda, Evie and Violet weren't the only ones out here. That was something at least. A small group huddled at the far end, smoking.

Two doors opened onto the broad patio overlooking the green and the Pearl River. Evie was guarding one and Violet the other. Safe for now, Ruby took a fortifying breath.

Beside her, Amanda said, "I'm proud of you for coming tonight. Peter has some nerve. Ninety percent of the people here are hoping you'll forgive him. As *if*."

"You gotta admit," Freddie Benjamin called after passing what was surely a joint to a girl Ruby didn't recognize. "Sending everybody that text. I still love her, man. It was borderline brilliant."

Jason Harding, who'd had a crush on Ruby most of his life, mumbled something, and then said, "You're lookin' good as always, Ruby. You, too, Amanda."

"Thanks, Jason."

"Backatcha, Jase." Wearing four-inch heels and a yellow sundress, Amanda rolled her eyes. In a quieter voice, she said to Ruby, "Missing Peter's grand entrance? Stellar. But you probably aren't going to be able to elude him all night."

It was well after nine by now. Only Ruby knew that the members of Gale High's graduating class of 2004 weren't the only ones who'd received a text from Peter. Ruby's had varied slightly from the others'. I still love you, baby. Give me a chance to prove it. Please.

She was almost afraid to check her phone again.

"He's coming this way," Violet called from her post at the nearest patio door.

"Come on, Ruby! The coast is clear over here," Evie exclaimed.

Ruby's phone vibrated in her hand. Her breath caught as she read the message. Instantly, she started for the door.

"Not this one," Violet called as she neared. "Go through the other door. The one by Evie."

"He's here," Ruby said.

"We know," Violet, who was seven months pregnant, replied. "Peter's heading this way. Half our class is right behind him."

"Not Peter," Ruby said, laying a gentle hand on Violet's baby bump. "Reed."

"Who?"

Leaving Amanda to explain if she so chose, Ruby darted inside on the onrushing breeze, her step light, her dress swirling around her thighs. Her hair, which she'd tamed with large hot rollers hours ago, fell in soft waves down her back.

The serene smile that tipped the corners of her mouth didn't falter as she passed the sea of faces she'd known all her life. Peter, tall and dark and smolderingly confident, was directly ahead of her now.

She blew past him so quickly he probably felt the current of air she left in her wake. A second collective gasp spread through the room just as a Bob Marley song began to play. Once upon a time "Satisfy My Soul" had been their song. Hers and Peter's, back when they had been a "couple." He'd thought of everything.

Darting around the last group of spectators in her way, she burst through the door, the hardwood floor of the banquet room giving way to the soundproof carpet in the hallway. Windows lined one entire wall, flooding the area with fading natural light. The stairs were directly ahead some thirty feet away.

And there, standing at the bottom, was Reed.

Her steps slowed as she neared, stopping altogether when she was six feet away. Behind her, the doors were opening and music and people poured into the hall.

Reed smiled at her. His blond hair was neatly trimmed yet slightly disheveled, his tie in one hand, his collar open at his throat, his pale green shirt a little wrinkled as if he'd been sitting in traffic for a long while.

Ruby didn't know how to proceed. Their "date" had come about only yesterday, and she hadn't talked to him about this. They hadn't rehearsed what they would say or how they would act or what they would do. They were going to have to ad-lib.

He started toward her, his stride long and effortless, and came to a stop less than an arm's length away, close enough to touch her, which he did, his fingers brushing her long hair off her right shoulder. "Maybe later you could tell me what I just missed," he said. "We have an audience, led by some dark-haired guy whose knuckles are dragging on the floor. So if it's all right with you, I think I'll kiss you."

She imagined she must have answered, imagined she knew, somehow, that his kiss would be part of the pseudo-date performance. She imagined that the way she raised her face and the way he lowered his appeared perfectly, exquisitely natural. But the moment his lips touched hers, her mind pulled the curtain on her imagination. Now there was only touch and taste and sound.

She took a small breath and inhaled the scent of warm leather and hot breezes and soap and apples, of all things. Heat shimmered off him, his lips firm and warm on hers, his jaw smooth beneath her fingertips, which meant she must have been touching him. Oh, yes, she was touching him. His skin was taut and slightly rough despite his recent shave, the bones underneath prominent and angular and solid. This wasn't sculpted bronze. This was living, breathing man.

He tilted his head a little, and she opened her lips slightly beneath his. Soft, muted sunset colors floated across her closed eyelids, pale yellow and sky-blue and lavender and coral, which was strange because the windows here faced east not west.

He made a sound deep in his throat. Barely audible, it was deep and dusky and sensual and furthered the sensation of floating.

She'd kissed other men. Some of them were very good at it. In a sense, she and Reed had *resisted* this very activity from the beginning. And yet the pressure of his lips, the way he moved his mouth against hers, his moist breath becoming hers, the taste of him, the feel of him, the fit, all of it felt as if they'd been born to experience this moment.

Her heart pounded, and the kiss changed subtly, like summer sprinkles that gradually gave way to summer rain. It was exploratory, mysterious yet achingly familiar somehow. She'd dreamed last night of a long goodbye. She'd never imagined such a perfectly beautiful long hello.

The kiss ended, stilling like a petal waiting to uncurl until the earth's atmosphere created a drop of dew. They drew slightly apart, their eyes opened, her hand fell away from his face and his fingers uncurled from her hair.

"Wow," she said quietly. "I wasn't expecting that. But wow."

He didn't quite smile.

And a little thrill ran through her, as if she'd done something slightly illicit, or at the very least naughty, and hadn't gotten caught. Actually, she *had* gotten caught, caught by half the graduating class of 2004, caught on at least nine camera phones. More than anything, though, she'd gotten caught up in Reed's kiss.

He took her hand with the first step, and it felt almost as intimate as that kiss. They started across the lobby, fingers twined, their strides smooth and matched. The crowd filtered back inside ahead of them, whispering, wondering what would happen next.

Peter held the door. Ruby wasn't expecting that.

"Who do we have here?" he asked.

She made the introductions and noticed that Reed was taller. Not by much, but a little. She realized it didn't matter. Peter was good-looking; she hadn't been kidding about the Jude Law and George Clooney combination. That didn't matter, either. His eyes were a brilliant blue, although, admittedly, they were tinged with green now.

She wasn't surprised he ignored Reed. That didn't really matter, either, because Reed didn't have to say a word. After all, he was the one who rested his hand lightly on her lower back as they walked through the door.

Behind them Peter was seeing red.

Reed dropped his tie into the first wastebasket he passed. As far as making an impression, he didn't believe a silk tie or anything else could top that kiss. He hadn't planned to do that, but now he didn't see how he could have done anything else. The memory of it had lodged in his bloodstream like a pulse. Ruby had tasted like wine, had sighed like a whisper, had felt tall and willowy and so incredibly soft. It wasn't something a man could forget.

Gale's banquet center was what he'd expected. It had high ceilings, fake pillars, round tables and chairs around the outer edges and a small dance floor on one end. It wasn't a large room, but it comfortably held the hundred or so people present tonight.

The lights weren't bright and the music was a little louder than it needed to be, which nobody seemed to mind. Everyone had to talk louder, but had gotten used to it. Most of them couldn't keep their eyes off Ruby. Reed knew the feeling.

She drew her hand out of his and hugged one of her old classmates the way women often did. It afforded him the perfect opportunity to look at her again.

Whoa had been his first thought when he'd seen her practically flying toward him across the lobby a few minutes ago. Leave it to Ruby to wear white. Not black, not red, not silver or gold. White.

Not a chaste white, either. In fact, it was far from that.

He didn't know a lot about fabric other than that he preferred to wear shirts made of fine cotton. Her dress was soft to the touch, whisper-thin and only slightly heavier than air. The neckline was a gentle sweep from shoulder to shoulder, collarbone to collarbone. It was low enough in the front to show off that delicate hollow at the base of her throat and a few inches of smooth, slightly freckled golden skin below it.

In the back it dipped lower. He didn't see a zipper; he didn't see how she could have gotten into the dress without one. At her waist was a sash in every muted shade of blue and green imaginable. The skirt skimmed her hips, the fabric gathered so softly it flowed like water when she moved. The hem stopped above her knees, quite a few inches above her knees, actually, and on her feet she wore sandals the same color as the beads and shells and pearls stacked one on top of the other around her neck.

Her hair waved loosely down her back. Way down her back. Without the tight curls it was longer than he'd realized. There were other attractive women here tonight. Ruby stole the show. And it wasn't because the most popular guy in the class who'd done her wrong wanted her back, although that appeared to be on everybody's mind. More than that, it was because she knew each and every one of these people. It seemed she'd tried and quit nearly every sport and club she'd joined. She hadn't been kidding when she'd told him she had trouble making up her mind. She'd moved away and come back, fallen for the same guy two or three times and evidently had humiliated herself endearingly. She thought they were all rooting for Peter.

Reed highly doubted that.

She introduced him to her friends, which was practically everyone. Reed knew how to hold his own in any social setting. He smiled and agreed and disagreed when he could do so amicably, but for the most part, he remained at her side, a quiet presence, slightly in the background. This was her party, after all.

There were the usual questions—*How have you been?* and *Where are you living?* and *What do you do?*—a lot of stories and much reminiscing about the good old days. He met her brother, Rusty; her BFF, Amanda; a heavyset friend named Evie and a very pregnant one called Violet.

There was a doctor and a lawyer, a musician and a guy named Freddie who spoke slowly and smelled like weed. And always, Peter laughed a little too loudly and managed to stay a little closer to Ruby than Reed would have liked.

Peter was waiting to make his move. Whether it was retaliation against Reed or an attempted reconciliation with Ruby was anybody's guess.

Leaving Ruby with a group of her friends, Reed waited his turn at the bar. Some guy named Todd talked tax laws with him and another one named Jason Harding looked especially crestfallen. Soon, Reed ordered a Sam Adams for himself and a margarita over crushed ice for Ruby.

Someone to his right nudged him, hard. "You're in my way."

Obviously Ruby's old flame was proud of his shoulders. Taking his half out of the middle, he ordered a Jack Daniel's on the rocks. Something told Reed that Peter worked hard for muscles like his and liked to show them off—arms, shoulders, chest, too, if the way he puffed it out was an accurate indication.

Reed didn't know if Ruby was watching from the other side of the room where he'd left her. He only knew he would have been hard-pressed to mimic Peter's sneer. One thing was certain. The jerk meant to intimidate.

Reed didn't intimidate easily.

"I don't know who you think you are or what you're doing here," Peter began. "Rocky, is it?" As if he didn't know Reed's full name, where he lived, what he drove and how much he earned by now.

Reed shrugged, as if bored. He may not have looked directly at him, but he knew enough from the bar fights he'd gotten caught up in with Noah that it was wise to keep one's potential opponent in his peripheral vision at all times.

"I'm sure you've heard I hurt her," he said bitterly, swirling his whiskey in his glass.

"Actually," Reed finally said, "Ruby has told me very little about you."

The bartender smirked. And so did the CPA and the shorter guy with the spaniel eyes. Score one for Reed.

"Yes, well," Peter the Great said with his customary sneer. "It's not surprising, given the fact that she only moved away two weeks ago. How well could you possibly know her?"

It looked to everyone within hearing range that this point would go to Peter. Reed took a drink from his longneck bottle. "And yet I'm the one she's with tonight."

Ha.

Score another point for Reed.

"You do not want to get in a pissing match with me, pal."

The pal rankled. Ruby had called him that more than once.

"You're right about that," Reed said, his Sam Adams in one hand and Ruby's margarita now in the other. "As far as I can see, there is no match. Skeeter, is it?"

The unofficial score was three to zip by the time Reed returned to the spot where he'd left Ruby five minutes ago. She wasn't there, though. In fact, he didn't see her anywhere in the room, and Ruby O'Toole stood out in a crowd.

A patient man, he stayed at the edge of the dance floor. Quietly nursing his beer, he waited for the belle of the ball to return.

Chapter Ten

The door swished shut quietly behind Ruby as she left the lounge. Someone had dimmed the lights in the hallway and in the adjoining banquet hall. Letting her eyes adjust, she paused for a moment and looked around. She didn't see Reed anywhere.

She'd planned only a quick visit to the ladies' room to run a comb through her hair and reapply her lip gloss. She should have known better than to underestimate what hubs of social activity women's restrooms could be, especially when there was an adjoining lounge with velvet settees and slipper chairs.

Since almost no one was dancing, the only location boasting more activity right now was the bar. She didn't see Reed there, either, though. Actually, she didn't see him by the punch table or the hors d'oeuvres table or with the small group made up of guests who didn't know anybody else. Maybe he was visiting the men's room. For guys, those were always quick trips, just one of the many differences in the sexes.

Wherever he was, she wondered if his ears had been ringing while she'd been gone. Funny, she'd expected everyone to ask about Peter. Instead, they were more curious about Reed.

Many of their questions had easy answers, which she'd readily given. She'd met him her second day in Orchard Hill. Yes, he was tall. No, not six-five, more like six-three. Yes, he was good-looking, too.

And okay, while they were on the subject, no, she hadn't shrunk, she was still five-ten and three-quarters, and she hadn't lost weight, either. No, she didn't know where he bought his clothes. Yes, yes, yes, he wore them well.

His shoes did look expensive, and no, she didn't know his shoe size. He'd gone to Purdue, and she didn't think he'd ever been married, and his eyes were dreamy, weren't they?

She'd hedged the more intimate queries, and at times she simply smiled. She couldn't help it if there was a dreamy depth in her eyes and a secret knowledge in what she didn't say. She was having a wonderful time, after all; she felt a glow deep inside, and it seemed to have started with that kiss.

Here in the banquet hall, Peter was talking to two friends from the old football team, Chad Wilson and Tripp Donahue. Although she pretended she hadn't noticed, she'd felt Peter looking at her much of the evening. His impressive biceps and trim waist, all that dark whisker stubble and those smoldering cobalt eyes were impossible to miss. He'd been part of the raucous group who'd drunk to the winning touchdown, his, that had earned the team a trophy and a permanent place behind glass in the display case outside the cafeteria at school. Once or twice she'd returned his smile. She wondered if he realized yet that it didn't mean anything.

It was getting late; everyone had to vacate the premises by midnight, which wasn't bad for a town that normally rolled up its sidewalks by nine. More guests were leaving all the time. Amanda was dancing with her fiancé, Todd; Violet and her husband had gone home a while ago. Evie, that little seductress, had ducked out with Max Hamilton, and Livia Holden was leaving this very minute with Jack Simon—or was that Lisa? Ruby never could tell those two apart. Rumor had it that Eric Gordon had sneaked out with someone else's date.

Abby and Chelsea had been right. Class reunions were major hookup fests.

Ruby hadn't given Peter his moment in the spotlight yet. She knew him, though, and any minute now he was going to take matters into his own hands.

She saw a movement across the room. Brock Avery, Gale High's former basketball center, and his girlfriend, a model named Fowler, just Fowler—that Brock always had been able to pick them—took a seat opposite the most-talked-about outsider here tonight.

There sat Reed, looking interested in whatever Brock and Fowler were saying. His pale green shirt was still tucked in, the sleeves now rolled up a few times at his forearms, elbows on the table, feet apart, one leg stretched out comfortably, basically a naturally delicious slice of man.

He laughed at something Fowler said, listened, said something in return. And so the exchange went.

It looked as if he was drinking a Sam Adams, but it could have been a Bud Light for all she cared. It wasn't his choice of beer that sent that interesting little flutter through her chest.

The bottle was halfway to his mouth when he turned his head and saw her. She started toward him, and even though his table wasn't far away, he was on his feet before she reached it. She wondered who'd instilled those incredible manners. Or were all Sullivans predisposed to fine conduct?

The O'Tooles, not so much, which Ruby demonstrated upon reaching Reed's side. Having already spoken to Brock and his gorgeous girlfriend, Ruby smiled in their general direction and looked up at Reed. "Is that margarita for me per chance?"

His chin came down just a little, and so did his eyelids. It was a dreamy expression, one that made her think about dreamy activities, bedroom activities.

"It's yours," he said, his voice low. "The ice melted. I can get you a fresh one if you'd like."

She shook her head and took a sip of the cool watery drink. "The place is clearing out. I didn't mean to be gone so long."

"Did you solve the nuclear crisis and discover a cure for the common cold?"

She took another sip, and another. "We're close, very close. Did you really call Peter Skeeter?"

Taking the drink from her hand, he placed it on the table next to his and said, "That's for me to know and you to find out. Do you hear that?"

Nodding, she remembered when he'd told her his favorite music was anything by Springsteen. "Was this song a personal request?"

"No, but I believe my patience is finally being rewarded." He took her hand and drew her with him onto the dance floor.

Stopping in a roomy spot, he faced her. They each took a step, meeting in the middle, her hand curling against his, his warm fingers lacing with her cool ones.

She'd taken dance in college. She could waltz, rumba, tango, jitterbug, and yes, she could even do the Macarena. Reed may not have known all those dances, but he knew enough to move his feet. And he knew where to put his other hand.

"You do realize," she said, close to his ear, "your touch is below proprietary and only slightly above Neanderthal."

He tightened his hold at the small of her back and drew her slightly closer. "Exactly where every guy in this room would like to be."

His voice was a low rumble, a quiet vibration that found its way into her ear, spreading in every direction, rippling outward and inward, pausing in unconnected places beneath her collarbone and breastbone, below her navel, bubbling like a science experiment along the insides of her hip bones before finally reaching her very center. She was still relishing the possibilities when someone tapped Reed on the shoulder.

Peter was cutting in.

Reed stiffened. Ruby did, too, and glanced from one man to the other. One was dark, the other fair, one determined, the other reluctant.

"It's all right, Reed," she said, and released her held breath. "Hello, Peter."

There was another moment's awkwardness, and then, his mouth set in a firm line, Reed nodded at Ruby, stepped back and let her go. With an indecipherable smile, she went from Reed's arms to Skeeter's—er, Peter's.

It was going to rain.

Reed knew the weather. He recognized the different cloud patterns, felt the shifting air currents and understood atmospheric pressure. The wind was changing.

Prophetic, perhaps.

It was going to rain. He could smell it, feel it, taste it. He tasted blood, too, but that was from nearly biting through his cheek.

He put a hand to the back of his neck. And forced himself to breathe.

From the dance floor he'd come directly to the patio. He couldn't claim to have refrained from looking back; but he'd looked back only once. Of the few dozen people still here, half had been watching him and all were probably wondering if they were going to get their promised scene, after all.

Lover Boy had had all night to make his move. Yet he'd waited until the deejay with the impressive sound system finally, *finally* put on a song by Springsteen. That rankled to beat hell.

Reed didn't relish the picture in his mind of Ruby deep in conversation with Tall, Dark and Handsome, *his* hand on her lower back now. They looked a little too cozy. Intimate.

Hell.

She didn't need Reed's protection. It was the honest-to-God truth. She was independent, self-reliant and would know where to slam her knee should the need arise. Besides, every guy here would come to her aid, and half the women, too. Peter Powelson may have been their former football star, but Ruby was everyone's friend.

The party was almost over. Reed didn't know how he felt about that.

He hadn't attended his ten-year class reunion five years ago. He didn't remember what excuse he'd given. He hadn't kept in close contact with most of the members of his graduating class. At the time, he'd been deep in negotiations to supply four varieties of fresh apples from Sullivans Orchard to the second-largest grocery chain in Michigan. Also there had been talk of an apple pickers' strike, the cider house had been getting a new roof and, as always, there had been hiring and firing and renovations and expansion and upkeep on buildings and equipment. And, of course, Noah and Marsh and Madeline had needed tending to. The truth went a little deeper than work or family obligations. He hadn't kept in close contact with members of his graduating class because he hadn't wanted to have to try to explain why he wasn't living in Miami or Seattle or, hell, Timbuktu. He hadn't wanted their pity. So he'd never given them a chance to understand.

Somehow, Ruby had figured it out. She'd put two and two together, and simply accepted that sometimes people's lives changed, and sometimes their lives changed them. She didn't pity him. She respected his choice, as he did, and that made him feel ten feet tall. Respect fed a man's soul. Perhaps even more dangerous, it made him feel understood.

He wondered what was happening on that dance floor. But she didn't need any more of an audience, and he didn't care to witness Peter's heartfelt, heartrending, soul-baring, deeply moving final play.

So as "Born to Run" wound down—why the hell it had to be Springsteen, he didn't know—as the last notes played, Reed stood on the patio overlooking an empty green and a meandering river, both lit by modernized antique gas lanterns on iron posts. He didn't put on a superhero cape or pound his chest with his fists. Instead, he let the most beautiful woman he'd ever known, the kindest and funniest and most capable, too, decide if she wanted to give a man she'd once loved another chance.

Reed fervently hoped she didn't. He fervently hoped Lover Boy didn't kiss her.

He wanted to be the one doing that.

"Mmm. Smell that?" Ruby asked as she and Reed strolled to his Mustang at the far end of the parking lot.

Finally, the reunion was over, and everyone except Sean Halstead, who was loading up his speakers, woofers, tweeters, microphones and the rest of his equipment this very minute, had already left. Not daring to let go of her dress for more than half a second in this wind, Ruby quickly waved to Amanda and Todd as they drove away.

"Reed? I was just wondering if you smelled that," she repeated.

"Asphalt?" he asked.

She nudged him with her elbow. The country club must have resurfaced the parking lot recently. It did smell of asphalt. That wasn't what she meant. Rain was in the air, but that wasn't what she meant, either. She was going to say it was the scent of happiness.

This was the second time she'd walked across this parking lot since the reunion had wound down. The first time she'd agreed to come out here with Peter. By the time Peter had driven away and she'd gone back inside, Reed had been talking to Sean while he packed up his computer and speakers and other music paraphernalia.

Since she'd ridden to the banquet hall with Amanda, Ruby had asked Reed earlier if he'd mind dropping her at her parents'. Although he'd said he'd be happy to, she hadn't actually talked to him since their last dance.

"Are you wondering what I said to Peter?" she asked.

"Who?" he said.

The wind whipped her hair across her face and there wasn't a thing she could do about it because it took both hands to hold her dress down.

"Okay," he finally said. "If you insist upon telling me, fine. Go ahead."

She smiled wryly. "That's for me to know."

His answering smile looked as if it might just crack his face. He'd been an amazing sport tonight. She had no idea how to thank him.

She'd been dreading this reunion. Everyone in that room had heard the entire sordid tale of how she'd let herself into Peter's apartment that day in April. She'd planned to leave him a seductive note, a red rose and—she was loath to admit this—her panties. Not the pair she'd been wearing, but a darling little see-through thong she'd purchased at Victoria's Secret especially for her escapade. She'd tried to wear a similar scrap of elastic and lace once, but such panties were strictly seduction ploys. Of course they came off easily. Who could stand to wear them?

Peter had been wining and dining her ever since they'd both found themselves back in Gale right after Christmas. She'd gone to work for her father and Peter had taken a position in hospital administration in nearby Traverse City. He'd been especially amorous of late, and that day she'd planned to leave the rose, the note and those panties on Peter's pillow.

She heard something upon closing his door, but it was an apartment, and she assumed the muted voices were coming from the neighbors. She'd actually felt a feverish and giddy sense of excitement as she'd tiptoed toward his bedroom. Odd that he kept the door closed when he wasn't home, but she opened it easily with a gentle turn of the handle.

The red rose and the note and—truth be told—the poorest excuse for underwear in the world fell to the floor where she stood just inside his bedroom. Instead of getting to leave her gifts on it, Peter's pillow had been propped under some other woman's hips. Not that that little detail registered at first. At that point all she could focus on was the woman's ankles crossed at the back of Peter's neck.

Ruby must have gasped.

And Peter had looked over his shoulder, giving her access to certain things she didn't want to see. Ruby remembered someone swearing—her—and someone calling her name—Peter. That was all she remembered, because that was when she spun around and let herself out. Of his bedroom, of his apartment, and eventually, out of his life.

Walking next to Reed tonight, she realized that Peter

hadn't been the right guy for her. Oh, he was tall and had beautiful eyes and wonderful pecs and washboard abs. Sure, he liked to show his muscles off in tight shirts, or better yet, no shirt.

He'd cheated.

Cheated.

And she'd become one of *those* women. Those wronged souls who blamed themselves for their partners' infidelity. For surely there must have been something wrong with Ruby, with her kisses or her lovemaking. Why else would Peter have strayed? For weeks afterward, she'd shown up at his favorite haunts, drove past his apartment and the hospital where he worked. She was a pathetic crybaby who hid under the produce stand at Meijer and plotted how she might win him back.

As if he was somehow worthy. As if she needed him in order to ever be happy again.

What happened to the girl who'd tried out for every sports team and joined—okay, and also quit—every club in school? What happened to the fiery young woman who took chances and made mistakes but in the process took a stand?

Tonight, laughing with old friends about old times, she'd looked across the room and found Reed looking back at her. And she'd discovered not the girl she'd been, not the woman she wanted to be, but the woman she already was.

Reed liked her. Simply. Truly. Liked. Her.

She'd seen it in his eyes.

Nothing was unforgivable, she'd told Peter a few minutes ago. Before his smile had gotten too cocky, she'd finished her statement. "But I don't love you enough anymore to find the energy it would take to work this relationship out, to learn to trust you again. That's too great a learning curve. It would take too much of *me* and there just wouldn't be enough of me left."

She was back to her old self. Only better. And now she really needed to let Reed get back to Orchard Hill and his life and reality. She wished there was some way to let him know how much she appreciated his show of confidence tonight, his quiet presence. He'd called Peter Skeeter. She would have loved to have been a fly on that wall. Just because she liked herself again didn't mean she was perfect.

"What's so funny?" The consummate gentleman, Reed opened the passenger door for her.

"Oh, nothing," she said. "Everything."

"It's good that you've narrowed it down."

The breeze had turned cool. It was the kind of late-night breeze that smelled of summer and asphalt and hinted of rain, the kind that caused people to stop what they were doing and tip their faces up and hold their arms out simply to feel it more fully. It was the kind of breeze that only occurred after midnight, the kind that made Ruby ask, "Did you just feel a raindrop?"

"For the last ten minutes," he said.

She smiled up at him, her hair swirling. He looked down at her, his shirt collar fluttering. She touched his arm. "I just want you to know," she said, "I'll never forget what you did for me tonight."

"Ruby," he said, his voice whisper-soft.

They would never know for sure who started it or how it began. One moment their gazes were locked. The next moment their lips were.

They met on a surge of heat and unbridled desire. They'd kissed before. Once. This was different. It was wild, unplanned but necessary. It was lips and tongues and breaths and moans and then all of those all over again. Ruby hadn't intended to do this, neither of them had. She hadn't meant to let the wind have its way with her skirt or for Reed to have his way with her mouth.

And yet the wind blew and the kiss swirled and a wild stampeding had started in her chest. His hands were all over her back, up and down and high and low, molding her to him. Hers were in his hair, gliding to his shoulders, pressing his chest, where his heart was stampeding just like hers.

Thunder rumbled in the distance. He groaned in answer deep in his throat, and the kiss became a mating of lips and tongues and the very wind that spun all around them. It went on and on and might have gone on forever.

But it couldn't, and finally, somehow, he dragged his mouth from hers. "Ruby."

"I know," she rasped close to his ear.

"I want to."

"I know," she said again. "So do I."

"But I can't. We can't. Not until I know. Maybe never. I can't ask you to wait. I can't do this."

"I know," she whispered. "I do. It's for the best. It is."

He drew away slightly, just a few inches, and looked at her, his storm-cloud blue-gray eyes meeting her desire-hazed green ones. And then his lips were on hers and hers were on him and his hands were on either side of her face and her palm was pressed against his chest, heat radiating off him in waves, his heart galloping beneath her fingertips.

The next time, *she* broke away. “Reed.”

He groaned.

“We have to stop.”

He touched his forehead to hers. “Yes, we do. You’re beautiful. You’re amazing. You’re right.”

Her hands went to his face, and then she was pulling him back to her, his lips to hers. His arms wrapped around her all over again, and he lifted her off her feet, pressing her backward against the solid car, levering himself against her.

If it were possible to make love through their clothes, they would have. He was hard where she was soft, and they both strained toward more, each in their own way, one seeking, the other wanting with everything she had.

Luckily, it wasn’t possible. Although it didn’t feel like luck. It felt like frustration and barriers they would have just as soon surmounted.

Still, they couldn’t make love. They wouldn’t make love. They didn’t.

What they did instead was take deep breaths and return to reality. Bit by bit, with a little awkwardness and great reluctance they untangled their hands and arms and she unwound her legs from around his waist and he set her back on her feet.

“I’d better get you home,” he said.

She pushed her hair out of her face and slipped into the car. He closed the door and went around to the driver’s side, climbed behind the steering wheel and turned the key.

For the first time in her life, she wished Gale were

a little larger. As it was, it took about two minutes to drive to her parents' house on Bridge Street, where she was spending the night.

Cinderella's coach had turned back into a pumpkin at midnight. Ruby's fairy-tale evening was ending in a similar way, but closer to one.

Reed didn't look at Ruby during the drive over streets in need of resurfacing, like so many other streets in towns all across America these days. Other than her giving him brief directions, they didn't speak. He concentrated on his driving, and did what he could to ignore the desire that had settled low and solid at his very core.

He couldn't forget the way she'd felt in his arms, pliant and warm and willing and so incredibly beautiful. He shouldn't have let things get that far out of control. And yet he'd been imagining it ever since he'd finally driven out of that traffic jam on the Pearl River Bridge, ever since he'd arrived at the reunion, ever since he'd seen Ruby rushing toward him in that white dress, her long red hair and blue-and-green sash flying behind her.

As far as he knew, she didn't look at him during the drive, either. Neither of them attempted small talk.

He could see a few sprinkles in the low beams of his headlights. The wind was still strong, but the clouds hadn't given up much rain yet.

She unfastened her seat belt before he'd brought the car to a complete stop in her parents' driveway. He threw the shift lever into Park and undid his. Whatever she'd been going to say went unsaid as she got out, as if she knew it would be a waste of breath to tell a Sullivan she would see herself to her door.

They met at the front of his car, the glow of headlights shining low and the porch light shining bright. "I've got it from here," she said at the bottom of the porch steps.

"What did you say to Lover Boy, anyway?" he asked.

She rolled her eyes, and he knew it would be a cold day in hell before she ever relayed the exchange to anyone word for word. It broke the awkwardness, though, so he wasn't sorry he'd asked.

"You're beautiful, Ruby. Outside and in."

"Good night, pal."

He watched her go up the steps. She was reaching for the screen door when his phone rang.

He grabbed the cell and looked at the screen. It was almost 1:00 a.m. And it was Marsh. Something had to be wrong.

Reed pressed the button and heard his brother say, "There's someone here who wants to talk to you."

"What?" Reed asked a little too loudly.

The next voice he heard was soft and sultry and decidedly Southern. "Reed, honey?"

"Who is this?"

"It's me. Cookie."

"What? Who?" he asked. "Did you say this is Cookie?" He had to listen hard in order to hear her confirm it. "Where are you?" He listened again, and like the parrot he'd obviously become, he repeated, "You're at the orchard? In Orchard Hill?"

"I came back for our baby, sugarplum."

"You came for Joey?" His gaze went unbidden to

the porch, and he saw Ruby's hand fall away from the door. She turned to face him as Cookie rattled off what sounded like some sort of explanation. The connection was terrible and his own heartbeat was so loud in his ears he couldn't hear most of what she said. "Put Marsh back on, would you?" he finally managed to rasp.

His brother's voice vibrated with the same intensity Reed was feeling. "I put her suitcases in the spare room."

In other words, she wasn't leaving with Joey tonight. Thank God for that. "I'm on my way," Reed said.

"We'll be waiting. Hey, Reed. The radar shows rain. Heavy rain. Drive carefully. I've got things covered until you get here."

The connection broke, and Reed's hands fell to his sides, his gaze on Ruby. She stood on her parents' front porch, the soft overhead light washing her in a golden glow. Or maybe that was his imagination.

He wasn't imagining the quaver in her voice, though, as she said, "That was Cookie?"

Nodding, he felt as if he owed Ruby an explanation, and yet he had no idea what protocol to follow. "Marsh said she showed up out of the blue insisting she'd made a terrible mistake."

The wind whipped Ruby's hair off her forehead and pressed her dress to her thighs as she held her skirt with one hand. She doubted Reed would leave until she was safely inside. The entire night felt surreal, somehow, and yet she knew she would never forget the way he was looking at her.

The low beam of his headlights cast his shadow onto the porch steps. She'd seen that stance before, feet apart, back straight, shoulders squared. With the light behind him, she couldn't see the color of his eyes. She felt his gaze, though. It was as if his fingers were actually trailing across her cheek, down her neck, across her shoulder, along her arm, to her waist.

She had no right to respond, and yet she did, warming, wishing, wanting. He'd called it the zing. It was more than that, at least for her.

He stared at her, and she at him, and neither of them knew what to say. She swallowed the lump in her throat as one thought played over and over in her mind. In one night she'd gotten over a man who would always cheat, and fallen in love with one who never would.

Oh, the irony.

Chapter Eleven

The storm raged as Reed left Ruby's hometown.

Even with his windshield wipers on high, he could barely see. Semis were parked along the side of the road and cars waited out the storm beneath overpasses. Slowing to a crawl at times, he kept both hands on the steering wheel, pressing toward home.

Rain came down in sheets, thunder boomed and lightning forked out of the sky. Not even the raging storm could keep him from thinking about what he'd just left behind and what he would soon encounter back home.

He drove out of the storm sometime after two. In the back of his mind he made a list of questions he would ask Cookie. He wasn't sure what to expect, but for the next hundred miles, Reed thought about what he would say, how he would say it and how it would feel if Cookie was indeed the mother of his son. On the one hand, it would mean Joey was his, and Reed deeply wanted that. It had seemed straightforward a few weeks ago. Nothing felt simple tonight.

His clothes were still damp when he pulled into his own driveway just after four o'clock. Steering around the fallen limb lying across his path, he parked where he always parked. His feet splashed through the residual puddles on the sidewalk as he went up the back steps and let himself in.

A television was turned low to an all-night weather station. Joey wasn't crying. So far so good.

There was a quarter pot of coffee left in the coffeemaker, the seldom-used sugar bowl was out and two mugs and an empty baby bottle sat by the sink.

The night-light was on in the nursery where Joey slept during the day. The crib was empty.

Feeling the effects of the long day and an even longer night that had no end in sight, Reed ran a hand through his hair and continued toward the soft murmur of voices in the living room. One belonged to his brother. The other one was vaguely familiar, as well.

Marsh was sitting in his favorite chair, his feet bare, his jeans ripped across one knee, his fingers strumming the cracked leather on the armrest, looking for all the world like something the cat dragged in. He jumped up the instant he saw Reed.

But Reed wasn't looking at Marsh anymore. His eyes were trained on a woman he hadn't seen in more than a year.

She wore pink jeans and a formfitting shirt. Her shoes, the right one tipped onto its side, sat on the floor next to the sofa. Her hair was a little longer than he remembered and perhaps lighter, too, but her eyes and smile were the same.

It was her, all right.

"Hello, Reedykins." With a bat of her eyelashes, she rose sinuously to her feet. "If you aren't a sight for sore eyes. It's been a while, hasn't it?"

His first coherent thought was that she could stand, and walk, and talk. She wasn't paralyzed or otherwise incapacitated, which was just one possible reason that might have forced a woman to leave a baby on a man's doorstep. He also couldn't think of any good reason for her to have kept their child's very existence a secret until two and a half weeks ago.

"Where's Joey?" he asked.

Her eyes widened innocently. "Why, he's in bed, of course. It's after four, you know."

Yes, Reed knew.

"Y'all must have a million questions." She was including Marsh now with her tender, quivering little smile.

Looking pointedly at Reed, Marsh said, "You two have a lot to talk about. I think I'll turn in." He started toward the kitchen and ultimately the back stairs.

There was an open staircase in this very room. With Marsh's selection of the other one, Reed knew his brother wanted him to follow him into the kitchen, where they might have a moment of privacy.

"Would you excuse me for a minute?" Reed said to Cookie.

"Of course, sugar. Take all the time you need." She sank back into the soft leather sofa cushion and curled her feet underneath her.

Marsh was waiting for him in the kitchen. "It is her, then?"

"It's the woman I— Uh, yeah. It's her. Did she tell you anything?"

Marsh put both hands on his head as if to prevent an explosion. "She's talkative, all right."

Reed remembered that about her. In fact, it was one of the reasons he'd kissed her the first time.

Marsh wasn't the type to elaborate. Sometimes getting information out of him was like pulling teeth. "Did she mention why she left Joey or why she came back now?" Reed asked.

Marsh shook his head. "She never got around to that, but Cookie isn't a nickname. And her last name is Nelson."

"How is she with Joey?" Reed asked very, very quietly.

"She hasn't seen him yet."

Reed met his brother's gaze. That didn't make sense. Finally he said, "Has she asked about him at all?"

It was Marsh's turn to sigh. "I offered to show her where he sleeps, but she said she didn't want to disturb him."

"Do you think she's telling the truth?" Reed whispered.

"About not wanting to disturb him? Hell, how should I know?" The refrigerator clanked on and the predawn breeze rattled the blinds at the kitchen window. Marsh scratched his stubbly jaw and yawned. "If you mean is she telling the truth about being Joey's mother, she offered to show me her stretch marks. No, I did not take her up on it. This is your baby."

Reed didn't miss his brother's grimace at the double entendre. He wanted Joey to be his as badly as Reed did, for his own good reasons.

"The truth is," Reed said quietly, "we don't know any more right now than we knew before she arrived. I left a message for Sam, but until we have proof, let's not let Joey out of our sight."

Marsh's relief was palpable.

Feeling an enormous surge of affection and gratitude for his brother, Reed said, "Hopefully we'll be able to fill in the blanks after I've spoken with Cookie. Meanwhile, I'll take this watch. Get some sleep."

"I think I'll do that." Marsh started to go, stopped. "How was the reunion?"

Reed thought about Ruby's friends and her laughter and how she'd contributed to all the newsy, breezy conversations, all the remember-whens, what-are-you-doing-nows. Ruby O'Toole put the joy in enjoyment.

He thought about Springsteen and how it had felt to see her dancing in Skeeter's arms. He thought about walking her to the car and the wind in her hair and his mouth on hers, and how the thrum of her kisses, her touch and her sighs was still in his bloodstream.

"It was fine. I had an okay time."

Marsh looked at him. And Reed very nearly groaned at the understatement.

His brother would never call him on it. That wasn't Marsh's way. He started up the stairs. Reed imagined he would stop at Joey's door, but he didn't have time to think about that right now. Instead, he retraced his footsteps to the living room for a little one-on-one with Cookie.

He noticed she wasn't sitting up anymore. He went as far as the center of the room and called her name. "Cookie?"

Her eyes were shut, her breathing quiet. Curled up on one end of the large sofa, she appeared to be sleeping.

"Cookie?" he said more sternly.

Her eyes remained closed and her chest rose and fell evenly, calling attention to her— Several terms came to mind, but he refused them all and turned his attention back to her face. She had a small round face, a narrow nose, lots of hair and fake eyelashes. She was cute—pretty, actually.

What game was she playing? Or did she have a good reason for her actions?

"Cookie, can you hear me?"

Nothing. Bending over her, he reached for her shoulder, only to pause, his hand suspended several inches above her. "Cookie?" he said louder than ever.

She didn't move a muscle.

"Cookie, wake up." He gave her shoulder a little shake. She was as limp as a rag doll. He tried again. All she did was sigh.

"Cookie, come on. Get up." If there was ever a time when he might take up swearing, it was now. He'd driven for hours through a torrential downpour, past downed trees and power lines, past accidents and flashing lights. The least she could do was sit the hell up and talk to him, dammit.

It was no use. Evidently one of those people who could sleep through a train wreck, she was out cold.

Straightening, he put his hand to his forehead, where tension was trying to expand his skull from the inside. The woman had one hell of a lot of explaining to do. He looked at her again and considered his options. Carrying her upstairs to the spare room did not appeal to him, and he didn't see what good it would do to sit here twiddling his thumbs while she slept. He faced the inevitable. His questions were going to have to wait.

Feeling as though he was suddenly all thumbs, he drew a plaid throw over her and turned out all but one lamp. Casting one last look over his shoulder, he went upstairs to bed.

He stopped in the doorway of Noah's old room. Light from the hallway stretched almost to the crib, where Joey was sound asleep. The floor creaked in the usual places as Reed went in and closed the door. He took off his shoes and peeled out of his damp clothes. After donning one of Noah's T-shirts and an old pair of sweats, he stretched out on Noah's old bed.

Noah's airplane posters were still tacked to the walls, and yet the room smelled of baby, milky and sweet and innocent somehow. Joey made little humming noises in his sleep, his breathing soft and fluttery. Utterly peaceful, this innocent baby had no idea his mother had returned.

If Cookie was his mother, that is.

Odd that she hadn't wanted to hold him after being away from him for nearly a month. Maybe she *was* exhausted from traveling, but even if she were dead on her feet, wouldn't she have wanted—needed—to at least check on him, to see him with her own two eyes, to prove that he was okay? Maybe she wasn't a good mother.

Or maybe he was looking for flaws.

The floors at Bell's looked fabulous. Everything was fabulous. Wonderful.

Peachy.

Ruby propped the tavern's back door open with a

chair to air out the lingering, unpleasant smell of polyurethane, and caught herself wondering how things were going at Reed's house. Oh no she didn't. She wasn't going to think about Reed and Cookie. Or Reed with Cookie. She closed her eyes because telling herself she wasn't going to think about it only made her think about it more.

She'd arrived back in Orchard Hill yesterday afternoon. She hadn't heard from Reed since he'd driven away from her parents' house. She hadn't texted him, or vice versa. She had no reason to. And vice versa.

All that kissing had pretty much made the friendship connection null and void. Perhaps some women could just be friends with a man they were in love with, but not Ruby. Unrequited love wasn't her style.

She had no one to blame but herself and even that wasn't doing any good. So. There was no sense wasting her time thinking about a few kisses and what had almost been. It was already Monday and she had too much to do to while away her time on what-ifs.

Later today she was interviewing her last candidate for bartender. In a pinch, Ruby could bartend, but she hoped that wouldn't be necessary. She planned to print and laminate the menu next, and then she would apply a coat of beeswax to the bar. And there were about a hundred other tasks to complete in preparation for the grand reopening of Bell's Tavern.

Most everything was on track. The shelves were stocked and her new waitstaff was ready to begin. The cash drawer had a lock, and she'd hired a short-order cook as well as a local band for Friday night. The full-size ad had run again in Sunday's paper and a smaller version had appeared in today's edition. Her online ads had garnered a great deal of excitement, too.

She wished she were more excited.

Hoping to generate a little cross breeze, she propped the front door open, too. She wondered if Joey remembered his mother, wondered if he'd sighed when he was finally in her arms again, home at last. She wondered if there'd been any fireworks yet. Not that she was worried about that. Why would she worry when she wasn't even thinking about Reed? Or Cookie. Or Reed and Cookie. Or Reed with Cookie.

She sighed, for all her determination couldn't seem to keep Reed far from her thoughts.

Methodically attacking the remaining items on her to-do list, she carried the Welcome to Bell's Grand Reopening banner to the front window. The moment she got there, it became clear to her that she had the worst timing in the world.

Reed was walking by.

She hadn't seen him in two days, which, from the looks of him, was how long it had been since he'd shaved. He was carrying Joey. The two of them appeared to be alone. She simply couldn't help wondering what had happened when he'd come face-to-face with Cookie.

Where was she, anyway?

He happened to be walking by, and he happened to look tired and slightly bedraggled. Ruby refused to drink in the sight of him. And she refused to duck and hide. She'd done that during the Cheater Peter debacle and she vowed she would never humiliate herself that way again.

Also, Reed had already seen her.

She definitely had the worst timing in the world. He didn't appear to think so, for his expression changed. He stopped and looked at her, and she swore he was glad to see her. Ruby had trouble drawing a breath. And yet she found herself reacting, her face relaxing, a smile lurking. The courthouse clock chimed on the quarter hour, two minutes late, as usual. They both smiled, and they might as well have been back in that parking lot after midnight, the wind whipping and rain threatening and their bodies warm and growing warmer all the time.

She supposed she shouldn't have been surprised he wandered inside. The front door was wide open, after all. It wasn't as if they were strangers or adversaries. She wasn't sure what they were anymore. Not just friends. Not lovers.

Joey's eyes widened adorably now that he was out of the sun. Reed's adjusted faster, blue-gray pools of appeal beneath sandy-colored brows.

"Hi," he said.

"Hey," she said at the same time.

A moment of awkwardness followed. And then he said, "We're meeting Marsh and Sam for coffee at the Hill in a few minutes."

We? Ruby thought. "Why is Sam still in town?" she asked.

He met her gaze. "There are some unanswered questions."

Which could have meant anything. Since it was followed by another unwieldy pause, she could only assume it meant something important. "Unanswered questions regarding Cookie?"

"Yes." He didn't elaborate, and she didn't feel she

had the right to ask. Odd, since she'd had no qualms about asking him anything. But that was before.

Before they'd kissed. Before she'd fallen in love with him. Before Cookie breezed into town on the tail of a storm.

Was Cookie Joey's mother? she wondered. Or wasn't she? Was she still in town? What reasons did she give for leaving him? For returning for him now? Ruby couldn't ask any of those questions, so she settled for something safe. "Does this banner show up from outside?"

Since he couldn't very well say what he was thinking, either, he said, "It does. Yes. Very well, in fact."

Neither mentioned the elephant in the room.

Needing to do something with her hands, she added more double-sided tape to the corners of the banner in the large window. He probably felt as if he had to say something to fill the void, and opted for "I heard you interviewed Bert Bartholomew."

She did that thing with her nose again. "He knew his liquor," she said. "I'll say that for him."

"But?"

Ruby felt him looking at her, and she swore he was thinking it was good to see her. It didn't matter that the rubber band was slipping from the ponytail at her nape or that her nail polish was chipped and there was a big tear in her T-shirt.

He. Genuinely. Truly. Liked. Her.

And vice versa.

She was in trouble. Deep trouble.

"I didn't hire him, though," she said.

"Bert worked for us for a while at the orchard. He kept a flask in his chest pocket." Moving Joey to his other shoulder, he said, "I suppose bartending would be a better fit for him than running the cider press. What time was the interview?"

"Nine this morning." She pulled a face. "I own a bar. Obviously I don't have a problem with people enjoying alcohol."

"Just not for breakfast?" he said.

He was being very agreeable. She thought he looked tired and uneasy, which wasn't like him.

Just then someone with a soft, decidedly Southern voice called through the open door. "Reedykins, are you in there?"

Reedykins? Ruby thought, as a petite woman wearing white jeans, a pink shell trimmed in faux leopard skin and four-inch heels joined them inside.

She stood close to Reed and glanced around. Spying Ruby, she said, "I do declare it's taken us half an hour to walk down the street. Reedykins knows everyone in town and everyone is just so friendly."

Ruby caught Reed cringing.

Reaching a delicate hand toward Ruby, the curvaceous blonde said, "I'm Cookie Nelson."

Reed cleared his throat and after a barely perceptible pause, completed the introductions. Naturally predisposed to like nearly everyone, Ruby had no intention of liking Cookie Nelson. It seemed to her that failing to tell Reed he had a child, and then deserting her baby with no explanation, was a good enough reason to hold a grudge against her. While Ruby was silently justifying her position, Cookie looked up at Reed. And smiled.

And Ruby was pretty sure it was as genuine as the

stars in her eyes. "My mama always said it's the curse of small towns, don't y'all agree?"

If Ruby could have found her voice she might have agreed, but it didn't matter. Cookie carried the conversation by herself. In almost no time Ruby learned that blue eyes ran in Cookie's dearly departed father's side of the family and her grandmother had loved apple pie, which apparently was some sort of a sign from heaven, since Reed lived on an apple orchard.

For an elephant in the room, she was very petite and friendly and quite pretty. Perhaps a year or two older than Ruby, she wore pink well, and that Southern drawl was almost contagious. She may have been a little ditzy and she may have talked a mile a minute about nothing, but she called Bell's Tavern "an adorable drinkery."

No matter what she'd done, Cookie Nelson wasn't going to be an easy person to dislike.

And Ruby wanted to dislike her.

"Y'all are opening on Friday? This Friday?"

Ruby's gaze swung from Reed to Cookie and back again. He wouldn't bring her, would he? "Yes," she finally said.

With a bat of her eyelashes, she gazed at Reed, and said, "We haven't been out yet. Do you think we could attend?"

"I don't think—"

Before he could finish, Cookie turned to Ruby and said, "We have a lot to work out, as you can imagine."

Joey let out a little squawk. The sound the baby made seemed to remind Reed where he was, what he was doing and that he had to go. His gaze found Ruby's. Sensing his reluctance, she swore he wanted to say something. The moment passed, and the trio left, Cookie taking two steps to Reed's every one and Joey riding contentedly in his favorite position at Reed's shoulder. Watching them go, Ruby thought it would be so much easier if the blonde bozo were easier to hate. It would be easier if Cookie were, too.

Was she Joey's mother or wasn't she?

Why was she in Orchard Hill if she wasn't? And why hadn't the private investigator moved on to his next case? It was all Ruby could do to keep from grinding her teeth together in complete frustration.

Casting a surreptitious glance over her shoulder at Ruby, Cookie daintily tucked her hand into the crook of Reed's arm. It was a possessive gesture if Ruby had ever seen one. Cookie Nelson wasn't stupid, not in the least.

And she wasn't going to be so difficult to dislike.

On Friday, Reed read through the contract on his desk. The terminology was important, the details even more so, and yet when he reached the bottom of the page, he didn't remember a single word he'd read. This was one time an eidetic memory would have come in handy.

The faraway drone of Marsh's chain saw carried on the warm breeze wafting through the open window. He'd gone out a few hours ago to clean up fallen tree limbs in the orchard. Noah and Lacey had returned from their honeymoon and were now in Traverse City visiting Madeline.

On Joey patrol this morning, Reed listened intently to the baby monitor on his desk. He was reassured by the baby's soft breathing and the occasional hum he made in his sleep, but distracted by the sound of narrow heels clicking across the hardwood floors.

Cookie's footsteps didn't stop until she reached the doorway of Reed's office. She wore jeans and a flowered top, the neckline low and the waist cinched tight. There was a provocative pout on her lips. "I made you a glass of iced tea," she said in her soft Southern drawl.

Reed put the contract down and flattened his hands on top of it. Sashaying closer, she perched daintily on the corner of his desk.

"It's iced tea, Southern style. Although I must say I can think of something a lot more fun to do while Joey's sleeping and we have the house to ourselves."

Reed ignored the overture and took a perfunctory sip of the icy beverage. It was syrupy sweet. Like her.

"It's an acquired taste, Reedykins. Maybe if you'd give it a chance."

She was pretty. She was provocative. She was even sweet. Perhaps she was right, and sweetness was an acquired taste.

But she wasn't telling the truth about Joey.

She had to realize that Reed, Marsh, Noah and Sam doubted her story, for they hadn't left her alone with Joey since she'd arrived. She'd been tearful that first morning. Crying daintily into a pack of lavender-scented tissues, she'd told them how sorry she was for leaving Joey that way and how afraid she'd been and how alone. Finding herself all alone, without family and few friends, she'd had the baby blues, she said. Reed had asked his family doctor about postpartum depression. It was a serious condition, so they'd all treaded lightly.

"Give me a chance, Reedykins?" she whispered

from her position on the corner of his desk. Reaching down, she laid her small hand on his arm, the action leaving him a clear view of cleavage.

Reed met her gaze instead, and held it until she looked away.

He could have learned to drink sweetened tea and to live with pink everything, with shoes in every room and gossip magazines on the coffee table. The Reedykins handle wasn't easy to swallow, but he supposed he could have learned to live with that, too. He might have been able to forgive her for abandoning Joey and for failing to so much as tell Reed she'd been pregnant. Perhaps in time he would have been able to forget.

But something was off with her story. And he didn't believe it had anything to do with postpartum depression. Sam was working on the case and they were all waiting for the results of the paternity test to arrive. Meanwhile, Cookie was evasive.

And seductive.

"It's the redhead, isn't it?" she asked.

Reed was saved from answering by Joey's cry. Cookie glanced at the monitor and slid to her feet.

"I'll get him," Reed said in no uncertain terms.

Her eyes narrowed, but she stepped aside and let him pass. Reed made a beeline for Joey's nursery. "Hey, buddy," he said from the side of the crib. "No wonder you're mad. You rolled over again. You don't like tummy time, remember?"

He picked the baby up, and instantly Joey quieted. Reed's heart swelled. His chest, too.

He'd watched Cookie closely with Joey. She was gentle with him, but until she produced proof that he was her child, Reed and his brothers weren't about to lower their guard where the baby was concerned. And she'd produced no proof.

She claimed she'd lost Joey's birth certificate when she'd been evicted from her apartment shortly after his birth. Sam had assured her, all of them, that that wasn't a problem. She could simply contact the county where Joey had been born and obtain another copy. As far as Reed knew, she hadn't even tried. Her memories of her pregnancy and Joey's birth were vague and inconsistent. Whenever Reed, Marsh, Sam or Noah asked pointed questions, her face crumpled and the weeping began anew.

Reed wasn't buying the act.

Laying Joey on the changing table, he was certain Cookie knew it. He unfastened the tabs on Joey's diaper. The instant the diaper was off, the baby kicked his feet in wild abandon. He'd first displayed the new little quirk two days ago. Already, he'd changed so much. He'd changed them all.

"I know," Reed said softly. "You love being naked. We're going to have a little talk about that when you're older."

Joey's gaze locked with Reed's and his grin widened beguilingly. He grasped two of Reed's fingers in his small, perfect hand. It made fastening the tabs on the new diaper more challenging, but Reed finished the task, disposed of the wet diaper and dressed him again.

Picking Joey up as if he'd been doing it all his life, he turned, and found Cookie watching him. She stood in the doorway, her blue eyes misty and her voice quavery. "It really is the redhead, isn't it?"

"Do you know what I think, Cookie?" he asked, starting toward her, Joey in his arms.

"What, sugarplum?"

"I think we should keep this about you."

A memory from Reed's childhood washed over him just then. His great-grandfather had been a well witcher. It sounded like voodoo, but in reality it was simple science, not magic. Holding a thin metal rod in each gnarled old hand, his grandfather had walked across a plot of land, north to south, east to west. When the divining rods crossed, he stopped. And invariably there beneath the ground the well-digging company found water.

Once, Reed asked how the rods knew. His grandfather had explained that water produced a different frequency, a different energy than dirt, rock and soil. And those divining rods sensed it the way an honest man sensed the truth.

There was a bit of his great-grandfather's wisdom in Reed as he studied Cookie's expression today. "Why are you here?" he asked.

She didn't cry into a lavender-scented tissue this time.

Wearing a pretty flowered shirt and a sad wistful smile, she gazed back at him, as dainty as a Texas bluebonnet. And just as hardy.

If Reed had been holding his great-grandfather's divining rods, they would have crossed. That was how close he was to the truth.

Chapter Twelve

"Is he here yet?"

Oh, boy, Ruby thought. Not this again. It had been a lot easier to pull off blasé when the he in question had been Peter. The atmosphere at Bell's Tavern was charged with anticipation. She'd been watching the door all night, and she wasn't the only one.

Rumor had it Reed was coming.

From her position behind the bar, she performed a quick scan of the room. The hardwood floors and the ornately carved bar were gleaming. The lights were turned low and nearly every table was full.

The live music was loud and the dance floor was crowded. Reed wasn't on it, though. He wasn't sitting at the bar or playing pool in the back. He didn't throw his cards on the table and yell, "Misdeal."

It was too early to call the grand reopening a complete success, but the waitstaff had barely had time to come up for air.

"Is he here yet?" Abby Fitzpatrick stood on tiptoe trying to see over so many tall people.

Ruby looked from Abby to Chelsea, and caught the dark-haired wedding planner averting her gaze. "What aren't you telling me?" Ruby demanded.

Chelsea studied her fingernails and coyly refrained from answering. Ruby knew nuances. Chelsea didn't want to lie.

Orchard Hill had an active grapevine, but this wasn't simply the rumor mill at work. Chelsea, Abby, Sam, Reed's brother Noah, Lacey and everyone else whose eyes were trained on the door expected something to happen.

Ruby understood how gossip traveled. Several people had seen her talking to Reed at Murphy's that night. Evidently someone had seen his car parked at the bottom of her stairs, too, and someone else had noticed him helping her carry boxes from her car into her tavern.

Reed and his brothers had grown up in this town. The Sullivans' past was tragic, their personalities alluring and their smiles tempting. In case that wasn't enough to cause hearts to flutter, someone had left an innocent baby on their doorstep. Nearly a month later, a dainty and very stacked Texan arrived claiming to be the baby's mother. Who could resist talking about that?

Ruby, that was who. She filled four glasses with beer on tap and lined them up on a tray. She was mixing her first Kerfuffle when the bartender she'd hired returned from a short break.

"Is he here yet?" Natasha asked as she donned her apron.

One of the waitresses rushed to the bar, saving Ruby from replying. "I need a Dynamite, a Howl at the Moon and two Fountains of Youth." She pointed her finger at Sam Lafferty but smiled at Ruby and said, "So is he? Here yet, I mean."

One by one, Ruby eyed the people she knew best in Orchard Hill. No matter what Chelsea, Abby, Sam and Natasha claimed, they knew something Ruby didn't know.

Bell's new bartender had straight black hair and striking green eyes and was taller than Ruby. With her straight black hair and striking green eyes, she was beautiful. At six-one, her height put her at a definite advantage. She had a clear view of the door. Ruby saw her eyes widen. A moment later, Ruby's widened, too.

Someone new had arrived. Someone wearing tight white jeans and a pink tank and five-inch heels. Oh, no. It was Cookie. Ruby felt the strangest compulsion to run. But there was no place to hide.

The noise level rose and a gasp sounded. That might have been Ruby. From her position at the end of the bar, she saw Cookie scan the room. The instant she spotted Ruby, she started toward her.

She was halfway through the crowd when another gasp carried through the room. All eyes turned to the door again. This time it was Reed who'd entered.

He scanned the room, too. And while the band began to play another song, his gaze landed lightly on Ruby.

Noah cut in front of Reed. He must have told his brother Cookie was here, because Reed's entire demeanor changed. Ruby watched as Reed caught up with the little Texan with the big hair.

Funny, Ruby hadn't been jealous of the bottle redhead in Cheater Peter's bed. She'd been shocked, disgusted, insulted, scorned, hurt, humiliated and about a hundred other unpleasant things, but not jealous. But then, she'd only *thought* she was in love with Peter.

Maybe this wasn't love, either. Maybe it was lust. Perhaps it was the condition that occurred to people who survived terrifying events like bank robberies or getting stranded on desert islands. What was it called? Stockholm syndrome. Wait, it wasn't that. That was when a person fell in love with her captor, and that took years to overcome. Hopefully it wouldn't take Ruby that long to get over Reed.

Bother.

Ruby had known for weeks that Reed was looking for the mother of his child. She'd known he was a family man at heart, but seeing Cookie and him together was harder than she'd thought it would be. It made her chest ache, and her stomach, too. And that made her mad. *Ha.* It seemed it wasn't going to take her forever to get over him, after all. In fact, she was thinking about clobbering him over the head with the bottle of whiskey Natasha was opening. Ruby wouldn't, of course. She'd paid good money for that Jack Daniel's.

While she was still weighing the pros and cons of violence and vengeance, a strong arm came around Ruby's shoulders. "Hello, gorgeous," Sam Lafferty said. "I haven't gotten up close and personal with a redhead yet tonight. If you know what I mean."

"No need to get poetic," she said sardonically. "You had me at hello."

With that, the notorious P.I. and famed carouser led her into a two-step around the perimeter of the dance floor. Ruby knew what Sam was doing, but he couldn't block Reed and Cookie from her view entirely.

They were talking now. Reed looked angry. Before Ruby got close enough to see Cookie's expression, Jake Nichols, the local veterinarian, cut in and spun her in the opposite direction.

Digger Brown cut in next, followed by someone named Josh and finally that guy Ruby had talked to at Murphy's the other night.

Her head was spinning by the time a man cut in for the final time. This one was tall and smelled of a woodsy aftershave and night breezes and apples, of all things. His eyes looked gray tonight, his hand at the small of her back possessive.

"Reed Sullivan," she said sternly. "What do you think you're doing?"

Chapter Thirteen

The first thing a woman learned in dance class was to let the man lead. After all, the true test of a dancer's finesse was to follow, regardless of her partner's ability.

But Reed wasn't dancing.

Music was playing, and other people were shuffling backward and forward, to and fro. Reed had assumed a dancer's position, his fingers twined with hers, one hand on the small of her back. But he was standing perfectly still, his eyes on hers.

She'd worn black tonight, and pinned her hair in a loose knot on the back of her head. As far as Ruby could tell, Reed hadn't noticed her outfit or her hair. Since he'd cut in on that last dance, he hadn't taken his gaze off hers.

"You have to move your feet to two-step," she grumbled.

She'd spoken, and in doing so, she'd moved her lips, which apparently drew his gaze to her mouth. Before she reacted to his nearness, to his heat and the strength in his arms, she said, "Where's Cookie?"

Tightening his hold, not loosening it, he said, "With any luck she's in the cab I called for her, on her way to the airport to use her one-way ticket to Dallas."

The Madonna Mamas were playing a song by Faith Hill. They sounded so much like the original it was uncanny. Strangely, Ruby could wrap her mind around that. But she didn't trust herself to analyze what Reed had said.

"Where's Joey?" she finally managed to say.

"He's home. With his father."

Her eyes widened, her mouth opened and her heart pounded. "You mean. Cookie isn't— You're not— Joey isn't—"

Reed shook his head.

He started to move, drawing her into the dance. But Ruby wasn't having it. "Joey—he's Marsh's?" she stammered, her feet planted firmly on the floor.

This time Reed nodded.

"Oh, Reed. I'm so sorry. So, so sorry."

"No, you're not."

She did a double take.

"At least I hope you're not," he added. "I'm not sorry."

She heard the depth of emotion in his voice. "I wanted him. I still do. I'd take him in a heartbeat if Marsh needed me to. I'm disappointed. Deeply. But I've had all week to come to terms with it."

"What are you talking about?" she asked. "You've known all week?"

"I didn't have any proof, but I was pretty sure the first night," he said.

The music was so loud Ruby missed whatever Reed said next. Abby must have stepped in, because the next thing Ruby knew, the band was taking five and Abby was rubbing her hands together at a job well done. No one was dancing this dance, anyway. Everyone, it seemed, was watching Ruby and Reed.

He lowered his hand from the dancing position to his side, but he continued to hold hers, his fingers warm, his thumb moving in a semicircle over her wrist. "I helped Cookie into a taxi an hour ago. She was supposed to go directly to the airport."

"Why didn't she?" Ruby asked, and that was only one of the questions blazing through her head.

"Because her ploy didn't work and because she's a drama queen, and maybe to take a year off my life."

"That I can see," Ruby said. "But then why did she finally leave?"

As if he hated to admit it, Reed said, "Because she's not entirely evil. She wanted to tell you something. You see, Cookie really is alone in the world. Like a lot of people, she struggles to get by."

Ruby was watching him closely, listening closely.

A waitress brought Ruby and Reed something to drink and Sam shooed another couple out of their chairs so they could sit down. While activity resumed all around them, while a card game was lost and a billiards game won, while the Madonna Mamas began to play again, and Natasha served up whiskey and pale ale, Reed told Ruby that when a friend of Cookie's relayed that a P.I. had come to the restaurant where they used to work and was asking questions about a waitress named Cookie who'd apparently left a baby on a doorstep in a college town in Michigan, Cookie remembered Reed.

"She and her friend did a little research online, and they found my family's orchard and they thought maybe there was an opportunity here. She swears she never meant to hurt anybody. It was just a little white lie."

"Claiming to be Joey's mother was just a little white lie?" Ruby asked.

"Her words not mine," Reed insisted. "She only intended to keep up the facade until I fell in love with her, or Joey's mother returned, whichever came first."

He took her drink from her hand, set it on the table and reached for her hand in his. "I couldn't possibly fall in love with her. I love you, Ruby. I love your Florence Nightingale tendencies and your mile-long legs. I love your wild hair and your eidetic memory and how unafraid you are to try new things. I love that you love everyone. And I'm hoping you love me."

Just then, the Madonna Mamas began to play "YMCA." People flocked to the dance floor. Ruby and Reed didn't join in.

"Remember when you asked me what my favorite color is?" he asked.

Although she nodded, she couldn't help wondering what that had to do with anything. "Not pink," he said.

Ruby felt it, that quiet little mewling inside, a shared smile and that delicious uncurling of rose petals.

"What's wrong?" he asked.

"Nothing. Everything. I was just thinking we still have two hours before last call. And now those two hours are never going to end."

"Who says we have to stay until closing?"

They got up together, and skirted tables and the edge of the dance floor and the bar. While the Madonna Mamas crooned the iconic song, Ruby and Reed sneaked out of Bell's.

Maybe sneaking wasn't the correct term. The two of them were hard to miss, her red hair and swaying hips, his masculine swagger and shirt so white it practically glowed in the dark. He turned Ruby into his arms before the door closed behind them, and covered her mouth with his. Already breathless, they started up the stairs hand in hand.

"Is there something you'd care to tell me?" he asked at the top.

"I can't think of anything," she said.

She knew what he was waiting for. She was waiting for the perfect time.

He swung her into his arms like a groom carrying his bride over the threshold. Ruby gave a little yelp, because it looked a lot easier in the movies. Maureen O'Hara's shin never banged against the doorjamb and Humphrey Bogart's hip never smashed into the doorknob hard enough to leave a mark.

But this wasn't the movies. This was real life. And in real life, Ruby laughed out loud and they both groaned a little in pain. Their gazes met, and their breathing deepened, and he loosened his hold and let her slide slowly down his body.

"Which way to your bedroom?" he asked.

She led the way. There, she switched on an old metal fan and a lamp with a fringed shade. He opened a window, she turned down the bed and finally they stood facing each other.

He laced his fingers with hers, palm to palm, and slowly went down on one knee. "There still isn't anything you'd care to say to me?" he asked.

"There is one thing," she said. "As long as you're down there, would you do me a favor?" He quirked one eyebrow. Oh, he had a dirty mind. One more thing to like about him.

"I dropped an earring earlier. I think it went under the bed. But never mind. Come here, would you? I'd like you to be standing for this."

He rose and stood feet apart, hands on his hips.

"You were saying?" she asked.

"Do you know when I knew I wanted to marry you?"

Her breath caught. "Actually, this is the first I've heard you want to marry me, but go ahead. I'm listening."

"It was the night I watched you eat a quart of ice cream by yourself."

It was the last thing she'd expected him to say. "You fell in love with me because I went overboard eating ice cream?"

"I fell in love with you because you don't do anything halfway."

"I thought you were going to say you knew last weekend when I was wearing that white dress."

He shrugged, and it was a marvelous shifting of shoulders and man. "That's when I knew I had to have you in my bed."

"Oh," she said. "Well, that's pretty, uh, I was going to say straightforward, but it occurs to me that I like a straightforward man."

He took both her hands in both of his and held them,

just held them. The fan whirred, and just like that, the lamp on the dresser went out.

"I think that's a sign," she said. "Did I tell you I'm superstitious?"

"The first time I saw you, you asked me what sign I was. You said I was a water sign, deep and moody."

"I really am sorry about Joey, Reed. I know how much you love him. Although I must say it is nice to know you're good with babies. I'd like to have a baby, your baby, maybe a few, maybe twins, a boy and a girl."

"Would you marry me first?" he asked.

"I'd want Father Murphy to perform the ceremony."

He inched a little closer, nudged her hair from her temple with his lips. "You want your old boyfriend to marry us?"

"That's what I like about you." Her voice was growing husky, dusky. "You always understand."

"That's what you *like* about me?" He was still waiting to hear her say it.

"There are a lot of things I like about you. You're a snappy dresser, for one. And underneath that cool, calm and collected persona is a streak of very uncivilized man."

He was feathering kisses along the side of her face, her cheekbone, below her ear and just beneath the ridge of her jaw. She pressed her body against his and kissed him, once, twice. His breath was a rasp as she tugged his shirt from the waistband of his jeans and undid every button. He was a patient man, but when she slid her hands underneath, pressing the fabric up and off him, he shuddered and took over.

"Do you know when I knew I loved you?" she asked as he whisked her silky black shirt over her head.

He caught her raised hands in his, and clasped her wrists together in his right hand. She felt shackled, and she swore she'd never felt such a delicious shudder go through her.

"This is the first I've heard anything about love," he said, his voice husky, his hips pressing against hers.

He was going to make her say it. She liked that about him, too.

"I knew I loved you when I heard you ask Nanny McPhee if she'd ever been spanked." He laughed, and even though she was serious, she didn't mind, because sometimes serious life was pretty funny.

"I've loved you every moment since, even when I hated you, even when I wanted to clobber you over the head with a perfectly good bottle of whiskey."

He lifted his face and looked at her, his eyes dilated in the semidarkness. "That sounds like true love to me. Is there anything else you want me to know right now, Ruby?"

"I can't think of anything off the top of my head," she said.

He placed her hands on his shoulders and whispered, "You're going to want to hold on for this."

She tipped her head back and smiled. But she did hold on, and on, and on, through kisses, and sighs, and murmurs and a serenade as old as time. Their remaining clothes came off slowly, shoes, slacks, her skirt and a pair of fine cotton panties.

He eased her onto her back on the bed, the fan whirring, the mattress shifting beneath their weight. He covered her breasts with his hands and covered her body with his. She was tall. He was taller. She was soft and unbelievably pliant, and he was hard and undeniably strong.

She was underneath him one minute, sprawled on top of him the next. She giggled when he found a ticklish spot, and he let all his breath out when she wrapped her legs around his hips.

He had her on her back so fast she gasped. She opened her mouth beneath his, and he began to move. The mattress shifted and the curtain fluttered at the window, their only music. She made a sound deep in her throat, until the shudders overtook her, and him.

Sometime later, he eased to his side and drew the sheet to their shoulders. Her long curly hair tickled his chin, and his short blond chest hair tickled her nose. They smiled in the near darkness, and it was as if the whole universe smiled with them.

"So this is love," he said.

"Who knew?" she agreed.

Not Reed, until he met Ruby, and not Ruby, until she met Reed.

Someone opened the door downstairs, and voices called to one another from the alley. Bell's grand reopening had been a huge success. Ruby was already looking forward to her next adventure. But no matter what she tried next, she was putting down roots here in this town where Johnny Appleseed once visited, where Reed's great-grandfather once discovered water, and his mother, rain. She was putting down roots with a man who knew how to make an entrance, and would always want to make an entrance with her.

They would never agree on ice cream and neither would want to cook, but he would read to her, sometimes from the newspaper, other times from one of the books stacked on his nightstand. She would love everyone in his family, even his great-uncle, the judge. And he would love her mother, and respect her father and tolerate her uncle Herb.

Later, she would tell him that someone had made her an offer to buy Bell's tonight. But for now, they touched, they enticed, they enjoyed, they aroused. They promised to be true and faithful, to love each other forever. She felt like a bride already, and it was better than in the movies. She made love to the man she loved, the man who loved her in return.

Her. And nobody else.

And him, and only him.

* * * * *

517/05